WILDER CREEK

LINDA SALVATO BUSSIERE

E M U
BOOKS

Acknowledgement
Many, many heartfelt thanks to Jim McLaughlin
who took time from his busy schedule
to proofread this book.
You're the coolest guy on the planet.

Published by
Emu Books
311 Route 119 West
Fitzwilliam, NH 03447

Designed by
Eric Stanway

WILDER CREEK

This book is dedicated to my beloved father
Giuseppi "Joe" Salvato
b. Aug. 21, 1922, Palermo, Sicily
d. Feb. 8, 2019, Beverley, MA
He proudly served with the 101st Airborne from 1941 – 1945
and always said "old soldiers never die, they just fade away."

CHAPTER ONE

Januery 16 1870
Deer Buford
Last time I saw you you talked bout gettin a ranch goin. Well me and Lydia are settled now in this heer New Mexico territory and its mighty pritty country. Lands goin cheep and grate for cows. I think it would do you well to consider comin out this a way. That is if you was sereus bout ranchin and reddy to give up rangerin and fytin Indians. You can stay with us ifn you decide to come out this way.

Lydias expectin and Im plum tikkled over the hole idea of bein a Pa. Hell I have already given up my wikked ways when I settled in with Lydia, mite as well go all the way. We got ourselves a nice place heer in Wilder Creek and Marshillin aint been diffikult since I done layed down the law. Saddle tramps, drunken cowboys, Meaxicans and what all, had to show them who was boss. Shure would be good to have a frendly face around. Hope you give some considerashun to what Im sayin. I know yule like it heer. Hell you wont get in no truble after all Im the law in this heer town.

Well thats all for now.
Your frend,
Hi

Colonel Buford McLeod, ex-Confederate soldier and Texas Ranger, reread the letter he received a few months before.
If Hi said the New Mexico Territory was a good place to settle, it was.

He and Hi Johnson had grown up together in San Antonio and were closer than brothers. Together they joined the Confederate Army, and then after the war the Texas Rangers.

A little over a year ago, Hi quit the Rangers and married his long time sweetheart Lydia Clark. Once he left the military life, he encouraged Buford to do the same.

At first Buford ignored the suggestion, but as time went by he started to reconsider. Hi planted a seed in his mind that grew into fruition, and at the age of 32 Buford decided to hang up his guns.

His decision wasn't just based on Hi's recommendation. Part of it came from the strange emotions he was feeling of late.

First there were the awful nightmares in which he repeatedly relived the violence and battles he'd experienced. His senses and adrenaline were growing more intense. Every loud sound made him jump, and he knew he could hurt someone as easily as if he were putting on his boots or taking a piss. There was no process for filtering in his mind. It all became second nature, and it frightened him. He hoped leaving the Rangers and being with his closest friend might calm him down.

His back side hurt from riding all day and he pitched camp for the night. Too exhausted to do anything else, he chewed some beef jerky, rolled up in a blanket, and went to sleep.

The next day he reached the territory and Hi was right, it looked just like Texas. Now he knew why they called this area "Little Texas."

It was past nightfall when he finally reached Wilder Creek and in the dark it didn't look like much. Ramshackle buildings lined the main street. The road was dry and rutted. It looked like dozens of towns he'd been to before. There were few people about, but he could hear a ruckus coming from down the main street. He knew from experience that it was coming from the local saloon, the only place open at this hour of the night.

He headed towards the noise and found the Longhorn Saloon. A couple of cowboys were standing out front, and he rode over to them.

"Howdy," he said, "can you tell me where I can find Marshall Johnson?"

"He's over at the jailhouse, yonder," one said pointing up the street.

"Much obliged."

When Buford reached the jailhouse, he found his friend fast asleep. Leaning back in his chair, Hi had one leg up on the desk, and his hat laid over his eyes. He emitted enough snores to raise the dead.

Buford studied him for a moment. Hi was short and wiry, with thin blonde hair and sparkling blue eyes. Friendly and charming, he was liked by both men and women. He was quick with a joke, always had a sympathetic ear, and could be persuaded to join in a friendly poker game or a drink. Before Lydia, he always found time for a prostitute, or soiled dove as he liked to call them.

Hi's relaxed demeanor was very different. Buford knew that he took everything too seriously. Business always came first, people made him nervous, and he had a rigid moral code. Everything for him was black or white with no shade of grey in between. Hi mellowed him out, and he was badly in need of that.

His musing over, Buford slapped his friend's foot and Hi was on his feet in a second, gun drawn.

"I see you ain't lost none of your quickness. Good to know after comin' through this here town."

"Buford, you old son of a bitch! You scared the shit out o' me." Hi stepped around the desk and clapped Buford on the back. "Good to see ya'! Get my letter?"

"That's why I'm here."

Hi's face lit up, "You aimin' to settle here?"

"Maybe."

"Well it's fine country for cows and with the price so high back east, them Yankees can't get enough of our beef. Yes sir! Ranchin's good business and folks is gonna' start comin' here and settlin' claims left and right. You got you a herd yet?"

"Yea. Shit Hi, can't tell you how many beeves was just roamin' the plains. Me and Tom rounded up a coupla' hundred head, like shootin' fish in a barrel. The only cows I had to buy was some good breedin' stock. Tom's got 'em now."

Long Horn cattle left to themselves during the Civil War roamed across the plains and multiplied at an astonishing rate; these maverick steers were known as beeves.

"How is baby brother, Tom?" Hi asked.

"Doin' fine. He's lookin' forward to ranchin' as much as I am. Can't say that your letter didn't influence me none. You might say you was my inspiration."

Buford yawned. "You look a might peaked." said Hi.

Yea, I'm pretty wore out. It's a far piece from San Antone. Is there a boarding house or hotel I can hole up in?"

"Yea, but you're not goin' to one, figured you could stay at our place."

"Lydia's probably pretty close to 'er time now, don't want to trouble 'er none."

"Yea, she's ready to calve any day now, but she'd be madder than a wet hen if'n I didn't have you come stay with us. She always likes to see Texas folks. Besides y'all be company for 'er tonight. I got men out trackin' down a horse thief so I gotta' stay 'round here and keep order."

Buford couldn't help himself and had to add another quip. "Yea, saw you at work when I come in."

"Don't give me no shit. I do my job. Just ain't gotta' pay attention right now. At least not 'til the boys get back with the varmint who stole them horses, that is if'n they don't hang the son of a bitch first. I reckon we have plenty of time. Let's go, you're comin' home with me."

Hi locked the jail house, and they set off.

They trotted side by side in amiable silence.

Buford was the first to speak. "Well Hi, you're lookin' good, Married life seems to agree with you."

"It does, god damn it, who would'a thought it?"

"Not me and that's for damn sure. I was messin' with you back yonder, but seriously, how you like Marshallin' here?"

"It's fine, though some days I have my fill of dealing with a bunch of assholes. Mostly drunks who don't know their ass from a hole in the ground. Ain't got no patience with 'em."

"Stop your complainin'. I know you thrive on this shit, who you foolin'. How many men you have to kill to let 'em know you was serious?"

"A few I reckon. No one who didn't deserve it. Had to let 'em know that I wasn't gonna' put up with their shit. Couldn't talk you out of ranchin' and joinin' me as a law man, could I?"

"Hell no!" Buford snorted. "I'm tired of lookin' over my shoulder all the time. That's why I'm here. Aim to settle down and get civilized."

Hi laughed. "You civilized? Never!"

"What you laughin' 'bout, you son of a bitch? Lydia civilized you, ain't she? A good piece of land will do the same for me."

"I reckon," Hi said, the look of amusement still on his face.   They soon reached a neat little house on the outskirts of town.

"Lord, Hi, this sure is fine. You build this?" Buford asked incredulously.

"Shit no! I tole' 'em when they hired me as Marshall that I needed comfortable quarters, and here it be. It's a beauty ain't it?"

"Yes sir, it is."

The two men dismounted and brought their horses to the barn.

"Any place out here I can wash?" Buford looked down at his dusty clothes with a frown. "I smell like a hog and don't want to greet Lydia 'til I'm clean."

"Pump house is yonder. I'll tell 'er, you're here. Y'all come in when you're ready."

When Buford entered the house, Lydia greeted him warmly.

"Colonel!" she exclaimed. "It's right nice to see you. Never thought I'd see any Texas folk again." She threw her arms around him hampered by the swell of her huge belly.

Embarrassed by displays of affection, he blushed and pushed her away gently, holding her at arms-length. She was a striking woman, tall with coal black hair, and large brown eyes. To Buford she looked prettier than ever, having the luminescent glow common to pregnant women.

He smiled warmly at her. "You're lookin' pert Lydia."

"As pert as a woman ready to birth can be, I reckon.", Lydia said with a gleam in her eye.

"This critter's gonna' be bunkin' with us for a while," Hi said.

"That is if it ain't no trouble. I can always stay in town."

Lydia frowned at him. "I wouldn't hear of it. Ain't Hi write you that you should stay with us?"

"He did, but you look close to your time. Don't want to be in the way."

"Colonel, you ain't gonna' be in the way and if'n you think I'd let you stay in town, you gotta' another thing comin'!"

Buford knew she was sincere. He'd always gotten along well with Lydia. She had a good heart, and a sweet nature; a perfect match for Hi. Unlike most women, she didn't make him nervous.

"Well I guess that's settled," Hi laughed. "Unless you wanna' get 'er riled and it ain't good to get a woman in 'er condition riled."

"I gotta get back to the jail house. Give the man somethin' to eat and show 'im to a bed."

"Lord Hi, ain't you got deputies? Let them work tonight."

"Damn, woman, I tole' you. They's all out after a horse thief. Ain't no one left in town but me. Now go on with you. Take care of old Buford here."

"Don't need no care, just a bed."

"Lydia will see to that. See y'all in the mornin'." Hi kissed his wife and left.

Lydia turned to Buford. "Lord Colonel, I can't tell you how good it is to see you again, it's been 'bout a year, ain't it?"

"Yea, 'bout that."

"You bein' here is gonna' be good for Hi, I swear the man pined for you."

Buford laughed. "We go back a long time. This is probably the longest we been separated since we was younguns."

"I bet your fierce hungry. You just set a while and I'll whip you up somethin' quick."

"Much obliged Lydia, but I'm more tired than hungry. All I wanna' do right now is sleep."

She led him to a comfortable room. "Is this fittin' enough for you?"

"This will do fine. Probably sleep on the floor anyways. Ain't used to beds."

Lydia looked at this bear of a man. Buford stood 6 feet 3 inches tall without his boots. His long auburn hair reached his shoulders. He sported a thick beard, which at present needed grooming. He had large brown eyes set under a protruding brow. He was handsome in a rugged, frightening kind of way. He intimidated a lot of people, but not Lydia.

She touched his arm gently. "Sleep where you want Colonel, we're just tickled to have you here."

Lydia closed the door, and Buford tried the bed. He fell asleep as soon as his head hit the pillow.

It was late morning when he awoke. He found Lydia in the kitchen.

"Well, sleepy head, looks like you found your quarters satisfactory."

"Sure did."

"Ham and eggs all right, Colonel?"

"Don't want to put you out. Don't feel right havin' you wait on me."

"I reckon I can still cook a couple of eggs. 'Specially for you. Don't forget how you saved my man's life."

Buford laughed. "Which time was that?"

"In San Antone, right after we got hitched. Don't you remember? That crazy cow poke from Abilene was ready to shoot Hi in the back, accused 'im of cheatin' at cards. I was never so scairt! But you kilt' 'im before he could squeeze the trigger."

"Oh, that time," Buford said matter of factly. "I didn't do that for Hi. Knew for a fact that he cheated that man. Killed the varmint on principle. Can't abide a man who'd shoot someone in the back."

Lydia laughed. "You can't fool me with that kind of talk. You would never let anyone hurt my man."

"Could never pull the wool over your eyes," he said with a smile.

She placed a dish heaped with eggs and ham in front of him and looked on with pleasure as he attacked it hungrily. She poured herself a cup of coffee and sat across from him.

"Vittles all right Colonel?"

"Couldn't be better. You're a damn fine cook Lydia."

Lydia cradled the hot coffee in her hands and gazed at

Buford. She thought that a good woman could save him, like she saved Hi. Once he was settled, she'd find him a wife.

Hi entered the kitchen all bluster and nervous energy.

"I thought you'd be home 'afore this," she scolded.

"Tarnation, woman. Men didn't come in 'til just a while ago. Buford, I tole' ya' they'd hang the son of a bitch 'afore I could bring 'im to trial.

"Couldn't you send word to me, 'bout you bein' late?"

Hi softened when he saw how upset she was. "Sorry darlin' but sent the boys back to cut 'im down. I wouldn'a cared if'n we had left 'im for the buzzards, but didn't think you'd approve, bein' a Christian woman and all. After they fetched 'im I had to make arrangements for a proper burial, fuckin' horse thief or not. Anyhow gimme' somethin' to eat. What Buford has looks mighty good to me, I'll have more of the same."

"Shouldn't give ya' nothin' scarin' me half to death," Lydia said with a smile in her eyes.

"Don't gimme' no grief, just put out some vittles."

Buford could tell that Hi was irritated, though he tried to hide it in front of Lydia. Instead Hi vented his wrath on him.

"And what the hell you doin' havin' breakfast now? It's almost noon! Thought you'd be out lookin' over some land."

"Hell no. Thought I'd just stay here and sit with your pretty wife."

"You jack ass. After havin' a real man what would she want with you?"

"A real man? You ain't implyin' Lydia's been unfaithful, are you?" Buford teased.

"You son of a bitch. I'm talkin' 'bout me."

"Oh. Well you said a real man, so I wondered..."

Lydia laughed to herself listening to their exchange. They scolded and insulted each other, but it was good natured banter.

"I already picked out a piece of land for y'all just in case," Hi said.

Buford laughed. "I knew that all ready. Why do you think I was lazin' around? But you can show me another time since you had a rough night sleepin' while your men went after a horse thief."

"You startin' that shit again? You're startin' to get on my fuckin' nerves. Do y'all want to see this piece I seen or not?"

"Sure. We'll go look at it when you're ready."

"Well I'm ready now, saddle up!" Hi said.

Thirty minutes later, they reached the place Hi had chosen. He and Buford rode around the claim. Mile after mile of plains, prairie grass, broken only by a few lonely clumps of pinion trees, shrubs, and the scruffy banks of a creek greeted Buford's eyes.

"Whataya' think?"

"Hate to say it Hi, but this looks real good. Perfect for cows."

"Ain't it though? You got plenty of water and space. Hell, there ain't another ranch for miles. Charlie Smith's the closest one, and he's some distance away."

"Whatta' 'bout the Indians?"

"You ain't gotta' worry 'bout them. Most of 'em have gone up north where it ain't so crowded. Got a wild band of Apache here and there, but ain't nothin' to lose sleep over." Hi looked longingly at the land and the gaze wasn't lost on Buford.

"Why don't you give up Marshallin' and ranch your-self?" he asked.

"Lots of reasons, I reckon. Don't think Lydia would take kindly to me bringin' 'er out here so far from town. And besides, cows is too much work. Bein' Marshall been right easy."

Buford smiled at his friend, "Reckon so. You can always shoot some son of a bitch, but killin' your cows wouldn't be profitable."

Hi scowled. "C'mon now, I ain't that bad! Ain't had no cause to shoot no one for a while. It was different when I come here, there was no law a'tall. It was no Abilene, but decent folk was scared to walk in the street. I changed all that and made this a safe place for sonsabitches like you to come and live."

"And I'm much obliged for it." Buford said. "Yes sir, while you was here scarin' drunken Mexicans and cowboys so I could live safe, I was on the border with fuckin' Kiowa and Comanches up my ass! Sorry I forgot, you had to deal with a horse thief." Buford couldn't let it go, nor control his mirth, and laughed heartily.

Hi gave him a scathing look and Buford laughed all the harder. He had missed his friend.

"Don't be an asshole. I ain't killin' Yankees, or hidin' in bushes any more waitin' for some fuckin' Indian, but I ain't grown as soft as you think."

"Sorry Hi, but you sure rile easy. Guess that's what happens when men like us retire. I know you ain't lost none of your blood lust, but you know how to live with it. That's what I aim to do, try to forget 'bout killin' and this ranch will be a start."

"Well let's go and stake your claim before the damn sodbusters come and get it."

Buford seldom was happy, but he was this day. He felt he finally had a future.

On the way back to town Hi told Buford the origin of Wilder Creek. It's founder, Jonas Wilder, had come from west Texas searching for new land to graze his cattle. Bordered by an off shoot of the Ute River it was fine grazing land. He was the first settler and named the area "Wilder Creek" after himself. Shortly after, he died of fever, but other settlers kept his name in memory.

When they finally reached town, Buford was pleased to see it was bigger than he'd first thought. It had all the services he would need to start his ranch. The town even had a doctor which was an unaccustomed luxury. A small, white church stood at one end of the long thorough fare. At the other end was a shabby boarding house, the jailhouse, and the Longhorn Saloon.

Behind the church was a group of neat little houses owned by Hi, the parson and a few store keepers. A few miles away was the Mexican community known as "the Village." Most of the Mexicans peddled their wares in town, while others worked as domestics. Spread out beyond town, were the ranchers.

After Buford settled his claim, Hi said, "This calls for a celebration. Why don't you and me go down to the Longhorn and have a drink. Besides, feelin' a little jumpy, could use a poke."

Buford gazed at him from beneath his thick brows. "Thought you said you ended your evil ways."

"Well I can't go botherin' Lydia in her condition, can I? A man has his needs. When Lydia's able I stay away from whores but now that she's not..."

Buford smiled. "Hi, you're still a hog. But I can't blame you, I could use a poke myself."

Hi laughed. "Glad you understan'. You're gonna' like what we got. A few months ago, two fine calico queens come here all the way from New Orleans. They sure can make a man smile. They was real fancy whores back in Louisiana but had to leave town right quick after a little trouble one of 'em had with a gambler. They was just passin' through but they made so much money here, they stayed.

When they entered the saloon, Hi was greeted warmly by Frenchie, the proprietor.

"Marshall," he said in his heavy french accent, "I'm glad to hear your men found that damn horse thief. He won't steal my horses again. A drink for you and your friend on the house."

"Much obliged," Hi said. "This here is Colonel McLeod, Texas Ranger. He come here to ranch."

Those that overheard studied Buford with interest. He and Hi had a reputation that proceeded them everywhere they went. Due to that, the towns folk were intimidated by Hi in the beginning. They soon learned he was a good man. Hi was a natural story teller, and having a captive audience, he often spoke of he and Buford's exploits.

"Howdy," Buford said, tipping his hat to Frenchie.

"A pleasure to meet you Colonel," Frenchie said with reverence.

"Where's your girls?" Hi asked.

"Lazy bitches! Probably upstairs sleeping. Business been slow today."

"Well, me and the Colonel aim to remedy that. Send for Emma and Jamie."

When Frenchie left, Hi said, "These are the two gals I was tellin' you 'bout. I prefer Emma, but I'll let you have 'er."

"Don't make no difference to me," Buford said.

"'Course not. You ain't much for women."

"Never said I was," Buford said quietly.

Two young ladies met them at the bar. One was a tall, willowy blonde, and the other a voluptuous redhead.

"Howdy ladies," Hi said, standing and sweeping his hat off gallantly. "This is my friend, Colonel McLeod."

Buford eyed the two women, ill at ease. "Howdy."

"Let's have some drinks over here, Frenchie!" Hi called out.

"You from Texas, too?" asked Jamie, the redhead, cozying up to Buford.

"Yes, ma'am. Come here to ranch."

"Don't get your hooks into 'im too fast," Hi said to her, seeing his friend's embarrassment. "I aim to spark you today."

"All right, Marshall," she said, switching her attention to him. He kissed her neck and she giggled.

Buford looked awkwardly at Emma. She had clear blue eyes and a cascade of wavy blonde hair that fell past her waist, her face was free of rouge. She looked innocent and respectable which he found disconcerting.

Emma tried to put him at ease. "What did you do in Texas, Colonel?" she asked.

"I was a Ranger."

"Just like this varmint, here," said Jamie fondly, squeezing Hi's leg.

"I'm ready," Hi said to her, downing his drink. They went upstairs, leaving Buford and Emma alone.

"How 'bout you Colonel?"

He didn't answer but placed some coins on the bar for their drinks, picked up his hat and followed her to her room.

Buford's sexual needs had always been satisfied by whores, but they still made him uncomfortable. Emma thought he looked like a rabbit caught in a snare and she found it appealing.

Closing the door quietly behind her, she went to him and kissed him softly. She slipped a hand up his thigh and cupped the mound between his legs. She wasn't surprised that he was hard but the size and bulk of what she felt made her shudder.

They undressed quickly, and laid side by side on the bed.

After a few moments of foreplay, Buford's need was great, and he got down to business.

When they were done, they both lay panting and sweating, thoroughly exhausted. After a while Emma said, "If you'd like to go again, Colonel, it's on the house."

"Much obliged," he said getting up and beginning to dress, "but I got a lot of work to do." He left some money on the bureau and tipping his hat, he left.

She lay back in bed, feeling light headed. "My Lord!" she thought, "if'n he ain't the best I ever had! He was skittish as a cat but reckon he would be, ain't too many women could take what he's got!"

When Buford went downstairs, he found Hi sitting at a table with some other men. Hi introduced him to Charlie Smith, Buford's closest neighbor; Clyde, one of the deputies; and Abel Platts, owner of the hotel.

"Lord, Buford, what took you so long? Forget where to put it?" The men at the table smiled but dared not laugh.

"No, I remember. I just ain't in a hurry like you, is all. How long was you up there, five minutes? You know Hi, there's times when it ain't good for a man to be quick on the draw."

The men at the table continued to smile uneasily. It would take a while for them to realize that Hi and Buford's animosity towards each other was harmless.

To their relief, Hi laughed. "Well, boys, it just don't do to give the Colonel here any shit. He'll cut you down any which way he can. Don't matter if'n it's with words, a gun or his cock."

Once their nervous laughter died down, Buford asked, "You men know if'n there's any one lookin' for work?"

"A few," said Charlie Smith. "There's that feller from Kansas, Josh Logan. He's stayin' at the boardin' house, yonder. Then there's that pathetic lookin' group of waddys over there," he said indicating a table at the far end of the room with four men sitting around it. "They come in yesterday. Don't know 'em but they might be suitable."

Cow punchers like these four men, worked for which-
ever ranch needed them during the busy cattle season. Once
it was over, they drifted here and there doing whatever odd
jobs they could find. The ranchers called these temporary
hands, "waddys".

"There's a few Mexicans 'round too, I expect. Reckon I
can find out," Hi added.

"You can have a couple a' my men and I think some of
the other ranchers can spare a man or two. I'll talk to 'em for
you. Round up don't start for a while," Charlie said.

"Be much obliged to y'all," Buford smiled. "Like to
leave at sun up day after tomorrow. Think you could gather
up some men by then? I'll pay 'em a fair wage."

"Sure, Colonel," said Charlie. "Where would you like
'em to meet you?"

Buford looked at Hi and said, "Reckon the jailhouse
would be just fine."

Hi sighed. "All right, let 'em all meet at the jail, but I'm
usually catchin' a snooze at that time of the mornin', and
none of 'em better wake me up!"

"Reckon I'll go on over and talk to those waddys,"
Buford said.

"I think they'll do," he said when he returned. "They're
on the way to Kansas but they can stay 'round a spell. Much
obliged for your help," he said to Charlie. "Like to stay for
another drink but got things to do. Nice meetin' y'all."

Hi got up, ready to leave as well. "I'll come with you.
Should be gettin' back to work, anyways,"

When they left, Hi said, "So what did you think of
Emma?"

"Huh?" Buford asked. He was thinking of the work that
lay ahead and she was gone from his mind.

"Emma! God damn, don't tell me she didn't make an
impression?"

"Oh! She was fine all right. I was saddle sore but the
work out she done give me took the kinks out a' my back."

"Well thank God, you can still appreciate a good whore.
Go do what you gotta', but don't be late for supper or Lydia
will have your hide."

Buford spent what was left of the afternoon buying supplies. He needed tools, lumber, hardware, cooking utensils and a number of other things. By the time he was done, he had a wagon load of goods. Next he went to the boarding house and asked for Josh.

"Who's askin'?" the surly clerk inquired as he hunkered down over a newspaper.

"Colonel McLeod."

The clerk stood up. "Oh Colonel! Pleasure to meet you, I'm Kramer Finn. Heard all 'bout you. Josh ain't here right now, he just left for the Longhorn."

"Just came from there, musta' missed him," Buford said. "Much obliged."

"Sure thing, Colonel," the clerk said with the utmost courtesy and respect.

"Goddamn, Hi!", Buford swore to himself as he went back to the Longhorn. "I ain't been in town 24 hours and everyone knows who I am."

The fact that he had gotten special treatment from the merchants, and curious stares from the folks he passed by, wasn't lost on him.

Hi liked to embellish and dramatize but most of his stories were factual. He spoke of how his friend had achieved the rank of Colonel at the age of 26 for outstanding valor at Gettysburg. He also told them that Buford could kill a man in the blink of an eye. By the time he was through, Buford's already impressive reputation had grown.

Back in the Longhorn, Buford asked Frenchie where he could find Josh. Frenchie pointed to a gaunt young man in his late teens or early twenties who sat dejectedly at a table alone, a glass of whiskey in front of him.

Buford walked over to him. "Howdy, I'm Colonel McLeod. Mind if I set a spell?"

"No sir don't mind a'tall. Name's Josh Logan." The two men shook hands.

"I'm a friend of Marshall Johnson's. Gonna be startin' a ranch here and I need a reliable hand. Charlie Smith tole' me you might be lookin' for work."

Joshua's long, lean face broke into a grin. "Yes sir, I need work bad."

"Know anything 'bout cows?"

"Yep, been 'round 'em all my life. My Daddy had a few."

"Where you from, son?"

"Little town, 'bout thirty miles south of Abilene."

"Why'd you leave Kansas?"

"I had my reasons," Josh said.

"You ain't in trouble with the law, are you?"

"No sir!" said Josh indignantly.

"Glad to hear it. Workin' for me ain't gonna' be easy. How hard do you wanna' work?

"I got two bits left Colonel. I'm lookin' for anything."

"Well if'n you want, I got plenty of work. First I need to build my spread then I gotta' go to San Antone for my herd. It's goin' to be a lot of long hours and hard work. I'll pay you forty dollars a month and found. That O.K.?"

Josh accepted. Thirty dollars was average pay and "found", meaning room and board would be provided. The forty Buford offered seemed like a windfall.

Buford could feel eyes boring into the back of his head, quick of reflex he turned and met Emma's gaze. She smiled sweetly and waved at him. Without acknowledging her he turned and continued his conversation with Josh. She was a whore and pleasure time was over. He finished talking with Josh and left the saloon.

Two days later the hired hands assembled at the jail-house. Charlie and two other ranchers, Zeb Converse and James Boutwell, had each sent three men. The group also included the four waddys, Josh, and four Mexicans hired by Hi.

Hi came out of the jailhouse when he saw Buford. "Well, you got sixteen men includin' you. That oughta' be enough," he said.

"Thought you was gonna' be sleepin'," Buford teased.

 Hi glared at him and pulled out his gun. "If'n you're gonna' start on that cocksuckin' horse thief again, I'm gonna' shoot you right here." Buford appreciated Hi's dramatics and laughed.

• • •

Phineas Cary, the merchant's son, rode up with a wagon load of Buford's purchases and Buford went to talk to him.

Hi turned to the group. "Thought I'd take this opportunity while the Colonel's out of ear shot to warn you men, don't fuck with 'im. He's my best friend and I knowed 'im all my life. He's a good man and there's none fairer, but if you try any funny business, he'll come down on you with the wrath of God. Get 'im riled, he's likely to shoot you. Y'all understand?"

"Yes, Marshall," they replied. Hi chuckled to himself at the look on their faces. He knew that Buford could be one mean son of a bitch, but he wasn't likely to kill any of them. But let them think it. Hi was the law in this town and he'd keep order in any way necessary.

By the end of the first day, Buford knew everyone by name and had a good idea of each man's character. During his years in the military he had learned to judge men well. He thought Josh was going to make a first-rate hand. He worked hard and didn't complain. One of the Mexicans, a small, brown man named Juan, was another hard worker. He was surprisingly adept with a hammer and always willing to help the other men. The waddys were good workers, too.

Although most ranchers built only what was needed at first and added structures as they went along, Buford, in his steadfast manner, decided to build his ranch all at once.

He planned to build a barracks and a cook house with a connecting area for saddles and the like. He wanted two big barns and several corrals. He hoped someday to be prosperous enough to raise horses as a sideline. Being a practical man, he knew there was more money in cows, and that would have to come first.

By the end of the first day, Buford was pleased. He had a good bunch of men, and things were coming along fine.

Juan appeared to be as good with pots and pans as he was with tools; he took over Buford and Josh's clumsy attempts to make a meal.

The workers ate around the camp fire. They didn't ask questions of each other, that would've been considered rude. Instead they enjoyed the conversation of men who shared a common goal.

Exhausted they curled up in their blankets to sleep.

Buford listened to their snoring. He was too keyed-up

to sleep. For years, as he'd sloshed through ankle-deep mud chasing Yankees, or sat in a thicket for hours waiting for Indians, he'd thought of a piece of land and a place he could call his own. Now he had one.

He hoped settling down would change him. A professional killer, he'd become cold and aloof. He felt as if he'd lost not only his heart, but his soul, and wanted to get his humanity back. As much as he would've liked to delude himself, he knew his frequent nightmares of battles and bloodshed was a bad sign.

The work was going steadily when a few days later, Hi came riding in. "Howdy girls," he said good naturedly. "How y'all doin'? Hot enough for ya' today?" The men wiped the sweat from their brows, mumbled a greeting, and went back to work. Hi rode over to Buford who was hammering in earnest.

"What the hell is that?" Hi asked.

"This here's gonna be the barracks."

"Haw, you don't know shit 'bout buildin'. Looks like a good wind'll blow the son of a bitch down."

"I'm doin' the best I can. Never said I knew nothin' 'bout buildin'."

"How the men workin' out?"

"Good. Besides, they couldn't be any worse than me at this goddamn job."

"Ain't that the truth. Emma was askin' for you. Wanted to know if'n you was comin' into town soon."

"Don't think so. Got too much to do here."

"Ain't I always tole' you that you work too much? A good poke now and then cleans the pipes out."

"My pipes is cleaned out, I only been out of town a couple a' days."

"Yea, but she likes you, I can tell," Hi teased.

Buford looked at Hi with a grumpy scowl and said, "What the fuck you doin' here anyhow?"

"I just come by to see how y'all doin'."

"Well you seen it."

"Yea, and your woodworkin' skills is worse than I thought."

• • •

In a few weeks most of the building was done, and Buford released the men who had been loaned to him by the ranchers. Only Josh, the waddys, and the Mexicans remained to finish the job.

As the work was drawing to an end, Buford gathered the men together. "Most of y'all know I got a herd of cows in San Antone. I gotta' go fetch 'em, and my brother Tom who's partnerin' up with me. I need some good men to help me. When we get back I'm gonna' need some top hands, and I'll keep y'all on. Josh already tole' me he's stayin'. He been 'round beeves his whole life. If'n you don't know nothin', me, Tom, and Josh will learn you cow."

The four waddys talked softly amongst themselves. Two of them, Phil Hughill and Jimmy Kelly came forward. "We'll stay, we sure could use the steady work."

Of the Mexicans, only Juan stepped forward.

"Colonel," he said, "I know nothing of cows, and don't care to learn. But I know lots of other things. I am good with a hammer. I can cook and clean and raise chickens and pigs. Please let me stay."

Buford smiled. "I reckon you know enough for me to sign you on. I'm obliged to y'all who want to stay. Enough jawin'. I don't know 'bout you fellers but I think some time in town will do us all good."

The men cheered. They were sick of work and being stuck out in the middle of nowhere. A trip to Wilder Creek was welcome.

The first thing they did was go to the Barbers for a bath and a haircut. Buford was pleased with his crew and thought a bonus of some new clothes would be appreciated. Their next stop was the haberdashery.

"I'm Colonel McLeod," he told the clerk. "These here are my men. I'd be much obliged if'n you could outfit 'em all and put it on my bill."

The clerk grinned, "Certainly, Colonel." New clothes for these men would bring in a bit of cash.

Buford was waiting for them when they came out. He inwardly smiled at their obvious pleasure but spoke in his gruff manner. "Everyone in this shit hole town knows y'all been workin' for me. Don't want 'em thinkin' I didn't pay ya' enough to have decent clothes on your back."

One of the Waddy's spoke. "We all knowed you paid us better'n than fair, this weren't necessary."

Before Buford could reply, Josh spoke. "Now that I ain't offensive, I'm goin' to the Longhorn and call on Miss Emma. It's been a long time since I had a woman."

Phil Hughill spoke up. "If'n I don't get to 'er first."

"Like hell!" Jimmy Kelly added. "She's gonna' be with me, soon as I walk in the door."

Buford smiled, "Now don't y'all go gettin' yourselves riled up over her, she's just a whore. They're only good for one thing, and one's the same as another."

Josh looked surprised. "Then you don't know Miss Emma."

"I know 'er," Buford said.

When they were outside the Longhorn, Buford paid them and said, "Y'all go along, I got some business to tend to. Don't get in no trouble."

"We won't," Josh said.

Josh, Phil and Jimmy entered the bar and sat at a table. As they waited for their drinks, Josh thought about his new boss. In the short time he'd known him, he'd grown to admire him. True, he was a hard task master and expected a good day's work, but he worked harder than anyone. The Marshall said Buford was a fair man and he was right.

Buford went to see Lydia and Hi. On the way he met Juan, who hadn't gone to the Longhorn since Mexicans weren't welcome.

Buford stopped to speak to him. "Hey Juan. You gettin' your affairs in order? Goin' to say goodbye to the wife?"

Juan answered. "I don't have no wife, Colonel. I have a mean old sister. She won't be sorry to see me go. My sister, she yells at me all the time. Tells me I am no good. I can't wait to get away from her." Despite his words, Juan already looked homesick.

"Shit, Juan. You ain't got no reason to look sorry. If'n it's yellin' you want, I do my share. You ain't gonna' be missin' your sister much when I get started on ya'."

Juan smiled. "Si, Colonel. I feel better now."

Buford grinned back. "We'll be leavin' from the Longhorn. When you're ready come fetch me there."

"Si," Juan said.

When Buford arrived at Hi's, an elderly lady answered the door. "Is the Marshall in?", he asked.

"Why you must be Colonel McLeod." The woman smiled and held out her hand. "I'm Alvira Gibson, the Parson's wife. Hi ain't here. Me and the midwife just delivered Lydia of a fine baby boy, not only ten minutes ago. We done sent the Marshall off as soon as the labor got bad. I expect he's off in town somewheres."

"A baby boy, ain't that fine. How's Lydia doin'?"

"She's doin' fine but think she'll do better when she sees 'er

husband. Do me a favor, if'n you see him, send him home."

"I'll find 'im," he turned and mounted his horse.

"Reckon if you can't find him, no one can," she said with admiration in her voice.

He nodded, embarrassed by her tone. "I'll do my best."

Buford went to the jailhouse but wasn't surprised to find Hi absent. Clyde, the deputy, greeted him. "If you're lookin' for the Marshall, he's at the saloon."

"I figured as much but thought he might be workin' for a change. Much obliged."

When he got to the Longhorn, Hi was already drunk. Buford made his way over to him. A plump brunette sat close to Hi, her arm around his neck.

Hi gave him a drunken smile. "How ya' doin'! This here's Sally. Lydia's reached 'er time and them old biddies run me out of my own fuckin' house, goddamn 'em."

"I come to fetch you."

Hi stood up, nearly toppling Sally to the floor. "She done have the baby?"

"She sure did. A fine boy."

"Whoohee!" yelled Hi. The crowd quieted at his outburst.

"I got me a boy!" he told them jubilantly. "Frenchie! Drinks for everybody!"

After they drank to Lydia and the baby's health, Hi headed for the door. Buford followed him outside.

"Sure am happy for you, Hi. You got a fine woman, and now a son." He slapped Hi on the back. "Sure am glad things turned out good for you."

Tears welled up in Hi's eyes. He sniffed and wiped them away, quickly. "It sure is somethin' ain't it? So many times I thought I'd never live long enough to have a youngun'. Shit, we been through some bad times me and you."

"That we have." Both men were silent but were thinking the same thoughts. They had defied death many times, and both were happy to be standing in the dusty street of Wilder Creek.

Hi mounted his horse and Buford patted him on the leg.

"Now you go on home to your family. I'll have a drink and poke a whore for you."

"Much obliged," Hi said. He turned his horse and rode fast for home.

Buford stepped back into the Longhorn and found his men. "That's one happy man," he said.

"Sure is. Nothin' like a youngun' to make a man feel his worth," Josh said.

"You got younguns'?" Jimmy asked.

"One."

"Well, I'll be," said Buford. "You ain't more than a boy yourself."

"Was old enough I expect."

"What you got?" Phil asked.

"A beautiful baby girl," Josh smiled.

"That's fine," Phil beamed.

"Yea, fine," Josh said sadly. "That's why I done leave Kansas. My girl, Elizabeth, was just 15 when I got 'er in the family way. I was gonna' marry 'er but her Paw told me he'd cut off my balls before we hit the alter. He didn't like me none and told me to skedaddle 'cause he weren't jokin'. I believed 'im, boys, and left with my balls intact but my fuckin' heart was broken."

Jimmy patted him on the back. "You'll be O.K. Ya' know what? You can have Emma, I'll get someone else. He and Phil got up and went in search for two other whores.

Buford looked at Josh. "Did you love 'er?"

"'Course I did! She's the love of my life. I'm thinkin' that if'n I ever get enough money behind me, I might go back."

"Well, I hope things work out for you." Just as he spoke Emma came to the table and Josh perked up.

"I ain't seen you for a while, Colonel."

"Been busy buildin' my spread."

"Yea, the Marshall tole' me it come out fine. You wanna' go upstairs?"

"Reckon I would, but I'll wait my turn. Josh been settin' here waitin' for you."

"Josh, honey. Would you mind gettin' one of the other girls?"

"Yes, Miss Emma, don't mind tellin' you I would," Josh scowled. "I want you."

"Go ahead," said Buford. "I'll wait."

She looked undecided for a moment and then said, "All right, Josh, let's go. You better be here when I get back, Colonel."

"Give you my word," he said.

Buford had another drink and in what seemed like no time at all, Josh came back. "Damn, that little gal can be a wild cat! She says she'll be down in a second, Colonel."

"Ain't in no hurry."

Maybe he wasn't, but Emma was and she was at his side in a moment.

"Ready?" she asked anxiously.

Buford looked at her. "You want to set a spell first? Let me buy you a drink."

"Maybe later," she said, "let's go."

Phil joined Josh at the table as Emma and Buford left. He said, 1"If'n I ain't mistakin' I think Emma's takin' a shinin' to the Colonel. See the way she looks at 'im?"

"Ain't nothin'" growled a jealous Josh. "She ain't particular. She knows he got money."

When Buford and Emma entered her room, she went to him and began to smother him with kisses.

"Whoa," he laughed. "What's all this? Give a man a chance to breathe."

She drew back, her face coloring. "I didn't mean no harm, Colonel, I know you're a hero and all but last time you was here, you was a tad skittish."

"Reckon, I was. I ain't what you'd call a lady's man and I ain't no hero. What kind of bullshit has Hi been spreadin'?" He suddenly felt angry and not just because of Hi. He didn't know his fear of women was obvious.

"He ain't tole' me much. Just said you was in the war and the Rangers together and you was a hero."

"Don't listen to that jackass. He likes to spin yarns."

Not for the first time she noticed the scars that covered his body and knew he was being modest. "Well, he said you was one of the youngest Colonels in the whole danged Confederate Army!"

"Reckon I was, but not 'cause I was a hero. When I got my commission all the good men was dead, and they had poor dregs to choose from."

When they got on the bed Buford, no longer felt shy. He made love to her with an expertise that came natural to him, even though his experience was limited.

Emma like him. He seemed different from her mundane string of cowboys. He gave her genuine physical pleasure, he had an air about him, confident and commanding.

She had grown to believe that all men were the same. They used her, caring only about their own needs. She knew this to be the nature of her profession and accepted it. Occasionally she had a man who treated her with tenderness or gave her pleasure, but they were few and far between. Never had she been with anyone like Buford.

When he got ready to leave, she hated to see him go, and chastised herself for it. She knew better. It didn't do in this business to get attached. Despite this, she offered him the poke free of charge.

"Wouldn't be right, Emma. This here's your work. I done took you and gotta' pay." He placed the money on her table.

"Ain't work with you, Colonel," she said with shining eyes.

He didn't answer but went for the door.

"Colonel!" she called out. He paused and looked back at her.

"Think you'll be comin' back to town soon?"

"Don't think so. I'm leavin' for Texas in a few days and

I'll be gone a spell."

"Oh," she said, disappointed.

"Damn, she's pretty," he thought. He looked at the floor and twisted his hat in his hands. "Well, might be in town one more time 'fore I go."

"Well, y'all come back and see me," she said. He nodded and left.

Buford joined his men and they drank and talked. A short time later Frenchie came over. "Colonel, I don't mean to disturb you but there's a greaser outside wishing to speak with you."

Buford went outside where Juan waited. "I'm ready to go Colonel," he said.

"C'mon in and have a drink with me and the boys then we'll be on our way."

"Oh no!" Juan said frightened. "They don't like us in there. There will be much trouble."

"You'll be all right. You'll be with me and the boys."

"I don't think so, Colonel. Gracias, all the same."

Buford scowled at him. "No wonder your sister yells at you all the time. I'm your boss and I'm tellin' you to come in and have a fuckin' drink."

Juan swallowed hard. Buford's look made arguing futile, and despite his trepidation, he followed.

Disparaging remarks greeted them when they entered.

"Ain't no greasers allowed in here, Colonel," one man said. "Reckon, you bein' new in town, you don't know."

"Well, he's in here now," Buford said, "and I aim to have a drink with 'im and the boys, then we'll be on our way."

He strode over to his table with Juan in tow. Phil, Josh and Jimmy looked at each other nervously. They knew there would be trouble though Buford seemed unperturbed.

"Frenchie, bring us a bottle," he said.

Frenchie hesitated not knowing what to do, but a scathing look from Buford set him in motion. He brought over the whiskey and an extra glass. All eyes in the room followed him.

Buford poured Juan a drink with a steady hand, though the Mexican's trembled when he picked up the glass.

"Well boys," said Buford, "a toast to you. You worked

hard and I'm obliged to y'all."

Before they could drink, a voice rang out from behind them. "Colonel! Get that fuckin' Mexican out of here."

Buford turned and looked at the young man who'd spoken.

"I ain't meanin' no disrespect, but as soon as we have this drink, we'll be outa' here."

"I guess you ain't understandin' my meanin'. That fuckin' greaser got to git."

"He will as soon as he has his drink." Buford turned back to his companions ignoring the angry man. The room turned suddenly quiet and an aura of tension hung in the room.

"Who is that pup?" Buford asked his men.

"That there's Zeb Converse, Jr. They call 'im, Junior," Josh said. "He got a bad temper and a big mouth. Only thing that saves his hide is his Daddy, Zeb Senior. He's a good man, loaned us his boys for buildin'. He helps everybody out, so's people let Junior run his mouth."

"Lucky for him," Buford said.

Emma was descending the stairs when she became aware trouble was brewing.

Despite Buford's calm, the men at his table were tense.

A drunken Junior stood up, nearly upsetting his table. "Fuck you, asshole! Did you come into this here town to help your friend Hi take over? My Daddy's been here since the beginnin', and I ain't aimin' to stand aroun' while you and that dumb ass Marshall take over the town. You think 'cause you both made names for yourselves rangerin' you can do what the fuck you want. I ain't havin' it."

Buford turned and looked at Junior. "Ain't tryin' to take over nothin' son. Like I said, let me and my boys have a drink an' we'll be outa' your way"

As soon as Buford turned towards the men at his table Junior pulled his guns, both aimed at Buford's back. Buford was aware that this green horn had made his move but didn't move a muscle. Instead he made a toast.

"Here's to us, boys, and a job well done."

A terrified Juan drank his shot and got ready to leave.

"Take it easy, Juan," Buford said pouring him another

drink.

"I've had enough Colonel."

"I'll tell you when you've had enough," Buford said.

Junior spoke again. "If that greaser ain't gone in a minute, I'm gonna' kill ya' both."

Juan got up from his chair and Buford grabbed his arm. "Finish your drink, Juan," he said calmly.

With shaking hands, the Mexican gulped the rest of his whiskey.

"O.K. son, you can put your guns away. My friend's leavin'." He looked at Juan. "Go on Juan, I'll be right out." Juan quickly exited; his face bathed in sweat.

Buford poured another round for the rest of his men. He saw that they were still looking over his shoulder at Junior.

"Them pistols still pointin' at me?" Josh shook his head in the affirmative.

Buford sighed. Looking into his drink he said to Junior. "You made your point. Now put them things away."

"I ain't made no point. Y'all gotta' understand that your name don't mean shit 'round here."

"You made that clear. If'n you don't put them guns down, you're gonna' be one sorry son of a bitch.".

"Yea, I'm scairt, you has been," Junior said.

Buford looked weary and shook his head. His men started to rise, readying themselves for trouble. "Stay put," he said softly.

Even though he was a big man, Buford could move like lightening. Before anyone knew what was happening, Buford had disarmed Junior. He pointed one of the guns at Junior's head and almost pulled the trigger before coming to his senses. He dropped his hands to his sides and took some deep breathes to calm himself.

He told a shaken Junior, "I swear to Christ kid, I don't care who your Daddy is, if you fuck with me again, I'll drop you where you stand. Now get the fuck outa' here before I change my mind." Although Junior glared at him, and tried to act tough, he left in a hurry.

After Juniors hasty retreat, the quiet room filled with conversation. The main topic was Buford and how he had handled the obnoxious young rancher.

Buford thought he'd caused enough of a ruckus for one night and he and his men left.

"Shit Colonel, I thought for a minute you was gonna' shoot 'im."

"I almost did," Buford said with a shaky laugh. "I hope that cocksucker keeps out a' my way or there might be heap of trouble."

CHAPTER TWO

The next few days were busy and the incident with Junior was forgotten.

He bought a good, sturdy chuck wagon and Juan filled it with the necessary supplies. Next, he went to the Smith ranch to a buy a "remuda"; extra horses for his trip.

Horses used for rounding cattle were called "cow ponies"; a mixture of mustang and cavalry horses. Small and strong, they displayed a great deal of "cow sense" when it came to directing and searching out cattle. However, they couldn't be ridden for more than four or five hours at a time, so extra horses were a necessity.

Buford and Charlie haggled over the price of the stock but each of them enjoyed it. It was part of the ritual. Buford got two horses at a ridiculously low price but paid more than was fair for a fine stallion. In the end, both men made out evenly.

After their business had been completed they lounged around the corral and talked about horses.

"I hope to bring back some horses of good breedin' stock," Buford said.

"It'll be fine if'n you do, Colonel. Can't get enough horses of good blood lines 'round these parts. Next spring, I'll be buyin' from you."

"Hope so. Nothin' pleasures me more than a good horse."

Charlie smiled. "Not even a good woman?"

"Never met one. Ain't been lucky enough to have a fine string of fillies like y'all." Buford was referring to Charlie's wife and five daughters.

"Well, Colonel, some of my fillies are old enough to foal, if'n you ever have a mind."

"Much obliged for the offer but reckon I ain't the marryin' kind."

•••

When Buford got back to the ranch he rounded up his men. "I thought you might like to go to town before we hit the trail."

When they reached town, everyone went their separate ways with the understanding that they would meet later at the Longhorn.

Buford set off for Hi and Lydia's to see the new baby.

Lydia opened the door, "Come see little James Buford," she beamed.

"James Buford? You give 'im Buford for a middle name?"

"You gotta' problem with that?" Hi asked.

"No, I'm plum flattered, just a might surprised."

Hi smiled. "Reckon long as he don't grow up nothin' like you it'll be all right."

Buford admired the infant from afar. "Sure is a cute little feller, ain't he?"

Lydia smiled. "He sure is. Don't know how I ever got along without 'im."

"Easy. You had Hi. He's just like a youngun'. He needs someone to watch 'im and keep 'im outa' trouble."

Hi screwed his face up in mock anger. "You son of a bitch! Let's get ourselves a drink and set out on the porch."

When they were settled out in the cool evening air, Buford said. "He's a fine boy, Hi. Sure seems strange for you to be a Pa."

"Sure does," Hi said in wonder. "A little over a year ago, I had nothin' and now I got a wife and chile'."

"You're a lucky man. Hope you realize it and settle down."

"What do you mean?" Hi asked defensively. "Ain't I settled? Hardly drink or play cards or nothin'. Only poked whores when I couldn't do Lydia no more."

"Hardly!" Buford laughed. "You slowed down some, that's for sure, but never knew a man who liked to drink and fuck as much as you. You was always free and easy in your ways. Now you got responsibilities."

"I know that," Hi snapped.

"Ain't tryin' to rile you. Just know you is all. You got a habit of gettin' bored with things after a while. Hope you don't get tired of what you got here."

"I don't think I will. I'll confess that I get itchy feet from time to time, but I could never leave Lydia. I seen some good times, but none as good as I've had with 'er. Now that we got the baby, reckon I'll be quite content."

Buford took a long swallow of whiskey. "Well, that's good to hear."

"I'm gettin' used to bein' settled in one place. Just like you, I'm tired of our old life. Been away from it over a year and it feels good."

"You're a lucky man," Buford said again with a sigh.

"Yep, I am. You could be, too. In fact, don't be surprised if'n Lydia starts paradin' a bunch of two legged heifers in front of you. She got it in 'er head that you'll make a good husband."

Buford laughed. "Lord Jesus! You know better'n that! I ain't worth a damn when it comes to women."

"True enough but you ain't no spring chicken. Even an ornery cuss like you is gonna' have to marry sooner or later."

"Hell, no! Ain't got the patience for a woman."

"You got a point there. Patience with 'em ain't one of your strong points. Lord, I've seen you hole up for hours waitin' for Yankees or Indians without battin' an eye. Seen the look that comes over your face with a pesky woman. You look like you want to shoot 'er and be done with it."

"Didn't think I was that bad."

"Hell, you ain't," Hi laughed. "Sure did miss you, you old son of a bitch. Glad you're goin' to be livin' here."

"Me too," Buford said. "Do me a favor, while I'm gone. Check on my ranch when you can. Worked too hard to let the goddamn Indians burn it."

"I'll keep an eye on it, but don't worry. Ain't had an Indian attack in close to a year. Reckon since I come along, they know where the bear shits in the buckwheat."

"Thanks to Hiriam T. Johnson, Texas Ranger," Buford said.

"Texas Ranger and Marshall. Don't forget that."

"How can I when you remind me every goddamn chance you get? Don't want to keep you out jawin' all night. Reckon I'll go on over to the Longhorn and keep the peace there for you."

"You got a big heart," Hi sneered.

"Don't I? Well reckon, now that you're all reformed and all, someone's gotta' keep the whores happy and Frenchie honest."

"You jack ass!" Hi laughed. "I can still do that, even though I'm tryin' to walk the straight and narrow!"

"You don't even know what straight and narrow looks like." Buford smiled.

"By the way," Hi said. "I heard about the ruckus with Junior Converse. You done good takin' that fuckin' pup down a peg."

"Yea, I really should'a ignored 'im, but he wouldn't keep his goddamn mouth shut. Honest to Christ, I almost shot 'im dead, him wavin' his pistols at my back. Good thing I caught myself in time. He's just a boy shootin' off his mouth. Didn't think he'd have the balls to pull the trigger."

"Well, reckon, you is gettin' civilized. In the old days, seen you shoot a man for less."

"Yea, well that was the old days. Y'all take care of your family, hear?"

"Yes sir, Colonel!" Hi said, brandishing a smart salute. When Buford got to the Longhorn, he saw Josh cozied up with Emma and tactfully went to the other side of the room, joining Phil and Jimmy. In a while he felt a gentle hand on his arm. It was Emma.

"Howdy Colonel," she said with a bright smile, "Josh tells me you're leavin' soon."

"Yea," he said.

"Sure gonna' miss you," she said.

He wondered how someone as sweet and pretty could be a whore. She wasn't course and tough like the others he'd known.

"Reckon, you'll have enough to think 'bout besides an old war horse like me," he answered.

"Gotta' say, it's been a pleasure bein' with you."

He flashed one of his rare smiles. "Much obliged for the compliment. You available?" he asked.

"I believe your name is the next one on my dance card," she laughed.

"I think you boys was right," Josh said after Buford and Emma departed. "Sure looks like she's got a hankerin' for the Colonel, don't it?"

"Yea," said Phil. "but what's it to you? Are you sweet on 'er?"

Josh's face turned red. "No."

"So what's the problem? Besides, I thought you was goin' back to that little girl who had your baby.", said Jimmy.

"The more I think on that the more I doubt her Paw would let me marry 'er. I reckon I do like Emma just a little bit," Josh sighed.

"Then take 'er off the line!" Phil said.

Josh didn't answer.

Buford and Emma made love twice. A few times she screamed loudly with pleasure and Buford scolded her. "Quiet there, Emma, don't want no one to think I'm hurtin' you."

When they were done he paid her and gave her a few dollars more.

"What's this for?" she asked.

"You're a good gal, Emma. Just a little extra. Believe me, you're worth it."

"Much obliged, Colonel. Why don't you wait for me and I'll come down with you?"

"No need," he said. "I'm goin' back to the ranch. See you in a coupla' months."

When he went downstairs he said to his men, "I'm leavin'. Stay if'n you want, long as you're back by sun up. We gotta' get our gear ready tomorrow."

"We'll come back with you," Jimmy replied.

They all rose to go, followed by a very drunk Junior Converse. When they were outside Junior asked, "Where's your greaser friend tonight, Colonel?"

"Left 'im at the ranch. You took offense last time and I didn't want to rile you again."

"Well, glad you learned your goddamn lesson," Junior

said, looking for a fight. His pride had suffered badly during their last altercation and he hoped to regain it.

A crowd began to gather thinking there might be trouble, and they didn't want to miss the excitement.

"I learned it all right," Buford said calmly. He mounted his horse and Junior stepped closer. "Is there anything else I can do for you son?" Buford asked.

"Don't think so."

Buford turned his horse and he and his men rode away.

"I don't trust 'im," said a scowling Phil.

"He's harmless. Just got a big mouth is all," Buford said.

"Mebbe'," said Jimmy. "He was really mad the other night and I hear he plans some mischief at the ranch while we're gone."

"Is that a fact?" Buford asked.

"That's what we heard," said Josh.

Buford turned his horse around and rode back towards the saloon.

"Where you goin'?" Josh called out.

"Back to see Junior."

He was in bad temper. Battle weary, all he wanted was to live in a small, quiet town in peace. He wondered why Junior wouldn't leave him alone. It seemed the young rancher was going out of his way to aggravate him.

"Reckon we oughta' git over there, in case he needs us," said Phil.

"From what I hear 'bout the Colonel, he ain't gonna' need us, Junior is. I think the Colonel's gonna' kill 'im sure," Josh said.

Back at the Longhorn, Junior strutted around. He had just chastised the Colonel in front of a crowd without repercussion.

Junior wanted to make a reputation for himself. What better way than to take on one of the toughest men in the territory? Because of his father's good reputation, he knew no one would bother him.

When Buford re-entered the Longhorn, all eyes turned towards him. They had a feeling his business with Junior wasn't finished.

"Colonel, you came back," said an exuberant Emma. He

pushed her aside gently.

"Ain't here to see you."

He walked over to Junior's table. "Can I speak to you a minute?" he asked politely.

"Can't you see I'm playin' cards?" Junior snapped.

Buford's nerves were already strained, and he lost his temper. Picking up the table, he threw it across the room where it smashed against the wall. Men and whores scattered in all directions.

"Reckon, the game is over," he said in a voice cold as ice.

Junior stood up in defiance and Buford quickly grabbed him in a choke hold and pulled him over to another table. "Sit down," he said shoving him roughly into a chair.

Buford stood before Junior; tall and menacing. "I heard you're thinkin' of doin' mischief at my spread while I'm away."

"You heard wrong," said Junior rubbing his sore neck.

"Good," said Buford, "'cause if anythin' happens to my fuckin' ranch, I'm comin' after you. You understand?"

Junior glared at him but kept silent.

"Do you?" Buford asked softly, pushing his coat away from his gun.

"Reckon, I do."

"Good." Buford said. He was heading for the door when Josh saw Junior draw his gun and aim it at Buford's departing back.

"Colonel!" he shouted.

Buford turned quickly and shot Junior in the arm. Junior screamed out in pain and dropped his gun.

Buford said to Josh, "Go fetch the doctor and whoever is in the jail house."

He walked over to Junior who lay on the floor writhing in pain. Blood seeped out from the fingers that Junior clutched around his wound.

"Shit," Buford swore softly. "You're gonna' be all right. I just grazed you. Let me look at that arm."

"Stay away from me," Junior yelled. The Converse hands that were present went to assist him. Buford looked at them, "Don't get skittish y'all. Didn't want to hurt 'im. He drew first."

Buford stood quietly while the rest of the crowd looked on.

"What y'all gawkin' at?" he growled. "Ain't you never seen a man shot before?"

Hi came in. "Who'd you kill now?" he asked Buford in exasperation.

"I didn't kill no one. Just winged Junior. He riled me some."

"What happened?" Hi asked Junior.

"It's his fault, Marshall. I was playin' cards and he come in and threaten me. I didn't do nothin'.'"

Hi looked questioningly at Buford.

"I heard he was gonna' do some damage to my ranch while I was gone, and I came back to talk to 'im. Afraid I lost my temper. Shouldn't have thrown that table." Buford pointed to the shattered piece of furniture that lay on the floor.

"Who's going to pay for it is all I want to know," Frenchie whined.

"I'll pay for the goddamned thing," Buford snapped. Just then, the doctor came in flushed with sleep.

"Where's the patient?" he asked, half awake.

"Over here," one of the Converse hands said.

Doc went over and examined him. "Wondered when you were gonna' get yourself shot, Junior. Nothin' for y'all to be concerned with, just a flesh wound." He looked at the Converse hands, "Bring 'im to my office."

Hi was angry. Clyde was the deputy on duty but didn't know what to do when he learned Buford was involved. Instead, he got Hi out of bed to deal with the situation. He was upset with Buford, but yelled at the men in the saloon instead.

"Didn't I tell y'all not to fuck with my friend here? It ain't no fuckin' miracle Junior got grazed. Buford coulda' shot 'im between the eyes just as easy. I'm countin' on y'all to see that Junior don't cause no trouble for 'im while he's gone."

Buford paid Frenchie and left. Emma tried hard to get his attention, but he didn't look her way.

When they were outside, Hi said, "You done shot 'im in

the arm on purpose, didn't you?"

"Shit Hi, 'course I did. Didn't mean to cause no trouble, but that's the second time that son of a bitch drew his gun on me."

"I ain't got no problem with you. Just wanted to make sure you ain't gettin' sloppy."

"I can see you're put out with me and I'm sorry for it, but Lord, Hi! Can't understand why that boy keeps fuckin' with me. His Pa ain't gonna' think I'm neighborly now, is he?"

"Naw," said Hi. "Junior's had it comin' for a long time. Besides, I'll go straighten things out with Zeb Senior. He knows his boy is a jackass."

Two days later Buford and his men left for Texas. The trip was long and hard but uneventful.

They finally reached San Antonio, hot and tired. Buford's younger brother Tom greeted them.

"Was wonderin' when you was gonna' get here," he said.

"It's a hell of a journey from Wilder Creek. Gonna' have a hell of a time gettin' the herd back. You still wanna' come back with me?"

"Yea. Ma and Pa are doin' all right, they don't need me. Time to strike out on my own. Ranchin' seems to be as good a way to make money as any."

"Hope so. Don't know if'n we'll make any or not."

"Don't matter. I can pay for my share," he smiled, "Besides I've grown attached to them cows."

Buford spent more time in Texas than he anticipated. He attended several cattle and horse auctions and built up his herd. He didn't hurry with things as he was reluctant to leave his family. He could count on one hand how many times he'd seen them in the past ten years.

It had been necessary for Tom to hire three men to help with the herd. Ira Lake, Daniel Muzzy and Bill Harper were all seasoned cowhands. They would need three more to drive the herd back to Wilder Creek.

Buford wanted men with fighting experience and he sought out Ezra Stearns, an old army buddy. Ezra had a steady job but accepted Buford's offer to be lead man. He knew of two ex-soldiers that would be suitable and Buford hired them. Jeremiah Norcross and Asa Jones joined the outfit.

When it was time for them to leave, Buford's mother wept.

"Lord, it was good to see you again, son," she said reaching up to hug him. "Come back soon."

She looked at Tom with tears in her eyes, "Know you gotta' go but it breaks my heart. It was a comfort havin' you 'round. You both take care of yourselves. Buford, you make sure no harm comes to your baby brother!"

"Aw, Ma!" Tom scowled. "I ain't no baby. I'm twenty years old."

Going back to the territory took a long time. Buford had a sizable herd to move and stopped often to round up mavericks and wild horses.

When they reached the "Nations," as the Indian territory was called, they encountered only a few. They were hungry and begged for food. Buford gave them a few steers and he and his men passed unmolested.

When they reached Wilder Creek, Buford gave a sigh of relief to see the ranch still intact. He got his men settled and then set off for town. He was exhausted, but he wanted to see Hi and get more provisions. He wouldn't allow himself the luxury of resting until all his business was finished.

Covered with trail dust, he entered town half asleep. He stopped at the jail house and was met by Clyde.

"Where's the Marshall?" Buford inquired.

"He's at the Longhorn."

"Why ain't I fuckin' surprised. Does he know how lucky he is to have a good deputy like you to cover his sorry ass?"

"Doubt it," Clyde smiled, "but I'll tell 'im you said so."

"Don't bother, I'll tell 'im myself."

When he entered the Longhorn it took his eyes awhile to get adjusted to the gloom. He was half blinded from the sun. In his haste to get back, he'd driven his men and herd unmercifully through the heat of a western summer.

"Well Hi, see you're hard at work," he said sarcastically.

"Jesus Lord, Buford, you smell like a fuckin' cow," he said wrinkling his nose. "Thought you had water at your place. When you'd get in?"

"Not too long ago."

"And you come straight here."

"Obviously," said Buford tired and in a bad temper. "Frenchie, fetch me a beer!" He put his long legs up on a chair. "My ass is sore as hell," he complained.

"But not too sore to come poke the lovely Emma," smiled Hi.

"Ain't that a'tall. Come to thank you for watchin' my spread and find out how young Converse is doin'."

"He healed up fine and his Daddy tole' me he ain't holdin' no grudge. He felt lucky you didn't kill the son of a bitch. He hoped it might teach 'im a lesson."

"Did it?" Buford asked.

"No!" laughed Hi.

"So long as he leaves me alone there won't be no more trouble. How's Lydia and the baby?"

"Doin' just fine."

Emma came downstairs and her heart skipped a beat when she saw Buford. She went over to him.

"Glad to see you back, Colonel," she beamed. "Got time for a poke?"

"Hell no! Ain't you got a nose? I ain't exactly pleasin'."

"I don't care 'bout that." She tugged at his arm playfully. "Let's go."

"Goddamn it, I said no!" he snapped. "I just come in to talk to the Marshall."

"If'n I wasn't a happily married man, I'd oblige you," winked Hi.

She smiled at him, "That's right kind of you, Marshall. I didn't mean to bother you, Colonel. Just was happy to see you."

"It's O.K. Emma. Had no call to yell at you. I'm wore out is all."

"You'll get used to this ole' jackass after a while," said Hi. "He's got a fearsome temper and it don't take much to rile 'im."

"I could get used to 'im real easy, temper and all," she laughed. "Now you boys behave yourselves," she said as she walked away.

"What ya' do to 'er?" asked Hi. "Every time I come in the damn place all she wants to talk 'bout is you. Askin' me all kinds of questions. Asked me if'n you had a woman!" he laughed. "Tole 'er the truth. Tole 'er you hate women!"

"It didn't seem to scare 'er off none," Buford smiled.

"Reckon not. Hell, not even the smell of you done that."

"Women are peculiar critters. Would never come to poke 'er lookin' and smellin' like this. Just come in to see you. I got a coupla' Texas boys back at the ranch who'd like to see you, too."

"Who?" Hi asked with interest.

"Well, there's Tom, and I done found Ezra Stearns."

"Good Lord, ain't seen them boys in years. Reckon, I'll come on over later. How many head you come in with?"

"Close to 2,000," Buford said proudly, "and that ain't includin' horses."

"Still that many left on the plains, is there? Or did you steal 'em, you ole' wily son of a bitch."

"I was gatherin' this here herd, not you. I got a lot of faults, but thievin' ain't one of 'em."

"I'm just jokin'. That's a lot of cattle. Didn't think there were that many."

"There was, even if'n I had to track a good many down. Wasn't 'bout to let all that Ranger experience go to waste," he laughed. "Bought about eight hundred head, too."

"Have any trouble gettin' back?" Hi asked.

"No. I was damn lucky. Weather was good. The Nations was quiet." He got up stiffly. "I gotta' get 'bout my business and get back to the ranch, I'm nearly wore out."

"You're growin' soft," said Hi. "Can remember a time when you spent months in the saddle without a whimper."

"Ridin's one thing, herdin' 2000 head is another."

"I tole' you ranchin's hard work. What you gonna' call your spread?"

"Don't know. I guess the McLeod ranch is as good a name as any."

"God, Buford, you ain't got no imagination. Ain't that book learnin' your Momma give you amount to nothin'?"

"Reckon not. Y'all come on over and see the boys, hear?"

"Sure will."

Buford went to various stores to get the provisions he'd need now that he was back. After he made his purchases and arrangements for delivery, he headed back to the ranch.

The swaying motion of the horse soon had him asleep in the saddle. He'd wake with a start occasionally but slept most of the way home.

When he got there everyone was asleep except Ezra and the men who had watch.

Buford went to the pumphouse to wash and then collapsed onto one of the bunks. He fell asleep in a second, oblivious to the sounds of snoring that surrounded him.

The next morning, he was woken by the sounds of happy shouts. Hi came storming into the bunkhouse. "All right girls rise and shine!" Ezra recognized Hi's voice immediately and it was a joyful reunion.

Tom introduced Hi to the new men and soon a bottle of whiskey was produced and passed around.

"What the hell you doin'?" asked Buford. "Put that bottle away, these men got work. Ain't everybody lazy like you."

"See what you're in for boys? The Colonel's one cranky son of a bitch! I got news for you Buford, the war's over and I ain't gotta' take orders from you. You don't out rank me no more. If'n anythin', I out rank you, 'cause I'm the goddamn Marshall."

"And he'll remind you boys of it every chance he gets," laughed Buford. "He don't do no work, though. He got a deputy who does it for 'im. The Marshall spends most of his day in the saloon, drinkin' whiskey, playin' cards, and settin' with whores."

"'Course, I spend my day in the saloon," Hi said with mock indignation. "If'n there's gonna' be any trouble, it's gonna' be there. Shit, never saw no one get shot for cheatin' at poker in a church!"

• • •

Life on the ranch got into a routine, one that Buford found difficult. Almost ten years of military service had taken its toll. He wasn't used to being in one place too long. Although he worked hard from sun up to sun down, he felt jumpy and high strung. He couldn't seem to relax and was wary of every sound and shadow.

Too restless to stay on the ranch, he went to town often. He visited with Hi and Lydia and always stopped at the Longhorn to see Emma.

Emma enjoyed the frequent visits and as time went by she grew fonder of him.

Hi was pleased to see him as well. "Sure glad you come to town a lot. Thought once you settled in you'd never leave the goddamn ranch."

"Truth to tell, I ain't settlin' in right. It don't seem natural to bunk in the same bed every night. You ever feel like that when you quit?"

Hi looked at his friend with compassion, but spoke light heartedly. "Yea, I did but I had Lydia to calm my nerves."

"Yea, reckon so."

"A man can't ride the range all the years we did and settle down right away. Thank God my woman saw me through it."

"Well, I don't need a woman to see me through this. Just gotta' get used to it is all. Damn," he laughed scornfully. "Didn't think retirin' was gonna' be so hard."

Buford, a master of discipline, soon had himself in check. He fought the urge to leave the ranch and eventually his visits to town decreased.

On one of his few visits, he met Junior and his father in the grain store. Buford felt awkward. He went to Zeb, Senior and introduced himself. "I'm Colonel McLeod, the one that shot your boy here. Real sorry 'bout it, too. How's the arm, son?" he asked Junior.

"Reckon I'll live," he grumbled.

"Good to meet you Colonel. There ain't no hard feelins'. You got a nice spread. I went out a few times to check on it. I wanted to make sure no Indians or riff raff troubled it," he said glaring at his son.

"That was neighborly and I'm much obliged," said Buford. "I want to thank you for the use of your men when I was buildin' it. Shoulda' thanked you before but ain't had an opportunity."

"It's all right, ranchin's hard work. I'm glad we finally met. You probably ain't met many of the town folks.

"No, I haven't. Met a few, though."

"I'm havin' a barbecue at my place next Sunday. I'd be pleased if'n you and your brother came."

Buford hadn't socialized with decent people in a long time. He didn't particularly care to either. He was used to the company of men and rough men at that. He would've refused the invitation, but he felt he owed this kind man something.

So it was that he found himself standing stiffly that Sunday in his best clothes, feeling like the jack ass Hi told him he was. He and Tom stood by the Converse's as a steady stream of people came by to meet them.

Tom's eyes glowed with excitement. More than a few attractive young ladies curtsied and blushed beneath the McLeod brothers gaze.

Tom looked up and winked at Buford. "Some mighty pretty girls here, ain't there? If'n I ain't mistaken seems like their Pa's want us to take notice of 'em."

"Feel like I'm at a goddamn cattle auction," he snarled.

"Be nice, Buford. You don't wanna' shame Ma," Tom laughed.

Tom was correct in his assumption. Either of the two handsome brothers would be a desirable mate for the single females of Wilder Creek and their fathers knew it. They had their own spread and would soon grow prosperous.

After that Sunday, they found themselves the most sought-after bachelors in the township. They were invited to socials, picnics and barbecues. Tom attended many, but Buford stayed home.

One Sunday as Tom preened in front of the mirror, he asked, "Why don't you come to town with me?"

Buford scowled, "One of us gotta' work. Lord knows you're off to some damn shindig just 'bout every Sunday."

"Stop your grumblin'. It's my day off, if'n I wanna' go to town I can. Besides, I'm a goin' to church. Ma taught us to respect the Lord's day."

"Your sudden urge to go to church ain't got nothin' to do with Charlie's girl, Hattie, does it?"

"Who tole' you that?" asked Tom, his face turning red.

"Hi, that's who. Says he sees you two makin' cow eyes

at each other."

"Lord, that goddamn Hi's worse than a woman for waggin' 'is tongue," cursed Tom.

Hi wasn't the only one watching. Lydia knew that Buford was being reclusive and thought she had to step in. She invited him to dinner and there was always a single female present.

Buford got so that he dreaded these torturous affairs. After looking at more than one lonely face over their dinner table he had to speak up.

"Lydia, I'm much obliged for the trouble you're goin' through, but I ain't of a mind to marry."

"What do you mean?" she asked innocently.

"If'n I can speak plain, every time you invite me for vittles, there's a gal here. I ain't smart 'bout these things but I think you're tryin' to get me hitched."

"I guess, I am," she laughed. "I thought I was doin' you a favor!"

"No, ma'am," he said. "I ain't interested."

"Why not, Colonel?"

"I'm too set in my ways. Maybe if'n I was younger."

"Nonsense, you're still young enough. How old are you? Reckon you gotta' be close to Hi's age."

"I'm older. Besides I ain't used to ranchin' yet. Ain't had a real home in a long time and I'm still feelin' a might skittish. Was right kind of you to try to help me, though."

Much to his relief, Lydia stopped her campaign and he could visit them in peace. He had only one need for a woman and Emma satisfied it on a regular basis.

Much to Emma's horror, she did the worst thing a woman in her profession could do; she fell in love. She didn't dare let him know for fear she'd scare him away.

If Emma knew anything, it was the ways of men. She knew Buford had an aversion to women and treated him accordingly. She felt he'd go to one of the others if she placed demands on him. So far, she was the only one he'd been with and she wanted to keep it that way.

Jamie chided her. "You ain't got no sense carryin' on like you're doin'. You don't mean shit to the Colonel. He ain't the marryin' kind and even if'n he was, it sure wouldn't be to no whore!"

After an absence of several weeks, Buford called on her. He was leaving for Abilene in a few days and came to town for supplies.

Jamie had spoken the truth and Emma's heart sank when she saw him walk in. "Jamie's right," she thought sadly, "He ain't the type of man who'd want the likes of me."

As he made his way towards her in the crowded saloon, she took a deep breath and put on a sunny smile. Unfortunately for Emma, her resolve melted as soon as the bedroom door closed.

• • •

The trip to Abilene that spring was pure hell. The weather was bad, and it rained most of the time. The trails were bogs of mud and small creeks and gullies were rushing rivers. Herds of cattle were backed up all along the trail. Hot meals were an impossibility, and everything was soaking wet. Both men and beasts were miserable.

They finally reached Abilene, cold, wet and miserable. Buford had mixed emotions about the large, noisy cattle town. As much as he hated the commotion his senses had come alive.

He and Tom took a room in the Drover's Cottage, a plush, three story hotel built by Abilene's founder, Joe McCoy. They had a herd to sell and everyone knew that most business in Abilene was conducted right there in the hotel.

Tom insisted that Buford do all the buying and selling. He would handle the men camped outside of town with the herd.   Buford met Victor West, an Ohio beef trader, in the lobby of the hotel.

Since Buford wasn't one for small talk, they got down to business and came to a price agreement in a short time. As they talked details, Buford smelled lilac water and heard a rustling of skirts come up behind him. "Father," a melodious voice said.

Victor stood up and Buford did also, turning to pay his respects to Victor's daughter. What he saw stunned him and rooted him to the spot. She was the most beautiful woman he'd ever seen. Small and delicate, with creamy white skin and jet-black hair, she looked like a porcelain doll. Her well-tailored day frock showed her figure to its advantage.

"I'm sorry to disturb you but Mother wanted to know when you'd be available for luncheon and sent me to ask."

"Colonel McLeod, may I present my daughter, Mabel?"

"Colonel?" she asked sweetly, "Are you a soldier?"

"I was," Buford said.

"The war?"

"Yea."

"Which side?" she asked demurely.

"Mabel, where's your manners? The Colonel doesn't have to answer to you," Victor said, embarrassed. "You must excuse her, sir."

"I don't mind, Victor." To Mabel he replied, "The Confederacy."

"Well I'm pleased to make your acquaintance any way," she bantered.

"Mabel!" Victor said, mortified.

The remark had no effect on Buford. "The pleasure is mine," he said sincerely. She could've told him to go to hell and he wouldn't have minded.

"If my daughter hasn't offended you, would you care to join us for lunch?"

"Reckon, I would," he said.

"Tell Mother that we'll meet in the dining room in 15 minutes and I hope you find your manners in the meantime."

When she left, Buford had a hard time concentrating on business. He couldn't get her soft violet eyes or alabaster skin out of his mind.

Mabel baited him all through lunch, but he remained unruffled.

"Mother," she said, "The Colonel fought for the south. Did you know that my father was a soldier, too?"

"No, I didn't."

"Yes, he fought for the right side.", she said with a sweet smile.

"Mabel, really!" said Victor exasperated. "What is the matter with you? You are being very rude to the Colonel. I'm sorry sir," he said.

"Don't apologize."

"Why do they call you Colonel?" she asked.

"When I left the army folks still called me "Colonel" and the name stuck."

"I've never met a Confederate Colonel," said Mabel. "There aren't many in Ohio."

"I reckon not," Buford smiled while Louise West blushed.

"You'll have to excuse our daughter," she said. "This is the first time she's traveled, and I fear she doesn't know how to behave."

"I'm not a child," Mabel said. "There's no need to apologize for me. Colonel, I don't mind telling you that I was an abolitionist".

"Lord!" groaned Victor, covering his face with his hands.

"Never cared for the idea of slavery myself," Buford replied.

"Really!" she said, her beautiful eyes wide. "But you fought for the south. Surely, you believed in your cause."

"I believed in Texas. When the state called for soldiers, I signed up. Just so happens that it's in the south. If'n it was next to Massachusetts, I'd have fought for the north. Didn't matter to me, I was fightin' for Texas."

"Father told me after the war, you became a Texas Ranger. It seems you have a great love for Texas."

"That's true enough," he said.

"Then why'd you leave? Father says your ranch is in the New Mexico Territory."

"Was gonna' settle in San Antone but a friend talked me into goin' to the territory. Damn good cattle land." Buford blushed. "Didn't mean to cuss in front of you ladies."

"Don't apologize. You seem like a very interesting man, Colonel," Mabel said.

He laughed, "Don't think so. I'm duller than dirt, but much obliged for the compliment. My friend in the territory, now he's an interestin' feller. Always wanted to be like 'im."

When lunch was done, Mabel said, "I hope to see you again, Colonel."

Buford, taken aback, just tipped his hat and made a hasty retreat.

That evening, Buford, Victor and Tom went to the Alamo Saloon. It was a beautiful place with polished brass, gleaming woodwork and long silvery mirrors. Tasteful renaissance style pictures of nude women hung here and there. It was a gentlemen's saloon, filled with well-dressed and affluent men. Those with a hankering for more excitement went to the district at the end of town for their pleasure. The towns people called it "the Devil's Addition".

"It was good of you to come out with me," Victor said. "My women folk were wearing on my nerves. They both read too many dime novels and wanted to see a cattle town. I don't know how they talked me into it. I'm especially sorry for my daughter's behavior. She was rude, and you were extremely gracious."

"It didn't offend me none. She's a lovely gal, Victor, you must be proud of 'er."

"I was until today!" he said. "After learning of your brother's military experience," he explained to Tom, "she had the impertinence to view her opinions of an issue now laid to rest. My wife and I were extremely displeased with her, but your brother was very understanding."

"She has good character. For a little thing she sure is feisty," Buford smiled.

Tom noticed the look that came over Buford's face as he spoke of her and smiled inwardly. "Good God!" he thought, "I think he's taken with her."

The next day Tom and Buford were outside the hotel talking when Mable came out. As soon as Tom saw her he knew why. Buford looked at her with eyes bright as new pennies and Tom was convinced his brother was in love.

During their stay in Abilene, they visited with the Wests frequently. For the first time that Tom could remember, Buford worked very little. He seemed to have no interest in anything except the diminutive Mabel.

For her part, Mabel was intrigued by the tall, rugged Colonel. She had seen the famous Wild Bill Hickok, Marshall of Abilene. She thought the Colonel far more dashing.

Much to his amazement, Buford realized he'd fallen in love. He never thought it would happen to him. Not knowing anything about love or nice women he grew confused and didn't know what to do.

He confided his feelings to Tom.

"Thought you was gettin' sweet on 'er," said Tom.

"She turned my head, that's a fact," said Buford, "never thought such a thing would happen. Don't matter much though, she's too good for me."

"Bull shit! Ain't every woman in Wilder Creek lookin' to get hitched to ya'?"

"None of 'em are as fine as Mabel. Besides, I don't know nothin' 'bout courtin'. I'd only make a jack ass of myself."

Tom remained silent. He knew that once Buford made up his mind about something it was useless to argue.

When it was time to leave Buford felt as if his heart would break. As he said good bye to the West's he longed to hold Mabel and kiss her good bye. Instead he kissed her dainty hand, much to Tom's delight. He was amused by his older brother's chivalrous behavior.

The trip back to Wilder Creek was much easier. The weather cleared and the creeks and stream beds returned to normal. Buford had only a few head of cattle and some horses that he'd bought. The small number of animals were easy to care for.

They encountered no Indians or other foes. A few men passed by that Ezra and Buford suspected to be rustlers, but the McLeod crew outnumbered them and were well armed.

Over the long miles back to the territory Buford thought of Mabel. He cursed himself for falling in love with her. He felt out of his league. He avoided women except for an occasional whore. Now he was in love with someone too good for him.

During the war he learned not to let his feelings get the best of him. When he saw his friends die in agony or killed a foe in battle it had eaten him up inside. As a defense, he shut off one emotion after another until his heart was as barren as the land he now traveled. Mabel had penetrated the shield over his heart and it hurt like hell.

When they got back to the ranch Buford worked harder than ever. It helped keep thoughts of Mabel at bay. He seldom went to town, not even to visit Hi and Lydia. However, his men went every Saturday night. One Sunday morning he overheard Josh say to Jimmy Kelly, "Damn it, Miss Emma was the best woman in the place and now she ain't pokin' no one. How can you work in a saloon if'n you ain't pokin' no more?"

When Buford left for Abilene, Emma missed him so much it hurt. She knew she was foolish when she stopped seeing other customers. The reason was more foolish still. She felt as if she were being unfaithful. She had enough money saved to hold her for a while, but knew she had to go back to work. He hadn't come to the Longhorn since returning from Abilene.

Buford's absence worried Hi and he rode out to see him. When Hi saw him he immediately sensed something was troubling his friend. For once he dropped his joking and sarcastic manner. "Buford, you look a wreck. Somethin' happen in Abilene?"

"No."

"Don't gimme' that bull shit. Somethin's wrong and I wanna' know what it is."

After a little more coaxing Buford poured his heart out.

"Ain't that a fuckin' shame. Finally meet the woman of your dreams and she ain't right for you. I know you're hurtin' but you gotta' go on. Hidin' out here ain't good for you. Let's go to the Longhorn and drown some of that sorrow."

Buford relented, and they rode to town.

When they got to the saloon, Emma lit up at the sight of him. "Colonel," she cried out, "was growin' worried 'bout you. Heard you was back but ain't seen hide nor hair of you."

"Been busy," he mumbled.

"How 'bout a poke," she smiled.

"Heard you went outta' business."

"When it comes to you my door is always open."

"Well, reckon, I could do with one. It's been awhile."

Buford followed her upstairs and some of the cowboys grew hopeful that she was back on the line.

Buford tried to lose himself in her young, slim body and took her again and again. When they went downstairs, most everyone had gone. Josh and two other anxious men were still there.

"Colonel, we didn't think you was ever gonna come down. I'm next Miss Emma, these two fellers is behind me."

"I'm sorry, Josh. I'm done for the night."

"I don't get it, Miss Emma. Are you back on the line or not?"

"Reckon I am but not tonight. The Colonel done tuckered me out. I ain't fit for no more customers."

The three men turned their gaze to Buford. "Don't look at me boys. I thought gals like 'er could spark all night."

"Tarnation," scowled Josh. "Reckon I'll go find Jamie." The other two men went in search of other girls.

When they were alone he snapped, "What the hell you doin?"

"Ain't doin' nothin'," she said her face coloring. "I don't feel like doin' it any more tonight. Besides, you spoiled me some. After bein' with you I don't care to be with no one else. I still ain't sure I wanna' go back on the line."

"That's just plum foolish. I ain't no different than anyone else."

"Maybe not, but you're enough man for me."

"Well, it ain't right. Reckon I better not see you no more."

"Why not?" she cried.

He had run out of patience and snapped, "Because you ain't gonna' make no money pokin' just me. I don't get to town much. What the fuck are you thinkin'? You're a whore, sparkin' men is your profession."

His obvious annoyance cut her to the quick. She tried to fight back the tears, but it was no use. Her lovely blue eyes filled, and they spilled down her cheeks.

"There ain't no need to cry," he said gruffly. "I hate it when a goddamn woman cries."

She sniveled and wiped her eyes.

"Don't know what kinda' foolishness you're up to."

She knew she couldn't tell him she was in love with him. It would make matters worse.

"I ain't up to nothin' foolish."

"I know there's some fellers who get stuck on a whore and don't want them seein' no one else. I ain't said or done nothin' to give you that notion, have I?"

"No."

"Good, cause' I don't feel that way. You're a nice gal and all but I ain't much for women. Only got one use for y'all and don't mind payin' for it."

"I know," she said. "I just figure I can poke who I want."

"Well, it ain't gonna' be me. It'll only cause hard feelins' and give people peculiar ideas. If'n you decide to work regular again, let me know."

She gave him a mournful look and her eyes filled with tears again.

"Jesus, Emma, cut that out," he growled. She turned and fled up the stairs.

On the rare occasions when Buford went to the Longhorn he avoided Emma and the other girls. He was through with women.

One day Jamie sidled up beside him as he stood at the bar.

"Can I talk to you a minute?" she asked.

"Sure."

"I don't know what to do about Emma," she sighed.

"What're you comin' to me for?" he scowled.

"You know why you danged fool! She ain't doin' no business and Frenchie's ready to throw 'er out!"

"Ain't none of my concern," he said quietly.

"All I'm askin' is for you to be a customer again, then at least she'd be earnin' somethin' and Frenchie might leave 'er be."

"Tole' you, Jamie, it ain't my problem. Be much obliged if'n you didn't trouble me no more."

"I tole' 'er you was one cold blooded son of a bitch!" she snarled and flounced away leaving the smell of cheap perfume in her wake.

It made Buford think of the delicate fragrance of lilacs and Mabel. "God damn, women!" he thought. "I got one I want and can't have, and one I can have and don't want!"

A short time later he turned and saw Emma sitting alone. She forced a smile and he went to sit with her.

"How you doin', Emma?"

"Doin' fine," she said lightly.

"That ain't what Jamie tole' me. She said Frenchie's

gonna' throw you out."

"Lord Colonel, I sure am sorry. She had no right to tell you my troubles. Don't you worry none 'bout me."

"Still ain't seein' no one?"

"Just can't bring myself to."

"Then you're in the wrong line of work."

"Reckon, I am."

He looked at her and sighed. Even though a seasoned whore, she had an innocence that made him feel sorry for her.

"Tell you what Emma, I'll start seein' you regular again but you gotta' know it don't mean a damn thing. This here's only business. You understand my meanin'?"

"Yea," she said her face growing flushed with happiness. It wasn't what she wanted but she'd take him under any terms.

"Well, then let's go," he said leading her upstairs.

It soon became common knowledge that Emma saw no one but Buford. When anyone complained to Frenchie, he'd say, "Take it up with the Colonel." He knew no one would dare.

One afternoon, Josh and Buford came to town for supplies. It was the middle of round up and they had little time to waste. As they passed the Long Horn, Josh said, "Sure is hot! A beer would taste mighty good."

"Reckon we can stop in for one," said Buford, "get the dust outa' our throats."

Emma greeted them when they entered.

"You come in to see me?" she asked, hopefully.

"Not this time, just passin' through," he said

"I'll take you, little lady," said a stranger at the other end of the bar.

"Much obliged but I ain't in business no more."

The stranger looked at her and then at Buford. "Well, sure coulda' fooled me. You asked him."

"That's different," she said.

"Is she your woman?" the man asked Buford.

"No, she ain't."

The stranger walked over to her. "Well, little lady, I got some money that says y'all gonna' come upstairs with me."

Emma tried to be gracious. "Much obliged for your kind offer but I ain't interested. Maybe one of the other girls..."

"C'mon' gal, I'm a losin' my patience," said the man pulling her roughly by the arm. "You know what, Frenchie? You got insolent whores."

At her resistance, he hardened his grip on her and yanked her towards the stairs.

"Let go. You're hurtin' me!" she yelled.

Buford had ignored them but now he spoke, "Let 'er be, cowboy. She don't wanna' go."

"You said she weren't yours. You ain't got nothin' to say 'bout this."

"She ain't mine and if'n she wanted to go with you wouldn't bother me none, but she asked you to leave 'er be. Let 'er go."

Up to this point Buford had been leaning on the bar. Now he stood up straight and turned to face the cowboy. Six feet four in his stocking feet, he stood six feet six in his boots.

The man looked up at him in awe and released his grip on Emma. He went back to the bar, finished his drink and left.

Emma rubbed her arm. "Woulda' been nice if one of y'all spoke up 'fore he hurt me."

"I woulda' Emma, but didn't think it was my place," apologized Josh. "Figured it was up to the Colonel!"

Buford glared at Josh and took Emma's elbow. He led her to an empty table where they could have privacy.

"Sit down," he said quietly though his eyes flashed with anger. She sat, instantly sorry for her angry remark.

"I done tole' you this was gonna' cause trouble. You done riled that cowboy. Worse yet, Josh thinks I'm obliged to you. Well, I ain't! I pay you for a poke and that's all. I ain't gonna' protect you or fight for you so don't expect it."

"Didn't mean to make a fuss. Reckon, I was just a little scared. The boys 'round here been disappointed but none of 'em been rough with me."

"It don't matter none. I'm goin' to Ellsworth soon and won't be 'round to pay you regular. Probably be best if'n you went back on the line."

"Don't worry 'bout me, I'll manage. Don't want to be a

burden to you, Colonel."

"Then don't be!" he snapped.

She knew he was angry at her and changed the subject. "Heard they threw all you cowpunchers outa' Abilene."

"They did but makes no difference to me. Besides, they brung old Joe's hotel down to Ellsworth on the railroad. Will be somethin' to see. Drover's Cottage is a big ole' place with a l00 stables. Musta' been a chore."

"Will I see you before you go?" she asked.

"Maybe."

"You must be gettin' ready to leave soon."

"We ain't finished roundup yet. Some of my herd got in with Charlie's and his in with mine. It's a big mess. That's why I'm just passin' through. Now you think 'bout what I said. You go back in business. I ain't responsible for you."

He went to see her a few days before he left. When they were done he paid her for her services and then some.

"Colonel! What's all this for?"

"Don't be gettin' ideas. Don't mean a damn thing. Just don't feel right leavin' you with nothin'. But tell you what, when I come back you better be doin' business as usual."

CHAPTER THREE

Cattle drives were never easy, but some were worse than others, and the trip to Ellsworth was brutal.

It started with Asa, who only a few days out, was bitten by a rattler. Fortunately, he survived but it left him sick and weak and unable to work.

Next, they lost a wheel on the chuck wagon while crossing a river with a strong current. The wagon tipped on its side sending most of their provisions rushing downstream.

To make matters worse the cattle stampeded not once, but twice. Once a herd stampeded, they often did it again and again. It was necessary to keep extra watch and the men worked twenty-hour shifts. Music soothed the nervous animals and the men sang until they were hoarse.

The strain began to show on the men and they complained, something a cowboy seldom did.

They finally reached Ellsworth, two weeks late, hungry, cross and tired.

The weary men stayed with the herd while Tom and Buford went in to Ellsworth to conduct business. Once the cattle were sold and delivered, the crew could go in to town and civilization. A good meal, a hot bath, and a loose woman were what they needed.

Ellsworth was now the center of commerce for cattle. Drover's cottage had been moved from Abilene to Ellsworth.

"By God, Buford, look at it! It looks just like it did in Abilene. Ain't nothin' different," said Tom

What he said was true. The hotel stood just as it had before. Its yellow paint gleamed, and the green trim stood out in stately prominence.

"How do you think they done get all that on the rail road?" Tom asked.

"Don't know how they managed. Know one thing. That Joe McCoy is one crazy son of a bitch," said Buford.

Seeing the hotel made him think of Mabel. He stifled the thought; it was pointless.

• • •

The next morning Buford went to meet Victor. The two men greeted each other warmly and got down to business. When they were done Victor said, "Would you and Tom like to join my family for dinner this evening?"

The word "family" gave Buford a jolt. "Much obliged, but we got other business to tend to. Maybe some other time," Buford said, hoping Victor didn't notice his discomfort.

He didn't. "I said I'd never bring my women folk again, but Mabel was quite taken with you. She nagged me until I couldn't stand it any longer."

Buford chuckled. "I don't think she's met too many rough characters."

Victor laughed. "I think it's more than that. If you can't join us tonight how about tomorrow?"

"Maybe. Don't know for sure," he said.

"You would honor us, sir," Victor said humbly.

Buford sighed inwardly. "All right. Reckon tomorrow would be fine."

"Splendid."

Buford walked to his room, his heart thudding in his chest and his mind in turmoil. Was it possible she might care for him? He decided he was being foolish.

Tom burst into the room. "Lord Buford! Guess who I just seen? Miss Mabel! Did you know she was here?"

"Yea. Victor tole' me. He said she wanted to see me. We're havin' dinner with 'em tomorrow night."

"I knew she took a shinin' to you."

"Bull shit. She just likes bustin' my balls 'coz I fought for the Confederacy."

"That ain't true. She was tryin' to get your attention," said Tom.

"Don't think so. She's nothin' but a spoiled brat and has 'er Pa runnin' in circles."

The next evening at dinner Buford was in a tizzy. In all

his years as a soldier and Ranger he'd never encountered a foe who frightened and confused him like the petite Mabel.

While they dined, she never took her eyes off him. She wasn't rude like last year. She hung on every word he said.

Her better behavior didn't sway him. Even if she did care for him it didn't matter. She was a lady and far above him. Since no good could come of it he decided to make himself scarce.

Although, he and Victor saw each other for business purposes Buford turned down the many invitations Victor extended.

One day Victor asked, "Colonel, have we offended you?"

"Hell no!" Buford said surprised.

"You no longer seem to desire our company, even though Mabel has behaved herself."

"No, Victor. None of y'all offended me, just the opposite. I'll be plain with you. I've grown right fond of Mabel."

"That's splendid! She feels the same."

"I doubt it. I think I amuse 'er, but I'm in love with 'er. That's why I been avoidin' you.

Victor looked him straight in the eye. "I'll be plain, too. She's very much in love with you. She's done nothing but talk about you for a year."

Buford's elation at this information was shattered by the reality of the situation.

"Makes no difference, she ain't the right woman for me."

"You could do worse than my daughter, sir!" said Victor in a huff, his feelings hurt.

"That ain't what I meant. She's too good for me."

"Surely, you don't mean that. You have a fine reputation. In fact, you're something of a legend."

"I ain't no legend. Killed me a bunch of men, is all."

"You were a fine soldier and lawman."

Buford laughed coldly. "Yea, I was. I was on the right side of the law but a killer is a killer. Worse yet, I have the stomach for it. I ain't no good for 'er."

"You don't give yourself credit. Zeb Converse speaks highly of you."

"Yea, and I shot his boy for sassin' me."

"A man does what he must. That life is behind you now. You're a rancher. It's time to settle down and have a family."

"I wish I could. After two years of ranchin', I'm still havin' a hard time settlin' down. Besides we're too different. Mabel is delicate and refined. I'm as crude as they come. I also got a powerful bad temper and I cuss a lot. I ain't hardly civilized. There's gotta' be decent men interested in 'er."

"There were but she dismissed them all. It's you she wants. I've indulged my daughter all her life. That's why I brought her. Knowing that you love her comes as a relief. I don't like to see my little girl disappointed."

"Even if'n I was an educated man, the territory ain't no place for 'er. You ever been out there?"

"No."

"Wilder Creek's a hot, dusty, hell hole of a town. It's hard and dangerous country. Mabel wouldn't like it much. My ranch ain't that far from town but far enough. She'd get lonely. It ain't no place for 'er."

"Have you ever heard that love conquers all?" Victor asked with a smile.

"Yea, but that makes no difference to a rattler or a Comanche. Do you want your daughter livin' out in the middle of nowhere with a man who still ain't civilized after ten years?"

"I know you wouldn't let any harm come to her."

"I wouldn't be 'round much. I'm out with the herd most of the time. I wouldn't be able to protect 'er and care for 'er like I should."

"I'll make you a proposition," said Victor. "Why don't you explain this to Mabel and let her decide? She's stronger than she looks."

Buford sat in silence for a long while. Everything was happening too fast. He'd convinced himself that he meant nothing to her. Now he didn't know what to do. He wanted her badly, but it didn't seem fair to subject her to a hard and lonely life.

"I can't Victor, I love 'er too much."

"Well if you love her, let her make the choice. You do want to marry her, don't you?"

"In the worst way," he sighed.

"Well then, it's settled. Come to our suite and talk to her."

Mabel was in the drawing room when they arrived. Victor led him to the door. Buford hesitated and took a deep breath. Victor gave him a reassuring smile. He opened the drawing room door and Buford entered alone.

Mabel looked up from the book she was reading, "Colonel!" she exclaimed. "To what do I owe this honor?"

"I ain't sure myself," he said nervously, twisting his hat in his hands.

"Do sit down," she said graciously. He looked uncomfortable and her heart went out to him.

"I ain't good at this sorta' thing," he apologized, "but I been talkin' with your Pa. He tole' me..., well, that you like me some."

"That's true," she said demurely. "I'm quite fond of you."

"Fond ain't exactly the word he used." Buford took a deep breath and said, "He said you love me. I love you, too. I ain't never loved no woman before, so I ain't sure what to do. Your Pa thinks we should get hitched but there's some things you oughta' know first."

"Why that meddlesome old darling!" she interrupted. "Hitched! Is he trying to peddle me off to you?"

Buford's face fell and he stood up quickly.

"Guess he misunderstood, or I did. Sorry I said anythin'. Meant no offense." He hadn't felt so humiliated since surrendering to the Union Army.

"Colonel," she said. "Not so quick! I didn't say I wouldn't marry you. Are you proposing?"

"Yea! No! Maybe!" he said flustered and agitated. "I ain't sure what I'm doin'. I'd be obliged if'n you didn't make it harder," he snapped.

His tone of voice startled her, and she looked at him with wide eyes.

He sat back down and sighed. "That's the first thing I gotta' tell you. I'm one mean son of a bitch. I ain't been 'round women much and don't know nothin' 'bout y'all, especially decent ones. I yell and cuss a lot and I got a quick temper. Don't think you'll find bein' married to me pleasant.

Other thing is where I live," and he told her of the loneliness and perils she'd encounter.

When he was done, he said, "Now, I reckon, I'm pro-posin'. That is if'n you got a mind to live in a God forsaken place with a cranky ole' critter."

Mabel was overwhelmed by his speech and had no response.

"Didn't think it would work out," he said, rising to leave for the second time.

"I'd be honored to be your wife," she called after him. He stopped in mid step and turned to face her.

"Even after all I said?"

"Yes. It sounds thrilling; cattle, horses, cowboys, Indians, and land as far as the eye can see. I saw some Indians once. They were dressed like us and friendly. Do the wild ones really paint their faces?"

"You probably saw scouts. They ain't all friendly. This is real Mabel, not one of your books. It's gonna' be a hard life."

Mabel sobered. "I'm not a stupid woman. I know it will be hard. I just want to be with you, no matter what." She regained her sense of humor. "When will we get hitched?" she asked with a laugh.

"Ain't givin' it much thought but reckon, the day we leave will be good enough."

"Why not before?"

"I want to give you time to think on this. It's probably gonna' be the worst notion you ever had."

"I won't change my mind," she said.

"If'n you don't, we'll be leavin' in a week. I hope that's enough time."

"Yes," she said, her eyes sparkling.

As he walked away, she said. "Aren't you going to kiss your betrothed good bye?"

He went back and kissed her chastely on the cheek.

"Surely, you can do better than that," she chided him coquettishly.

He took her challenge and drawing her close he kissed her passionately.

When he released her she was flushed, and breathless.

When Buford left the room, Victor was waiting for him.

"Well?" he asked.

"She's agreed to marry me," beamed Buford.

"Splendid! When will the wedding take place?" Buford told him of his plans.

When he went back to his room, he told Tom.

"Told you, didn't I? I knew she wanted my dashin' brother," he said with good humor.

"I didn't think so. Victor tole' me different. The next thing I knew I was in his suite proposin'. Damn! It sure happened fast."

Once the initial shock wore off, Buford realized he had a lot to do. "Tarnation!" he thought, "we ain't even got a decent place to live!"

He hurried to the telegraph office and sent Hi a wire informing him of his impending marriage. He also asked him to hire Ziggy Schulz to build a comfortable house for his bride. Ziggy, a master carpenter, had moved to Wilder Creek last winter.

The days that followed found Buford busy. He brought Tom with him to a jeweler to pick out a ring. He also bought a wagon which he hoped would be comfortable enough for Mabel during the long miles back to Wilder Creek.

Mabel couldn't have been happier. Although Buford was rough around the edges, she thought him the most wonderful man in the world. He had made a name for himself and she would be proud to be his wife. Tall, strong and handsome, he reminded her of the heroes in the dime novels she devoured, even though he chastised her for it. She looked forward to her new life, hard as it might be.

On the day they were to leave, a hasty ceremony was held in the West's suite. Mabel looked beautiful and Buford's breath caught in his throat at the sight of her. Even as he spoke his wedding vows he couldn't believe that he was marrying this lovely, well-bred lady. As much as he hungered for it, there was no time or privacy to consummate the marriage.

He was amazed at how quickly the large wagon filled with trunks. He was ready to say something to his glowing bride, but Tom shot him a furtive glance and he kept quiet.

Their journey back to Wilder Creek started peaceful

enough. The weather was hot but fair and they encountered no one else on the trail. The wagon, loaded as it was, moved slowly and Buford was certain his men were unhappy at the pace. Besides that, he had them fanned out around the wagon as added protection.

One morning, Ezra came thundering up to the wagons.

"Indians, up yonder!" he said.

"Apache?" Buford asked.

"Can't tell. They're too far away. Either Apache or Kiowa. One thing I know for certain is they ain't peaceful."

"Indians!" cried Mabel in delight.

Ezra and Buford glanced at each other. It was obvious that Mabel had no idea how serious their situation was.

Buford looked around and saw some rocks and a small stand of cotton wood trees. "We'll hold 'em off there. Call in the men." Ezra hurried off.

As Buford brought the wagon to the trees Mabel said, "When they get close, can I see them?"

"Jesus Christ!" he bellowed. "This ain't no picnic. I want you to get in and stay in this fuckin' wagon. Don't come out 'til I tell you to."

"Colonel!" she said shocked. "Must you use profanity?"

Buford lost his temper and made no effort to hide it.

"You're more bothered 'bout my language than that we might all get kilt'. Before they kill you, they'll have their way with you, now do what I say!"

He had a fierce expression on his face and she did as she was told. He hid her as best he could amongst the items in the wagon.

The men rode in and Buford shouted out orders.

They had just got in position when the first war yells greeted their ears. Out of the dust thundered over a dozen Kiowa warriors. Buford could see the fear on the faces of his men. "Steady boys," he said reassuringly. "Don't shoot till they come into range."

They got closer and he and his men fired their first volley. Three Indians fell. The others came on through a hail of bullets but only two more found their mark. When the Kiowa reached the copse of trees they jumped from their horses and fought Buford and his men on the ground.

Buford fought like a man possessed. His precious wife was only a few feet away. When he was no longer surrounded, he took stock of the situation. Dead Indians littered the ground. Josh, Daniel and Ezra were still engaged, fighting for their lives. He didn't see Tom or his other men. He noticed two Kiowa going for their horses. Taking careful aim, he shot them both.

He was running to help the others when he saw Tom laying on the ground, his throat cut from ear to ear.

Buford didn't stop but ran faster. Lunging through the air he came down hard on the Indian who struggled with Josh. Grabbing the Kiowa by the hair, he pulled his head back and slashed his neck, almost severing it in his fury.

Mad with rage, Buford lost sight of everything but the remaining Indians. Ezra had defeated his foe, but Daniel still struggled. Taking careful aim, Buford shot the Kiowa in the head.

"Much obliged," gasped Daniel, scrambling from beneath the dead Indian.

Now that the fight was over, some of Buford's men looked at him in awe. They had never seen anyone fight so ferociously.

Buford walked over to Tom and knelt beside him. "Oh Tom," he moaned softly and closed his eyes in an effort to squeeze back the tears. When he regained his composure, he stood up.

"Anyone else dead?" he asked Josh who stood nearby.

"No, but Jimmy caught an arrow. Asa's with 'im over yonder," he said, pointing with a shaking hand. "Rest of us is cut up some but we'll be all right."

An arrow protruded from Jimmy's shoulder and Asa was trying to pull it out.

"Fuckin' thing don't wanna' come out," he said.

Buford tried and Jimmy let out a groan. "Ain't gonna' neither," Buford said, "We better leave it in."

"Do you think we should?" asked Asa.

"It's stuck on somethin'. If'n we yank it out or push it through, we're gonna' kill 'im sure."

"If'n the Colonel thinks it should stay in, listen to 'im," pleaded Jimmy, sweat from the heat and pain streaming down his face.

"If we ride hard we should reach the ranch in about two days. I think we should wait and get Doc."

Jimmy grimaced but made no response.

"Make 'im as comfortable as you can in the chuck wagon," he instructed Asa.

He went back to his brother where most of the men had gathered. Some of them wept.

"Want we should bury 'im?" asked Josh, wiping the tears from his dirty face.

"No. We'll be hittin' McLeod land in a few days, bury 'im when we get there."

The men stood by quietly not knowing what to say or do. They were still dazed by their ordeal. Even Ezra, a seasoned soldier, seemed affected. His hands shook badly as he rolled a cigarette. Buford was the only one who appeared calm. Devastated by his brother's death, he couldn't mourn. Ten years of warfare taught him to deny his grief. He picked Tom up gently and placed him across his horse, then went to the wagon, where a terrified Mabel peered out.

When he reached her, she threw herself in his arms and began to sob. He hugged her tightly and buried his face in her hair. After a moment, she realized her head rested on a blood-soaked shirt and she drew back in revulsion. "God!" she wailed and sank to the ground. He didn't know how to comfort her and gestured to Juan to go to her.

Buford sighed and went to join his men. He studied them, taking in their injuries with an experienced eye. Outside of Jimmy, he saw bad cuts and bruises but nothing life threatening.

"I'll give you boys a few minutes to clean up but then we gotta' get goin'."

Buford took off his shirt and threw it aside and went back to the wagon. "Juan, go tend to the boys." Buford washed his face and hands and put on a clean shirt. Mabel sat at the edge of the wagon, her face buried in her hands. He sat next to her and she looked up at him.

"I'm sorry about...Tom," she said.

"Reckon it was the Lord's will," he said dryly. His face was hard, and it frightened her.

He wanted to hold her but was afraid she'd reject his embrace like before. Instead he spoke harshly to her. "I tole' you this was no fuckin' picnic. Now you know what I was talkin' 'bout. Is this like your fuckin' dime novels?"

She looked at him with fearful eyes. His words cut her like a knife, especially since he was right. She realized she had acted like a fool. He sat quietly by her side. He knew he should say or do something after her ordeal, but didn't know what. She couldn't bear the eerie silence and spoke. "Are you hurt, Colonel?"

"Banged up some but I'll be all right."

"The men look like they need a rest. Do you plan to travel far today?"

"Yea. We got to. Jimmy ain't gonna' make it if'n we don't. Reckon, we should get goin' now."

As he got up to leave Mabel called out "Colonel!" She was desperate for reassurance and wanted him to hold her but when he turned around to face her she changed her mind. His face was set in a fierce scowl. "Never mind" she said softly.

He asked Ezra to look after Tom. At first, he was going to tie him to the back of the wagon but realized it would upset Mabel.

They set out and Buford rode by the wagon where Mabel sat deep in thought. She'd never been so frightened. When the fight was over, the sight of the carnage made her vomit.

Now as they rode along, he hardly spoke. She wished he'd react to the horror they just experienced. "His brother was just killed," she thought. "How can he be so calm?"

It was long after dark when they made camp. The group spoke little. Too weary and upset to eat, they went to sleep early. This trip had been a disaster since they left the ranch.

Buford woke them at dawn. "Time to go," he said.

The men got up groaning. Their wounds were sore, and they were stiff from fighting and fatigue.

Josh said, "Lord, Ezra, think the Colonel's tryin' to kill us. I feel like shit. Another hour's sleep would do me a world a' good."

Some of the men agreed. Yesterday had been hellacious.

"C'mon' girls," Ezra chastised them. "Stop your whinin'.

Especially y'all," he said to Asa and Jeremiah, "thought y'all was in the war."

"We was and I don't mind fightin'," scowled Jeremiah, "but this ain't the war. Don't see why we gotta' go on at such a pace."

"We gotta' get Jimmy back 'afore he dies." Ezra said solemnly.

Later that afternoon Ezra rode over to the wagon. "Colonel, we gotta' do somethin' 'bout Tom. He's startin' to stink. I'm havin' a hard time keepin' the bugs away."

"We'll be hittin' McLeod land soon, we'll bury 'im then."

"You ain't gotta' smell 'im," Ezra mumbled as he rode away.

Mabel was horrified by this exchange. They were talking about a human being, though one would never know it. "What kind of monsters are these western men?" she wondered. The ones she'd read about were tough, but honorable. Ezra talked about Tom like he was a piece of meat and Buford still hadn't shed a tear.

At sundown they reached the furthest edge of the ranch.

"Reckon, we can bury 'im now," Buford said. "Was gonna' wait 'til we got closer, but this'll have to do." He and his men scratched out a shallow grave in the hard, dry earth.

Mabel saw Tom for the first time since he'd been killed, and the bile rose in her throat. The hot sun had swollen and blackened his body and he was covered with flies.

They put him in the hole and covered him over with rocks. Now they stood around the grave waiting for Buford to say something. He cleared his throat and said, "I ain't got the words. I'll bring the Parson back for a proper service. No sense wastin' time. I reckon if'n y'all don't wanna' bury Jimmy too, we get goin'." He left the group and walked back to the wagon. Mabel followed behind.

Josh exclaimed, "Don't this beat all. I can't believe the Colonel didn't say a few words over ole' Tom. Kinda' gives me a fright. There's some that say he's cold, but never believed it 'til now. Reckon he's as hard as they say."

Ezra came to Buford's defense. "He ain't bein' hard, he's bein' smart. He's thinkin' of Jimmy. Ain't no use spendin' time with the dead when you got the livin' to care for. Now you heard the Colonel. Time to get movin'."

"Still seems peculiar," said Josh.

Buford had been afraid to say more than he did. He would've broken down, something he wouldn't do in front of them. During the war he learned that a commanding officer had to maintain his composure, no matter what. This wasn't the army, but he was their boss. To him, it was the same.

Jimmy was growing worse. The wound was red and swollen and he was delirious with fever. Concerned for his wellbeing, Buford drove the outfit on mercilessly. It was after midnight when he let them stop. They were on the trail again before sun up.

With every passing mile, Mabel felt she had made a mistake. She had never been so uncomfortable. She was also apprehensive about her new husband. It troubled her that he thought saying a prayer over his brother was a waste of time.

The men knew Buford wanted to get Jimmy back quickly, but few thought he'd survive no matter how fast they traveled. They were bone tired and needed sleep and time to tend their wounds, but he wouldn't allow it. He drove them on almost beyond endurance. And they reached the ranch by noon.

Mabel's heart sank when she saw the ramshackle group of buildings sitting out in the middle of a flat, parched piece of land.

"I'll be damned!" Buford swore.

"What is it?" she asked.

"Look yonder," he said, pointing to a two-story house set apart from the other buildings.

"Oh!" she cried, her hope renewed, and her weariness forgotten.

He pulled the wagon up in front of the cook house and helped her down. She stretched and looked towards the house that sat some distance away.

"It's lovely, Colonel! May I go look at it?"

"Sure. I'll be over in a minute."

The men were greeted by Phil and Ira, who'd stayed behind with the cattle not ready for market. They were stunned by the bruised bunch before them.

"What the hell happened to y'all? Where's Jimmy and Tom?" Phil asked.

"We run into some Indians, two days ago. They kilt Tom and Jimmy's in the wagon, near dead." Josh replied.

"Jesus Lord!" said Phil, hurrying to the wagon. Jimmy was like a brother to him. He found Buford there, tending to him.

"How is he?" he asked anxiously.

"Ain't good. I want you and Ira to bring 'im to Doc's. Be careful of that arrow in 'im. Couldn't get the fuckin' thing out. You get along now, ain't got no time to spare. I'll be in town later. Stay with 'im 'til I get there."

After Ira and Phil left, Buford joined Mabel who was talking with Ziggy.

"Colonel!" said Ziggy in his heavy German accent, "it's wonderful to see you again."

"Looks fine, Ziggy, doesn't it?" he asked Mabel.

"It's beautiful!" Mabel said for indeed it was. Built in the fashionable Victorian style, it had turrets and lovely "ginger bread" trim.

"You like it? I am so glad."

"Didn't think you'd get it built so fast," said Buford.

"It's not done yet, but pretty soon. You can live in it though. Come inside and see," Ziggy said proudly.

On the first floor was a kitchen, dining room, living room, two bedrooms and utility room. Upstairs were five more bedrooms.

"Sure is big," said Buford.

"Not so big. It will look smaller when it's finished. Besides, when the Marshall told me you were getting married I thought you'd need lots of room for children!"

Buford smiled. "I ain't aimin' to have as many youngun's as you. He's got eleven!" he said to Mabel.

"You must be very proud," she said.

"I am. Seven of them, fine strapping boys. I'm teaching them all I know so they can take over for me when I am too old to swing a hammer."

"If they are as skilled as you, we'll have the prettiest town in the territory!" beamed Mabel.

"How long 'til it's done?" Buford asked

"Two, three days at the most. But you can sleep here at night, it's dry."

"Much obliged but I don't think my wife will be comfortable," said Buford. "If'n it's only a couple of days, reckon we can wait at the hotel. I got things to do in town any way."

"Couldn't we stay?" Mabel asked hopefully.

"Think we'd be better off at the hotel, darlin'. We ain't got a stick of furniture and we'd only be in the way. Let Ziggy do 'is job."

"You come back in three days, and it will be done," Ziggy promised.

"Well Mabel," Buford said, as they walked back to the cook house, "think you can stand bein' in that wagon a little longer? Town ain't that far."

"I'm too tired to care where I go, as long as I can rest when I get there."

"Well the hotel ain't fancy but it's got a bed."

By the time they reached it, Mabel was so weary she could hardly stand. Buford got them the best room and that wasn't much.

After they were settled he said, "I got some business to tend to. Why don't you get some sleep."

"That would be heavenly," she said yawning.

"I won't be long." He brushed his lips across her forehead and left.

Mabel loosened her clothes, removed her shoes and laid down on the lumpy bed. Every muscle in her body screamed from the long journey. Try as she might she couldn't stop thinking of the Kiowa attack. As she drifted off she knew she'd have nightmares.

Buford stopped in to see Hi.

"Buford, you son of a bitch! Where's your bride?"

"Back at the hotel."

"What's the matter? Don't y'all like the house?" Hi asked with concern. He could tell that Buford was upset.

"The house is fine. It ain't finished yet and we ain't got no furniture. We'll be stayin' here in town a spell."

"How was Ellsworth? Bet you missed the excitement of old Abilene."

"Had enough excitement. We was attacked by Kiowa two days ago. Jimmy's hurt pretty bad. He's over at Doc's. On my way to see 'im." He stopped unable to go on. "They kilt' Tom," he said softly.

"Damn!" swore Hi, stomping his foot. "Fuckin' Indians. Only good one's a dead one. Ain't I always said that?"

"Kilt' 'em all," said Buford.

"Damnation, Buford. This is sorry fuckin' news. Damn!" Hi got up and paced his office. He didn't want Buford to see the tears that rolled down his cheeks. He stood with his back turned until he could pull himself together. After a while he said, "Ain't no way to start off married life, is it?"

"Sure ain't." Buford said glumly. Neither of them spoke, each lost in his own thoughts.

"How's Mabel holdin' up? She must've been some kind of scared," said Hi breaking the silence.

"Yea, she was. After she's had some sleep she might be feelin' better. The trip was hard on 'er. I reckon I'll gone on over to Doc's and see how Jimmy's doin'.".

Buford walked to the door and said, "I done buried Tom out at the end of the ranch. Want the Parson to come and say a few words over 'im." He sighed, "Should go to the Smith place and tell Hattie."

"When you get done with all that, come back here. We'll go to the Longhorn for a drink. Reckon you'll need one."

When Buford got to Doc's he found Phil and Ira waiting for him anxiously.

"How's he doin'?" Buford asked.

"Not good a'tall," Phil said mournfully. "Doc's still tendin' to 'im. Said he wanted to see you."

Buford went to the door and knocked softly. "It's Colonel McLeod," he said.

"Come in," said Doc.

Buford was appalled by Jimmy's appearance. His skin was white, and he was unconscious. He no longer had an arrow protruding from him but that was the only improvement.

"He ain't lookin' good," Buford said quietly.

"He's not, poor fellow."

"Reckon, I shoulda' pulled that arrow out," Buford said

feeling guilty.

"Heavens no!" cried Doc. "You did the right thing. If you'd forced it, he would've died. If he lives, he'll have you to thank."

"I ain't done nothin'. Tended enough arrow wounds to know it might kill 'im but looks like he's gonna' die anyway."

"Maybe, but at least you gave him a chance," said Doc with respect.

"I'm stayin' over at the hotel for a few days," said Buford, uncomfortable with Doc's demeanor. "If'n you need anythin' let me know. I'll be back tomorrow to see 'im. You need my men?" he asked.

"No, Colonel. By the way, sorry to hear about Tom. Phil told me."

"Much obliged," said Buford, sadness and fatigue etched on his face.

"There's good news, too!" Doc said brightening. "Heard you got yourself married."

"Yea."

"Well give that woman a fine healthy son and name him after your brother."

Buford went out and dismissed his men. "Ain't nothin' we can do. Doc took out the arrow and Jimmy's still alive but it don't look good. I'll come and see 'im tomorrow. Y'all go on back and help the rest of the outfit. Reckon they're pretty wore out. Rode 'em hard tryin' to get Jimmy here."

After that Buford went to the Parson's and made arrangements for a service. Next, he went to the undertaker for a head stone. His heart ached as he wrote out the words he wanted on it.

It had been a hard day for him, but the worst was yet to come. He still had to tell Hattie. When he got to the Smith ranch he found Charlie outside with the horses. He called out to Buford.

"I understand congratulations are in order. The Marshall done tole' me you was gettin' married. Now if'n I can get that brother of yours to wed my Hattie..." He stopped when he saw the stricken look on Buford's face.

"That's what I come to talk to you 'bout," said Buford. He dismounted and tried to speak but a lump rose in his throat. He walked away until he could compose himself.

Charlie knew something bad happened. He kept his distance and left Buford alone.

After a moment Buford went back to him, "Tom's dead," he said.

Charlie's face paled and his eyes filled with tears. "No! What happened?"

"We was attacked by Kiowas a couple of days ago. I reckon Hattie ought to know. Tom was aimin' to propose to 'er when he come back. Carried 'er picture with 'im everywhere." Buford remained silent too distraught to go on. "Buried it with 'im." he whispered.

Tears streamed down Charlie's face. Although Buford didn't shed a tear, Charlie could see he was broken hearted.

"He's buried on the ranch and I'm gonna' have a service for 'im if'n you think Hattie might wanna' come."

"We'll be there. He was a fine man, your brother."

"That he was. They didn't come no better," said Buford struggling with all his might not to weep. He said no more but got on his horse and left.

He went to the hotel to check on Mabel. She was sound asleep, and he didn't disturb her. He went to the desk and sent a wire to his family, then he went to the jail house and met up with Hi.

"Ready for that drink now," he said.

When they entered the Longhorn, Buford saw Emma sitting at one of the tables. She smiled, and he tipped his hat. He hadn't thought about her once since leaving Wilder Creek. She went over to them.

"Howdy, Emma," said Hi.

"Howdy Marshall. Heard you got married," she said to Buford.

"Yea. Got hitched in Ellsworth."

"I ain't never heard you mention no woman before," she said.

"Didn't think you'd be interested," he said.

"Interested? You son of a bitch!" she cried drawing the attention of those around them. Before Buford could reply, Hi grabbed her by the arm and led her away.

"What's ailin' you, Emma? This ain't like you! Ain't you

heard the Kiowas kilt' Tom? The Colonel's had a bad time of it. You best let 'im alone for now."

Emma straightened herself with dignity. She was embarrassed by her outburst.

"I'm sorry, Marshall. Ain't been myself lately. Tell 'im I'm sorry 'bout Tom. Didn't mean to cause 'im more grief."

"You're a good gal, Emma," said Hi.

Her eyes filled with tears and he threw a comforting arm around her. "I know you're takin' this bad. Ain't easy to have the man you love wed another."

"Ain't that," she said wiping her eyes. "Reckon I might as well tell you what's ailin' me. I'm havin' his baby," she blurted.

"Lord Jesus!" swore Hi. "What a mess!"

"Don't I know it," she said sadly.

"Why'd you let it happen?"

"I didn't let it happen! It was an accident," she said in indignation.

"No offense, Emma, but you been on the line a long time and ain't never had no trouble before," he said.

"Didn't want no trouble now. I was careful like Jamie taught me. Don't know how it happened."

"What are you gonna' do?"

"I don't know."

"Shit," Hi swore. "You gonna' tell 'im?"

"Do you think I should?"

"If'n you do, best you wait awhile. He's got a lot on his mind right now."

"I'll wait," she sighed and retired to her room.

"What the hell was that all about?" Buford asked.

"Reckon, she feels like a woman scorned," Hi answered.

"Don't know why. Always tole' 'er I was under no obligation."

By the time Emma reached her room, her face was colored a deep red. She was mortified at the scene she'd caused downstairs. What must the Colonel and everyone think? She hadn't intended to make a fuss.

Buford had been gone a few months when she learned she was pregnant. It was apparent she conceived the last night they lay together, though she had used precautions.

She would never trap a man in such a low-down way. Once she got over the initial shock, she thought it might work to her advantage. She hoped he might accept the child and her as well. Her hopes were dashed when she learned of his marriage.

She gazed out the window to the dusty street below. The sound of music and laughter floated up from downstairs and she felt terribly alone. If not for Jamie, she'd have no one. The money Buford had given her before he left was gone and Jamie supported them both.

"You ain't gonna' get no help from the Colonel," Jamie scolded. "Didn't I tell you not to get involved with that son of a bitch? You're pregnant and he's married. Fine kettle of fish you got yourself into!" Emma's life had never been easy. She thought of her past.

She'd grown up in a dirt shack in Tennessee. Her mother was dimwitted and her father a drunkard. He beat Emma and her mother any time he was in a foul mood and that was often. As she grew older and prettier, he started to make sexual advances. Emma could live with the beatings but not with that.

When she was fifteen she ran away with a Confederate soldier on his way back to Louisiana. He promised to take care of her and she couldn't leave her unhappy home quick enough. She awoke one morning in a shabby hotel in New Orleans, to find her soldier and his things gone.

It frightened her to be alone in the crowded town, but she wouldn't go home. She was penniless and tried to find work. She wandered the city, but unskilled and illiterate she could find no employ.

One day she passed out in the street from hunger. When she came to, she was in a lavish bed in one of New Orleans finest bordellos. Jamie had seen her fall and gone to her rescue. The kind-hearted prostitute nursed Emma back to health.

Through Jamie she found a job she was good at. Her looks and personality made her a favorite and she made lots of money.

One night Jamie got into an argument with a gambler. The man drew his knife and attacked her, trying to cut her face. Jamie carried a small gun in her ample bosom and managed to pull it out and shoot him at point blank range.

Fearing the law, she fled, and Emma went with her. Emma would not stay in New Orleans without her friend and savior. They decided to go to California and on their way passed through Wilder Creek.

The men were thrilled to have two pretty and experienced whores in their saloon and paid them handsomely. Tired of traveling, and satisfied with their earnings, the girls decided to stay.

She sighed, her musings over. Jamie was right. The Colonel was married, and she was in a world of trouble. She debated whether she should tell him. After much thought she decided to. She didn't expect or want any help from him, but it was his child and he had a right to know.

CHAPTER FOUR

When Buford returned to the hotel he found Mabel awake and refreshed.

"My goodness, Colonel!" she exclaimed. "You should get some rest. You look like you're ready to collapse."

"Reckon, I am. Could use a little shut eye. You must be hungry, though. Wanna' get some vittles?"

"I think you should get some sleep first."

"Reckon that ain't a bad idea. You don't have to call me Colonel, you can call me by my Christian name."

"I know, but I like calling you Colonel."

"Too tired to argue with you," he said pulling off his boots and stretching out on the bed. He was asleep in seconds.

Mabel busied herself unpacking. She caught sight of herself in the mirror and gasped. She was dirty, and her hair was all askew. Grabbing a brush, she went about making herself presentable. As she groomed she couldn't help thinking of all she'd been through since leaving Ellsworth.

An inquisitive woman with a quick mind, she'd enjoyed seeing new places and the "untamed" west. She had felt strong and brave, like the pioneer women she'd read about.

In the beginning the worst part of the trip had been her discomfort. The wagon's hard boards bit into her back. It was worse at night and she found it difficult to sleep. The Colonel slept outside, his rifles and revolvers beside him.

At first, she thought his vigilance extreme but now she realized she'd been naive. He'd told her they might encounter danger and she had laughed. The events of the past few days had shown her the reality of her situation quickly.

Once again, she had to wonder if she'd done the right thing in marrying him. His coldness and indifference frightened her.

She felt queasy and nervous for another reason as well. They had yet to consummate their marriage and tonight would be the first time they slept together. A tightness filled her chest when she thought of it.

Her mother had delicately explained what would be expected of her although it might be distasteful. "Men have their needs, and as a wife it is our duty to honor them." Mabel looked at Buford. He was a huge, ferocious looking man and a chill went up her spine.

When Buford awoke he was disoriented. He didn't recognize the strange room at first but then it flooded back. He thought of Tom and wished it was a horrible dream.

He sat up and saw Mabel sitting in a chair gazing at him. She looked beautiful in the afternoon light and his heart tumbled in his chest. He studied her tiny figure and dreaded what lay ahead.

It would've been difficult to say which one of the two feared what was to come more. "I sure need a washin' bad," he said. "Amazin' you could stay in the same room with me."

He went to the wash stand and began to undress. Mabel colored and jumped up from the chair.

"I think I'll go downstairs and see what's for dinner," she said.

"No need to," he said, oblivious of her embarrassment. "From what I hear, ain't gonna' be any good."

Before she could reply there was a knock on the door. Relieved at the distraction, she answered it.

It was Hi. "Lord!" he thought giving her a quick once over, "You must be Mabel. I'm Hi Johnson."

"Hi!" she exclaimed, "Come in. I've heard so much about you!"

He entered the room and pointed at Buford. "Knowin' that varmint, it probably was all bad."

"Quite the contrary. The Colonel has nothing but praise for you."

"Musta' been drunk, when I tole' 'er that," Buford scowled. "What the hell you want, anyways?" he said in mock annoyance. "Can't a man have time with his wife the first night back in town?"

"Reckon not. Lydia got to thinkin' 'bout the fare ole' Bart serves and sent me for you in a hurry. Hope I ain't too late."

"No," said Mabel.

He looked at her appreciatively. "I hope you don't mind my sayin' this Mabel, but you sure is a beauty. How in tarnation did that ole' hog snare you?"

"You must watch what you say about my husband," she smiled. She saw the playful sparkle in Hi's eyes and enjoyed the light-hearted banter.

"Sure, gonna' be hard!" He answered. "Lydia wants you should eat with us. Gotta' confess she can't wait to meet you."

"That would be lovely," she replied.

When Buford was ready they set out for the Johnson home.

Lydia stood on the porch and watched them approach. When they drew close, she was taken back by Mabel. Hi told her she was a fine lady and it was apparent.

Dinner was a relaxed and comfortable affair and the two women got along well. Mabel admired the baby and was in awe of Lydia's home making skills. The small house was well tended, and dinner was delicious. Mabel thought Lydia was like the women in her novels, rough but hard working and honorable.

Lydia in turn marveled at how graceful and refined Buford's wife was. She'd never seen such fair skin and lustrous hair. Mabel's hands were small and delicate and looked unused to work. Lydia worried that Mabel might not adjust to life in the territory.

They had a pleasant time under the circumstances. Although Hi did his best to lighten the situation, Tom's death hung over them like a cloud. When it was time to leave Lydia invited Mabel to come back on the morrow to spend the day with her.

On the way back to the hotel, Mabel and Buford were quiet, each filled with trepidation of what was to come. When they reached their destination Buford said, "Why don't you go on up and get settled. I'll stay down here and talk to Bart for a spell."

Mabel climbed the stairs with shaking legs. In their room she washed and put on her night clothes. She unpinned her hair and it fell to her waist in long, luxurious waves. She was shaking badly as she climbed into bed.

Buford came in a short time later, a bottle of whiskey in his hand. He looked at Mabel and his heart sank. She looked so small and frightened he didn't think he'd have the nerve to touch her. He sat in a chair and poured himself a generous glass of whiskey.

"Are you coming to bed, Colonel?" she asked in a shaky voice.

"You ever seen a man nekkid' before?" he blurted.

"Of course not!" she replied.

"Well, I reckon the sight of me is gonna' scare you. I been banged up some."

"I'll turn the lamp down," she said, trying to muster her courage.

"They say the first time hurts bad for a woman."

"I know. That's why I want to get it over with!" she cried.

"You want some whiskey?"

"I never touch spirits."

"It might help some."

"No."

"Well turn that lamp down. Don't want you boltin' outa' the room."

He undressed in the darkness and slid into bed beside her. He took her in his arms and began to kiss and caress her gently. She trembled for a short time but soon responded.

When he finally penetrated her, she gasped but made no other sound.

"You all right?" he asked when he was through.

"I'm fine," she lied. Although he tried his best not to hurt her, she felt bruised and battered.

"You want that whiskey now?" he asked.

"Yes, that would be nice."

"Figured you would," he said getting up and walking gingerly around the pitch-black room. Without thinking, Mabel lit the lamp and gasped at his nakedness. He'd been right. If she'd seen him before she would have run in terror.

"Turn that danged thing off."

She turned down the lamp and he managed to find his way back to bed, whiskey in hand. She drank it gratefully. "Mother was right," she thought, "This is horrible!"

• • •

Buford couldn't sleep.

He had just made love to his new wife and he should've been happy, but Tom's death put a damper on things. He thought about Mabel, too. He was sure she regretted her hasty decision to marry him.

She had been looking at him strangely since the Kiowa attack. He knew from the start she wasn't cut out for life on the range and assumed that was the problem. It never occurred to him that it was his aloof behavior that bothered her.

As he lay there, morbid thoughts filled his mind. He thought of his mother in Texas. She'd told him to take care of Tom and he had failed her. It made him feel guilty.

"This ain't no good!" he scolded himself. He was a master at burying his emotions, but Tom's death was difficult to ignore. He got up and paced the room, taking deep breaths to regain his composure. It didn't help, and before he knew it he was crying gut wrenching tears.

Mabel stirred, and he quickly grabbed a handkerchief and wiped his tears away. He didn't want her to see him like this. When he calmed down he slid back into bed.

In the morning when she awoke, he kissed her gently on the lips and reached for her. He needed to lose himself in her lovely, young body but she drew away.

"How you feelin' this mornin'?", he asked, trying not to show his disappointment.

"Sore and tired," she answered.

"I'll bring up a tub for you. Reckon a hot bath'll make you feel better."

"That would be wonderful," she beamed.

Buford was aware of his nakedness. "Uh...Mabel, you might want to look the other way. I gotta' get up and I ain't got no clothes on."

"Don't be silly, after all, you're my husband." The initial shock of seeing him naked last night had worn off.

He got up and she studied him in the morning light. She marveled at his muscular frame and noticed the many scars that covered his body. She was careful not to look at other parts of his anatomy.

"Were you wounded during the war?" she asked.

He began to slip on his clothes and didn't notice her scrutiny.

"A few times."

"Tell me about it," she said.

"They ain't nothin'," he mumbled. "Besides, ain't all from the war. Got my share with the Rangers."

"You're very brave," she said with admiration

"No. Just did what I had to. You stay put while I fetch the tub."

He and Bart brought the large metal tub upstairs. When they reached the room, Buford dismissed the old man. "I'll bring it in," he said. "The wife's a bit skittish. Go down and fetch the water and I'll help you in a minute."

"New brides, eh Colonel?" Bart asked with a twinkle in his eye.

The two men made numerous trips up and down with pails of hot water.

When the tub was full, Mabel got out of bed. Buford looked at her longingly and couldn't get over how beautiful she was.

"Is there something wrong?" she asked, noticing how he stared. She wasn't aware that her nightgown clung to her provocatively.

"No," he said, "Only that you're the prettiest woman I've ever seen." He looked down at his hands feeling foolish.

"Why thank you, sir!" she said. She couldn't help but smile. Her big, rugged husband was blushing like a school boy.

"Reckon you'll want some privacy so I'm gonna' go see Jimmy."

"Fine," she said. "I'll be ready for breakfast when you come back."

Buford found Jimmy still unconscious but alive.

"He's not out of the woods yet," said Doc. "He survived the night but the wound's festerin'. I'm not sure he'll pull through."

Next Buford stopped in the jailhouse to see Hi.

"Damn!" exclaimed Hi. "You said she was pretty, but I never reckoned for what I seen. I ain't gotta' tell you that she's too fuckin' good for you, do I?"

"No," said Buford. "She's definitely better'n I deserve but it ain't no different with you. You ain't worthy of Lydia, either."

"True enough," said Hi. "Speakin' of women, when you get a chance go talk to Emma."

"What the fuck for?" Buford scowled. "I ain't got nothin' to say to 'er."

"Mebbe' not, but she might have somethin' to say to you. Ain't no rush. When you get the chance."

"She done said enough. Cussin' at me yesterday! She got some nerve!"

When Buford got back to the hotel Mabel was dressed and sipping on a hot cup of coffee. A tin of biscuits was on the small table beside her.

"It was rude of me not to wait for you," she apologized, "but I was famished. I sent down for some coffee. Let me get you a cup."

The big iron pot was heavy, and the hot liquid splashed on her hand as she poured.

"Oh!" she cried dropping the cup and putting her injured hand to her mouth. Buford was by her side in a second.

"Let me look at it," he said putting her tiny hand in his.

"I'm so clumsy," she laughed. "It's nothing really. Don't fuss." She wouldn't carry on even though her hand stung painfully.

He looked at it closely. It was red where the coffee had scalded but the burn wasn't serious.

She felt uncomfortable by his closeness and her pulse raced. "I'm afraid my domestic skills aren't much," she laughed stepping away from him. "At home we had two servants."

"I'll get you some. Most of the rancher's wives got a Mexican gal or two."

"No, Colonel. I want to keep my own house. I'll be with Lydia today. Perhaps she can teach me a few things."

After they ate, Buford left her at the Johnson home and went to the ranch.

He found it a beehive of activity. The men were rested and there was much to do after their long absence.

"How's Jimmy?" Phil asked Buford.

"He's alive but Doc still ain't sure he's gonna' make it. Why don't you go on and see 'im. I'll have Ezra find someone to take your watch."

"Would be much obliged, Colonel. Me and Jimmy come a long way together. He's like kin."

Buford went to find Ezra and the herd.

Ezra had everything running smoothly. Buford talked with the cowboys for a while and then went to see Ziggy.

"Colonel!" said Ziggy, climbing down from the ladder. "She will be ready soon. One more day."

"Good. The sooner the better. Can't abide the hotel."

It was late afternoon when he returned to Hi's house. Lydia and Mabel sat in rockers on the front porch. It was a tranquil scene, but he found no comfort in it.

"Colonel!" said Mabel excitedly. "Lydia is going to let me prepare dinner tonight. Isn't that grand?"

"Reckon it is. Much obliged, Lydia," he said.

"Think nothin' of it," she said. "I'll teach 'er to cook. You always liked my vittles."

"That I have. When you expectin' Hi?"

"Not for a while yet. Come and set with us."

"Think I'll go on down to the jail house and see 'im."

When he left, Lydia sighed. "What a pity. He's all tore up over Tom."

Mabel looked at her with wide eyes. "How can you tell? Frankly it bothers me how little it seems to affect him."

Lydia shook her head. "You don't know the Colonel yet. That's just his way. He don't wear his heart on his sleeve."

"I'm aware that you know him better than I, but you didn't see him! His own brother was murdered by savages and he didn't bat an eye. He and Ezra talked about Tom smelling! Then when we buried him the Colonel said he couldn't waste time on saying anything over his grave."

"Believe me when I say the Colonel is hurt. He's holdin' his sorrow inside."

Mabel smiled, "Thank you for telling me that. I think I'll learn more from you than how to cook." Not for the first time she thought of how little she knew about her husband.

At the jailhouse, Hi went out of his way to cheer Buford. He told him humorous tales about the townsfolk and ribald stories of goings on at the Longhorn. None of them had any affect.

Hi was getting disheartened when Clyde came in. "'Bout time you got here," he grumbled.

"Yea, the Marshall's been workin' hard all afternoon tellin' me stories," said Buford.

"Sorry to hear 'bout your brother," said Clyde awkwardly.

Buford nodded.

"C'mon Buford, let's go. We got two beautiful women waitin' for us. See you in the mornin' Clyde."

As they approached the Johnson house, the smell of burnt food greeted them.

"What the hell?" swore Hi. "What's gotten into Lydia?"

"Ain't Lydia, it's Mabel. I expect she's cookin' us dinner. Smells like shit don't it?" Hi was glad to see Buford smile. He hadn't been able to coax a grin from him.

"Sure does. Hope she's better in her other wifely duties," laughed Hi.

"Like her cookin', she needs practice."

"And you're just the man to give it to 'er, too," said Hi with glee.

At the table, the two men looked askance at their plates while Mabel beamed. Hi was ready to inquire what it was, but a dark look from Lydia kept him silent.

The meat was burnt in places and raw in others. The vegetables were different colors of soggy matter.

Buford and Hi picked at their food.

"What's wrong?" Mabel asked. "Is my cooking that bad?" She smiled, but tears lay under the surface.

"No, Ma'am!" said Hi. "It's fine. Just that Fanny Bell come to the jailhouse with a pie this afternoon. Reckon me and the Colonel et' our fill."

"Oh," she said relieved. Buford shot Hi a grateful glance.

When they were ready to leave Lydia said, "Why don't

you come on over and cook supper again tomorrow?" Hi scowled at her but she paid no attention.

"I'd like that very much," said Mabel.

"I don't know 'bout that Lydia," said Buford. "Me and Mabel got furniture and what not to buy for the house. Reckon, it'll be past dinner time when we're through."

"Never you mind. We'll wait. Mabel ain't gonna' learn to cook if'n no one shows 'er."

That night when they got back to their room, Mabel joined Buford for a night cap.

When they were in bed, he reached over for her and she moved away.

"Damnation," he swore silently to himself.

"Mabel?" he asked in the dark.

"Yes?"

"You want me to take another room?"

When she didn't answer, he got out of bed and went to the window. In the still night air, he could hear the music coming from the Longhorn down the street. He wished he could go for a drink and pretend nothing had changed. Tom was still alive, and he wasn't married to a woman who shunned him.

After last night, Mabel was afraid of him. Although she anticipated that it would be awful, it had been worse than she imagined. She knew she was a disappointment to him.

"There's no need for you to leave. Come back to bed," she said finally.

When he returned, he lay there not daring to touch her. He sighed deeply. Grateful, she was ready to go to sleep when she heard him sigh again. Gritting her teeth, she rolled over and placed a tiny hand on his chest. The hair on it felt soft and silky and not unpleasant. She moved a little closer to him. It was all the encouragement he needed.

In the morning they breakfasted on Abel's hard biscuits and strong coffee. Buford decided he better get used to inedible food.

He went to Doc's while Mabel got dressed. He had no idea it took a woman so long to get ready.

He was glad to find Jimmy conscious.

"Howdy Colonel," he said weakly. "Much obliged to

you."

"For what?"

"Doc says I'm gonna' pull through 'cause of you."

"It wasn't nothin'. All I done is leave that fuckin' arrow in."

"Yea, well Doc said if'n you had fucked with it, I'd be dead."

"Learned a long time ago to leave it in if'n it's stuck. Happened to me once. Couldn't get the fuckin' thing out no matter what we done. Finally, Hi had to cut it out. Almost met my maker that time. Left a hell of a scar but I'm still here." After a short visit, Buford returned to the hotel.

Mabel looked stunning in a new bonnet and dress and he smiled. She'd been very accommodating last night, and he thought it added to his feeling of well-being.

They spent most of the day in the general store, where Mabel breathlessly rushed around picking out furniture, pots and other household paraphernalia.

They made it back to Hi's in time for her to cook another dreadful supper. That night she gave herself to him willingly.

The next morning, accompanied by Phineas and two wagon loads of goods, they left for the ranch.

As Ziggy had promised, the house was finished, and the men moved the furniture in.

Buford had a hard time controlling his temper. They had no sooner placed things where Mabel asked, when she'd change her mind. As a result, they moved furniture from one place to another for hours.

When they were finally done, Mabel left the men and went to the kitchen.

"Damn it to hell!" swore Buford. "Ain't never seen a woman change 'er fuckin' mind so much!"

• • •

The next day at dawn, a mournful procession followed the Parson to the end of the McLeod ranch. The ride would take all day and they wouldn't get to Tom's grave until just before dark. Despite the inconvenience, many people came to pay their respects. The good-natured Tom had been a favorite in Wilder Creek.

As the Parson began his eulogy, crying could be heard in the crowd of mourners. Buford stood by stoically and listened, grief clearly etched on his face. Mable put her arm through his and snuggled up closer. When she did, she felt his body trembling. This was the first time she had seen visible proof of his loss.

After the service they made camp. The sorrowful group huddled around the campfire speaking in hushed tones.

"I'm restless," Mabel said to Buford. "would you walk with me awhile?"

He didn't answer but taking her arm they walked far from the campfire.

When Mabel was sure they couldn't be seen or heard she hugged Buford tightly. He didn't respond but stood woodenly with his arms by his side. She laid her head on his chest and began to rub his back with a soothing motion. In a while he returned her embrace. She couldn't see him in the darkness but felt his body shake as he cried great sobbing tears.

In the morning they broke camp and made their way back to the ranch, reaching it at sundown. Juan and the women prepared a large meal in the cook house. After eating their fill, everyone went home.

It was a very tired couple who went to the newly completed house. Despite her sadness, Mabel felt a sense of well-being. Her husband had finally showed her he was human. Lydia had been right; Buford didn't show his feelings in front of others. She felt flattered that this rugged man could show her his emotions. he lked through the elegantly furnished rooms. "

"Well, I'm going to bed," she said, yawning. "I didn't sleep well last night. I never dreamed that sleeping in a soft bed would become such a luxury. It was something I'd always taken for granted."

"I'll be there in a minute," he said.

"Don't take too long," she said coquettishly.

"I don't know why Mother said it was terrible," she thought to herself. "I'm beginning to like it."

Buford walked around his new home and felt sick to his stomach. He couldn't get over all the furniture and knick-knacks that seemed to fill every inch of space. He felt like he was suffocating. He went out and looked up at the clear night sky filled with stars. "Can you see me Tom? If'n you can, I bet you're hee-hawin' like a fuckin' mule." He continued to stare up at the sky, silent tears streaming down his cheeks.

The next morning Mabel bustled around her well equipped kitchen. Breakfast was bad, lunch worse, and dinner all but inedible.

Although she tried very hard Buford could see that her housekeeping skills were poor. After a week of burnt hands, broken dishes and horrid food, he'd had enough. He would've starved if he didn't sneak to the cook house for some of Juan's cooking from time to time. It was apparent they'd need a maid.

"She's tryin' God love 'er but she ain't much of a cook or anythin' else for that matter," grumbled Buford. "She can't keep a fire goin', can't make a bed, can't do nothin'. You know any woman in the Village who might need a job?" he asked Juan.

"My sister Rosa. She can use the work."

"You still home sick after all this time?" Buford chided.

"Oh no, Colonel! My sister, she's difficult, but she's a good housekeeper."

"Reckon, you oughta' fetch 'er then," sighed Buford.

So it was that Juan's sister, Rosa, came to work for them.

From the first day she arrived, she and Buford didn't get along. She didn't speak English and he insisted Mabel teach her. Much to his dismay, his wife became fluent in Spanish instead.

"How's she gonna' learn English if'n you don't teach 'er?"

"Have a little patience, Colonel. She'll learn in time. Besides, you've been around Mexicans all your life," she answered sweetly.

"I know their gibberish, but this ain't Mexico. It's the goddamn United States. and it's time she learns the language," he said scowling at her.

"Oh, you can be so silly at times," she said, his glare lost on her.

She smiled to herself inwardly. Perhaps she didn't know

how to cook or clean, but she quickly learned how to manip-
ulate her husband. She wasn't intimidated by his moods.
She used all her feminine whiles to intimidate him instead.

Buford loved her more than anything. It wasn't just
her beauty but her disposition as well. She had no fear of
him. He'd never met anyone who seemed unaffected by his
moods. It both annoyed and pleased him.

Although Buford told Victor he wouldn't be around
much, he couldn't bear to leave her. He stayed back at the
house. He was fortunate to have trustworthy and competent
men.

With Jimmy injured, Tom dead and Buford staying
home the outfit was down by three men. Buford hired Barn-
abas Cary and Reuben Buzzell. Ezra was pleased with the
new cow punchers and Buford was satisfied that things
were running smoothly.

He spent all his time working with his horses. The barn
and corrals were close to the house, so he was nearby if
Mabel needed him. He was glad to have the time to break in
mustangs and concentrate on breeding new stock.

Although Rosa taught Mabel to cook and clean, she
grew lonely and bored. She asked Buford to take her to town
frequently, claiming she had errands to run.

When she was done she'd visit with Lydia. Although
Buford could find business to tend to, he was annoyed at
being gone from the ranch so often. One day he went to the
Longhorn. He'd hadn't been in since the day he returned
from Ellsworth.

Emma walked over to him and he was surprised at her
condition.

"Was wonderin' when you was gonna' come in," she
said.

"Ain't got no call to. Lord, Emma didn't know you was
in the family way."

She smiled. "You ain't half as surprised as I was!"

"Who done this to you?"

She took a deep breath, "You did."

"What?" he asked incredulously. "You sayin' it's mine?"

"Yea."

"Jesus, Emma! Could be anyone's. Besides, even if'n it is

mine, I always tole' you I ain't beholdin' to you."

"Don't fret. I ain't askin' for nothin'. Thought you might want to know is all." Squaring her slender shoulders, she turned and walked away.

Before Buford knew what he was doing he called out to her and she came back. He pulled out a hand full of bills.

"I know this baby ain't mine, but it wouldn't be Christian to leave you like this."

She looked down at the roll of money he handed her. "This is right kind of you," she said, tears of relief glistening in her eyes.

Buford left and went to the jailhouse to see Hi. "You seen Emma lately?" he asked Hi.

"Just left there."

"Did you know she was havin' a baby?"

Hi laughed, "Pretty hard to miss."

"She says it's mine."

"Yea, she tole' me."

"When?"

"Day you come back to town."

"Why didn't you tell me?"

"For Christ's sakes, Buford. You was tired and just buried Tom. Didn't think it proper."

"Goddamn, fuckin' women!" Buford growled. "I know it ain't mine."

"'Course it is. She been with nobody but you."

"I was on the trail to Ellsworth. Been close to six months since I touched 'er. It ain't mine I tell you."

"Happened before you left mebbe'. She looks like she's six months gone."

"How the fuck do you know?" Buford asked.

"I know 'cause of Lydia. You ain't gotta' worry 'bout Emma. She can take care of 'erself."

"I ain't worried ,'bout 'er. Just gets me mad that she says the kid's mine."

Hi didn't reply. He knew once Buford made his mind up about something there was no changing it.

●●●

Try as she might, Mabel was having a hard time adjusting to the isolation of the ranch. After she'd used up every excuse to leave the ranch, she confessed to Buford she was lonely, just as he had warned.

He indulged her, although he resented the time away. His work left undone, he spent days on buggy rides, in town and at other social events.

He missed the days when he worked hard, ate with his men out of metal plates and crawled into bed, dirty and exhausted. Now he squired Mabel around, clean and in his best clothes.

One afternon as Mabel visited with Lydia he sat with Hi in the jailhouse. Hi said, "This is the life, ain't it Buford? We're both settled down with two fine gals."

"Yea, we're lucky I guess," sighed Buford.

Hi's mischievous eyes turned serious. "What's wrong? Don't marriage agree with you?"

"I hate it!" he answered standing up and beginning to pace. "Look at me here in these dandified clothes and it ain't even Sunday! I should be out workin' now 'stead of settin' on my ass. Come into town today 'cause Mabel wanted to visit with Lydia. I ain't fittin' into it right, Hi."

"You jack ass. Marriage takes some gettin' used to. You think I didn't feel like you? Me and you done lived hard, fightin' and killin' for so long. Settlin' down ain't easy."

"It was different for you. You done left the Rangers and got married all at once. You know I still ain't right. I ain't used to the bunkhouse, now I'm sleepin' in a house with fuckin' satin pillows. What the fuck?"

"We lived hard for a long time. Mebbe' you should tell 'er how you feel. Put your foot down. Tell 'er you got work to do. Hate to say it, but mebbe' you should show 'er that McLeod temper."

"Done showed her a coupla' times. Didn't do no good. She ain't afraid of me none."

"Well, I'll be!" laughed Hi. "Good for her. You knowed she wouldn't like being holed up on the ranch. She needs a youngun' to keep 'er busy. As I was sayin' to Lydia just the other day..." he was interrupted by Clyde who came rushing in, frightened and out of breath.

"Marshall, I just come from the saloon. There's a bad bunch down there. They just come in and was askin' after you and the Colonel. Says they got unfinished business with y'all. Says they knew you when you was both Rangers. They's shootin' up the place and got Frenchie and the girls scairt' bad."

"Who are they?" asked Hi.

"Don't rightly know. They didn't say."

"Reckon, we better go down there," Hi said to Buford.

When he and Buford entered the saloon, they found six drunken men shooting the globes off Frenchie's lamps.

"What's goin' on here!" Hi yelled over the din of bullets and breaking glass.

The men stopped firing.

"Heard y'all wanted to see me. Do I know you?" Hi asked.

One of them, Joseph Potts, grinned.

"Well, well boys, looks like we found 'em. Why Ranger Johnson my feelin's is hurt. You don't remember me? How 'bout you, Colonel?"

"Reckon I do. You and your boys robbed a bank in El Paso. Remember chasin' you to the border."

"Yea, that's right. Ceptin' you're forgettin' one thing. You killed my brother and Ranger Johnson here, kilt my best friend. My brother was only sixteen. Y'all left my friend's wife a widow with five kids."

"Bank robbin' is risky business," said Buford.

"So ain't rangerin'," Joseph sneered.

"That it is," said Hi, "but we ain't broke the law. You and your gang done that."

"I see you're still a law man," he said to Hi.

"Yep."

"Well, I don't give two shits for the law," said Joseph. "My brother was unarmed when you shot 'im. I been lookin' for you two a long time."

Buford smiled coldly. "Unarmed? Out of bullets mebbe' but not unarmed. He run out shootin' 'em all at me. He was reloadin' when I kilt 'im. Wasn't gonna' give 'im another chance to shoot at me."

"You're right," Hi said to Joseph. "As I recall, I was the one who kilt' your friend. It would seem a man with a family oughta' know better than to ride with outlaws. Besides, we didn't kill no one in cold blood, y'all was shootin' at us. I reckon you're sorry you missed."

"Well, ain't plannin' on missin' this time," said Joseph drawing his guns. He was fast, but Buford was faster and shot him dead. That's when all hell broke loose, and a gun fight ensued.

Hi and Buford dove for cover. They instinctively fell into sync. They'd been in so many campaigns together, they fought side by side like a well-oiled machine.

Besides Potts, they killed three more men. The last two surrendered.

Buford's adrenalin was pumping hard and he felt exhilarated. It had been a long time since he and Hi had fought outlaws together. They led the men back to the jail house through an admiring crowd of on lookers.

When they were locked up Buford looked at Hi and grinned. Hi started to laugh and Buford joined him. They laughed until tears streamed down their cheeks.

"Well, look at your Sunday go to meetin' clothes now!" said Hi choked with laughter. Buford looked at his clothes. He was a mess. He'd hit the floor of the saloon hard and had rolled out of the line of fire. His good coat was covered with dirt, manure, ash and spilled beer. He smelled as bad as he looked.

Hi continued to laugh. "That's why you're so happy, Buford. You love lookin' and smellin' like a hog."

"You ain't so clean neither," Buford said with mirth. "How you gonna' explain that there two-inch hole in your hat to Lydia?"

"What?" asked Hi, sobering. He loved his hat. He took it off and looked at it. "Goddamn it all to hell!" he bellowed.

He walked to the cell which held the two men.

"Look at my fuckin' Stetson, you sons of whores! This here's a hangin' offence and I'm gonna' make you swing for it!"

The men believed him. They were young and had been startled by the fighting prowess of the two older men. They believed the two ex-rangers would be easy prey but calculated wrong. Now seeing the murderous gleam in Hi's eyes, they feared for their lives.

When the fight was over, pandemonium broke out in town. Witnesses to the gun battle ran here and there telling others.

Clyde came in. "Done took care of the dead, Marshall, and broke up the crowd. Anythin' else I can do?"

"Yep. You can stay here and keep an eye on these varmints. I'm takin' the afternoon off. Gonna' go home to clean up and see my woman."

One of the townsfolk had stopped by Lydia's to tell her and Mabel of their husband's adventure. "Lord, you shoulda' seen 'em," the observer said with a smile. "The Marshall and Colonel took care of them outlaws lickity split!"

Though Lydia knew Hi was all right, she was still filled with unease. She dreaded the day when someone would come with bad news.

Mabel, on the other hand, was thrilled. When she first came to Wilder Creek she'd been pleased by the attention she received. Everyone treated her kindly and with extreme courtesy. She was the "Colonel's wife" and worthy of respect.

"I swear, they coulda' got themselves kilt!" said a flustered Lydia.

When the men arrived both women flew into their arms.

"You're gonna' be sorry you done this," said Buford pushing Mabel away gently. "I'm a might dirty."

"I don't care," she said, embracing him again.

CHAPTER FIVE

After a few months, Buford still wasn't used to marriage. The only thing he liked about it was waking up to Mabel every morning. After all the years of living rough, the lavish house was a nightmare. It was no place for a cattle man. He left trails of dirt on the floors, carpets and furniture. Rosa cleaned behind him cursing in Spanish.

Mabel wasn't settling well either. She was lonely and restless. They attended social outings amongst the ranchers and townsfolk, but they were few and far between. Buford had put his foot down about spending so much time away from the ranch.

"Damn it, Mabel. I can't keep runnin' off every time you wanna' go somewhere. I tole' you before we got hitched you'd be lonely out here."

She had to admit he was right. She began to learn from Rosa in earnest and felt a sense of accomplishment when she could run the house almost as well as the Mexican woman. She also took up hobbies to keep herself busy.

• • •

One day as Josh helped him with the horses he said, "If'n you got nothin' else for me to do later, reckon I'd like to go into town. Aimin' to see Miss Emma."

"Ain't she expectin'?" Buford asked.

"She done have the baby a few months ago. A fine boy, too. She's back in business again."

Buford hadn't seen Emma since the afternoon she'd told him the baby was his. He'd put her from his mind, a feat he was more than capable of.

"If'n Ezra got nothin' for you, reckon it'll be all right. Glad to hear that Emma come to her senses."

"Ain't as glad as I am," Josh beamed. "Have to say, Colonel, broke my heart when she didn't pleasure no one but you."

"That's all in the past."

"Yea, notice you don't go to the saloon no more."

"Ain't got no call to. I ain't a gamblin' man, only went in before for whiskey and whores. Now that I'm married ain't got no need for whores and I can drink whiskey at home if'n I have a mind to."

Josh wondered if the Colonel knew Emma's child was his. For many months she serviced no one but him. Josh had tried to buy her services many times and she always refused. He had no doubt that Buford was the father.

• • •

That afternoon when her chores were done, Mabel decided to watch Buford break in horses.

The first time she witnessed this bone jarring process she had cried out in fright every time he fell off the bucking animal, although it didn't faze him in the least. He got up, wincing and limping and climbed back in the saddle. They bit him frequently and many a night she'd apply salve to the vicious wounds.

After watching a few times, she grew used to the harshness of the procedure. She enjoyed the battle of wills between man and beast. In the end, the wild creatures became docile as lambs.

She reached the corral in time to see Buford take a bad fall.

"Goodness, Colonel! Do be careful!"

"I swear, this son of a bitch is gonna' kill me yet," he laughed, getting up and dusting himself off.

Mabel admired the big, black stallion. "He's a beautiful animal. When he's broken in might I have him?"

"No, ma'am! He's a bad one. Josh wanted to break 'im but I wouldn't let 'im. Ain't no one gonna' ride this ornery bastard but me, even after he's broke. Juan named 'im Diablo and he's livin' up to his name. Daisy's good enough for now."

Mabel had never handled a team and wagon nor rode a horse before coming west. Buford was teaching her both. The horse he gave her was a sweet-tempered horse named

Daisy. She told Buford she was ready for a more vigorous horse. "You ain't ready," he said.

She leaned against the railing of the corral and admired Diablo. He was the most splendid horse she'd ever seen.

Buford climbed on the stallion twisting its ear hard to distract him. He was no sooner in the saddle when the bronco began to kick and buck as if possessed.

He threw Buford again and again. Bleeding from the lip and favoring his right hand, Buford refused to give up. He dug his spurs deep into Diablo's side to subdue him, but the horse was mean and stubborn and didn't submit.

After a few excruciating hours, Diablo gave in and Buford rode him easily.

As Mabel watched them trot around the corral, she thought her husband was wrong. Diablo didn't seem menacing at all.

"Look at him!" she exclaimed. "He's just as calm as can be. Now may I ride him?"

"Lord, Mabel. I already tole' you no! I don't trust 'im. I don't know if'n he'll ever be broke in. He's just lettin' me think it for now."

Mabel waited for Buford as he put Diablo in the barn. He limped heavily as he walked back to her.

"Fuckin' horse!" he swore blackly. "If'n he didn't settle down think I woulda' shot 'im."

"I hope you're only joking. He's a fine animal." She began dabbing at the blood on his lip with her handkerchief.

"Don't fuss," he said, brushing her hand away. "Ain't the first time I been banged up bustin' broncs."

"You're as stubborn as Diablo," she replied.

She was growing used to his quick temper and foul moods. Even his cursing ceased to bother her. No matter how hot his temper flared she remained cool and calm. She knew he was putty in her hand. Her stomach fluttered when she thought how tender this hard, cold man could be.

He stopped walking and broke her train of thought. "What's the matter?" she asked.

"My goddamn leg done kinked up on me. Just need a second for the spasm to pass. You go on. I'll meet you inside."

She put her arm around his waist. "Here, lean on me."

"I can't lean on you. I'm twice as tall as you! Besides I ain't no baby! Reckon I can make it to the fuckin' house on my own," he snapped.

"Lord, you are so pig headed!" she said suddenly exasperated. "Why won't you let me help? You and your foolish pride!"

He glared at her. "Ain't foolish and it ain't pride. I'm just used to takin' care of myself is all."

"Fine!" she said and left in a huff.

Buford smiled at her retreating back. "Lord, she's got spirit!" he thought. "Mabel," he called out. She turned and looked at him. "Didn't mean to get you riled. But this here is just part of, what do you call it? Oh yea, my rugged individuality!"

Mabel stomped back to the house without replying. She knew better than to offer her help, so why was she angry that he refused?

She was no longer angry when he finally entered the house, his face red from exertion.

"Rugged individuality, indeed!" she laughed.

• • •

That night Josh entered the Longhorn cleaned up and ready to sport. Emma was busy, and he had to wait. When she came downstairs, he rushed to her side.

"Howdy, Miss Emma," he said courteously. "How 'bout a poke?"

"Sure. Y'all go on up and wait for me. I'll be along directly."

"Don't take too long!" he said dashing upstairs.

Emma went to the bar. "Frenchie, give me a drink," she said softly.

"Sure, Emma," he beamed. "Business has been good for you lately, no?" She was one of his favorites again.

He'd almost thrown her out when she saw no one but Buford, and again when she got pregnant. He was glad he hadn't. Now that things were back to normal, she was making a lot of money for them both.

She sipped at her beer. "Yea, business been good but it's sure tirin' me out. Ain't used to it. It's been a long time since I done poked the whole danged town!"

"When you were stuck on the Colonel, we all warned you," he scolded gently. "Even the Colonel himself!"

She sighed. "I shoulda' knowed better but I couldn't help myself. I made a mistake and now I'm payin' for it."

"Everyone's paying!" Frenchie joked. "Perhaps you are not a happy woman but soon you will be a rich one!"

"I hope so. I gotta' take care of my boy." She finished her beer and wearily climbed the stairs.

• • •

A few days later, Buford was cutting rails for the corral. Spring was still a month off, but it was blistering hot. He stopped to wipe the sweat from his brow and noticed a group of riders approaching. He couldn't tell who they were, but knew it meant trouble.

As they drew closer, he could see Hi, Clyde, Charlie Smith, Zeb, Junior and a few others. He put down his saw and walked over to greet them as they reined in.

"What's goin' on, Hi?" he asked.

"Apache," Hi answered.

"Saw 'em this mornin'," Charlie said. "Went out after one of my cows and saw a whole danged passle of 'em. Sons of bitches was steelin' my cattle! I went straight to the Marshall and he put this here posse together."

"We're goin' after 'em and thought you might want to come," said Hi.

"How many you reckon there was?" Buford asked Charlie.

"Don't know for sure. Maybe a dozen, maybe more."

"I'll get some of my boys. The more men, the better."

Hi said playfully, "Hell, Buford. We don't need no more men. Me and you was famous Indian fighters, remember?"

"If'n you think you can take on all them Indians yourself, go ahead. Me and the boys will come along and watch."

Buford went to the barn for a horse and his guns. Josh was in there grooming the horses.

"Josh, we got Indian trouble. Apache stole some of Charlie's beeves. I'm goin' to fetch Ezra and some of the boys. I'm leavin' you in charge. I want some men 'round the house and make sure they're heavily armed. I don't want Mabel left alone. I want you to stay with the herd."

"All right, Colonel," Josh said with a sigh of relief. After the Kiowa attack, he was glad he didn't have to go.

Juan came out of the cook house as Buford led his horse out of the barn.

"What is it, Colonel?" he asked.

"Apache were on Charlie's ranch this mornin' and stole some of his cattle."

"They were probably hungry," said Juan.

"Since when you been on their side?" Buford snapped.

"I'm not on their side but it's true. Little by little they are losing their hunting grounds."

"They got plenty of fuckin' huntin' grounds north of here. They ain't got no call to steal our cows."

Juan disagreed but kept silent. The gringos had a habit of taking land that didn't belong to them. They had taken land from Mexico, now they would take the Indian's. He could understand their rage. The government broke treaties and slaughtered their women and children.

"I don't think them Indians are gonna' stick 'round after stealin'. I'd be much obliged if'n you'd go on over to the house and stay with the women folk. I got men coverin' the house, but I need a good man by Mabel's side to protect 'er."

"Si, Colonel." Juan smiled. He was devoted to Buford. Many gringos made him feel inferior, but Buford treated him as an equal and trusted friend.

Buford mounted his horse and joined the others. As they rode out, they met up with Ezra and more of Buford's outfit. Satisfied with their numbers, they went in search of the Apaches.

At lunch time Phil went to the house for Juan.

"Josh wants you to bring the grub to us. He don't want no one to leave the herd. Just in case."

"I told the Colonel that I would watch the women."

"Don't know what to tell you," Phil replied. "Josh is in charge. The Colonel don't think them injuns' are still 'round but Josh ain't takin' no chances. The Colonel would be mighty mad if any of his cows was stolen."

"Si, the Colonel told me he didn't think we'd have trouble. I'm sure the women can stay on their own for a while. There are still many men watching the house. Besides," he laughed, "even an Apache is no match for my sister."

Juan told the women of his plans. "Stay in the house until I get back." He handed Rosa a rifle. "You know how to use this if you have to."

"Have any Indians been spotted?" Mabel asked in alarm.

"No, Signora. The men are watching but have seen nothing. There's nothing to worry about."

"Go about your business," Rosa said in Spanish. "The Signora will be safe with me."

After Juan left Mabel sighed. "When I was in Ohio, I thought it would be exciting to see real savages. That is until the day the Kiowa attacked. I was never so frightened in my life. Do you think we're safe?"

"Si. The Colonel would never have left you if he thought you were in danger."

"I suppose you're right." Mabel gave a nervous laugh. "Look at my hands, they're trembling. I feel like a fool."

"You need something to keep your mind busy," said Rosa. "Come. We'll work on the quilt."

"I don't think I could. With these shaky hands I'll prick myself with every stitch. I'm afraid to leave the house but I can't stand being inside. I wish I could ride Daisy. Riding always eases my mind. I'm sure I'll be all right if I stay in the corral. I know the Colonel has men all around us."

"Then you ride. I'll come with you and bring this," Rosa said, patting the rifle beside her.

When they reached the barn, Mabel was surprised to see Diablo. "I wonder why the Colonel didn't take him?" She wasn't savvy enough to know that he wouldn't take such a head strong horse when tracking Indians.

She went over and patted his sleek head. "I'd love to ride you, but my husband won't let me," she cooed.

In her strong-willed fashion, she decided to saddle him. Juan and Buford were gone, and they would never know. She felt certain she could handle the stallion if she stayed in the corral.

She mounted Diablo and walked him around. Though spirited, he behaved beautifully. "I knew the Colonel was wrong about you!" she said aloud.

Rosa wasn't concerned about Mabel's choice of mounts.

She didn't know Diablo was forbidden. Instead she walked around the perimeter of the corral with an ever-watchful eye.

As Mabel went around the corral, her nerves quieted. Suddenly off in the distance she heard the crack of a rifle and Diablo reared and bucked. He lurched around and around. She tried to hold on but didn't have the strength or experience. Losing her grip, she tumbled off the huge animal's back. It all happened swiftly but it seemed to Mabel as though it took her a long time to hit the ground; then everything went black.

Rosa's attention was drawn by the gun fire. She looked in the direction from which it came expecting to see Indians. She heard the commotion in the corral and tore her eyes away from the horizon just in time to see Mabel fly off the horse.

"Dio!" she cried and ran to her.

She panicked. Indians were coming, and her mistress was hurt. She dragged Mabel in the barn and bolted the door behind her.

She laid her on a bed of straw and chafed her wrists, staring at the closed barn door all the while. She expected a savage to come bursting through at any moment.

When she looked at Mabel again blood was trickling from her nose and mouth. Her face was white and her breathing unsteady and shallow. Rosa tore off a piece of her petticoat and staunched the flow of blood.

After a while, she heard a rider approaching and grabbing her rifle, ran to the window. She saw a cloud of dust and then Juan's wagon came into view. He didn't appear to be in a hurry and she was puzzled. Wasn't he aware that he was in danger? She unbolted the door and ran outside.

"Juan, quickly!" She cried, waving her apron.

He slapped the reins hard and reached the barn in a moment. He reined in and was out of the wagon before it stopped. Rosa beckoned him inside the barn.

"We heard gun fire and the Signora's horse threw her. What happened? Have the Apache come?"

"No, it was one of the hands. His gun went off by mistake. It nearly started a stampede. The other hombres were angry. Not as angry as the Colonel will be. The Signora does not look good."

They carried her to the house and put her in bed. Rosa washed the dirt and blood from her face.

Juan looked on in sorrow. He would never forgive himself if anything happened to her. "I should never have left her," he said miserably.

"What could you have done? It was the fault of the gringo with the gun. Even if you were here, the horse would have thrown her."

"I did not think Daisy so skittish."

"She didn't ride Daisy. She was on the big black one."

"Diablo!" Juan cried. "The Colonel won't let anyone ride him. If I'd been here, I would have stopped her."

"It is too late now. Quickly, get the Doctor!"

Juan hurried out. A short time later he was back with the doctor.

Doc went in and began to examine Mabel. Rosa took Juan aside. "Go feed the men," she said to him. "It is past their supper time."

"I brought it to them this afternoon, so I wouldn't have to leave the Signora again. Why did I go?" he wailed. "I should never have gone!"

"Stop it!" Rosa snapped. "Build up the fire and turn up the lamps. Make the Doctor something to eat."

"How long has she been unconscious?" Doc asked.

"About three hours."

"Were you with her all that time?"

"Si."

"Did you notice her movin' her arms and legs?"

"No Doctor. She lays like the dead," she said, crossing herself.

"She took a bad fall. She's got a bump on her head but no broken bones. Makes me think she hit the ground head first and that worries me. Hopefully she'll just have a headache and a few aches and pains. I'm leavin' some laudanum. If she's not right when she comes out of it, send for me right away, otherwise give her enough to make her comfortable.

He closed his bag and got ready to leave. "The men were still out when I left town. I'll send the Colonel home as soon as they come in."

"You better come with him," said Rosa. "I have a feeling my brother and a few of the other hombres are going to need you when he learns of this."

He looked at her solemnly. There definitely would be hell to pay. The Colonel loved that woman beyond reason and anyone who harmed a hair on her head was in trouble.

He didn't voice his opinion. Instead he spoke with a reassurance he didn't feel. "Accidents happen. The Colonel will understand."

When Doc got back to town, he stopped at the jailhouse and told Clyde. "If the Colonel comes here, tell him to come see me. It's urgent."

It was the middle of the night when Buford came back to the ranch, his horse in a lather and near dead with fatigue. After seeing Doc he'd driven his mount harder than he should.

He jumped from the saddle and took the stairs two at a time. He ran into the bedroom and saw Juan and Rosa sitting beside Mabel.

His heart caught in his chest. Her face looked as white as the pillow she laid on. He stood at the foot of the bed and stared at her helplessly.

He glared at Juan with a murderous gleam in his eye. "What the fuck happened here?" he said between clenched teeth.

Juan winced and spoke with a shaking voice. "Diablo threw the Signora."

"Diablo! What the hell was she doin' ridin' 'im? Of all the goddamn stupid things to do. Why didn't you stop 'er?"

"I wasn't here, Colonel."

Buford's face screwed up in rage. "Why the fuck not? I tole' you to stay with 'er, didn't I?" he roared at the hapless man.

"Quiet," said Rosa. "You are in a sick room! She needs…" He shot her a withering glance and her mouth snapped shut.

"I brought the men their noon meal. Josh thought they should all stay with the herd."

"So, you left my wife instead?" he asked in disbelief.

"I was gone only a short time. When I came back, she

was like this. I didn't know she would ride that devil horse!" Tears rolled down Juan's cheeks and he couldn't go on.

"Were you with 'er?" he asked Rosa.

"Si. She was riding in the corral when a gun went off and the horse threw her." She didn't want to give him any more details.

"Who's the fuckin' idiot who fired the shot?" he growled looking from one to the other.

"Reuben, the new man, but it was an accident. The men were armed in case of the Apache. When he sat to eat, he put his rifle down and it went off," Juan said wiping his tears with the back of his hand.

"Lord, Jesus Christ!" swore Buford pacing back and forth. He was filled with rage.

"Get outta' here, both y'all. I'll stay with 'er."

He sat beside Mabel and took her hand. "Oh Mabel," he moaned.

He cursed fate for this wretched day. They had tracked the Apache all during the long, hot afternoon only to lose their trail at Ute Creek. It took them all night to get back to Wilder Creek and they arrived in town tired and disgusted. Buford had already been in a bad mood and after talking to Doc he'd taken leave of his senses.

He decided that if Mabel died, he would kill everyone responsible. Juan, Reuben and Josh would feel his wrath. His thoughts were broken by a knock at the door.

"What do you want?" he said in a cold voice.

The door opened a crack and Josh peered in, his face chalky white. "It's me and Reuben, Colonel. The men just come in and tole' us what happened."

Buford's face was twisted with fury. "Get the fuck outta' my sight. I'll deal with y'all later."

Josh felt as if his bowels were filled with cold water. "Sure, Colonel." He closed the door quietly.

On the way to the bunk house, Josh said, "We sure is in for it."

"Yea, but it was a mistake. Bad luck for everybody all the way 'round," Reuben said.

"I ain't sure the Colonel will see it that way."

"What do you think he'll do?" Reuben asked anxiously.

He hadn't been with the outfit long and didn't know what to expect.

"Don't know for sure, but whatever it is, ain't gonna' be pleasant."

"Maybe we should skeedaddle now. Don't think I wanna' hang 'round and find out."

"Nah, I've knowed the Colonel a few years. He might whoop our ass, but I don't think he'll kill us."

"I hope you're right, or we're fucked."

All the rest of that night, Buford sat by Mabel's side willing her to open her eyes. He refused the food and coffee Rosa and Juan offered. The only thing he wanted was a bottle of whiskey. It calmed him down and by dawn he came to the conclusion that no one was to blame but Mabel. She'd disobeyed him, and this was the result. The fact that she'd done it while he and Juan were gone convinced him of her treachery.

As the first light of dawn filled the sky, he looked out the window and saw Diablo, still in the corral. Sight of the animal increased his fury.

His hand instinctively reached for the gun at his side. Full of concern for Mabel he'd not thought to remove his gun belt. He strode out to the corral and aimed at the horse, then slowly brought the gun down. Diablo was too fine a horse to kill. Like his men, it wasn't the horse's fault his wife had been so careless.

When he went back to the house, Mabel had come around. Rosa was with her.

"I'm sore. What happened?"

"Goddamn horse threw you. Can you move?"

She wriggled her legs and arms. "Yes, but it hurts." She tried to lift a hand to her throbbing head, but she was too weak.

"You gave me a fright. You been out a long time!"

"Have I? I don't remember anything."

"You got on that fuckin' Diablo! Tole' you not to. As soon as my back was turned you went and rode 'im."

"Please don't shout. My head hurts."

"Sorry darlin,'" he said softly. "Here drink this." Lifting her gently, he gave her the laudanum. "It'll help with the pain."

She sputtered at the foul taste. "I'm thirsty," she croaked. Rosa left the room for some water.

Juan knocked softly on the door. "The Signora, is she all right?"

"Yea, she's gonna' be fine. Juan, I'm sorry I lost my temper with you. You're a good man. It wasn't your fault she rode that fuckin' horse."

Juan said, "I should've never left her." Buford was ready to protest when Mabel interrupted.

"I feel awful," she wailed.

"Reckon you do, but you're gonna' heal up. Don't seem to be no permanent damage. You ain't lost the use of your limbs and you ain't addle brained."

"Thank God, for that," she said quietly. He already had.

Juan left and came back with the water and a tray bearing coffee, cold ham and biscuits for Buford. His stomach was twisted in knots, and he wasn't hungry.

"Rosa is getting tea and broth for the Signora. I brought this for you. You should eat."

"Ain't hungry." He supported Mabel's head and gave her small sips of water.

Rosa came in with a bowl of clear broth and some tea. "I'll give it to 'er." He took Rosa's hand before she could withdraw. "I'm much obliged to you for savin' my wife's life."

Rosa was shocked by this admission. "It was nothing."

Buford fed Mabel. After a few mouthfuls of broth, she said. "I don't want any more. I feel queasy."

"Just a little more," he coaxed. "You gotta' get your strength back."

After a few more sips, she said. "I can't. I hurt too much to eat. I feel as if there's a knife in my head."

"Reckon, I can give you more laudanum." He gave her another dose. "Now try to sleep. I'll be right here if'n you need me."

The laudanum did its job and in a short time, she was asleep. Going over to the window and looking out, he thanked God again and silent tears of relief coursed down his cheeks.

When Mabel woke Buford was still by her side, a cold

cup of coffee clenched in his hand.

"How's your head?"

"It still hurts but not as bad as before."

"Good. You hungry?"

"Yes, famished."

"I'll get Rosa to bring you some vittles."

When he entered the kitchen, Juan and Rosa looked at him with concern. He looked exhausted. He hadn't slept in two days. He stumbled back in the room followed by Rosa. She bore a tray with tea and a dish of stew. Like before Buford took over.

Rosa stayed in the room and said, "I'm glad you are well. I prayed for you. I prayed for the Colonel, too. He hasn't slept or eaten in days."

Buford looked over his shoulder at Rosa. "Goddamn it, I'll eat and sleep when I'm fuckin' good and ready."

His kind words forgotten, Rosa glared at him and left the room.

"Poor darling," Mabel said. "I'm all right now. You need to rest."

"It ain't the first time I stayed up a few days."

"I insist," she said firmly. "Rosa can stay with me."

"I ain't tired," he lied.

When Mabel had eaten the last of the stew, Buford gave her more laudanum.

He gazed at her in the afternoon light. He wanted to tell her how afraid he'd been and how much he loved her, but he kept silent. She might think him a coward.

As the laudanum spread through her system, the pain lessened, and she noticed the empty whiskey bottle.

"Oh, Colonel!" Mabel laughed weakly, "Did you drink all that?"

"Reckon, I did. Calmed me down."

"And I thought you were just tired."

"I tole' you I'm fine."

"You're not fine. You haven't eaten or slept and you're drunk!"

He scowled at her but remained silent.

"Don't look at me like that," she scolded. "I insist that you lay down. How can you help me if you're half dead yourself? Come to bed."

"Afraid I'll roll on you or somethin'."

"Lord, you're impossible. Go sleep in the bunkhouse or somewhere. Anywhere! You look like you're ready to fall over."

"Reckon, you're right. I'll get Rosa to stay with you. If'n you need anythin', have 'er fetch me."

"I will, now go!" He kissed her on the lips and departed.

He went to the bunkhouse where he encountered Josh and Reuben.

"Juan said the Missus is doin' good," said Josh.

"Yea she is. I'm sorry for how I treated y'all. I didn't mean no harm. When I saw Mabel layin' there I got pretty riled. I thought about it and saw she was the one who was wrong. She had no call to ride Diablo." He sighed. "I never thought a woman could fuck me up like this."

When Josh and Reuben left, Buford collapsed on a bunk. Empty and stagnant in the heat of late afternoon, it smelled of cows, horses and unwashed men. It had a comforting effect on him and he fell fast asleep.

He didn't awaken when the men came in for supper. They smiled at the sight of his large frame sprawled on the bunk. He still had his boots on and snored loudly.

"Good to see the Colonel in here again," laughed Ezra. "Never thought I'd miss the ole' pain in the ass."

"Sure glad, Miss Mabel's gonna' be all right," said Josh.

"Ain't we all," said Asa. "Glad he didn't shoot y'all."

"Ain't as glad as I am," said Reuben.

As each day passed, Mabel grew stronger. After a week, the pain in her head began to subside and things went back to normal.

• • •

One night at dinner Buford said, "It's roundup time and I gotta' go out with the herd. I'll be leavin' day after tomorrow and won't be back for a week or two."

"Must you?" asked Mabel.

"Ain't got no choice. It's our busiest time of year. Besides, I'll be goin' to Kansas after that. Might as well get used to me bein' gone."

Mabel didn't want him to go. Try as she might she

found the ranch lonely, even with Rosa as a friend. It would be sheer hell without him.

"Colonel..." she began.

"I don't wanna' hear it. I tole' you and your Pa 'bout this. I gotta' go and that's all there is to it," he said in a cold voice.

She didn't speak to him for the rest of the evening and he remained silent as well.

As they undressed for bed, he could feel her eyes boring into him. "Goddamn it, Mabel, stop starin' at me like that!" he said testily.

"I can't help it," she wailed. "I don't want you to go!" She burst into tears and Buford softened immediately.

He took her in his arms. "Don't cry. You know I can't stay with you all the time."

"If I let you go on the roundup, can I come, too?"

He released her.

"If'n you let me go?" he asked angrily. "I don't need your fuckin' permission to go anywhere!"

She ignored the profanity. "I mean..." she said flustered, "I can help. I can cook and tend to the men."

"That's Juan's job. Round up ain't no place for a woman! Are you loco"?"

"I just want to be with you," she said crying all the harder.

He didn't soften this time, instead it made him angrier. "I don't wanna' talk 'bout this no more."

She could tell he was angry, but she wasn't concerned. They'd be retiring for the night and she would have the advantage.

As soon as they got in bed, he turned away from her. She began massaging him trying to loosen the knotted muscles in his back. After a while she could feel him relax. He rolled over and reached for her. It was close to dawn before they slept.

The next morning, he spoke with Ezra.

"You think you can handle roundup? Mabel wants me to stay with 'er. Shouldn't give in but I can't help it. Besides, I'll be away long enough when we go to Kansas"

"Me and the boys can do it. We won't let you down,"

said Ezra.

That night at supper Buford didn't talk about it and Mabel dared not bring it up. She didn't know if he was going or not. They were sitting in their ornate parlor when Ezra came in.

"Me and the men got everything ready. Don't you worry none. You got good cowpunchers who know how to cover the dog. We won't miss any. We'll round up every single cow. You got my word."

"I know you boys will do a good job."

When he left, Mabel couldn't help but smile in victory. Once again, her husband had succumbed to her will.

Buford looked over at Mabel. She had a satisfied grin. Realization struck him like a thunder bolt. She had used her feminine wiles to get her way.

A few weeks later, the men came in with the herd and Buford went to work. There was still a lot to do. Some cattle had to be castrated and others needed their horns cut. A tally needed to be made and wounds and parasites tended to.

During this time Mabel found out she was expecting. She debated whether to tell Buford and decided not to. She didn't want him to stay home because of her condition. She thought she'd convince him in her usual way. If she failed, she'd tell him.

A few nights before he was to leave for Kansas, Mabel broached the subject. "Colonel, do you have to go? Can't Ezra do business with my father?"

Buford was tired and out of sorts. He'd been working fifteen hours a day getting the herd ready. "Jesus Lord!" he said. "I ain't lettin' no one else sell my cows," he said sharply, "I'm puttin' my foot down this time and I ain't changin' my mind."

"Whatever you think best," she sighed.

His temper flared. "Don't you start with me, woman!" he stormed from the house. He came back hours later when he thought she'd be asleep.

Mabel lay awake worrying. She couldn't persuade him to stay unless he was in bed. She was relieved when he returned and got in beside her.

She touched him gently and he sat up with a jolt.

"Leave me be, I ain't in the mood tonight."

"I don't know what you're talking about.".

"I ain't lettin' you have your way with me no more! It ain't a proper way to make a man change 'is mind."

She grew indignant. "I should slap your face for saying that!"

"Go ahead," he retorted. "Rather you do that than paw at me!"

"Paw at you!" she cried. "You insult me!" She rolled over in a huff, trying to get as far away from him as possible.

Buford could hear her crying in the dark. His resolve began to weaken but he fought the urge to hold her and apologize.

"Gettin' as bad as Hi," he thought, "do anythin' for a poke."

Mabel fumed all the next day. He had cut her to the quick and she felt humiliated. She decided not to tell him about the baby. Let him go to Kansas without knowing. She was too angry to care.

Supper that night was uncomfortable. Mabel was furious and made no attempt to hide it. Buford put down his fork and sighed. He'd be gone a long time and didn't want to leave with bad words between them.

"I'm sorry darlin'. Didn't mean to hurt your feelins' none. This here is business and it's somethin' you're gonna' have to get used to. Maybe next year you'll have a baby to keep you company."

She looked at him with a start. Should she tell him? "Colonel, there's something I have to tell you. I'm...I'm..." she faltered and changed her mind, "I'm going to miss you."

"I know."

She didn't cry the morning he left, but there was no mistaking the mournful expression on her face.

CHAPTER SIX

The first couple of days out Buford worried about Mabel, especially after the incident with Diablo. He wondered if he could trust her. He'd been harsh with her and hoped she'd learned her lesson. He had to nip her willfulness in the bud.

He worried about outside dangers as well. The rancher's wives were vulnerable this time of year. It was common knowledge that the men were away on drive. Desperados and Indians were always a threat.

Buford left Jimmy and Asa at the ranch this year. The last drive had nearly killed them both and he thought they earned a reprieve from the grueling journey. Besides, they were capable men and he felt better leaving Mabel and the ranch in their care.

Mabel had made lots of friends and he knew she'd have a steady stream of visitors to ease her loneliness. The women took advantage of their husband's absence and visited back and forth. Hi and Lydia promised to see her often and Hi vowed he would watch over her.

As was his way, he made himself stop thinking about her. He had taken every precaution before leaving and now there was nothing he could do. To dwell on it was a waste of energy. Besides, he had too many other things to worry about.

As the trip progressed, he found himself enjoying the drive. He'd been cooped up long enough and it felt good to ride the range.

One morning as they were breaking camp, Daniel came over to him.

"Uh...Colonel, some of the horses are gone."

"What do you mean they're gone? You're the wrangler,

what the hell happened to 'em?"

"I don't know. I had 'em all secure for the night but they was gone when I woke up."

"Who had watch last night?"

"Josh, Phil and Ira."

"Get 'em over here."

The three men followed Daniel back with trepidation.

"You hear or see anythin' last night?" he asked his brows furrowed in anger.

"No, sir," they answered as one.

"Well either you boys is sleepin' on watch or we got ourselves some fuckin' professional horse thieves 'round."

Buford walked over to where the horses had been. He squatted down and studied the tracks. He could tell how old they were by the number of insect trails that crossed them.

"There's four of 'em," he said, "and they ain't that far ahead. Reckon we better go after 'em."

"Is it Indians, Colonel?" asked Josh, worried.

"Don't think so."

The men rode hard through most of the morning.

"I think we should let 'em go, Colonel," said Ira. "We're losin' time. Shoulda' caught up to 'em by now, I reckon."

Buford glared at him. "We'll be catchin' up to those cocksuckers soon enough. Besides, you men was careless and we're gonna' track 'em if'n it takes us all fuckin' day. I don't take kindly to horse thieves."

Not too long after, they saw them in the distance.

"There they are," said Buford. "C'mon boys, let's get after 'em."

"Hope they ain't Indians," Josh said again.

"They ain't," answered Buford.

They rode fast and soon shortened the distance.

The horse thieves became aware of their pursuers and started firing.

Buford pulled out his rifle and squeezed off a shot. One of the horse thieves fell.

Buford took careful aim and fired again. Another man hit the ground.

One of the thieves' bullets found its mark and Josh's horse whinnied and fell. Josh and the horse rolled together and lay in the dirt.

"Son of a bitch!" Buford swore.

He squeezed the trigger of his Winchester again. An expert marksman, he had no trouble bringing down another man.

The last man fell, and Phil cried out. "Got 'im!"

Ira and Daniel rode on ahead to gather the stolen horses while Buford and Phil went back to Josh.

Josh was standing up, dazed but unhurt. He brushed the dust from himself.

"You all right, Josh?" asked Phil.

"I'm O.K. but, Jesus, that was close. The sons of bitch's kilt' my fuckin' horse!"

Ira and Daniel came back with the stolen animals. "What are we gonna' do with the bodies?" Ira asked.

"Leave 'em for the buzzards," said Buford. "They ain't fit for nothin' else. Can't abide fuckin' horse thieves."

Josh saddled one of the recovered horses and they headed back to camp. They got back at supper time. Josh watched as Buford took a generous portion of stew from Juan's pot. "Lord," he said. "Can't believe the Colonel. He done kilt' three men and he's hungry!"

"Killin' always makes the Colonel hungry," joked Ezra. "Durin' the war, seemed he was always hungriest after a battle. One time, after a particularly bloody one, saw the Colonel eat a whole cow hisself." Ezra was trying to get a rise out of Josh and it worked.

Buford decided to stay put for the night. The cows were near water and he saw no reason to move them out. One day wouldn't make a difference.

Buford thought of Tom often. This was the first drive he'd made without him. Kansas wouldn't be the same and Buford was glad Victor would be there. They were kin now and it would help ease his pain.

Once again Buford stayed at the Drover's Cottage. Victor was on the porch waiting for him when he arrived.

"Colonel, it's good to see you again. I was sorry to hear about your brother," he said quietly.

"Much obliged. It's hard bein' here without 'im."

"I imagine it is. Tom was a good man."

"That he was," said Buford, the tears threatening to spill. "How's Mabel?" asked Victor trying to dispel the gloom.

Buford smiled. "She's fine. I got a package for you from 'er."

"That's grand. Louise will be pleased."

"Did she come along this year?" Buford asked.

"Heavens, no! I only brought the women along last year because Mabel wanted to see you. Since her mission to win your heart was successful there was no need for my wife to come. A cow town is no place for a lady."

Buford turned serious. "I wouldn't bring Mabel again after the Kiowa attack. I ain't never been so scairt'. I been in my share of fights but with Mabel in harm's way, well…." His voice trailed off.

"It was a risk you warned us about. I had no doubt you would protect my daughter."

"I tole' you I ain't no hero, I'm a fuckin' killer and I'm good at it. If'n I wasn't I don't wanna' think of what mighta' happened."

Victor could see a strange glint in Buford's eyes and quickly changed the subject. "You just arrived. How thoughtless of me to keep you out here talking!" he apologized.

"That's all right." Buford smiled. He excused himself and went to his room.

The next morning Buford stopped by Victor's room. "Here's that package," he said.

"Do I have time to open it, or are you in a hurry for breakfast?"

"Got plenty of time."

The wrapping was torn and dirty, but the contents were still clean and dry. Victor opened it and took out a quilt.

"Lord!" he said, "Did my Mabel make this?"

"Yea, she did. It's somethin' ain't it?"

"I see she's learning some domestic skills."

"Yea, and it ain't been easy for either of us," Buford smiled. "No offense Victor, but I ain't 'et more horrible vittles in my life than what your girl served up. Everything tasted like shit. Had to get 'er a maid, the only way we could live decent."

"Yes, Rosa. Mabel writes of her often."

"I'm sure she does. I think Rosa's a pain in the ass but Mabel's fond of 'er. She's the one who taught Mabel to make this here."

"Well, it's lovely. Louise will be surprised."

"I believe there's a letter with it," Buford said.

"I'll read it after we conduct our business."

When Victor returned to his room, he anxiously tore open the letter. He was surprised to learn that Mabel was expecting a baby.

She wrote, "Please don't mention it to the Colonel! I'll tell him when he returns. You are aware how important it is that he meets with you. I was afraid he'd cancel his trip if he knew. Besides, he'd only worry, so not a word! But oh, Father, isn't it glorious news?"

Victor was faced with a dilemma. "What should I do?" he wondered. "Drat, that daughter of mine! Her husband has every right to know of her condition. What a fool she is!"

Later that afternoon the men met again.

"I read Mabel's letter." Victor said with concern.

Buford noticed and said, "I suppose you know she took a bad fall from one of our horses, but she's right as the mail now."

"Yes, she wrote us of her lack of judgement," Victor said clearing his throat. "That's not what's troubling me. Once again, my daughter has placed me in an awkward position. She asked me not to tell you, but I must. She's going to have a baby."

Buford looked as if he'd been struck. "A baby," he whispered.

"My foolish daughter didn't plan on telling you until you got back."

"Why the hell not?" Buford asked, his heart pounding in his chest.

"She didn't want to interfere with our business. She knew you'd stay home if she told you. I can't believe how pig headed that girl can be! I hope you're not angry with her."

Buford, still stunned by the news, shook his head, "No, I ain't mad but sure is puzzlin' that she didn't tell me. Women! I swear, Victor, I'll never understand 'em."

"Don't try, Colonel," laughed Victor, "it won't do you any good. Take this advice from a man who's been married over twenty years."

"I gotta' go back," said Buford, with an astonished look on his face.

"My thoughts exactly. That's why I told you. I can handle things here for you. Do you still have that fellow, Ezra, in your employ?"

"Yea, I do. He's with the herd."

"Well, he seems like a sensible man. I'm sure between the two of us we can take care of your affairs."

The shock finally wore off and Buford cracked a huge grin, "Goddamn! I'm gonna' be a father. I have to confess, your little girl's been actin' strange lately. Reckon that's the reason."

Buford got Ezra and the three men settled down to work. When things were arranged to his satisfaction, he got ready to leave.

He went to a jeweler and bought a gold necklace with matching ear bobs and then went to pay his men.

"I gotta' go back to the territory and I'm leavin' Ezra in charge. Don't think I have to tell y'all to be careful. See you fellers when you get back."

When he left Daniel said, "I bet he's hurryin' back to be with Mabel. He sure is growin' soft."

"That ain't so," said Ezra.

"But we just got here and he's leavin' all ready," said Josh.   "Y'all done got paid. Why the Colonel is leavin' ain't none of your business," said Ezra.

• • •

Travelling alone and with no animals to tend to, Buford made it back to the ranch in good time.

Mabel was surprised to see him. "Colonel" she exclaimed throwing herself in his arms. "I didn't expect to see you for another month yet!"

He crushed her to him and then loosened his hold. "Why didn't you tell me?"

"Tell you what?"

"'Bout the baby!"

"Goodness! I should've known better than to tell Father.

You aren't cross with me, are you?"

"No, just wish you tole' me. Woulda' saved me a heap of travellin'."

Her eyes snapped with anger. "When I asked you to stay home you made it very clear that you had to go to Kansas and made quite a fuss about it."

"I didn't know you was in the family way. If'n you'd tole' me I coulda' made other arrangements. Had to anyhow."

"You wouldn't stay home when I asked you to. It should have made no difference whether I was having a baby or not."

Buford was tired and tried to ignore her obvious anger. All he felt was concern. "You feelin' all right?"

He looked thoroughly exhausted and she softened. "I'm sorry for not greeting you properly." She wrapped her arms around her and he leaned down for a kiss.

"You didn't answer my question," he said still holding her close.

"I get a little queasy now and then but that's to be expected. Enough about me! Let me get you some coffee. It's so good to see you! I've missed you so!" She hugged him again.

As they sat in the kitchen drinking coffee, Buford noticed a glow about her and thought she never looked more beautiful. He wanted to take her to bed right then and there.

"Mabel, can I...can we...you know," he stammered.

Her face colored. "Yes."

"You sure?"

"I asked Lydia and she said we could for a little while."

"Damn it, Mabel! You asked Lydia? Everybody in town knows 'bout this here baby 'cept me!" he yelled.

Mabel wasn't happy about the way things were turning out. She had yearned for him while he was gone. Now he was back and in one of his moods. Her hormones were wreaking havoc and she burst into tears.

"You're impossible! And to think I missed you! Lydia is the only one who knows. I made her promise not to tell anyone, not even Hi. If you weren't so self-righteous I would've told you!"

"Self-righteous? Me? What the hell you talkin' 'bout?"

he scowled, his temper flaring.

"Weren't you the one who accused me of seducing you? I didn't tell you about the baby because I knew you'd say I was using my feminine wiles to keep you home!"

In her fury, she threw her empty coffee cup at him. Her aim was poor, and it sailed over his shoulder and crashed to the floor. Jumping up from the table she fled to the bedroom, slamming the door behind her.

Buford sat at the table, dumbfounded.

Rosa came in, "Welcome home, Colonel. It is good to see you back early," she said with an ironic smile.

"Don't fuck with me. I ain't in the mood. What the hell's wrong with 'er?" he asked. "She loves me then she hates me." He looked lost and confused.

"The baby. It makes some women mucho loco."

"Should I go to 'er?"

"Leave her for a while and let her calm down. It's nothing. It will pass."

"Lord, Jesus Christ!" he swore. "She threw a cup at me!" he said flabbergasted.

"You will have to have patience for the next few months. It will not be easy for a man such as you."

"Damn!" Buford swore again as he left the house.

Rosa smiled and shook her head. For the first time, she felt a twinge of tenderness for him. He'd asked her advice and his uncertainty touched her.

He knew he'd hurt Mabel's feelings with his comment about seduction, but he hadn't realized how much. She hadn't told him about the baby in fear of another snide remark. He felt guilty and ashamed. He'd bring her the present he bought and apologize.

As he walked back to the house he thought of what she said and his guilt turned to anger. She knew she was pregnant and kept it to herself out of spite. "That's why she didn't tell me! Of all the devious, hare brained, schemin'..." he muttered to himself.

He strode into the house and went to the bedroom. He tried to enter but the door was locked. "Mabel, open up!" he bellowed.

"Go away!" she said.

He was furious. He stepped back a few paces and kicked out with a powerful leg. The door flew open and banged against the wall. Mabel cringed.

"I know I shouldn't get on you now, but you get me madder than hell! You didn't tell me 'bout the baby 'cause you're a spoiled brat. If'n you wasn't in your condition I'd take you over my knee!"

Tired as he was, he stormed from the house and left for town.

He found Hi at the jailhouse and complained to his friend. When he was finished Hi said with a chuckle, "Lord! She sure is a feisty thing, ain't she?"

"Feisty ain't got nothin' to do with it! I can't trust 'er! I tole 'er not to ride Diablo and she done ride 'im any way and nearly kilt' herself. Then she don't tell me 'bout the baby, but she made sure to tell her Pa. She knew he'd tell me."

"Ever think you give 'er no choice?"

"What are you talkin' 'bout?"

"Buford, I knowed you all my life. There's only two ways 'bout things, far as you're concerned; your way and the wrong way. You're stubborner than a fuckin' mule! Once you make up your mind 'bout somethin' there ain't no changin' it. Mabel got no choice but to do things behind your back. You been married a year and you still don't know shit 'bout women! They got their own mind, Buford, whether you like it or not."

Buford continued to fume.

"Let's go to the Longhorn and have a drink," suggested Hi.

"I don't go in there no more."

"Yea, and why's that? It's 'cause of Emma, ain't it? She scairt' you away tellin' you 'bout her baby! See what I'm sayin'? Nobody can talk to you!"

"How many times do I gotta' tell you that kid ain't mine? She got herself pregnant while I was in Ellsworth."

"You seen 'er just before you left, didn't you?"

"So?"

"Probably got 'er in trouble then."

"That's bull shit."

Hi sighed. "Well, I think it's yours and so does she. That's your fuckin' problem. When women talk to you plain, you don't like it. Mabel got no choice but to lie to you!"

Buford glared at Hi beneath furrowed brows. "Let's go have that drink," he snapped.

The Longhorn was nearly empty when they arrived. Jamie, Sally and a few of the girls sat around one of the tables, passing the time with a friendly game of poker. Emma was upstairs with the baby.

"Look what the wind blowed in," said Jaimie, in a low voice. "It's been a long time since the Colonel set foot in here. Hope Emma don't see 'im." The words were no sooner out of her mouth when Emma came downstairs.

Emma's heart skipped a beat when she saw Buford. It had been a long time since she'd seen him last. With a bright smile she went over to him.

"Jesus Christ!" swore Jamie, "there she goes. Emma!" she called out with a hint of warning in her voice. Emma and Buford both turned to her. The look on Buford's face sent a chill down Jamie's spine and she decided not to interfere. She looked down at her cards. "He got somethin' up his ass and that's for sure," she said.

"It's good to see you, Colonel," Emma beamed. "How you been?"

"All right. How 'bout you? Heard you had a baby boy."

"Yea I did. He sure is somethin'.."

"What you name 'im?"

She looked down embarrassed. "Tom," she said softly. "I was always fond of your brother."

Buford was startled but recovered quickly. "That's a good name, Emma. Reckon Tom would be proud if'n he knew."

"You men here on business or pleasure?" she asked.

"We're here to drink," Hi laughed. "The Colonel's woman is givin' 'im trouble!"

Buford shot a scathing glance at Hi. "Ain't no one's business but my own," he growled.

"Don't suppose you come in for a poke?" she looked at Buford hopefully.

Hi answered. "Hell no! He's a married man now and it don't fit into his moral code. Ole' Buford here has peculiar notions 'bout right and wrong."

"Be much obliged," Buford said taking her arm. He shot another dark glance at Hi and the couple departed.

"Well, I'll be damned!" said Jaimie. "He's goin' upstairs with 'er!"

"You ain't as shocked as I am," said Hi.

When they were in her room Emma said, "Come see our baby, Colonel. He's a beauty!"

"Christ, Emma. I tole' you he ain't mine! Reckon I should leave."

"No, don't!" she cried. "Didn't mean no harm. Come look at 'im' any way."

Buford studied the baby asleep in his crib.

"He's a nice lookin' boy, Emma, but he don't look like me or my kin."

She thought it best not to answer.

They settled down to business and Buford took her again and again. It had been a long time since he'd been with her and he couldn't get enough. All the anger and frustration of the past year came out with the intensity of his love making. When they were finished, he doubted he had the strength to stand.

He cradled her tenderly in his arms. "Glad you come to your senses and went back to work," he said.

"Not for long. I'm savin' some money and then I'm quittin'. A saloon ain't no place to raise a chile."

"Ain't that bad. Knowed a few men that was raised in saloons and whore houses. Didn't seem to hurt 'em none."

"Just the same, ain't bringin' Tom up 'round a bunch of whores. Gonna' save me some money and open a bakery."

"A bakery!" Buford exclaimed. "Why a bakery?"

"Don't know much, so ain't got much of a choice. I only know two things; how to fuck and how to bake."

"Jesus, Emma! Watch your mouth!"

"Sorry, Colonel, didn't mean to offend you none, but that's the truth of it. Yep, had to look the truth straight in the eye after I had little Tom, but never mind 'bout me. What you doin' here? Didn't think I'd ever see you again. You gonna' be comin' in often?"

"Don't think so," he sighed. "Shouldn't be here now,

'cept my wife got me so all fired mad!"

"Oh, revenge," she said softly. "Don't reckon I care much. Always liked bein' with you no matter what the reason."

Buford noticed the deepening shadows.

"Lord! Sure is gettin' dark. I best be gettin' home."

"It was fine to see you. Know you won't be wantin' no more pokes but hope you'll come in for a drink now and again. I won't trouble you none. Promise!"

Buford looked at her. He always thought that she was too nice a girl to be a whore.

"Maybe I will."

He left a large sum of money on her bureau and left.

When he went downstairs, Hi was gone. Buford stopped by the jailhouse on his way out of town.

"Damn, Buford! Didn't think you had it in you. Don't you beat all! Who was you spitin' when you went with Emma, me or Mabel?"

"Spitin' nobody. Just seemed like the right thing to do at the time. Ain't gonna' make a habit of it."

After Buford left, Emma was filled with mixed emotions. She'd been happy to see him but now that he was gone she fell back into despair. His presence had churned up feelings that were better left alone. She'd been foolish to ask him to come back.

She often scolded herself for telling him about the baby. It had achieved no purpose but to put a bigger wedge between them. She'd missed him during the long months he'd stayed away. Now that she'd seen him, she only felt worse. His presence brought home the helplessness of her situation.

She took some comfort in the thought that he was fond of her. He'd seemed genuinely pleased to see her and made love to her with more than his usual passion. She supposed it might not be bad if he came in occasionally for a drink. The pain in her heart would lesson in time. She would have to be content to be his friend.

It was dark when Buford reached home. Mabel was in bed and sound asleep. As he undressed, he found the jewelry box in his pocket. He'd forgotten all about it. He slid into bed beside her, deep in thought.

Hi's remarks went through his mind. Did he force Mabel to deceive him?"

He was still asleep the next morning when Mabel awoke. She looked at him in the early light and watched his chest rise and fall in the steady rhythm of sleep.

Yesterday was the first time she'd ever been afraid of him. She still trembled when she thought of the look on his face as he kicked in the door.

After he'd stomped out of their room, her fear had turned to anger. When it was dark, and he hadn't returned she grew worried. During the long anxious hours she waited, she had ample time to think. She'd concluded that she was at fault and vowed to make it up to him.

She got up and went to the kitchen. After fixing him a tray with eggs, bacon, toast and coffee she returned to the bedroom.

"Colonel?" she said softly. He opened his eyes and sat up. She placed the tray in front of him.

"I'm sorry," she said, her eyes brimming with tears.

Her manner surprised him and he didn't know what to do. She mistook his hesitance for anger and looked away, not meeting his gaze. He put the tray on the bedside table and took her in his arms. She clung to him and sobbed.

"Shh," he said softly. "Don't cry, sweetheart."

"I've treated you dreadfully," she moaned. "You have good reason to be angry with me."

"Maybe, maybe not. I went and seen Hi. He gave me hell, I don't mind tellin' you. Says I force you to lie. Do I?"

"I don't know. I'm so confused. All I know is that I love you!"

He kissed her softly and much to his surprise he got aroused. "Didn't think I had nothin' left after yesterday," he thought to himself. Mabel kissed him passionately and one thing led to another. The breakfast she prepared grew cold and greasy beside them.

Tranquility ensued until a few weeks later when they went to town. Buford dropped Mabel off at the general store while he went to get grain. She'd just entered and her attention was caught by a display near the door. It was then she overheard a conversation that wasn't meant for her ears.

"Hear we might have a bakery in town soon," Charlie Smith's wife, Joanne said.

"I ain't heard nothin' 'bout it," answered Alvirah Gibson. "Sure would be good to have one. Sometimes it's so hot, I can't bring myself to bake."

"Ain't gonna' change things much. Heard it was one of the whores from the Longhorn that was gonna' open it. Can you imagine! Like any decent woman would go there!"

"Mercy! Which one of those sluts is thinkin' of it?"

"I'm not sure. Oh yea! The one they call Emma."

"The one who had the Colonel's baby?"

"The very one. Don't want to bring her bastard up in a whore house."

The women rounded a corner and saw Mabel. Her face was white and she held onto a shelf for support.

"Mabel!" Alvirah said, rushing to her with concern.

"When you come in? We didn't know you was here!" explained Joanne.

"Is it true?" Mabel asked in a trembling voice.

"Lord, we put our foot in it now, ain't we?" Joanne said to Alvirah.

"And me a Parson's wife. I shoulda' knowed better than to spread vicious gossip."

"Is it true?" Mabel asked again.

"Come and sit down, dear. You've had a terrible shock," said Joanne.

When Mabel was seated Joanne continued. "Ain't no use lyin' 'bout it. One of the whores down to the Longhorn had a baby durin' the winter. Some say it's your husband's, but no one knows for sure."

"I feel faint," said Mabel, sagging in her seat.

"Lord, Joanne, see what you done?" scolded Alvirah taking smelling salts from her reticule.

Buford walked in as they were tending to Mabel. He panicked and reached their side in a second. "Mabel, darlin', you all right?"

She glared at him. "I'll be fine. Don't concern yourself."

He looked at her with a mixture of confusion and worry. Joanne swallowed hard and said, "Colonel, can I speak to you a minute?"

He looked down at Mabel. "Not now, Joanne, Mabel needs me."

"You go on," said Alvirah. "I'll tend to 'er. Joanne got somethin' to tell you."

"I..." he started to reply but Mabel interrupted. "Go!" she snapped.

Joanne led him outside. Next to the Johnson's, she and Charlie were the McLeod's closest friends. Despite this, she was afraid to tell him of her and Alvirah's faux paus.

"Colonel," she said her face growing red, "Alvirah and me spoke of matters we had no right to."

"Get to the point, Joanne. Don't wanna' leave Mabel too long."

Joanne took a deep breath. "We didn't know Mabel was in the store and we was talkin' 'bout Emma, the whore who's gonna' be openin' the bakery. We mentioned she had your chile and Mabel heard us. If'n you hate us for it, I don't blame you. We was danged fools!"

"Damn it to hell! No wonder she's put out with me!"

"I don't know what to say, Colonel. I'm ashamed of myself!"

"You should be!" Buford scowled. "Damnation, you women and your foolish tongues. Ain't my baby, and folks got no right to be sayin' it is. See what you done?"

Joanne didn't answer.

Buford paced back and forth on the board walk in front of the store. He stopped and said to Joanne, "When I took Mabel to your place a few weeks ago did she say anythin' to you 'bout the baby?"

"She didn't know 'til just now. I'm real sorry, Colonel! We didn't know she was there! She musta' just come in!"

"Not that baby! Our baby!"

Joanne drew in a sharp breath. "Mabel's...?"

"Yea, she is. That's why I come back from Kansas so quick. Now she's madder than a wet hen. Dang it to hell!"

He stood large and menacing before her. A tall woman, Joanne felt intimidated by his huge size and cringed.

"I'm sorry," she mumbled.

He brushed by her and went back in the store. He glared at Alvirah. "You done shoppin' Mabel?" he asked.

"I suppose I am," she said coldly.

"Let's get along, then," he said. He tipped his hat at Alvirah and Joanne who stood huddled together.

"Ladies," he said sarcastically.

When they were in the wagon, Buford slapped the reins harder than necessary.

"Mabel, I'm sorry 'bout what happened, but you gotta' know there ain't no truth to what them hens was sayin'. It ain't my kid."

"Why did they say it was? Have you ever been with that woman?"

"Ain't gonna' lie to you. I visited 'er regular 'til I married you. I was in Ellsworth when she got in trouble. Think she said it was mine 'cause she had the notion I'd take care of 'er. I sure surprised 'er when I come back a married man. I swear to you Mabel, it ain't mine! She's a whore. Could be any one's."

Mabel looked relieved. He spoke with such conviction she couldn't doubt him. "She's dreadful to be spreading such awful stories!"

Much to his surprise, Buford grew defensive, "Ain't that a'tall! Emma's a nice gal, for a soiled dove. She didn't mean no harm. It's the townsfolk who can't keep their damn mouths shut!"

Mabel felt jealous although she knew she shouldn't. Surely her husband had been with other women besides her. "Is she pretty?"

"Yea, reckon she is. Don't look like no whore, can tell you that. Look's wholesome."

"Do you still see her?" she asked softly.

Buford answered without thinking. The time he'd spent with Emma meant nothing to him. "Just seen 'er once."

"Oh," she said in a strangled voice.

He looked at her. "Don't mean nothin'. She's a whore for Christ's sake! When I seen 'er it was no more than scratchin' an itch! Ain't makin' excuses for myself but I was a might put out with you at the time."

"You're right, Colonel. It's no excuse. I think you're loathsome!" Tears streamed down her face.

"Goddamn it, Mabel. Coulda' lied to you. Coulda' tole

you nothin', but I ain't like that!"

"Was it the day you came back from Ellsworth and we quarreled?"

"Yea."

"Oh! You're vile. I was worried sick about you and you were with a...a...whore!" She could barely say the word.

"Don't know why you're carryin' on so. Don't mean nothin'."

"Maybe not to you, but it does to me!"

They rode on in silence, Mabel's muffled tears the only sound. "Aw, hell," he thought to himself.

When they got back to the ranch, she locked herself in the bedroom.

"Mabel! Open the goddamn door," Buford shouted.

"I won't!" she called out. "You're beastly!"

Furious, he turned on his heel and departed. He couldn't keep breaking the door down. His carpentry skills were poor, and it had taken him a while to fix it after he kicked it in last time.

That night, Mabel didn't come out for supper.

"Might as well bring 'er vittles to 'er," he said to Rosa.

After dinner, she remained in the sanctuary of their room and Buford decided to sleep in the bunkhouse. The men were still out on drive and it was empty except for Asa and Jimmy.

The next day, Mabel was absent for breakfast, lunch and supper. Buford ate alone.

He said to Rosa, "Damn it. If'n she don't wanna' see me, she don't have to. Reckon I'll bunk with the men and eat with 'em, too. Prefer their company any way!"

Asa and Jimmy wondered why the Colonel was staying at the bunkhouse but didn't ask. They could tell by the miserable look on his face that he must be having trouble with his wife.

Every day Buford went to the house hoping to see her, but she hid herself away from him.

After a week, he could stand it no longer and sought out Rosa. "Where's Mabel?" he asked.

"In her room. When she hears you come she locks herself in. She does not wish to see you."

"Is she feelin' all right?"

"Si. The baby does not give her trouble, but you do!" She said coldly.

"Don't rile me, Rosa!" he snarled. "Tell 'er I want to see 'er."

"I will not! She is angry with you!"

Buford paced back and forth trying to calm himself. His anger finally abated, and he sighed. "I need your help, Rosa."

"You need no one. Stubborn like a burro, you are. Why should I help you?"

"Because I'm fuckin' desperate is why! Shouldn't even be talkin' to you but I got no choice. Do you know why she's mad at me?"

"No. It is none of my business."

"Well Mabel's bein' plum foolish. She's mad 'cause I spent one night with a whore."

"You are a married man and soon to be a father. You should not go with other women, even a whore." Rosa said crossly.

"I didn't go with another woman. I went with a whore and it don't amount to a hill of beans. She's mad 'cause this whore had a baby and she heard it was mine. It ain't and I tole 'er so. I only seen this whore once since we been hitched. Mabel didn't take kindly to it and she's been avoidin' me ever since."

Rosa glared at him and shook her head.

"I'm outa' my mind over this here. I love 'er and I can't stand it no more. Don't know what to do, 'specially since she locks me out of our room. Can't keep kickin' the fuckin' door in!"

"I don't like what you did, but for her sake I will help. Would you like me to talk to her, Colonel?"

"I'd be obliged, Rosa. Can't take much more of this."

"Go tend to your chores and I will speak to her."

After he left, Rosa went to the bedroom and knocked softly. "He's gone, Signora."

Mabel came out. "Thank goodness! I can't bear to look at him."

"I know, poor man!" said Rosa, shaking her head sadly.

"What do you mean?" asked Mabel, feeling betrayed.

"He's a beast!"

"Si. But beasts have hearts, too."

"Not him! Do you know what he did? He went with a...one of those women at the Longhorn. It was the day he got back from Kansas and we argued. I was sick with worry when he didn't come home and all the time he was enjoying himself!"

"Yes, he told me. I don't blame you for being angry, but you are being too hard on him. He is in agony. If you could have seen him just now! He looks like a man in hell. It is killing him that you will not see him."

"He deserves to suffer! When I think of him being with her and then coming home to me, I feel so...so...I don't know!" She started to weep.

"Ah, my little one," Rosa said, holding her in a motherly embrace. "You have much to learn about men. They all see that kind of woman at one time or another. There are those who make a habit of it. He told me he was with this woman only once. Do you believe him?"

"Yes, I do. If anything, he's honest."

"Forgive him then. She means nothing to him. My own husband had a Signorita he used to see once a week."

Mabel looked at Rosa in amazement. "That didn't bother you?"

"Yes, but I knew my Miguel loved me. He saw her only for pleasure, but she meant nothing to him."

"I'm sorry that I don't feel like you. I think if the Colonel truly loved me, he would never have done such a thing."

"Dio! You are such a child! You are the only woman he loves. Before he married you all the women wanted him. Good women, too. And why not? He had a ranch and is very handsome. He would have none of them! He told Juan, "I will never marry." Then he met you. The Colonel loves you and you are a fool to doubt it!"

Mabel sat deep in thought. "Yes, you're right. I'm being silly. I know he loves me."

"Then go to him. He is sick with sorrow. Can you not find it in your heart to forgive him?"

"I might if he said he was sorry!"

"Sorry for what? Yes, it hurts us, but you still don't

understand! These women are like dirt beneath a man's feet. You should not treat the Colonel so harshly."

Mabel sighed and said, "I'll go to him. Where is he?"

"Where do you think? With his horses."

Mabel wiped her eyes. "Do I look all right, Rosa? Maybe I should wash my face and comb my hair..."

"You look fine, just go!"

When Mabel reached the barn, she peered inside. Buford was in one of the stalls grooming Daisy. A shaft of late afternoon sun came through the window near where he stood, and she could see the suffering on his face.

Buford felt a presence behind him and whirled around quickly, startling her.

"Mabel! Didn't mean to scare you. Didn't know if'n you was friend or foe. Been a civilian nigh on three years and I'm still skittish."

She remained quiet and he returned to his work. He didn't know what to do. He was afraid that he'd do or say something wrong and she would run from him again.

Mabel made the first move and went to the stall.

"I'm sorry about the way I've been acting," she said. "Rosa says it's because of the baby, but that's a poor excuse!"

He put down the brush and gathered her in his arms. "Don't apologize, darlin'. It ain't you, it's me. You got yourself one idiot of a husband."

"Oh no. I think you're wonderful! I have from the first time I met you. I still remember it clearly. You took my breath away!"

He laughed but didn't reply. Compliments made him uncomfortable. He was satisfied just to hold her close. The smell of hay and horses, the warm afternoon sun and her small, voluptuous body had a tranquil effect on him.

A few days later the men came in from Ellsworth and Ezra went to the house.

"Afternoon Ma'am," he said to Mabel. "Is the Colonel in?"

"No, he's at the Smith ranch. One of their mares foaled this morning and was having a hard time of it. Charlie's not back yet and Joanne sent for the Colonel. He's still there."

"Reckon, I'll see 'im when he gets back."

"Is everything all right, Ezra?" Mabel asked. "Were you and Father able to take care of the Colonel's business?"

"Yes, Ma'am. Everythin' went fine."

• • •

At the Smith ranch, Joanne and Buford worked side by side. Joanne had been shy about asking for his help but had no choice. She didn't have the skill or the strength for this difficult birth. He'd come right away and didn't appear to be angry with her.

Joanne hadn't seen him since the incident at the general store and she still felt bad about it. She never intended to hurt Mabel.

She and the other women were fond of her. Elegant and lady like, Mabel never put on airs. She endeared herself to them by seeking their advice on several house hold matters. She also seemed oblivious to the power she held over her rugged husband.

The townsfolk enjoyed seeing Mabel and the Colonel together. He treated her as if she were made of glass. When he helped her from their wagon his huge hands all but obscured her tiny waist. It made them smile to see the big, rough Colonel so gallant and considerate of his diminutive wife.

After two grueling hours Joanne and Buford finally delivered the colt.

Buford wiped the perspiration from his face with a bandanna. "Lord, thought we was gonna' lose 'em both!"

"Ain't that the truth! Woulda' too, if'n not for you. I'm much obliged to you. Can I get you some coffee?"

"Reckon, I could use some."

When they were seated in the kitchen with steaming mugs before them, Joanne said. "I'm real sorry 'bout shootin' off my mouth, Colonel. Charlie's gonna' be awful mad when he hears of it."

"Don't reckon he will unless you and Alvirah tell 'im. As far as I'm concerned it's over and done with."

"That's Christian of you. Hope we didn't 'cause you too much grief."

"If they only knew," he thought. Aloud he said, "Don't let it trouble you none. I'm the one should be apologizin'. Had no call to yell at you like I did."

CHAPTER SEVEN

As Mabel's pregnancy advanced Buford doted on her and gave in to every whim. Often he'd find himself ready to explode but a look of warning from Rosa kept him in check. It did no good to lose his patience. His temper had never bothered her before but now the least little thing brought her to tears.

When her moods got too much for him, he'd go to the Longhorn for a drink. Hi was in the saloon one afternoon when he came in.

"Howdy Buford. How's Mabel feelin'?"

"Just fine."

"She's ready to calve soon, ain't she?"

"Yea, and I'll be glad when it's over. She sure can get 'erself in a mood."

"All women do. Lydia was one pain in the ass when she was carryin' J.B. She's kinda' disappointed that we ain't been able to have another but I'm glad. Don't want to go through that bull shit again! You in here to see Emma?"

"No. Come in for a drink."

"Bet you ain't had a poke in a long time. Thought you mighta' come in for one."

"No. I ain't been sparkin' Mabel but ain't got no business with Emma neither."

"Sure don't understand you Buford. You go with Emma when you ain't got no call. Now you got reason to and you won't."

"Well, Mabel found out 'bout last time and she nearly skinned me alive!"

"How'd she find out?"

"I tole 'er."

Hi nearly choked on his beer. "What?"

Buford told him what happened in the general store.

Hi still looked incredulous. "What's that got to do with you sparkin' Emma now?"

"Mabel asked me if'n I was and I tole' 'er the truth; only once." He laughed and shook his head. "She was so fuckin' mad I thought she might cut my cock off!"

"Lord Buford, you sure is somethin'!"

"Well I just come in for a drink. Reckon I'll go home. I don't like leavin' Mabel."

He was no sooner gone when Emma came downstairs, little Tom in her arms. She went to Hi.

"Thought I heard the Colonel."

"You did, he just left."

"Oh," she said dejectedly.

"Lord, little Tom sure do look like 'im, don't he?"

"He does. I wish the Colonel could see it."

"It wouldn't do any good if'n he did. He's a hard man."

"I know he ain't beholdin' to me. I only wanted 'im to know he had a fine son. I ain't gonna trouble 'im no more. Mabel's givin' 'im a baby soon."

"That she is. Seen 'er the other day and she's ready to drop."

"Kinda' hoped he'd come lookin' for relief but he ain't."

"You know why he ain't been in to spark you?"

"I ain't got no idea."

"Remember the last time he was with you?"

"Sure do."

"Well, he done tole 'er' 'bout it! Ain't he a jack ass?"

"He sure is, but I love 'im any way."

"You're wastin' your time."

"Don't I know it! She sighed. "Even if'n he wasn't married, he wouldn't want me 'cause of what I am."

"That ain't so. Mabel's the only woman that ever broke that mustang! Outside of 'er, he don't love no one. Wouldn't matter what line of work you was in. He ain't got no tenderness in 'im."

"Go on! He's bettern' that!" Emma said in his defense. "Don't he help folks? When anybody needs 'im ain't he always there for 'em?

"That ain't what I mean. I know bettern' than anyone

that he's a good man, but he's cold as ice. He ain't got no love in 'im 'cept for Mabel."

"I still don't think you're givin' 'im his due but it don't make no difference."

"No it don't and it never will. He's too fuckin' stupid to realize you bedded only him for a good long time. Any other man would know, but not him. That's why he don't believe the kid's his."

"True enough, but it hurts that he thinks I'm lyin'"

• • •

It was an unusually hot day in November when Mabel went into labor. Buford sent Juan off to the Smith ranch for Joanne, a competent mid wife. It was Mabel's wish to have Lydia with her when the time came, and Buford sent Josh for her.

While they waited, Buford held Mabel's hand. She could see he was beside himself with worry and tried to stifle her cries of pain.

"Colonel, I think you should go now," Rosa said. "This is woman's business."

"I'll stay 'til Joanne gets here."

"Well, here I am," Joanne said, sweeping into the room. "Now you git! I'll let you know when your baby's born. Might take a spell, first babies always do."

Buford tried to work but couldn't keep his mind on anything. Occasionally he heard Mabel scream which completely unnerved him.

When Lydia got there an hour later, he was pacing up and down in front of the house.

"Lord Colonel. You're gonna' wear a hole in the ground if'n you don't stop a'pacin'," she laughed.

"Can't help it. Sure is nerve wrackin'."

"Thought you might think so. I stopped at the jail house to fetch Hi. He'll be along soon to set with you."

"Much obliged, Lydia."

"'Til he gets here why don't you go visit with the boys in the bunkhouse."

"Reckon, that's a good idea," he agreed.

When he entered Josh was the only one there. He smiled. "Colonel, you look like you need a drink. I got a bottle right here."

"I need more than that, but it's a start. Hearin' Mabel screamin' is the worst fuckin' sound I ever done heard." Josh handed him a bottle and a glass. Buford's hands shook badly, and the liquor splashed around the glass.

Josh looked at him in surprise. He recalled how steady Buford's hands had been as he poured drinks with Junior's guns pointed at his back. Josh had never seen him vulnerable. He'd been cool and calm through gunfights and Indian attacks but now he looked as if he would fall apart.

"Here, let me," Josh said. "You ain't got no call to worry, Colonel. Everythin's gonna' be just fine."

"I know I'm actin' like a jack ass but Mabel's so small." "Don't mean nothin'. My girl in Kansas was just 'bout a baby 'erself when she had mine. Everythin' turned out all right."

Hi came in a short time later. "Howdy girls! Jesus Christ, Buford. Look like you seen a ghost! Don't tell me you're nervous!"

"Yea, I am. This sorta' thing don't happen to a man every day!"

"Sure it does, just not to ole ornery sons of bitches like you."

Hi had brought a bottle and after several more glasses of whiskey, Buford calmed down. The three men sat in the bunk house talking and drinking.

As the hours wore on Buford went out often and looked towards the house. When he heard Mabel scream, shudders ran up and down his spine.

"Should she be yellin' like that?" he asked Hi with fear in his eyes.

"Sure! This here is normal. Lydia bellowed like a wounded heifer. Just like you, it riled me, that's why them old biddies threw me outta' my own house. Lydia come out all right though, there ain't nothin' to worry 'bout'."

"Mabel's such a little bitty thing, I knew this was gonna' be hard for 'er."

"Naw! She ain't that little. You're such a big critter everybody looks small!"

Buford stepped out of the bunkhouse in time to see Lydia come out to the porch. His heart filled with joy. He took a step forward and stopped dead in his tracks.

Instead of coming for him as he expected, Lydia put her face in her hands and bowed over. Her shoulders shook with her sobs.

Buford's blood turned to ice water and he sprinted to the house.

When he was by her side she looked up. Her face was pale, and tears streamed down her cheeks.

His heart lurched in his chest and he'd never known such fear.

"What's wrong, Lydia? Is it the baby?"

Unable to speak, she shook her head yes.

"Goddamn," he said, squeezing his eyes shut to hold back the tears. "I better go see Mabel."

Lydia grabbed his arm. "Colonel, Mabel's...gone." He looked at her in disbelief and rushed into the house.

When he got to the bedroom he found Joanne cleaning the baby and Rosa tending to Mabel. Both women were sobbing.

His face was as white and hard as marble. His body shook as if he had the ague. "I wanna' be alone with 'em," he said.

"We're almost finished," said Rosa through her tears.

"Now!" he roared so loud and fierce that both women scurried out. He slammed the door behind them and locked it.

He gazed down at Mabel. A faint smile curved her lips.

He turned to the cradle and stroked the tiny body of his son. His legs gave out and he crumbled to the floor in a heap of tears. After a while he got up and sat on the bed. He picked up the cold, lifeless body of his wife and held her close to him.

None dare disturb him and he stayed like that for hours. He started at the loud knock on the door.

"Buford, it's me," said Hi. "Let me in."

"Go away!"

"C'mon, Buford! Let the women finish their work. In this heat it ain't no good to wait."

Buford opened the door and Hi drew in his breath.

He was startled beyond words at Buford's transformation.

They'd witnessed and done things that would turn the hardest man to jelly. Buford had weathered them all. Now he looked like a man who'd been to the pits of hell. In the few hours since Mabel's death, his hair had turned totally white.

Hi recovered and said, "C'mon' Buford come with me. Me and you'll have a drink." He took him by the arm and led him away. Buford stumbled along beside him like a man walking in his sleep.

He didn't acknowledge his men who waited to pay their respects. They knew he'd take this hard but no one expected the glassy eyed, white haired man who shambled by them.

Rosa, Joanne and Lydia went back to the bedroom and Hi brought Buford to the parlor and poured him a generous glass of whiskey. Neither of them spoke.

After a while, the women came out and Lydia motioned to Hi. He stepped out of the room with her.

"Mabel and the baby's ready to be laid out. Maybe you should go see the undertaker and the Parson. Looks like the Colonel ain't gonna' be able to. We best get 'er buried tomorrow."

Hi looked back at Buford who sat with his head in his hands.

"I don't think I should leave 'im alone."

"I'm goin' home. I'll make the arrangements," she said, still weeping. Joanne left too.

He went back to Buford. "The women are gone, but I'll be bunkin' with you tonight."

Buford got up.

"Where you goin'?"

Buford didn't answer but went to the bedroom and locked the door.

"Aw, hell," Hi said softly.

Buford stayed there all night despite Hi's many attempts to get him to come out. Finally, as the first light of morning reached the sky, Hi curled up on the fancy sofa in the parlor. It was far from comfortable, but he fell asleep immediately.

Lydia woke him later that morning. News travelled fast and besides the Parson and undertaker, several of the ranchers and towns people were there as well.

"Where's the Colonel?" she asked.

He pointed towards the bedroom. Lydia looked drawn and tired and her shoulder's sagged. "Oh," she said quietly. "He been there all night?"

"Yea," said Hi. "Can't get 'im out. I'll try again."

"No let me." She took a deep breath and knocked loudly. "Colonel, it's Lydia. Can I come in?"

Buford didn't answer but opened the door and let her enter. Mabel and the baby lay as they had when she left yesterday. Lydia put a comforting hand on his arm and he stared at her as if she were a stranger.

"Why don't you go out and have some coffee with Hi," she said soothingly. He looked past her at the bodies on the bed and walked out. When he left the undertaker had the casket brought in and set to work.

Hi put an arm around Buford and they went to the kitchen where a tearful Rosa served them coffee. Hi was afraid for his friend. Buford hadn't uttered a word since he'd thrown the women out of the bedroom yesterday.

He sat and drank his coffee but didn't pay any heed to the bustle that went on around him. Alvirah, Joanne and many of the area women were in the kitchen, cooking for the large crowd that had assembled outside.

When the undertaker came out and whispered in Hi's ear. Buford didn't seem to notice. "Where you want to bury your family?" Hi asked. Buford looked at him but didn't respond. "Want me to pick a spot?" he asked. The silent Buford looked down and studied the contents of his cup.

Hi sighed and went out to find a burial plot.

Although it was hot, the air felt good. He studied the ground and decided on a place. A grove of pinon trees stood a short way from the house and he thought it would be suitable.

Many of the town's folk greeted him. "How's the Colonel, Marshall? There gonna' be a service?"

"Yea, there'll be a service. The Colonel ain't hisself but reckon he'll get by."

Hi went back to the house and sent some of Buford's men out to dig a grave.

When they were finished the Parson came out followed by Buford's men bearing one casket. Lydia thought Mabel would want to be buried with her baby beside her. They placed it in the freshly dug grave. Buford and Hi sat in the kitchen while the activity went on around them. When everything was ready, Hi said. "C'mon' Buford, it's time to go."

Buford didn't seem to understand but stood up and followed Hi outside. There was a collective gasp from the mourners at Buford's appearance, and a moan when the huge man's knees buckled, and he fell to the ground. Hi and Josh pulled him up and supported him as they made their way to the gravesite. When they were all assembled the Parson began his eulogy. Buford stood like a man in a trance.

There were those who wondered if he knew what was happening.

After the service the house filled with people and the women served food and coffee.

Still in a stupor, Buford didn't speak or acknowledge any one. Hi led him to the bedroom. "Why don't you try and get some sleep."

Buford looked at him dumbly but went and laid on the bed. Hi shut the door behind him as silent tears streamed down his cheeks. He'd known Buford all his life and the way he was acting now terrified him. He vowed he wouldn't leave him until he recovered.

After a few days Buford came out of his fog. Hi went back to town feeling certain that in time his friend would overcome his grief.

He closed up the house and dismissed Rosa. He couldn't bear to stay there without Mabel. He returned to the bunkhouse and the company of his men.

Always a reticent man he became more aloof. He spoke no more than he had to, and his eyes were dull. He went about his chores by rote and his men grew alarmed.

Buford knew he couldn't think beyond matters at hand, whether it be a task, a meal or his bunk. If he did, he'd go insane. The dreams he had at night were proof of that.

After the Civil War, he suffered from nightmares. In

them he experienced battles over and over again. He saw the blood and heard the agonized cries of the wounded through the cacophony of guns and cannon. Sometimes the dead got up and pointed an accusing finger at him, other times they moaned softly to him, "Why me, Colonel? You were in charge. Why did you kill me?" The dreams varied but the theme was the same; death, destruction and guilt. They were horrible but infrequent.

After Mabel died, he had them every night but now they had a new twist. As he stood in the battlefield, he not only heard the sounds of battle, but a woman who began to scream. It was soft at first but grew in volume until it seemed it would shatter his eardrums. It was Mabel, screaming her life away in order to bring his son into the world. Like the others she cried out, "Why me? Why did you get me pregnant? Why did you kill me?" She had joined his nightmare world of ghouls.

He awoke from these dreams with a start, sweat streaming down his body. He would stay up for days at a time trying to avoid them but eventually, exhausted, he'd fall into a deep sleep and relive the horror again and again.

He became a recluse and never left the ranch. If he needed business done in town, he'd send one of his men.

Charlie, Hi and some of the other townsfolk came to visit but they found his silence and lusterless eyes disconcerting. "Give 'im time", the womenfolk said.

One day it was necessary for him to go to town. Hi spotted him from the jailhouse window and ran outside.

"Howdy! Sure is good to see you away from that fuckin' ranch."

"Ain't stayin'. Had to go to the bank. I'm goin' back now."

"Naw! C'mon', let's go down to the Longhorn for a drink." Buford gave him a gloomy look.

Hi realized he'd been too exuberant for his solemn friend. "Let's have a drink," he said softly.

"All right. Just one."

Hi sighed with relief. He was growing more worried about Buford every passing day. He looked and acted like a walking corpse and Hi feared for his friend's sanity.

When they entered the Longhorn, Emma had to stifle a cry.

She couldn't believe the tall, skeletal figure before her was the Colonel. He was a shell of the man he'd been.

She put on her best smile and greeted them. "Howdy, Marshall. Colonel."

"Howdy," said Hi. Buford tipped his hat but didn't speak.

"Sorry 'bout your wife and boy," she said quietly.

"Much obliged," he said.

Behind Buford's back, Hi motioned for her to get away. He was afraid her presence might upset him.

She gave Buford's arm a gentle squeeze and left.

A few boisterous cowpunchers sat at a table. Unemployed waddys, they were passing through on their way to Albuquerque.

Of the five, four were decent men. The other, a man named Ethan, fancied himself a gun fighter. They were drinking heavily and growing louder and louder.

Buford's appearance was not only startling to those who knew him but to strangers as well. He'd lost a lot of weight and his clothes hung on his tall frame. Dirty and unkempt, dark circles surrounded the eyes in his chalk white face.

"Good God!" Ethan said, "What in tarnation is that thing over yonder! That is the sorriest excuse for a man I ever seen." He drew Buford to the attention of his comrades. They didn't want trouble and urged him to sit down and be quiet to no avail.

"Hey Marshall! What's the matter with your friend? He done look like he's dead and don't know enough to lay down."

The men with him looked embarrassed.

Buford ignored the comment but he'd taken to ignoring everything. Hi went to the table and said menacingly.

"The man lost his wife and chile'. Show some respect!"

"Sorry Marshall, didn't mean no offense. Looks like he should be in the ground with 'er is all!"

"Shut your fuckin' mouth or I'll throw your ass in jail," Hi said.

Ethan didn't reply and Hi went back to the bar.

After a while Ethan started talking again, even though his companions continued to get him to behave.

"Yes sir. Some men sure go to pieces when they lose a woman. Like that feller. He looks like the angel of death hisself', don't he? Hey Mister! You the angel of death?"

Buford turned slowly and glared at the man, his dull eyes turning to burning coals. He strode towards the table and Hi scurried to put himself between Buford and the cowpuncher.

"Now, Buford!" said Hi putting up a hand. "These here boys was just leavin'. Weren't you boys?" The men nodded yes, but Ethan couldn't be stopped.

"I ain't goin' nowhere. I ain't afraid of ghosts," he sneered.

Buford pushed Hi out of the way and grabbed Ethan by the throat in a vice like grip, cutting off his wind. Ethan lashed out but his blows had no effect. Buford punched him in the jaw with a bone shattering right that sent Ethan crashing to the ground. He picked him up by the neck and began to squeeze.

Hi shouted at him. "Buford! That's enough!"

Buford let go and Ethan rubbed his throat, gasping hard. "You're crazy!" he said in a hoarse whisper. He dropped his right hand and reached for his gun.

Before he could draw, Buford dove and knocked him down. The gun flew out of Ethan's hand and skittered across the floor.

Buford continued to pound him mercilessly, even though Ethan tried to get away from the brutal assault. Hi jumped on Buford's back trying to stop him. As strong as he was, he was no match for an enraged Buford.

"Don't just stand there, boys. Help me!" he said to Ethan's companions. Even with the other four men, Buford wouldn't stop pounding the nearly unconscious man. Hi knew if he didn't do something soon, Buford would beat the man to death.

Hi drew his gun. "Hate to do this," he said and gave Buford a hard crack on the head. Buford slumped down on top of the frightened cowpuncher.

Hi rolled Buford off Ethan. The cowpuncher lay there,

his face a bloody pulp. His companions picked him up.

"Sure sorry 'bout this," said Hi. "Didn't know he was gonna' go off on 'im like that. 'Course' mebbe' he'll learn some fuckin' respect. I suggest you get outta' town before my friend comes to."

When Buford regained consciousness, he was in Emma's room. She looked down at him, her face filled with concern.

"My head," he complained. "What the hell happened?"

"You went loco and almost kilt' one of them cowpunchers downstairs. Woulda' too, 'cept the Marshall knocked you cold."

"I gotta' get home," he said.

He got up and the room started to spin. He put his hand to his head and leaned against the bed post until it stopped.

"Colonel, you all right?" Emma asked in alarm.

"Just dizzy. I'm O.K."

"Maybe you should stay awhile," she said.

"Much obliged but I gotta' git."

"If'n you're feelin' up to it, the Marshall wants you to stop at the jailhouse." He didn't answer, but tipped his hat and left.

He was upset that he lost control. He'd almost killed a man and had no recollection of it. If not for Hi he would have. The only thing he remembered was the cowpuncher calling him the angel of death; the very thing Buford dreamed about every night. Didn't the dead come back in his dreams night after night to remind him?

He didn't stop to see Hi. All he wanted was to get back to the ranch.

The next day Hi came to see him.

"How you feelin'?" Hi asked.

"Did you have to hit me so fuckin' hard?"

"Ain't had no choice. What the hell's wrong with you? The man had a nasty mouth and deserved a whippin', but Lord, Buford! You wouldn't stop! Five of us tried to take you off'n 'im and it was like we wasn't there."

"Don't let it bother you none," said Buford. "Don't plan on goin' into town no more, no matter what."

Hi rode back to town, more troubled than ever.

Emma worried about him as well. It hurt her to see what

he'd become. She supposed she'd never see him again as she would be leaving the Longhorn soon. Ziggy was already refurbishing a vacant building for her bakery and she looked forward to a new life.

Jamie thought she was making a big mistake. "Who the fuck is gonna' come into your bakery? No decent women."

"I didn't expect any decent women," Emma argued. "There's a bunch of hungry cowboys 'round. There's also a lot of big ranches. If'n the womenfolk don't know I laid up with their men, they might give me an order."

Two months later, Emma found herself situated in her bakery.

As she anticipated, some people came in but business was still poor. She was glad that she'd put some money away to keep her for a while.

As word spread of her past, business ceased almost totally. Her only customers were the cowhands from neighboring ranches and a few strangers. Her common sense told her to leave and move to another town, but she couldn't. Her best friend was here as well the man she loved.

She did have one steady customer; Josh Logan. Often, he spent all the money he had on baked goods. She knew he was in love with her although she didn't offer him any encouragement. He was a sweet man and Emma felt bad that she couldn't return his affection.

One day he proposed to her and she thought it time to tell him of her feelings.

"You flatter me by askin' for my hand, Josh, but I don't love you that way. I think you're a first-rate person and I really am fond of you, but not in a marryin' sense."

"That's all right, Miss Emma," a crestfallen Josh replied. "You don't have to love me, just let me take care of you and the boy."

"I wish I could Josh, I really do." She replied.

With a glum expression on his face, he left the shop. The bell on the door tinkled at his exit and the cheerful sound made Emma's heart sink. "I wish I could marry you," she thought. "If'n I did, it sure would take me outta' a world of hurt."

• • •

Hi was pleased that Emma was trying to earn an honest living. If not for an accident of fate he doubted she ever would've become a soiled dove. She might've turned out different if a Christian woman had found her in the street instead of Jamie.

He stopped in her shop from time to time and it bothered him to see it empty day after day.

One day at the dinner table he said to Lydia, "I want you to go to Emma's bakery."

Lydia looked at him appalled. "I will not! I ain't buyin' nothin' from that whore!"

"That ain't fair. She's tryin' to make a new life for 'er boy and no one's givin' 'er a chance."

"Sorry, Hi. I ain't goin'."

"Have it your own way. If'n you won't go, I will."

Lydia sat quietly, deep in thought. She knew Hi had been with Emma when she worked at the Longhorn. Even though Emma seemed done with that business, Lydia didn't want Hi visiting her shop. Besides she was curious about the fallen woman.

"All right. I'll go."

"Y'know what, Lydia? You're the best woman in the world."

The next morning Lydia went to the bakery, loitering outside awhile so the other women in town could see her. After she thought enough people had noticed she entered the shop where heavenly aromas greeted her.

Emma was in the back room when the bell on the door sounded. She came rushing out and was surprised to see a woman at the counter.

"Howdy!" Emma said.

Lydia was surprised at Emma's appearance. She was pretty, and her blonde hair and clear blue eyes gave her an angelic quality.

"Howdy," she replied. "I'd like two loaves of bread and some donuts if'n you got any."

"Donuts just come from the fryin' pan and are still hot," said Emma with a smile. "How many you want?"

"A dozen would be good."

Emma disappeared and came back with a sack of warm,

fragrant donuts. "You want one now?" she asked. "They'll be cold by the time you get home."

"Reckon, I can wait," said Lydia.

"You sure? I got a pot of coffee on the stove. Thought maybe you'd come in back and set. Have a cup of coffee and eat some of these donuts," Emma said hopefully.

Lydia thought a moment and decided to stay. It was obvious that the woman was lonely. Whether it was this or curiosity that kept her there, she didn't know.

"All right. Expect it can't do no harm," she said and followed Emma to the back.

The back of the shop held three small rooms; a kitchen, sitting room and bedroom. Emma led her to the kitchen and Lydia noticed that it was spotless.

"Reckon, I should introduce myself," said Lydia. "I'm Lydia Johnson, the Marshall's wife."

Emma's silky brows rose. "Well I'll be. I know your husband!" Color came to her face and she amended, "The whole town knows the Marshall! Please sit down," she said indicating a rocking chair. She walked to the stove and poured two steaming cups of coffee.

"I reckon you know who I am," she said forlornly.

"Yea, I do, but makes no never mind to me. Where's your boy?"

"He's nappin' in the bedroom, yonder." She gave Lydia a cup and held out a dish of donuts.

"I'll take one from what I bought," said Lydia.

"No please," cried Emma. "I got plenty and don't think I'll be sellin' 'em."

Lydia gazed at Emma. She could see no evil in her guileless features.

"If'n you don't mind my sayin' so, you sure don't look like no whore. Not many of us seen you before. You ain't never been out on the porch, callin' to the men like the others."

Emma looked embarrassed. "No," she said. "I ain't never done that. The men knowed where to find me. There's younguns' and decent folks on the street. Didn't think it proper to let 'em see me."

This pleased Lydia and she said, "Give you credit for

tryin' to bring up your boy right. I got a boy, too, but reckon you know that."

"I do. I was there when the Colonel come in to tell 'im he had a son. The look on his face is one I'll never forget. The Marshall loves you heaps, Mrs. Johnson, but reckon I don't have to tell you that."

"Call me Lydia. He thinks a lot of you, too. Tole me you was a nice gal. He's the one who sent me here. Truth to tell, I only come 'cause I was curious. I'm glad I did. My husband's right, you ain't bad a'tall."

Emma blushed. "Why, right kind of you to say so, Mrs. Johnson...uh, Lydia."

The two women fell into easy chatter. After a while, little Tom's lusty yells could be heard from the next room.

"'Scuse me," said Emma. She got up and went to the bedroom and came back moments later with her child.

Tom was a year and half old and his features were growing pronounced. Lydia was stunned to see how much he resembled the McLeods. He had Buford's eyes and coloring and resembled Tom in other ways. She didn't voice her opinion.

"Ain't he precious!" she said.

"He is to me," beamed Emma. "Don't know what I'd do without 'im."

"You're a good woman to mend your ways. You can count on me comin' in regular."

"I'm much obliged," said Emma.

So began Lydia's campaign to help Emma. She told every woman who'd listen how good Emma's baked goods were.

"Can't believe it Lydia," said Fanny Bell, one of the rancher's wives. "You doin' trade with one of those women. Probably been with your man and mine too!"

"So?" said Lydia. "Ain't sparkin' no one's man now. She's tryin' to live a decent life. People change."

"Not that type!" Fanny responded.

"Well, ain't askin' you to send your husband in. If'n you don't trust 'im go yourself!"

"Well, I'll be, Lydia," Fanny said in huff. "Good thing I know you're a God fearin' woman, otherwise I'd be shocked."

"I am a God fearin' woman and didn't Jesus hisself' have a whore for a friend? If'n He can forgive that sort, so can I. Ain't tryin' to preach to y'all but I see it as my Christian duty to help the lamb that's gone astray!"

Fanny pondered this and decided Lydia was right. She became a regular customer as well.

Lydia gave the same opinion to all those who questioned her judgement. She was pleased to see that she made a point to some of them and business got better for Emma, but it was short lived.

One day Hi went to see Buford. The only time he saw him was when he went to the ranch. Buford hadn't gone to town since the incident with the cowpuncher.

When he found Buford he said, "You ain't seen a couple of desperados 'round have you?"

"No. Don't reckon I have."

"I'm lookin' for two men. One's tall, young, with dark hair. The other's short, old and fat. If'n you or your men see 'em, bring 'em in."

"All right," said Buford.

Hi was in a bad mood. "Lord, Buford, you are a sight! You look and smell no better than a fuckin' saddle tramp."

"So what. If'n I see those two men I'll bring 'em in," Buford said turning away.

"Where the fuck you goin'? You ain't gettin' rid of me that easy." Hi said. "I swear Buford, I ain't never seen you such a mess. It breaks my heart!"

"Sorry to be a burden to you," Buford said coldly.

"I don't even know why I come to see you when I do. You're sorry company."

"Then don't come no more. Don't care for your company neither. All you do is gimme' opinions and advice that I don't want. Don't even know why you bother."

"You got the gall to ask me that? Do all the years we been friends mean nothin' to you? Mabel been gone six months and you still ain't right in the head! You ain't dead but you sure ain't alive neither. Goddamn freak of nature is what you are."

"You done, Hi?" asked Buford testily. "You always think

you got me all figgered out, don't you?"

Hi lost his temper and shouted, "Damn right and it's 'cause I know you bettern' you know yourself. I'm disappointed in you. Sittin' here wallowin' in self-pity. You used to be a man now you ain't nothin'! You lost more than your wife. You lost your balls, too."

"Don't matter none. You got enough balls for both of us."

"Ain't got no patience for you today. If'n you see those two men, bring 'em in."

"What they do, Hi, disappoint you?" Buford asked sarcastically.

"Don't fuck with me. They beat up Emma, that's what they done. They went to the Longhorn lookin' for 'er. When they heard she wasn't on the line no more they went to the bakery. She refused 'em and they beat 'er real bad. She ain't pretty no more. I hope I get my hands on them fuckers!"

"Well go along and find 'em. I got work to do," Buford said turning his back on Hi.

Hi was furious. "Well, you ain't got to worry 'bout me givin' you advice you don't want. Ain't comin' here no more."

The next day Buford and his men started round up. As he was cutting sign he came upon some tracks. He followed them and came across two men breaking camp.

"You men must be strangers in town otherwise you'd know this here is private property."

"Yea, we is," said the younger one. "Didn't mean no harm. We was just movin' on."

They fit the description of the men Hi was looking for and Buford said, "You men been in town lately?"

"Us?" said the older one nervously. "No. We was just passin' through. We're on our way to Texas."

Buford noticed one of the younger man's hands. It was swollen and fresh scabs dotted it.

"What happened to your hand, son?"

"Nothin' much. My horse got ornery yesterday. Had to show 'im who was boss."

"You men know a gal named Emma?" he asked, a fierce look in his eye.

"Don't reckon we do," said the older one, the fear plain on his face.

"I think you're both fuckin' liars," said Buford. In a blink of an eye he drew his guns and shot them both. He left their bodies for carrion and went to town. He didn't want Hi to waste time looking for them.

When he entered the jail house Hi said, "Well, my words done sunk in. Good to see you in town even if'n you ain't cleaned up none."

"This ain't no social call. I found them two men."

"Good! Where are they? You leave 'em outside?"

"No. I kilt' 'em. Just wanted you to know." Buford left before Hi could speak.

A few days later Jamie came to the ranch looking for Buford. She saw a group of men sitting around the chuck wagon having their noon meal, but he wasn't among them. When she reined in she was greeted by cat calls.

"Sure is fine for you to come all this way to service us!" Jimmy called out.

"Ain't here to see you. Where's the Colonel?"

"Don't make no never mind," said Asa walking to her. "C'mon' down from that horse, woman, I got somethin' to show ya'!" The other men laughed as Asa unbuttoned his pants.

The men, intent on harassing Jamie, didn't hear Buford ride up behind them.

"What the hell's goin' on here?" he growled.

They turned and the jovial mood melted. Even in his wasted state he looked tall and mean in the saddle.

"I was just goin' to help Miss Jamie offn' 'er horse," Asa said.

"Well, ain't you the gentleman! What was you gonna' help 'er off with?" he said looking at Asa's open pants. Asa's face grew crimson.

Buford turned his attention to Jamie. "What do you want?" he asked impatiently.

"Got a message for you from Emma," she said pulling a letter from her bosom.

He rode up and took it. "Much obliged," he said.

Her errand completed, Jamie glared at Asa and galloped

off.

The men looked at Buford, curious about the letter.

"What y'all gawkin' at?" he asked. "Finish eatin' your vittles and get back to work."

He rode a distance away from them and opened it.

"Deer Colonel,

Jus want to thank you for killin them 2 men who hert me. Them bastids deserv to die for what they don to me.

Much oblyged. I had Jamie set down these wurds coz I dont no how. Your frend, Emma

Buford crumbled it and threw it to the ground. He hadn't killed those men for her. He needed an excuse to hurt someone and she'd given him one.

That night he lay awake thinking of what Hi said. As much as he hated to admit it, his friend was right. He didn't feel alive, but he wasn't dead either. It was time he tried to ignore the demons that pursued him.

Hi made him realize that he had to make a choice. Death was out of the question; suicide was cowardly. That left living. Buford summoned up all the courage he had and proceeded to get his mind and body together.

A week went by and Hi hadn't returned to the ranch. He'd kept his word; he wasn't coming anymore. Buford would be leaving for Ellsworth soon and decided to visit Hi before he left.

Lydia was surprised when she saw Buford ride up to the house. He was clean and neat and his eyes looked less vacant.

"Colonel!" she said warmly, "Do come in."

"How you been, Lydia? Ain't seen you for a spell."

"It's been awhile but ain't you a sight for sore eyes! C'mon' in and have some coffee. Hi's puttin' J.B. to bed."

Hi came out of the bedroom. "Jesus, Lord, if'n it ain't Buford." A smile lit his face and made his blue eyes sparkle. "Sure is nice to have you payin' a social call again."

"Yea."

"Took my words to heart, didn't you."

"Some of 'em. Go on and gloat. Get it fuckin' over with."

"Ain't gonna' trouble you none. Sure am glad to see you

lookin' better! Looks like you even gained a few pounds!"

Buford looked around the small but neat living room and swallowed hard. "This ain't easy. Ain't been here since Mabel... She sure loved to visit with y'all."

"I know," said Hi softly. "But you're here now and I'm happy to see you."

The two men talked for a few hours then Buford rose to go.

"You leavin'?" asked Hi.

"Yea. Gotta' round up more cattle in the mornin'."

"You been to see Emma?"

"No," said Buford, puzzled. "Why should I?"

"I knowed you always been fond of 'er. Thought you mighta' gone to see how she's doin'."

"Ain't crossed my mind."

"Well, go and see 'er. Reckon she'd appreciate a friendly face. Might comfort you some, too."

"I'll go and see 'er but don't get no ideas, Hi. You of all people oughta' know better. I never did set much store in women, whores in particular. Mabel..." his voice faltered. He cleared his throat and took a deep breath. When he regained his composure, he said. "It was a goddamn miracle that I fell in love a'tall."

"True enough. That's 'cause you're a cold blooded varmint."

Buford got a hard gleam in his eye. "You're right and I ain't never gonna' try to change that again."

Buford found the bakery and knocked on the back door.

"Who is it?" Emma called out.

"It's Colonel McLeod."

"Be right there," she said. It seemed to Buford that it took a long time for her to answer the door.

When it finally opened, he couldn't believe what he saw. Emma's face was swollen beyond recognition. Ugly gashes covered her scalp, forehead and cheeks. Both eyes were blackened and closed shut. She had a shawl drawn tightly around her shoulders, but her hands and arms were visible, and they were as bruised as her face.

"Come in," she said her pulse racing at his unexpected visit.

He came into the tiny kitchen and sat down.

"Got your note," he said.

"Yea, Jamie tole' me she give it to you."

"You sure is a mess."

"Did me good, didn't they? Much obliged to you for sendin' them to hell! Guess I won't have no more trouble. Doubt any one will want me now. Like you said, I'm a mess."

"Didn't mean it that way, Emma. Besides, that ain't true. Ain't Josh sweet on you? Ain't been payin' close attention but gathered that fact from my men."

"Yea, reckon he was. When I opened my bakery and stopped whorin' he come 'round when he could. He even proposed marriage to me. He's a good man and I was plum flattered but he ain't for me and I tole 'im so. Ain't seen 'im much since."

"Momma!" little Tom called out.

"Comin' baby." Emma got up and began to feel her way into the next room. "Can't see too good but I'm learnin' to get around," she said.

Buford jumped up and took her gently by the arm. "C'mon' Emma, I'll help you." He guided her to the bedroom.

"Thirsty!" Tom said when he saw his mother.

"All right," she said. "I'll fetch you some water."

"You set with the boy, Emma," Buford said. "I'll get it."

The sight of the disfigured Emma and the toddler who depended on her made him angry. No man had a right to hurt a woman that bad. Not even one with a past like Emma's.

He brought the water back and Tom drank it.

"Y'all go on back to sleep," she said tenderly, tucking in the baby as best she could. "I got company now, but I'll be in soon."

Buford guided her back to the kitchen and said. "Christ Emma, sure am glad I kilt those fuckin' varmints. Wished I made 'em suffer 'stead of killin' 'em clean."

"Just glad they're dead," she said.

"You got any body to help you?"

"Jamie does when she can, but other than that I been doin' for myself. The other girls want to gimme' a hand but

I don't think it's a good idea. Finally got the decent women in this town on my side. Don't want to ruin it. I don't think they'd approve of seein' whores comin' in and out all day. Jamie comes at night, mostly."

"What about Lydia, the Marshall's wife? He tole me she likes you. I'm sure she'd help if'n you asked 'er. I know she got the other womenfolk to trade with you, mebbe' they can take turns."

"Yea, that's true, Lydia helped me. Shamed the other women into comin' to my shop, but this here's different. None of 'em been beatin' down the door to help me. Reckon comin' to my shop is one thing, takin' care of me is another."

What neither of them knew was that the women held Emma in contempt again. Her mishap with the cowboys proved to them that there was no room in their town for a reformed whore.

"You gotta' do somethin'. Ain't fair to the boy. You can't manage."

"Ain't got much choice. I been doin' for myself all right."

"I had a woman named Rosa used to work for me. I'll see if'n she can come and stay with you."

"Much obliged Colonel but I can't pay 'er. Got just a little money left and don't know when I'll be able to go back to work."

"Don't fret Emma. I'll pay 'er wages."

"Can't accept it, Colonel. Can't even poke you no more and earn it!" Tears began to stream from her swollen lids.

"Aw, Christ, Emma. Stop you're cryin'. Don't want nothin' from you. If'n it makes you feel better, pay me back when you can."

"You always was good to me," she said wiping her puffy eyes.

"Just bein' Christian, is all. Don't think more of it than it is," he said gruffly.

"I ain't," she said.

"I'll send Rosa over in the mornin'. She's a pain in the ass but she's bettern' nothin'. Goin' to Ellsworth in a day or two but I'll see you when I get back."

"Much obliged," she said. "I'll pay you back every penny."

"Anythin' I can do for you before I go?"

"No. Was on my way to bed when you come."

"I'll take you in."

"Ain't no need," she said.

"Lord, Emma! You ain't grown so respectable that an ole friend can't help you to bed."

She smiled for the first time in days. "Guess not. Didn't want to be a burden to you."

"You're always sayin' that, Emma, but you been a burden moren' any woman I know!"

Her smile faded and tears filled the creases of her lids.

"Don't start bawlin'. Didn't mean to hurt your feelins'." He strode over and picked her up.

"Ain't no need to carry me," she said. "I can walk."

"It'll be quicker this way," he said. As he held her in his arms he felt the first stirrings of passion and scolded himself. He set her down on the bed and left.

CHAPTER EIGHT

The next day Buford sent Juan to fetch Rosa and bring her to Emma's.

Although Buford liked Emma, his help wasn't motivated by any special affection, for in truth he had none. It was her situation that drew his pity.

• • •

He and Charlie would ride herd together this year. Charlie suggested the idea to him. He knew Buford's return to the cow town where he married Mabel would be painful, as well as his reunion with Victor West.

They started out at dawn the next day and Buford was glad for the company. Two weeks out, Buford and Charlie rode ahead scouting for water. They came down a steep rise and found a wagon train that had been ambushed by Indians. Broken wagons and dead bodies littered the landscape.

Charlie shuddered at the carnage, but it had no effect on Buford. He'd seen such sights many times.

Ezra and John, Charlie's lead man, met up with them and dismounted.

"Lord almighty!" said Ezra.

Buford studied the ground. "This happened a few hours ago. Means who ever done this might still be close by," he said.

"How can you tell?" asked Charlie fighting to keep his breakfast down.

"Lots of ways."

"Who you figure it is?" Charlie asked.

"Comanche," Buford answered.

Charlie felt his hair stand on end. "These folks are all dead, Colonel. We best be movin' on."

"Maybe so, but think I'll take a look 'round. Might be

someone still alive. If'n you ain't got no stomach for it, go back and tell the men to keep an eye out," Buford said gruffly.

Charlie looked stricken and Buford changed his tone. He'd meant no offence. "I ain't callin' you no coward, Charlie. This is a sight to sicken the hardest men but I seen this here a hundred times. Go warn the men."

Charlie and John rode back towards the herd.

As he and Ezra walked from corpse to corpse Buford thought their efforts futile until Ezra called out, "Colonel! Think I got a live one here!"

Buford went over and looked down at the man Ezra found. Scalped and full of arrows, the poor wretch still lived.

"Well, I'll be," said Buford. "He must be one tough son of a bitch."

Buford looked at the man's wounds. The arrows were in his arms and legs leaving his vitals intact. With Ezra's help he pulled them out. Buford ripped off the bottom of his shirt and poured water from his canteen. He bathed the wounds and then covered the poor man's scalp with the cloth.

"We'll take 'im along with us. Ain't nothin' more we can do. If'n he lives it'll be God's will," Buford said.

The herd appeared over the rise and Buford saw Juan and the chuck wagon. He whistled loudly and waved him forward.

Juan came as fast as he could, and Ezra and Buford placed the man in back of the wagon.

Charlie rode up. "You found one. I can't believe it!"

"Don't think he's gonna' live long, but we'll do what we can," said Buford. "Let's get a burial detail goin'. Ain't right to leave these poor souls for the birds."

Covering their faces with bandannas to keep out the stench and the dust, several of the men began to dig in the hard, dry earth. After a few hours all the dead were buried, and the men continued on the trail. The two outfits went along carefully, watching all the time for Indians but none appeared.

"I sure hate comin' through the Nations," Charlie said with a shudder.

The man was still alive when they reached Ellsworth

and Buford turned him over to a doctor's care.

Buford's meeting with Victor was as Charlie expected. The two men mourned the loss of their beloved Mabel and Buford wept openly and unashamed. This surprised Charlie who'd never seen him cry. This and the heart wrenching sorrow of their meeting had his own face wet with tears.

It was difficult for the two distraught men but they got through their business. Buford grew melancholy, but the jovial Charlie kept him from sliding back into his silent, all engulfing grief.

One afternoon Victor met Charlie alone in the foyer of the hotel. "I'm worried about the Colonel. It's not just his white hair, he's a changed man. Victor said.

"That he is." Charlie replied, "When your daughter died he lost his mind. He's startin' to come out of it though. He's gettin' better."

"He is?" Victor asked incredulously. "Good Lord! If he's better now than he must have been..." he shrugged at a loss for words.

Charlie shook his head knowingly. "Ain't never seen no body carry on like he done. Didn't say two words to no one. Didn't eat or sleep. Didn't wash or leave his ranch. It was pitiful. He ever mention a feller named Hi Johnson to y'all?"

"Often."

"Well, he went to Buford's ranch one day and give 'im what for. Shamed 'im into comin' 'round I think. He tidied hisself up and he's eatin' again. He put on a few pounds and though he still don't look good, he looks a heap bettern' he did. I swear Victor, you wouldn't a' knowed 'im a few months ago."

That evening Charlie talked Victor and Buford into going to one of the saloons that lined the long, crowded street. He thought it would do them good to get out of the hotel.

They visited one of the less seedy establishments. It was crowded with ranchers, gamblers and cowboys. Some of Charlie and Buford's men were there and they greeted them when they entered.

Charlie noticed Josh and Jimmy sitting at a table with four men. Two appeared to be gamblers and the profession of the other two was hard for Charlie to discern. He thought they might be gunfighters. All of them seemed slick and disreputable.

"Hope your men don't have no trouble with that crew," he said to Buford. "Looks like the boys might be outa' their league."

Buford looked where he pointed. "I don't know. Jimmy's good at poker. His daddy was a gambler and taught 'im all he knowed. He's so good, he can't get no one in the outfit to play with 'im. He'll be all right."

They continued their conversation and a short time later heard voices raised in anger. Jimmy and one of the gamblers were out of their seats, glaring and yelling at one another nose to nose.

"Lord," said Charlie, "I knew it!"

"Don't fret," said Buford. "I won't let nothin' happen." He went over and grabbed Jimmy by the arm, pulling him away from the gambler.

"You got a problem, Jimmy?" he asked.

"Your damn right I do. This son of a bitch says I'm cheatin'."

"How do you explain winnin' every hand since you sat down?" asked the furious gambler.

"I been lucky!"

"Lucky? Why you..."

"Settle down you two," snapped Buford. "Why don't you come back to the table with me," he said to Jimmy. "You too, Josh."

"Like hell he will!" said the irate gambler. "He ain't leavin' with my fuckin' money! Who are you anyways his pappy?"

"I'm his boss. I'll take my men outa' here and you can go on with your game. I don't want no trouble with y'all."

"Well you already got it," said one of the men at the table. He got up and pushed aside his jacket exposing the butt of his gun.

"Sit down, son. Already tole' you I don't want no trouble."

"And I'm tellin' you it's too late."

The man was right. Buford's attitude shifted in a split

second. "Well, then either use them guns or sit down," said Buford pushing his own coat aside.

The piano player stopped and the crowd in the saloon quieted. The air hung thick with tension. Jimmy and Josh stood behind Buford ready to back him. Men from the Smith and McLeod outfits got up and took strategic positions around the room. They were ready for trouble.

The man gazed down at Buford's gun and then up to his face. A leering grin spread on his weasel like countenance.

"I do believe you're serious, pappy," he said.

Buford didn't reply but looked at him coldly.

"What do you think, boys?" he asked the men at the table. "Does pappy look like a gunfighter to you?"

They guffawed. "Yea, he looks real mean," said one.

Tall and gaunt, Buford had lost his intimidating presence.

"I'm tellin' you for the last time," Buford said quietly. "Use them guns or sit the fuck down."

The man reached for his gun and Buford shot him. He pivoted and pointed at the others.

"Any of you got anythin' you wanna' say?" he asked.

They looked at him in amazement and none spoke except the gambler.

"I ain't got no trouble with you, Mister. My problem's with your man there. He cheated, and I want my money back."

"Give 'im his money," Buford said to Jimmy, without looking at him. His eyes and his gun were still pointed at the men around the table.

Jimmy threw the money down and protested, "But Colonel, I didn't cheat. I won it fair!"

"I know, but it ain't worth no more bloodshed. Give it back. Bothers me to see a gambler whine like a woman."

The gambler's face turned red. "Watch your mouth. If'n you didn't have that pistol in your hand, I'd show you who was a woman."

"Go ahead," snarled Buford, holstering his gun and lunging at the gambler in one swift motion. The man's eyes grew wide with surprise, but he lashed out and hit Buford square in the jaw. Buford staggered back.

"Who's a woman now?" the gambler said with a nasty smile.

Just like in the Longhorn, Buford took leave of his senses and went at his foe in a fury. He threw a powerful right to the gambler's stomach knocking the wind out of him. The gambler doubled over, and Buford boxed his ears. The man fell and Buford reached down to haul him to his feet.

He felt a strong hand grab his shoulder and he whirled around ready to strike. The glitter of a star on the man's vest brought Buford back to earth and he dropped his fist.

"Gotta' take you in, Mister," the Sheriff said.

"What for?"

"You done kilt' a man."

Buford laughed. The sound was cold and harsh. "Man? That weaselly varmint over there?" he gestured to the man lying on the floor, a neat bullet hole in his head.

Buford had an insane look in his eye and it filled Victor with dread. He wasn't sure what his son-in-law would do next. He didn't think Buford would hurt the Sheriff, but he couldn't be sure. He strode over to them and said, "Sheriff, that man drew first."

"Then how come his gun's still in the holster?" asked the law man.

"He didn't get that far," shrugged Buford.

"Find that hard to believe. That there is Coyote Pete," said the Sheriff. "He's fast."

"Reckon, he weren't fast enough," Buford said dryly.

Charlie joined them. "Don't know who he is," he said, "but he done drawed first. Y'all seen 'im didn't you?" he asked the other patrons.

"That's right Sheriff, ole' Pete, went for his gun first," said one man. Others agreed.

"What about him?" the Sheriff asked pointing to the gambler. His friends had picked him up and he sat with both hands over his bloodied ears.

"Oh, him? Reckon he just riled me some."

The Sheriff studied the three men. They looked prosperous and respectable. It was obvious by Victor's speech that he was a gentleman.

The Sherriff said, "All right everyone, show's over. Billy,

take Pete outa' here. I wanna' talk to you," he said to Buford, leading him to a table. Victor and Charlie followed. The piano player struck up a lively tune and things returned to normal.

"Ain't he somethin'?" asked one of Charlie's men as they walked by. "Always heard the Colonel was good in a fight but Jesus!"

"He's the best," beamed Josh. "Y'all see them varmint's faces when he shot their friend? Thought they was gonna' shit their britches."

When they were all seated the Sheriff asked, "Who are you men and where you from?"

After introductions were made, he said, "So you're Colonel McLeod. I done heard 'bout you. You used to be a Ranger. You the same feller that brought that poor devil to Doc's?"

Buford nodded.

"Thought you was one and the same when Doc tole' me, except his description of you didn't seem to match. Heard you was a big feller with dark hair."

"Gettin' older," Buford said.

"Don't seem to have slowed you down none. Heard 'bout your friend, too. What's his name, Jackson?"

"Johnson. Hi Johnson," Buford answered.

"That's the one! I'm a Texas boy myself. They say you and Johnson was two of the best Rangers we ever had. Just signed on as Sheriff a few months ago and heard you come here regular. Was hopin' to meet you. Wish it was under better circumstances."

"You ain't bringin' me in for this here, are you?" Buford asked.

The Sheriff sighed. "No. I'm sure ole' Pete deserved what he got. Just seems peculiar that he never got his gun out. He done kilt' more men than you can shake a stick at. Never figured he'd lose in a draw."

"The Colonel is extremely adept with a gun himself," said Victor. "If I didn't see it, I wouldn't have believed it either. I'm impressed, Colonel. Your reputation is warranted."

Buford didn't acknowledge Victor's comment.

"You mind tellin' me what happened?" the Sheriff asked.

"That feller over there holdin' his head, accused one of my boys of cheatin'. I went over to get my man and take 'im outa' here. I didn't want no trouble. Pete took offense and went for his gun. He gave me no choice. Then I made Jimmy give 'is money back to that gambler. Didn't want no touble."

"That's Bobby Monroe," said the Sheriff. "He's a bad sort. Goes from cattle town to cattle town. Coyote Pete and them other fellers travel with 'im. Two gamblers and two gunfighters. Not a nice crew. If'n you give 'im his money back why did y'all fight?"

Buford sighed, "That was my fault. Lost my temper and insulted him. Didn't have no call to."

"I think you did," said Charlie. "Jimmy won that money fair and square, he ain't no cheater."

"Reckon, but there's no harm done," said the Sheriff getting up to leave. "There won't be no more trouble?"

"Not if'n people leave me be," said Buford.

"Word travels fast. I don't think anyone will bother you. It was a pleasure to meet you." He turned to leave.

"Sheriff!" Charlie called out. "That man we brung in. He still alive?"

"Yea. The Colonel did a good job patchin' 'im up."

● ● ●

The way home was a nightmare. The men were used to harsh conditions. They'd gone through a lack of water before, but this was the worst. A sudden drought dried up the usual streams and water holes. The men sucked on bullets in an attempt to ease their thirst. Buford worried about the cattle he'd bought in Kansas. If they didn't find water soon, they'd go blind.

They finally reached Wilder Creek and water.

Buford let his men and animals get their fill. Once hydrated he let his men rest but didn't allow himself or the livestock that option. He took the extra day and a half to bring the cows to the ranch.

Once back with everything settled, he felt restless and decided to go in town to see Hi.

He found his friend at the jailhouse and awake. Buford

teased him. "Well I'll be damned. You ain't got no deputy workin' for you and you ain't sleepin'."

"Fuck you, too." Hi said with a big smile on his face. "You're lookin' pretty good. I do believe gettin' away from this fart of a town agreed with you. You almost look human again."

"Good my ass! Didn't have no water most of the trip. Me and Charlie lost some fine animals on account of it."

"Still, you look good. Your face ain't that funny white no more. You got some color to you."

"Hard not to get some when you're in the saddle day after day without a bit of shade. Times I thought we wasn't gonna' make it."

"Well, you did. You always come through in a tight spot. Except when it comes to women."

Buford could tell by Hi's face that he had something on his mind. "Hi, if'n you got somethin' to say, wish you'd speak plain." "Been by to see Emma?"

"No. Was goin' there next."

"Glad you come here first. Things ain't goin' good for 'er and I know she won't complain to you. A couple of days after you left town, Rosa up and left 'er."

"What?" said Buford, his temper starting to rise.

"Yes siree! Reckon Juan never tole' 'er who she was nursin'. When she found out she left."

"Never had no use for that woman!" Buford scowled.

"She never had no use for you neither. Said she wasn't gonna' help no whore, 'specially yours."

"I'm gonna' go to the Village and wring 'er neck!"

"Don't waste your time. Emma don't need 'er no more. Besides, I already been to the Village. Rosa's more stubborn than you! Wouldn't come back no matter how I begged. Got me riled and I give 'er a piece of my mind. Worst of it is I couldn't get no one to help 'er when Rosa got done."

"Didn't Emma have a Mexican gal, used to do chores for 'er when she was at the saloon?"

"Yea, but she went back to Mexico when Emma opened 'er bakery. I'm tellin' you, I tried. I couldn't get no one."

"How 'bout here in town? No one lookin' for work?"

Hi snorted. "C'mon' Buford! You know ain't nobody

gonna' work for Emma."

"How 'bout the decent women. Can't they give 'er a hand? They was goin' in 'er shop regular."

Hi sighed and shook his head. "Somehow them stupid women got the notion that goin' into the bakery was dangerous after what them two varmints did. Lydia says they're afraid to go in. Some of them bitches even said this here was Emma's penance for bein' a fast woman! You ever hear of such a thing?"

"Of all the danged shit I ever heard..." Buford spluttered. "What about Lydia? She won't go in either?"

"No, and it's a great disappointment to me. She's just as bad as the rest. Emma tried to manage 'erself. Then one day she fell with the baby and Tom got a nasty bump. After that she was desperate and let the whores help 'er. Seein' them go in and out ruined any chance Emma had for a normal life. I ain't surprised 'bout the other women, but I thought Lydia was better than that."

"Don't sound like Lydia. She's got a forgivin' heart."

"Guess she don't and this here's been a sore spot between us."

"Women." Buford said in disdain.

"It didn't help Emma any when the whores came to help. Every time one of 'em went to Emma's, the men carried on, callin' out and actin' like fuckin' baboons! Well, it's over and done with. Emma's healed up for the most part. Got some nasty scars and says she sees funny outa' one eye. Gets dizzy spells and head aches, too, but she gets by."

"She done have 'er share of trouble," said Buford.

"And you give 'er most of it!"

"How you figure that?"

"Are you really that much of a fuckin' idiot? You gotta' know how she feels 'bout you."

"No, I don't. You already tole' me she loved me and I made a fool of myself. If'n you're referrin' to 'er givin' me cow eyes all the time, yea, I know. She always done that."

"You wanna' know why? She's got feelins' for you.

"Well, I think you're wrong. She never said nothin' 'bout it. Tole' me lotsa' times that I pleasured 'er some. Figured that's why she looked at me like that."

"Pleasure 'er my ass. Probably says that to everyone."

"She ever say it to you?"

Hi's face turned red. "Ain't gonna' discuss what me and Emma talk 'bout in bed."

"Have it your way. She never tole' me she loved me. Only thing she ever said was that the kid was mine."

"Mebbe' 'cause he is."

"Or maybe 'cause' she thought I'd marry 'er. Reckon she didn't figure on me bein' already hitched."

"Lord Buford, you got no sense a'tall! She knew you was married 'fore she tole' you. She had nothin' to gain by it."

"Thought of that, too. Maybe she was bein' spiteful."

"You're a jack ass! Emma ain't the spiteful kind and you know it. I'm tellin' you it's your kid! She wouldn't poke no one but you. Why you bein' so stubborn 'bout this here? All you gotta' do is look at 'im! Everyone in town knows he belongs to you. Has Emma ever lied to you before?"

"Just once."

"And when was that?"

"When she tole' me little Tom was mine."

Hi smashed his fist down on his desk and glared at Buford. "Lord you rile me at times, you really do! You are one pig headed son of a bitch!"

"Well, if'n you're gonna' get all put out, reckon I'll just leave."

"Wish to hell you would. I might beat some sense into you if'n you stay!"

Buford left but decided against seeing Emma. If Hi was right it would be best to keep his distance.

When she first told him about the baby, he wondered why. Whatever her reason, he hadn't dwelled on it. He'd been a newlywed at the time and had thoughts for only his bride.

Emma peered out her window and saw Buford walking down the board walk deep in thought. She grabbed a shawl and ran outside.

"Colonel!" she called out.

Buford looked up, his reverie broken. "Damn," he swore softly.

He crossed over to her. "How you been, Emma?"

"Gettin' along," she said with a smile. "You wasn't 'bout to leave town without callin' on me?"

"Afraid I was. Just got back and I'm fuckin' tired. Seen the Marshall and he tole' me you healed up fine. I can see that for myself."

"C'mon' in and have some coffee and a cinnamon bun. Josh tole' me once that you was fond of 'em, and I just took 'em outa' the oven."

"I'm much obliged but I really gotta' git."

She tried to hide her disappointment and smiled. "Well, if'n you can't, you can't. Since decent folks won't come to my bakery I've been kinda' lonesome."

He looked at her but didn't reply.

"Don't make 'im feel sorry for you!" she chastised herself. Out loud she said, "Sorry, Colonel, don't mean to be a burden to you," she clapped her hands over her mouth and laughed. "I said it again! Last time I seen you, you gimme' hell for it. If'n you got a minute I'll get them buns and you can take 'em with you. Share 'em with your men."

Her earnest expression touched him and he said, "Never you mind Emma, reckon I can set and eat them rolls here."

They went to the kitchen and he watched as she bustled around. Her wounds had healed well thanks to Doc's expert hand, but she had scars on her forehead, chin and over her right eye. They were visible but not disfiguring.

"Hi tole' me 'bout the trouble you had with Rosa. If'n I get my hands on 'er, I'll..."

"Don't blame 'er, Colonel! She did nothin' wrong. She set much store by Mabel, so she didn't like me none. Can't blame 'er."

"She's an ornery critter and always was," he said.

"Shouldn't complain but it's the other ladies in town that make me feel bad. I didn't want the girls at the saloon to help me at first. After I fell and hurt Tom I had to do somethin'. Just wish these ladies could see it my way."

"That's why I come in, Emma. Wanted to talk to you. People here ain't never gonna' accept you. Why don't you leave Wilder Creek and go somewheres else? This is a big territory. Go open your bakery in another town where no one knows you. Makes more sense than stayin' here."

"I thought of it but where would I go? Sooner or later I'd be sure to meet up with someone who knows me. Once word got out I'd be ruined and have to move on again. I can't run from my past. I'm stayin' right here and show these women that I changed my ways. They'll realize it in time. Ain't seen none of the girls since I been well, not even Jamie."

"What you gonna' live on in the mean time? You ain't doin' much business."

"No, I ain't but things is gonna' get better. Now that all the punchers is back from Kansas they'll be comin' in again. Things'll pick up. I don't need much to live on."

"I ain't got nothin' to do with you stayin' 'round, do I?"

She looked at him in surprise. "No," she lied. "Why'd you think that?"

Buford was embarrassed. "Never you mind. No reason. I best be goin'. If'n you got any more of them buns I'd like to buy 'em."

"Got a whole passle of 'em."

"I'll take 'em all. How much?"

"You ain't gotta' pay me."

"Jesus Emma. I'm doin' business with you here! You ain't gonna' make no money, if'n you give your goods away." He paid her and left.

Buford fumed all the way back to the ranch. As he suspected, Emma didn't love him. He had given her money a few times and that was all. He had made a fool of himself asking her if she stayed in town because of him. He'd give Hi a piece of his mind the next time he saw him.

"What's he up to?", Buford wondered. "Is he tryin' to make a jack ass outa' me? I know that son of a bitch wants to get me and Emma together. She needs a man and he thinks I need a woman."

His anger suddenly left him, and he laughed out loud. It was a cold and empty laugh and held no mirth. "The jokes on him! I ain't never gonna' feel for no one again, 'specially no whore."

By the time he reached the ranch, all thoughts of Hi and Emma were gone.

He settled back into his old routine and tried not to think of Mabel. For the most part he was successful. It was his way not to dwell on things he could do nothing about. She was gone, and he couldn't change it. A twinge would hit him occasionally, but he'd busy himself with work and soon the memories would fade. He had locked his heart away, even to her.

He went to town occasionally but didn't go to the bakery. His face turned crimson when he thought of his last meeting with Emma. He decided not to say anything to Hi, instead he wanted to let the embarrassing incident drop.

A few times he passed Emma on the board walk but didn't stop to speak to her. He tipped his hat and went on his way.

Emma for her part hated to leave the bakery. Although some of the men greeted her, the women gave her a wide berth and snubbed her. She held her head high, seemingly oblivious to the dark looks the ladies shot her. She kept her composure until she got home, then with the door safely closed behind her, she'd crumble into tears.

"How long until they forgive me?" she wondered.

If not for little Tom she would've died of loneliness. She'd severed all ties with her old friends. If she saw them on the veranda of the Longhorn or passed them on the street, she didn't acknowledge them. They knew she had to shun them and understood.

One day Buford was in the general store when she came in. He couldn't help but notice her cold reception and the rude attitude of the clerk.

Buford tipped his hat. "Mornin' Miss Emma."

"Mornin', Colonel," she said politely.

Emma made her purchases and left quickly. "Strumpet!" said one woman as the door shut behind her. If Emma heard the remark, she ignored it.

"Imagine!" said the woman to the other patrons, "She walks down the street bold as brass, wheelin' 'er bastard in front of 'er. She might try to act like decent folk, but she ain't and never will be."

"Maybe that ain't so bad," said Buford quietly. "If'n y'all are decent folks, she's better off the way she is."

The woman looked at him with surprise. She was one of his admirers and didn't believe the rumors that the child was his. She thought Buford too fine a man to take up with the likes of Emma. His remark took her off guard and she didn't know what to say. He tipped his hat and bid her good day before she could recover.

When he stepped outside, he watched Emma make her way down the board walk, pushing Tom in his carriage. Most of the women, seeing her approach, quickly crossed the street.

"Well, I'll be," he thought to himself.

He decided to stop in and see her.

When Emma got back to the bakery, she removed her hat while silent tears ran down her cheeks. She heard the bell on the front door and wiped her eyes.

"Colonel! What a nice surprise."

"After seein' you in the store, thought I'd stop in. How's business?"

"Could be better."

"Those ole' heifers are still givin' you a bad time I see."

"Yea, reckon they will for a while. They'll come 'round sooner or later."

"You're more certain than I am. Still think you oughta' leave town."

"Ain't runnin' no more. Been runnin' most of my life and it ain't done me no good. Had trouble with my Pa in Tennessee so I run to New Orleans. Had trouble there and come to Wilder Creek. Had some bad luck here, too. Don't matter where I go, trouble seems to follow me."

He gazed at her and sighed. He could tell she'd been crying and her dress, though clean, was beginning to show wear.

"Well, I aim on givin' you some business. Juan ain't got time to do the bakin'. Figured on orderin' everythin' we need from you. Could you bring it to the ranch a coupla' times a week?"

Her face lit up. "Sure! I still got a horse and wagon. What do you want?"

He had a lot of men to feed and placed a large order. "Bring it on over whenever it's ready and give it to Juan. He's usually in the cook house. Better pay you now. Don't know where I'll be when you show up."

"Much obliged, Colonel. You done saved my hide so many times..." her voice trailed off.

"Ain't doin' it to save your hide a'tall'. The ranch's gettin' bigger and I have more important things for Juan to do than bakin'. Don't know why I never thought of this before," he said gruffly.

"Got some of them cinnamon rolls out back. You want one?"

"Much obliged but I gotta' get back."

"Maybe I'll see you when I bring your goods," she called out as he left.

"Maybe."

She had no trouble finding the ranch and was impressed with its size. She couldn't get over the beautiful house and thought it a shame that it sat empty.

Juan greeted her warmly.

"Hello, Miss Emma. The Colonel told me you would be coming."

"Hope you ain't mad I took one of your chores away," she smiled.

"No, Signorita. Not at all. Dio! I have a half dozen others I wouldn't mind getting rid of."

Buford wasn't there but she hadn't expected him to be. "I'll be comin' here twice a week. Surely, I'll run into 'im sometime," she thought happily.

Week after week went by without her seeing him. He left the money for his purchases with Juan.

It was a cold, blustery day and the sky was filled with dark clouds. Tom was dressed warmly but Emma had nothing but a light shawl. She shivered in the chill wind as Juan paid her and his heart went out to her.

"Do you have time for a cup of coffee?" he asked.

"Be much obliged. Sure is a cold one today."

They sat in the cook house and chatted. Little Tom sat on the floor at Emma's feet and played quietly.

Emma began to feel one of her headaches coming on and knew she had to get home.

Since the men beat her, she'd suffered with them frequently. The headache came first, followed by dizzy spells and nausea. A few times she'd almost fainted and kept a vial of smelling salts with her. In her haste to get to the ranch, she'd left them at home.

"Gotta' get goin'," she said.

"You feel all right Signorita? Your color is not so good."

"Just a headache. Probably best that I get home and lay down awhile. I'll be all right." She rose to leave and passed out.

"Dio!" cried Juan rushing to her side. He wanted to put her in the bunk house but was afraid to leave the baby alone. He was wondering what to do when Josh came in.

"Lord! What happened here?" he asked.

"Miss Emma said she had a headache then she fainted. Bring her to the bunk house."

Josh picked her up gently and carried her to his bunk. He sat beside her and chafed her wrists.

Juan came in with Tom. "I'll sit with her. Maybe you should take care of her horse. I think it'll be awhile before she's able to leave."

Josh nodded. He kicked at a stone as he walked to Emma's wagon. He felt angry and frustrated. It was clear that Emma needed someone and he wished she had accepted his proposal of marriage. Heartbroken, he continued to visit the bakery but didn't bring up the subject again.

She came to and sat up. "Where am I?" she asked, incoherent at first.

"You're in our bunk house, Signorita. You fainted."

"I remember now. My head hurts like the devil. Reckon I should be goin'. Got some laudanum back at the store and it helps some."

"You are in no condition to make the ride back. What would happen to your boy if you fainted on the way home?"

Josh came back in. "How you feelin' Emma?"

"I'm feelin' poorly but I hate to stay. If'n the Colonel comes in from the herd he's gonna' get riled. You know how he feels 'bout women. Maybe one of you could follow me back to town?"

Josh beamed. "I'll be glad to!" She got up and almost fell again. Josh reached out to steady her.

"Signorita! I beg of you, stay here and rest awhile. You are not well. Josh can take you back later."

"Reckon, I got no choice. Don't think I'll make it back the way I'm feelin' now, even with Josh's help."

She lay back down on the bunk and Josh covered her with his blanket.

The men left, shutting the door quietly behind them.

Josh fumed. "Goddamn it, I'm worried. Didn't know 'er spells was that bad. She needs someone to take care of 'er."

"She should've married you when she had the chance," Juan said solemnly. The men confided in him and he knew how Josh felt about her. "Perhaps you should ask again."

"Don't think she'll change er' mind. She don't love me and tole' me plain."

"Is it still the Colonel?"

"Yea," said Josh sadly. "Says she don't but any fool can see she does."

Josh went to the barn to work with the horses and Juan went back to the cook house. It was close to noon and the men would be coming in for lunch.

He placed the toddler in the middle of the floor and surrounded him with saddles. With his make shift play pen in place, he started to cook.

When the men arrived, they grinned at the sight that greeted them. Juan sat in front of the bunk house with Tom on his lap. He sang a song in Spanish and bounced him on his knee in time to the music.

"That's Emma's kid, ain't it?" Phil asked.

"Yea," answered Josh. "She come here this mornin' and took ill. We got 'er inside."

Tom had his mother's sunny disposition and he beamed at the men.

"Let me hold the little feller for a while," said Asa.

The men retired to the cook house for their meal. Little Tom's antics amused them and he was the center of attention.

A short time later Buford rode in. When he entered the bunkhouse he was surprised to see Emma curled up in Josh's bunk, sound asleep.

He stormed into the cook house. "Can anyone tell me what the fuck Emma's doin' in the bunkhouse?"

Juan answered. "She fainted this morning. I thought it

best she stay until she felt better."

Buford saw Tom in the men's midst and scowled. "You been watchin' 'im all mornin'?"

"Si, Colonel."

"Damnation! You got work to do. I ain't payin' you to watch no baby!"

"I could not leave him alone," Juan shrugged.

"Soon as she's feelin' better," Josh said, "I'll follow 'er back to town, if'n it's all right with you. She tried to leave and almost fainted again."

"That woman is a pain in my ass," snarled Buford. He picked up a biscuit and went to leave.

"Well, can I?" Josh called out.

Buford turned, a dark scowl on his face. "Reckon so, but make it quick. This outfit done wasted enough time with Emma and 'er kid today."

After he was gone Reuben said, "He sure is contrary."

"In what way?" Ezra asked.

"Well, he done helped Emma by orderin' all this here, so why's he mad if'n Josh and Juan is helpin' 'er now?"

"He ain't buyin' it to help 'er out. He's doin' it so Juan has time for other chores. Reckon, that's why he's peeved. Don't expect you got much work done this mornin', Juan," said Ezra.

"No, I did not," he answered.

A few hours later Emma woke up. She found Juan and Josh in the barn. Tom napped in the hay close by.

"How you feelin'?" asked Josh.

"I'm right as the mail. Reckon I can go back to town by myself."

"Don't mind takin' you," Josh said. "The Colonel says it's O.K."

"Much obliged, but it ain't necessary."

Juan spoke up. "What harm can it do? Let Josh go back with you."

"Ain't that often I get an afternoon off Josh smiled. "You'd be doin' me a favor by lettin' me accompany y'all." She relented and they set off.

When Josh came back from town he went to the bunk house and the bottle of whiskey he kept there. He had need of a few drinks.

Mile after mile he thought of how different things would have been if she'd consented to be his wife.

As much as he admired the Colonel, he was put out with him. He showed no sympathy for Emma today and his hard manner grated on Josh.

"If'n he wasn't such a tough natured critter he'd know it was up to him to take care of 'er. He's bein' stubborn 'bout the kid. He don't think it's his when anyone can see it is."

When the men came back for supper, they found Josh drunk and melancholy.

"What the hell's this?" Buford snapped when Josh reeled from the bunk house.

"Reckon, I had one too many," Josh slurred.

"Reckon you did. Get your chores done?"

"Don't think so. Took Emma back to town."

"She get you drunk?"

"Hell no! What're you blamin' 'er for?" Josh said testily. "You don't think much of 'er do you?"

"I don't like your tone," said Buford, his temper beginning to flare.

"Well, that's too goddamn bad. I don't like yours neither and I don't like the way you treat 'er."

"It ain't your fuckin' business how I treat 'er or anyone else."

"Well, it is!" Josh said, looking close to tears. "I love that little gal and she won't gimme' the time of day. She loves you! She done have your baby and you don't give a damn!"

"That's enough," Buford said menacingly.

"No it ain't, Colonel. You're gonna' hear what I have to say whether you like it or..."

Buford reached Josh in two strides and cracked him hard across the face.

"I ain't hearin' no more. Go sober up before you really get me riled."

Josh touched the corner of his mouth. When he brought his hand down, his fingers were sticky with blood.

Buford's face was dark with rage and his huge hands were balled into fists at his sides. Back to his proper weight he looked fierce and Josh decided not to push the matter further.

He stumbled back to the bunk house and threw himself on his cot, weeping silent tears of rage and shame.

Buford looked at the other men and shook his head. "Said it once and I'll say it again, that woman sure is a pain in my ass."

The next morning Josh felt like he'd been kicked in the head by a mule. He looked in the cracked, dirty mirror hanging on the bunkhouse wall. His lip was swollen and a large bruise covered his cheek.

Josh went to the pump house and stuck his head in a barrel of cold water. It eased the ache in his face and cleared the cobwebs from his mind. He spotted Buford washing on the other side of the room and walked over to him.

"Can I talk to you a minute?" he asked Buford.

"Go ahead."

Josh studied him Buford's large frame and bulging muscles. He wondered what made him pick a fight with this giant of a man.

"I'm sorry 'bout last night. Don't remember much 'cept I was outa' line."

"Reckon you was."

"I had no right to talk to you like that. I reckon you probably want me to go."

"Only if'n you want to. I'd hate to lose you. You're one of my best men."

"No, I'd like to stay on. You been real good to me and I had no call...usually me and you get along pretty good," Josh said rubbing his face gingerly.

"Yea, we do. Didn't mean to hit you so hard, but couldn't let you get away with sassin' me in front of the men. I gotta' keep order here." He looked at the mournful Josh. "Reckon you're still sweet on Emma."

"Reckon, I am," Josh sighed.

"Maybe you oughta' try courtin' 'er."

"I done tried. She don't want me."

"I don't mean hangin' 'round the bakery like a love sick calf. I'm talkin' 'bout courtin' 'er. I'm the last man who knows anythin' 'bout such matters. Ask the Marshall, he's the lady's man, or he used to be."

"I might just do that," Josh said brightening. "Reckon,

she kinda' scared me a little. Didn't want to push 'er none."

"Emma's a lotta' things but she ain't nothin' to be afraid of. Now if'n you want 'er, go after 'er proper."

"Much obliged for the advice, Colonel." Josh walked off with a spring in his step.

"If'n you won't leave town, Emma, I'll marry you off. Reckon I won't have no peace 'til I get rid of you somehow," Buford thought.

CHAPTER NINE

Josh took Buford's advice, and after consulting with Hi, he went to town every chance he could. Dressed in his best clothes he always brought Emma a trinket or flowers.

She was pleased to see him but as his visits grew more frequent and the gifts more plentiful, she felt obligated to speak up.

"Josh, gotta' say I'm obliged to you for the attention and all, but it wouldn't be fair to let you go on this way."

His face fell but he spoke cheerfully. "Just bein' friendly, Emma. Ain't gonna' trouble you with talk of marriage."

"I know how you feel, and it don't make me happy to hurt you none."

"I imagine you do, loving the Colonel all this time," he replied.

"Is it that obvious?"

He laughed. "Sure! The whole dang town knows it.

"Well," Emma said exasperated. "How come he don't see it?"

"Ya' know the Colonel. He don't know shit 'bout women."

"Reckon, you're right."

To change the subject Josh said. "Charlie Smith is havin' a shindig this Saturday. Wanna' come with me?"

"Are you loco? I couldn't. I ain't accepted by decent folks."

"It's 'bout time you was. You ain't never done nothin' to 'em."

"Nothin' but bed their husbands. You can see how that might put a woman out, can't you?"

"Reckon, so. But they was friendly enough when you opened your bakery."

"Yea, before I got beat up. After that I guess they figured I was nothin' but trouble. Those ole' hens didn't take kindly to me takin' up with my ole' friends."

"Well that's plain foolish! You needed help with Tom and done what you had to. If'n them heifers helped you, you wouldna' had to turn to the whores."

"Reckon so, but that ain't the point. There'll be trouble if'n I go. Besides, ain't got no one to set with Tom."

"Maybe I can get Juan or one of the other boys to watch 'im."

"Don't put yourself out. I can't go. I wish I could though. Ain't never been to no decent party. Is the Colonel goin'?"

"Don't think so. He ain't much for socializin'."

When Josh got back, Buford noticed his gloomy mood.

"Go and see Emma?" he asked.

"Yea."

"How's things goin'?"

"Not well a'tall. She still don't want me."

"Give 'er time, son. She'll come 'round."

"Don't think so. I wanted to take 'er to Charlie's shindig but she won't go."

"Probably for the best. The women folk don't like 'er none."

"Well she won't leave this fuckin' town so's the only way she's gonna' get accepted is to stop hidin' from 'em." Josh scowled.

"Maybe you're right."

"Sure, I'm right! The women who were goin' in 'er bakery thought she was nice enough 'afore she got beat up. I think they can like 'er again. Don't matter though. She ain't got no one to watch the kid."

Buford thought about it. "You know Josh, I think there's some sense in what you're sayin' and I'm prepared to help y'all. We'll get Juan to watch Tom and the three of us'll go to Charlie's for a while. Most folks 'round here don't gimme' trouble."

"I don't think she'll go."

"I'll go talk to 'er," Buford said.

When he got to the bakery, Emma greeted him warmly. "Howdy, Colonel! Ain't seen you in a spell. What can I get for you?"

"Nothin'. Come to talk to you 'bout Charlie's shindig."

Her pulse raced. Was he going to invite her? "Oh?" she asked trying to hide her excitement.

"Josh tole' me he asked you to go. Think you should."

She was disappointed but didn't show it. "Yea, he asked me, but I said no. I don't think it's a good idea. Besides, I ain't got no one to stay with Tom and nothin' to wear."

"Juan can stay with your boy." He reached in his pocket and drew out some money. "I'll buy you a dress."

"I can't do that. I've taken enough of your money. I can't go and that's that."

He sighed in exasperation and shook his head. "If'n you're foolish enough to stay in town, you might as well try bein' part of it," he said gruffly.

"I got too many reasons not to go," she said turning away from his harsh gaze.

"I tole' you I'll get you a goddamn dress and Juan can watch the kid."

"Why's it important to you?"

"Ain't important to me a'tall. But it is to Josh and to you. You gotta' face them heifers. I'll be there to make sure no one gives y'all any grief."

She thought awhile. "In that case I'll go."

"Well then take this here money for a dress."

"There ain't no need to buy me nothin'. The girls have plenty."

"C'mon' Emma. Buy yourself somethin' new. I can afford it."

"That's right kind of you but I reckon I could get a dress from one of the girls and fix it so it don't look so whorish. You know I can't go to the saloon. Would you fetch one for me?"

"Jesus, Emma you know how I feel 'bout those women," he scowled.

"Never mind then. I didn't wanna' go anyhow."

Buford sighed and left for the Longhorn. When he arrived Hi was there.

"Howdy Buford, what brings you to town?"

"Come to see Emma."

"You don't say? Ain't gettin' any ideas, are you? Josh ain't gonna' like it none. He been courtin' her these past few months."

"I know that, you jack ass! You think me and Emma...?" he laughed. "You're just tryin' to get me riled. Josh wants to take 'er to Charlie's shindig. She tole 'im no and I come to talk 'er into it."

Hi stared at Buford intently. "You ain't serious 'bout this here?"

"Sure am."

"Well if'n you do you're gonna' have a stampede of women on your hands."

"I know. Hope I'm doin' the right thing. Besides I'm sure Emma ain't gonna' be the only woman there that don't have a past."

"True enough but them women are what you call discreet. What you got to gain by this?"

"Nothin'. Tryin' to help Josh out. It was his idea. He thinks since the heifers liked her when she opened the bakery, they might come 'round."

"I know for a fact they won't and it's Emma who's gonna' have

"Damage is already done. Can't see how it could get worse. A bad time."

Ain't you and Lydia comin'?"

"I gotta' work."

Buford looked skeptical. "For once you're gonna' fuckin' work?"

Hi chuckled. "I do once in a while."

Buford talked to Jamie about a dress and she came downstairs with a large box.

"Here's your dress, Colonel," she teased.

"What are you givin' it to me for?"

"I can't bring it over there!"

He sighed. "It's gettin' dark. No one will see you."

"I ain't bringin' it. Me and the girls got 'er in this mess and we ain't 'bout to make it worse."

"I'm goin' by on my way home," said Hi. "I'll take it to 'er."

• • •

Saturday, before his men left for Charlie's, Buford talked with them.

"Y'all know that Josh is bringin' Emma. Want you men to help 'im out some. Hope you'll ask 'er to dance. This here outfit's gotta' stick together."

The men went directly to the Smith ranch, but Juan, Josh and Buford went to Emma's.

When she opened the door the three men stood gaping. She'd never looked lovelier. Her blonde hair was piled high in soft curls and her pale green silk dress suited her coloring.

"Y'all gonna' stand there all night?" she asked with a laugh.

"You sure do look fine!" Josh said appreciatively. "Reckon I'll have the prettiest gal there."

"Do I look all right? I had to alter it some. It ain't too plain, is it?"

"You look good Emma, let's get goin'. I ain't got all night," Buford snapped impatiently.

Buford let Josh use the wagon and handed Emma up to him.

"I'll ride on ahead," Buford said. "Don't dilly dally."

The party was in full swing when they arrived. Joanne and Charlie stood behind a large table laden with food and drink. Hands from the other ranches stood in small groups talking and others danced with the few women present.

Joanne's eyes nearly popped from her head when she saw Buford, Josh and Emma.

"What the hell?" she scowled. "This ain't gonna' do, Charlie. Tell 'em to take that slut outa' here."

"I ain't gonna' do no such thing. Emma's a nice gal. Josh is courtin' 'er and it wouldn't be right. After all, we let the other men bring their women. They ain't whores but they ain't virgins, neither."

Charlie strode to them with a large smile.

"Howdy! You're lookin' pretty tonight, Emma."

"Thank you, Charlie. Ain't causin' no problem bein' here am I?"

"Hell no! C'mon' over and meet my wife."

"I know 'er. She used to come in the bakery," Emma said nervously.

"Then come and say hello," Charlie said taking her arm.

Emma's heart pounded in her chest. She was afraid of the reception she'd receive.

"Evenin' Colonel, Josh," said Joanne not acknowledging Emma.

"Evenin'," they both answered.

"Joanne, you remember Miss Emma, don't you?" Charlie asked.

Joanne glared at him and he glared back. He gave into his strong-willed wife often but not this time.

"Evenin'," Joanne said stiffly.

"Evenin' Mrs. Smith. You done a fine job. Everything looks real nice."

Joanne didn't answer. "Charlie, I gotta' go back to the house for a minute." She turned her back and walked away.

It was an awkward moment and Emma's face fell. "Maybe I should leave," she said.

"I won't hear of it," said Charlie. "May I have this dance?"

His kindness made her feel better and she smiled. "Much obliged," she said. He swept her into the group of dancers.

Josh and Buford looked at each other. "Maybe this wasn't a good idea."

"No Colonel. We done right." Josh said angrily.

"Now Josh, I want you to keep calm. Ain't gonna' help Emma if'n you fly off the handle. These are all good men here, and they'll help Emma. Reckon any trouble you have is gonna' be with these fuckin' heifers."

"I know that."

Charlie brought Emma back and she and Josh went to join the others.

"Joanne don't like this much," said Buford.

"No, but I don't give a damn."

Hi walked over to them with a smile.

"What are you doin' here?" Buford asked. "I thought you wasn't comin'."

"I come to watch Emma make her debut into society!"

The three men sat at a table drinking and talking. Joanne never returned from the house but none of the men were surprised. She hadn't made a fuss, but she was showing them how she felt by her absence.

Buford watched Emma and Josh out of the corner of his eye. They seemed to be having a good time and he saw nothing to make him think otherwise.

When Josh made introductions some of the girls greeted her coldly and some not at all.

Charlie's daughter Hattie was mortified and took a few of the girls aside.

"I ain't one to find fault with the Colonel or his men but to bring a whore to our shindig is just plain awful."

Her sister Maryanne joined the group. "The menfolk sure are glad that floozy's here. Y'all see 'em? Bowin' and scrapin' like a bunch of baboons!"

Hattie's new beau came to fetch her for a reel and the other girls went back to their escorts. They were angry but remained silent.

Emma hadn't expected a warm welcome from them, so she wasn't disappointed. If anything, she felt relieved. They hadn't been kind but none had made a scene. She was feeling too good to worry about it and happy to be dancing outside in the warm spring night. Her eyes sparkled and her face shone with excitement.

Buford couldn't see anything unseemly. He noticed a few women huddled in a group, but it had been only for a second and he thought no harm would come of it.

After an hour he called to Josh. "Me and the Marshall are leavin'. You and Emma seem to be doin' all right."

"We are. Ain't no one troublin' us. Reckon there's no need for you to stay." Charlie promised to help Josh champion Emma's cause if it became necessary and the two men left.

Buford could've gone directly back to the ranch but thought he'd ride back to town with Hi. He wanted to see how Juan was getting along.

"I know you didn't plan on goin' tonight. It was right nice of you to come. and keep the peace." Buford said.

"Don't mention it. You know how I feel 'bout Emma. Besides, I thought with the two of us there, folks would think twice before speakin' out."

"Reckon it worked. Outside of Joanne, things went

smooth."

In town, they parted company and Buford went to the bakery. He found Juan outside vomiting.

"You ailin', Juan?"

"Si! I think I ate too many of Miss Emma's cakes."

"Where's the boy?"

"Sleeping."

"Hate to leave you like this. You gonna' be all right? You look a might pale."

"I don't feel so good, but I'll be all right." Juan turned and retched again.

"You say the kid's sleepin'?"

"Si. A few hours now."

"He still in diapers?"

"No."

"Reckon I can handle 'im long as he's asleep. Why don't you go on home."

"Gracias, Colonel. My stomach feels ready to burst."

After Juan left, Buford went inside and sat in the only comfortable chair Emma had. He stretched his long frame out and fell asleep.

Back at the party, Josh was having a good time. He was proud to be with Emma. The other men, following the McLeod outfit's lead, treated her with respect.

The jealous women looked on as she captured the attention of almost every man there. They would've been surprised to know that it was her sweet nature and not her past that made her popular.

After a few hours, they could bear it no longer.

"I don't know 'bout you," said one young lady, "but I ain't stayin' here with that fast woman another second. I'm askin' my man to take me home, while I still got 'im!"

Another agreed. "I'm with you. I have an idea," she giggled, "let's all say we have headaches. Serve 'im right if'n we all leave at the same time. Let 'em dance with each other!"

One after another pleaded ill and asked their escorts to leave. When the last woman left, the Smith girls bid the men goodnight.

"I'm afraid all the excitement set my head to poundin'," Hattie said theatrically. Her sisters snickered and followed her to the house. No female remained except Emma.

Charlie was furious. "Goddamn it! I knew there'd be mischief tonight! It's peculiar how they all started ailin' at the same time."

"Oh!" Emma said in dismay.

"That's all right," said Ezra. "Don't let 'em bother you. Reckon them hens is jealous."

"Josh, you gotta' take me home!"

"Why?" asked one of the Converse hands. "We'd all be powerful pleased if'n you stayed. It ain't much of a shindig if'n we ain't got no one to dance with. You're a damn sight prettier than a heifer branded feller."

The men laughed. Often, shindigs consisted of all males. With no women present, a few men were picked out and "heifer branded." These unfortunates would wear an apron or tie a scarf around their arm and dance the female part.

"I'd like to, but I couldn't. If'n I stayed it wouldn't look proper. The women made their point."

"Reckon they did," said Charlie.

"Well if'n she's leavin' reckon we'll all go. After dancin' with real women I don't feel like dancin' with no man!" said one of Charlie's hands.

Emma was close to tears most of the way home. She'd known her presence had bothered the other girls. Now because of her, the party had broken up early.

She and Josh were surprised to see Buford's horse tied outside the bakery.

"Hope everythin's all right!" said Emma, jumping from the wagon and rushing into the house.

She was puzzled but relieved to find both Tom and Buford sound asleep.

"Don't know what happened to Juan," she said, "but things seem all right."

"Reckon, I should wake 'im," said Josh.

"I wouldn't, Josh. He seems to be sleepin' real peaceful, like. Besides, don't think I stirred up any of the boys, but think I'd feel safer if'n I had a man here. After last time..." her voice trailed off and she touched the scars on her face.

"I'll stay with you, Emma. We'll wake up the Colonel and send 'im home."

"Seems a shame since he's already asleep."

Josh's heart felt heavy in his chest. He sighed loudly, and the mournful sound wasn't lost on her.

"I'm much obliged to you for bringin' me. I ain't never gonna' forget tonight no matter how it turned out. I felt like Cinderella and you was my Prince!"

"Well, I suppose if'n you want the Colonel to stay, I'll get along."

"Wait, Josh," she said as he turned to leave. She went to him and gave him a soft kiss on the cheek. "Thank you for a wonderful time."

He gave her another mournful look and left.

Emma turned around and studied the sleeping Buford. She got a blanket and covered him.

At her touch he woke with a start. He looked at her ample bosom as she leaned over him. He shut his eyes quickly and feigned sleep.

She straightened out and gently pushed his long, thick hair from his face. "Sleep well," she whispered. She was ready to withdraw when he took her hand and kissed it.

Her pulse raced at the feel of his lips and her face colored. She thought he'd been asleep. He stood up and crushed her to him.

With Tom in bed there was no place for them to go and Buford took her there on the floor. He knew he was making a terrible mistake, but she was as eager as he. Her touch had set off an explosion inside him and he had to have her.

When they were through, he said, "I'm sorry, Emma. I don't know what come over me. Shouldn't have done that."

"It's all right. I wanted to. It's been over a year since I had a man."

"Been a long time since I had a woman. Reckon that's why I lost my head. Shoulda' gone to the saloon and seen one of the girls. Had no call to bother you. Ain't helpin' you be respectable."

"Don't matter none. I ain't never gonna' be looked on as respectable. Folks 'round here, ain't never gonna' change. You been sayin' that all along and you was right." Her face was sad.

"Someone bother you?" he asked sharply.

"After you and Hi went back to town, the gals decided they was feelin' poorly and left. All at the same time! I was the only woman there. Me and Josh left directly but I'm sure there'll be talk."

"Damn," he swore softly. "Reckon I done you and Josh no favors."

"But you tried and I'm grateful," she said with a smile.

He looked at her. Now with his passion spent he was ashamed of himself for what he'd done. He felt as if he'd violated her, though she'd been willing.

"I better go Emma. Wouldn't do for folks to see me here."

On the way home, he chastised himself. He felt he'd betrayed Josh. "What the hell was I thinkin' tryin' to get them two together?" he thought. "That ain't bad enough but I go and poke 'er! Ain't gonna' get rid of 'er that way. God, I'm a jack ass!"

The next morning, he apologized to Josh. "I'm sorry 'bout last night. Emma tole me what happened. Hope none of the boys are riled with y'all for the women leavin'."

"No, but the way those fuckin' women was actin' riled the boys some."

News spread fast about Emma attending the Smith shindig and the women leaving. Stories grew about her staying alone with men from four outfits. Had she no shame?

Emma thought things couldn't get worse but as usual for her, they did.

One day as she walked to the general store, three burly cowhands stepped in front of her.

"Lookee here, boys," said one. "It's Emma! How you been Emma?"

"Just fine. Ain't seen you boys in a spell."

"Don't come to this part of the territory much. I hear tell you're a respectable woman now."

"Tryin' to be."

"This your kid?"

"Yea. This here's little Tom."

"Well, I'll be. You're still lookin' good," one of the men said looking her up and down in a lewd manner. "Seems a shame to waste all that talent you got. Whatta' you say?"

"Yea, how 'bout it?" one of his companions asked.

"Sorry boys. I been outta' business for a spell. Nice to see you again." She tried to push her way through, but they stood in her way.

"You too good to pass the time of day with us?" one of them leered.

"No, but ain't got no more to say to y'all. I best be about my business. Now if'n you'd just let me by, I'd be much obliged." She tried to push forward again and one of the men shoved her back roughly. Her eyes grew wide with fright and little Tom started to cry.

The street wasn't crowded that time of day and few people were around. Some of the women gathered and looked on smugly.

"Just what that hussy deserves," commented Joanne Smith.

The men who walked by chose to ignore the situation. They had no desire to tangle with the mean looking cow-punchers.

Abel Platts, the hotel owner, thought differently and sent one of his men for the Marshall. At the same time, Buford stepped from the general store.

He looked down the street and saw the backs of three men standing across the boardwalk. It was apparent they were blocking some one's way. Curious, Buford walked down to them.

As he drew closer he heard Emma say, "Please let me pass. I don't want no trouble."

Buford lengthened his stride and was there in a second. Taller than the men he stood behind, he looked over their heads at Emma, "These men botherin' you?"

She hated to start trouble, but it seemed unavoidable. She sighed, "Reckon, so."

They turned around to face him. His size didn't seem to daunt them. "Why don't you men go 'bout your business," Buford said.

"Who the hell are you?" one of them asked.

"Just a friend of Emma's. Now let 'er pass."

The man looked at his two companions and laughed, then lunged at Buford.

Buford grabbed him and one of the others. He banged their heads together with a loud crack. They fell to the boardwalk unconscious.

The third man stepped over them and threw a solid punch to Buford's middle.

Emma watched in horror as a brawl ensued. The few people in the street came together to watch the vicious fight. Buford's foe was no stranger to sparring with his fists and he held his own.

Hi and his deputy came over just as Buford bettered his opponent.

"What the hell's goin' on here?" he shouted.

Buford looked up from the bleeding man he held in the dust.

"Just tryin' to teach these varmints some manners, is all," he answered spitting a stream of blood.

"Well, let 'im go. I'll deal with this here."

Buford let go and stood up. He reached down and picked his hat up from the ground. He brushed it off nonchalantly.

"All right folks!" Hi called out. "The Colonel's done fightin' for today. Get on with your business." The crowd dispersed, and he looked down at the cowboy who sat in the street holding his jaw.

"Heard you and your friends was botherin' Emma," Hi said.

The man didn't answer.

"Mebbe' you'll find your tongue in the jailhouse. Clyde bring these varmints in." Clyde helped them up and led them away.

Tom was howling in fright and Emma held him in her arms, trying to comfort him.

"You all right?" Buford asked from split and swollen lips.

"Yea, I'm fine. I'm obliged to you."

"Well, I ain't," fumed Hi. "Lord Buford if'n you wasn't my friend your sorry ass would be in jail! Can't you come to town without causin' a ruckus? At least once a year you come in and tear the fuckin' place up!"

"Just keepin' you on your toes." Buford tried to smile

but his lacerated lips made it look more like a grimace. "Can I go back to my ranch, now? Or are you gonna arrest my sorry ass?" he asked with sarcastic humor.

"Lord! I don't know 'bout you. You're such a jack ass!" Hi said. He looked at Emma. "You sure you're all right?"

She nodded. Hi tipped his hat and turning his horse around, headed back to the jail house.

"You're bleedin' pretty bad, Colonel," Emma said.

"Just a few cuts."

"Come to the bakery and I'll tend to 'em."

"That ain't necessary."

Now that the fight was over he felt uncomfortable with her. He thought of the last time he'd been with her and her naked body came to mind. He was furious with himself but lashed out at her instead.

"Christ Emma! Them men coulda' hurt you," he snarled.

"Wasn't much I could do."

"There is somethin' you can do, goddamn it. Leave town. Josh tried to make an honest women outta' you and you won't have 'im. Why are you bein' so fuckin' stubborn?" his tone was soft but menacing.

She started to tremble. She wasn't in the mood to hear this.

She was perfectly aware that their intimate moment had meant nothing to him. He'd let his passions get the best of him and she'd taken advantage of it. Still, the annoyance he now displayed had her close to tears.

"Thanks again, Colonel," she said stiffly and walked to the general store.

Buford watched her and swore. "Fuckin' women! I'll never understand 'em!"

Busy with roundup, he didn't have an opportunity to go to town after that. A few weeks later he left for Kansas, Emma far from his mind.

When he got back, the Bell Star, a new saloon had come to town. Out of curiosity Buford went in. Hi greeted him.

"Howdy Buford. See you caught up with me. You been to the jailhouse?"

"What the hell for? You ain't never there!" Buford joked. "This here your new office?"

Hi laughed. "No. Still keep regular hours at the Longhorn. This here's a beauty though ain't it? Look at the whores! They sure are fine."

Buford looked around him. The interior of the saloon was superior to the ram shackle bar Frenchie had. The few women he saw were indeed pretty.

"Bet Frenchie don't like this none."

"No, he don't. This here's progress though. Thinkin' of hirin' another deputy. Thought I'd wait 'til you got back. You interested? Since you like fightin' so much thought you might want the job."

"No. Ain't interested. Had my fill with bein' a law man."

"All right," Hi sighed. "Don't know why I asked you. Knew you'd say no. Been by to see Emma?"

"No but I was goin' to. Gotta' place an order."

"Don't know if'n she's able."

Buford sighed. "Now what the hell happened?"

"Nothin'. Don't get put out! Them headaches she gets is growin' worse."

"Wish she'd move the hell outta' town or get hitched. Don't know why she's bein' so stubborn."

"She's bein' stubborn? How 'bout you! When you gonna' accept some responsibility for your boy?"

"Shit, Hi. Don't start on that again. It's growin' tiresome."

"Well you got an obligation. He's your's whether you like it or not and his Momma needs help!" Hi stopped talking. He could see that Buford was angry.

"Reckon I don't share your opinion. See you 'round." Buford strode out of the saloon.

He fumed as he made his way to the bakery. "Obligation!" he thought. "I ain't under obligation to nobody!"

When he entered the bakery, he noticed she didn't look well. She'd lost even more weight and had dark shadows under her eyes.

Tom, now nearly three, came from the back room and walked to Buford. He looked up, nearly tumbling backward.

"Howdy!" he shouted.

Buford smiled and looked down at the little boy. "Howdy," he replied shaking the little hand.

"The Marshall tole' me you ain't feelin' well," he said looking back at Emma.

"Get some pretty mean headaches, but I'll get by."

"You feel up to bakin' me my usual order? If'n you don't, that's all right. Take anythin' you can manage."

"No. I'm right as the mail. Ain't done much business since all you punchers been gone. Sure could use the money."

"Well, don't put yourself out."

Tom continued to stare at Buford. He leaned over and said, "How you doin' little feller?"

Tom grinned at the attention. He ran around to his mother and coyly hid behind her skirts.

It made Emma smile and feel warm inside. It was the first time the Colonel had ever acknowledged her son.

Tom peeked around her clean white apron and beamed at him.

"He's turnin' into a fine boy, Emma. You should be proud."

"I am," she said stroking the boy's hair.

Buford didn't notice that it was the same shade as his own.

"I'll bring this order out soon as I can."

"Don't push yourself." He placed some bills on the counter. "All right if'n I pay you for a month in advance?"

Her eyes lit up. "Would be fine." She reached out to take it with a trembling hand.

Her face grew a ghostly white and she swooned, hitting the floor hard. Buford rushed to her and Tom burst into tears.

"Jesus!" Buford said. He picked her up and carried her to her room. Tom followed behind him, wailing. The din drove Buford to distraction.

"Hush now! Ain't no need to cry. You're Momma's gonna' be all right," he said gruffly, frightening the little boy more.

Buford rushed outside. The first woman he saw was Alvirah Gibson and he called out to her.

She went to him. "Good afternoon, Colonel," she said looking in disdain at the shop behind him.

"Emma took sick and I need your help. Stay with 'er boy while I fetch Doc."

"I will do no such thing! How dare you ask?" she snapped.

Buford's quick temper flared.

"Alvirah, don't rile me," he said drawing himself up to his full frightening height. "Thought you was a good Christian. I'm askin' you to set with 'er boy for five minutes. Now get in there before I lose my patience!" His eyes flashed and Alvirah scurried into the shop.

When he and Doc got back to the bakery, Tom had stopped crying. He sat contentedly on Alvirah's ample lap.

Doc went to the bedroom.

"How is she?" Buford asked Alvirah. She got up and placed Tom in the chair she'd vacated.

"I don't know," she said tersely. "Didn't see 'er. The boy was here in the kitchen when I come in and here we stayed. You didn't ask me to watch 'er, just the boy."

Buford was about to reply but she cut him off. "Good day Colonel," she said and left in a huff.

Doc came out of the bedroom.

"Emma's all right. She's tired and not eatin' right."

"What?"

"The boy looks well enough. My guess is she don't have the money to feed 'er and the boy, too. She's goin' without. That's probably why she has those headaches. Would you set a spell with 'er and the boy while I get 'er a hot meal?"

"Reckon, so," Buford said deep in thought.

"Damn," he swore to himself. Tom scrambled down from the chair and ran to the bedroom. Buford followed.

Emma had come to and she smiled weakly.

Buford scowled at her, his eyes full of anger. "Doc, said you ain't been eatin'."

"I own a bakery. 'Course I'm eatin'."

"I ain't talkin' 'bout bread, Emma. When's the last time you had real vittles?"

She kept silent.

"I'm talkin' to you," he hissed.

She lay on the bed cuddling with Tom.

"I feed Tom proper. He's a growin' boy and gotta' eat

good."

"Is that what's goin' on here? You gotta' starve yourself to feed your boy?"

"I ain't exactly starvin'."

Buford strode back and forth in the tiny room. "Lord, Emma. I really don't know 'bout you. I thought Mabel was head strong, but you beat all! Sometimes I feel like hog tyin' you and bringin' you to a new town myself!"

"Sorry Colonel. Don't mean to put you out. Don't see you hardly a'tall, but when I do, I'm usually in trouble."

"Ain't that the truth. You'd have no trouble if'n you moved somewheres else."

Doc came back before Emma could reply.

"Can I leave, now?" Buford asked him.

Doc noticed Buford's furrowed brow, a telltale sign that he was perturbed. "Sure."

Buford turned on his heal and stormed out of the bakery, nearly knocking Hi off the boardwalk.

"Jesus, Buford. What's the matter with you? Heard Doc had to come down here. Emma feelin' poorly again?"

"Yea. Goddamn fool! Know why she's been ailin'?"

"My guess would be the beatin' she got."

"Wrong. She ain't eatin'. Starvin' 'erself so she can feed 'er boy."

"Well, I'll be," Hi said softly. "Why didn't she come to me for help? Me and her is ole' friends!"

"You're gonna' have to ask 'er that, 'cause I surely don't know." Buford brushed by Hi and made his way to the general store. He ordered a large quantity of food and had it sent to the bakery.

Buford was surprised to see Emma bright and early the next morning. She'd come to the ranch with his full order.

He didn't help her from the wagon and she got down herself. "Surprised to see you today," he said.

"I'm feelin' better."

He brought the baskets into the cookhouse and Juan emptied them. When he came back out Emma handed him some money.

"What's this?" he asked.

"Payin' you back for all that food," she answered.

"Don't want it. You ain't gonna' get ahead if'n you don't keep it."

For the first time, Emma's voice held a hint of frost. "Ain't acceptin' your help no more. Seems clear to me that you don't like givin' it."

"Aw, Emma..."

"No, I mean it, Colonel. You ain't obliged to me. Thanks all the same."

She scrambled back up into the wagon and slapped the reins. The wagon lurched and went on its way.

Buford stood dumbly looking at the money in his hand. It was the crisp new bills he'd given her yesterday for his order.

"Goddamn it, to hell!" he swore and called out to her.

She heard him but ignored it. She cracked her whip and sent the horse into a gallop. Buford jumped on his horse and went in pursuit.

He had no trouble catching up to her although she tried to outrun him. He shouted for her to stop but she glared at him and came down harder with her whip. In a fury, he rode up front and grabbed the horse buy it's bridle and eventually the wagon came to a stop.

He was beside himself with rage. "What the fuck's wrong with you?" he roared. "Tryin' to kill yourself and the boy? Why wouldn't you stop?"

"Don't want the money back. That's what you followed me for, ain't it?"

"Lord, Emma. You do try me. This here's why I get riled at you. I paid you fair for my goods. The food was just somethin' I done. How am I gonna' get my bread if'n you're half dead?"

"It ain't that. I don't need your fuckin' money. You look down at me and you always did! You make me feel dirty and cheap."

Emma seldom lost her temper and now that she had, she felt ashamed and looked away. Buford didn't know what to make of it and remained silent. His horse snorted and broke the uncomfortable silence.

Buford looked down and saw one of her empty baskets close at hand. Quickly and silently he slid the money into it.

"Take the fuckin' money. If'n not for you take it for the boy. Now go on. Don't let me keep you."

She flicked the reins and headed towards town. Buford watched her for a while and then rode back to the ranch.

"Damnation, never seen Emma that riled before!" he thought to himself. In his fashion, he didn't dwell on it and she slipped from his mind.

After that, they saw each other occasionally either in town or at the ranch. Buford would tip his hat politely but never stopped to speak with her.

Emma chastised herself for her foolish outburst. Her anger had accomplished nothing and now he wouldn't talk to her.

A few weeks later Hi came to the ranch, Tom in the saddle in front of him.

"Howdy, girls!" he called to the men gathered together for their noon meal. "Where's the Colonel?"

"Here I am," said Buford coming from the barn. "What you got there?" he asked Hi.

"What's it look like? It's Tom."

"I know that! What's he doin' with you?"

"Emma's feelin' poorly. She got pneumonia. Doin' two jobs got 'er run down."

Emma's bakery business had continued to fail. She supplemented her meager earnings by taking in laundry from some of the local outfits.

"So? You come all the way out here to tell me that?"

"'Course not! Let me finish. Emma's feelin' poorly and I tole 'er I'd watch the boy. When I got back to the jailhouse the place was turned upside down. I ain't got time to watch 'im after all. Thought you could do me a favor and keep an eye on the little feller."

"Come again?" Buford asked not sure he heard Hi correctly.

"You heard me. I can't watch the boy so I brung 'im here to you."

"Can't you find a woman to watch 'im or bring 'im back to Emma?"

Hi snorted. "Can't. Emma's sicker n' a dog and what woman's gonna' watch a bastard?"

"Don't know, Hi, but it ain't my fuckin' problem!" Buford steamed.

"Watch your language in front of the boy," scolded Hi.

"Well, dang it! Don't know where you get these foolish notions. You volunteered to watch 'im, not me!"

Hi got down from his horse. "I know that, but it ain't workin' out. You gotta take 'im," he scowled at Buford.

Hi took Tom down from the saddle. "This here's the Colonel. You know 'im, don't you? He's a jack ass!"

"Jack ass!" Tom said happily.

Hi guffawed. "That's right! See Buford? The boy learns quick!"

"Ain't keepin' 'im here. I'm followin' you right back to town."

"Go ahead, I won't be there. Got business to tend to. Besides, it'll be good for the boy to be 'round men. Ain't good for 'im bein' with his Ma all the time."

"I don't care."

"Don't I know it!" Hi said exasperated. "But that ain't the point. I'm leavin' 'im here and I'll pick 'im up later."

Hi jumped in the saddle and raced away.

Buford's eyes narrowed, and he hollered out, "Hi, you come back here!" Hi turned and waved but kept on going. The dust closed over him and he was lost from sight.

"Goddamn son of a bitch!" Buford swore out loud.

"Jack ass!" Tom said pointing to him.

"Hush!" Buford barked and Tom looked at him with frightened eyes.

Buford sighed and studied the little boy. For a second he saw something familiar but the thought passed as swiftly as it had come. He smiled at him and said in a softer tone, "Well little buckaroo what am I gonna' do with you? You're just a little tad pole!"

Buford looked off and saw his men getting ready to get back to work.

"Hold on there!" he shouted, striding towards them. "Which one of y'all wants to watch the kid?"

"Not me," they all mumbled and walked quickly to their horses and chores.

"How 'bout you Josh."

"Don't think so, Colonel. You hired me on to watch cows not younguns!"

Buford grew irritated. "Juan. Looks like you got the job. Take this little varmint here and keep 'im under your wing."

"It will be a pleasure. Tom and I have grown to be friends. Right, amigo?"

"Si!" Tom said.

Buford looked surprised. "He knows Spanish?"

"A little. I teach him a few words here and there."

"Well, keep 'im outta' my way," Buford said.

Hi congratulated himself all the way back to town. He'd make Buford realize Tom was his one way or another.

Several hours later when he went back to get Tom he was disappointed to find Buford gone.

"Where's the Colonel?" he asked Juan.

"Out riding line."

"Did he spend any time with the boy?"

Juan laughed. "The Colonel? No!"

When Hi brought him back to the bakery, Tom babbled a blue streak. Although the three-year old's words were unintelligible to Hi, Emma understood.

She looked at Hi, her eyes bright with fever and anger. "Did you bring him to the Colonel's?" she asked incredulously.

Before Hi could respond, Tom answered, "Si."

CHAPTER TEN

The next time Emma went to the ranch to bring the bakery order she had trouble getting little Tom to leave.

He began to cry and hold out his arms to Juan. "Amigo!" he cried.

Emma said gently. "Amigo has work to do, honey. He's too busy to watch a little boy. Looks like my boy's takin' a shinin' to you," she smiled. "Never seen 'im fuss like that."

As she turned the wagon around Tom twisted in his seat and once again appealed to Juan. "Amigo!" he cried pitifully. It was more than Juan could bear.

"Stop Signorita!" he shouted running to the wagon. "Can he stay? I'll bring him home after chow. I promise to take good care of him."

"That's right kind of you but the Colonel wouldn't like it."

"I know, but he's never here. He doesn't come off the line. When he does, he doesn't stay long. As long as I get my chores done, he won't mind."

"You sure?" Emma asked.

"Si. Please Signorita!" Juan pleaded although he was sure of no such thing.

Emma relented. "All right. I reckon it'll do 'im good to be 'round a man." She handed Tom down and went on her way.

Much to Juan's relief Buford missed the noon meal. He hoped he could feed the men supper and head to town before Buford came back in the evening.

Juan doted on the little boy and they enjoyed a pleasant day. He showed Tom how to throw grain to the chickens and feed the pigs. Tom was well behaved and didn't hinder Juan as he went about his tasks.

After dinner, Juan quickly saddled a horse. He was in a rush to leave before Buford returned, but was unsuccessful. He could see him approaching and knew it would be foolish to run.

"What's he doin' here?" Buford snapped, pointing at Tom.

"He and Emma came this morning and he wanted to stay."

"So you let 'im."

"Si, Colonel. He's a good boy and I did not think it would do any harm."

"Well you was wrong. Don't want 'im here," Buford said angrily.

"All right Colonel. I will not do it again. I will bring him home now."

"I will," said Buford. "I gotta talk to Emma 'bout this. I don't want this here to happen again."

"No, Colonel! She didn't want to leave him. She knew you'd be angry. Please don't say anything to her. I'll take him back."

"Pass the boy up to me, Juan."

Juan did as he was told. He learned a long time ago that Buford was not a man to argue with.

During this exchange, Tom looked at both men with wide frightened eyes. It was clear to the child that he wasn't wanted, and the tall man was angry. Now as Juan handed him to Buford, he started to cry.

"Amigo!" he called out.

"Good bye little friend," Juan said with a smile. "Don't cry. The Colonel is taking you back to your Momma. I'll see you in a few days."

Buford sighed as he trotted off with the squirming child. He looked down at him and again saw something familiar in the boy's face. "Looks like someone I know but can't put my finger on who," he thought.

"Stop your cryin' buckaroo. I ain't gonna bite you," he said quietly. He awkwardly stroked the boy's hair.

Tom ceased his sniveling and soon the gentle motion of the horse had him fast asleep.

When Buford got to the bakery Emma was surprised to

see him.

"Where's Juan," she asked nervously, taking the sleeping toddler.

"Left 'im back at the ranch. I wanna' talk to you," he said.

"Let me put Tom to bed first." She knew by the look in Buford's eyes that he was angry.

She came out of the bedroom and straightened her shoulders in determination. She wasn't going to let him upset her.

"What is it you wanna' talk to me 'bout?"

"Don't take kindly to you leavin' the boy at the ranch," he said coldly.

"I didn't think you would. I was mighty surprised when Juan insisted. Shoulda' knowed better."

"Yea, you shoulda'. Don't do it again."

His obvious contempt for her and her child made her furious. She took a few deep breaths to calm herself. When she finally spoke, her voice trembled.

"Me and you used to be friends, Colonel. Lately seems that you don't like me or my boy none."

"Well, truth to tell Emma, I don't need this shit. If'n you don't wanna' start over somewhere new, I can't make you, but stop shovin' your boy in my face."

Her anger mounted, and her face grew flushed. "I'll never leave 'im there again. You have my word."

"Good." He tipped his hat and left.

She was steaming mad even though she knew he was right. She had no reason to stay in town except for her love for him. A love that was eating her alive and putting a strain on their already fragile relationship. Good to her word, Emma never left Tom again.

One morning as Buford groomed his horse he felt a quiet presence behind him. He turned and saw little Tom staring at him.

"Where's your Momma?" he asked.

Tom pointed outside.

"What you doin' here?"

"See hosses," Tom said, his eyes all aglow.

Buford looked at the little boy and sighed. "Well, c'mon

over. If'n you wanna' see 'im you might as well come up close," he said irritably.

Tom went over and looked up at the stallion Buford was brushing. "He's big."

"Yea, reckon he is. You wanna' pat 'im?"

"Yes!"

Buford picked him up and held him close to the horse. Tom patted its side.

"Nice hoss," he smiled.

Emma and Juan stood conversing in front of the cookhouse. Emma glanced down and saw that Tom was gone.

"Tom?" she called turning around and glancing in all directions. "Juan, did you see where he went?" she asked in panic.

"No, but don't worry, he couldn't have gone far." They spread out and began searching for him.

Buford had just set Tom on top of the horse when Emma came in.

"There you are," she said, relief flooding through her. "You gave Momma a scare! Sorry, Colonel. Didn't mean for 'im to pester you." Her tone cold.

"No harm done."

"C'mon' Tom we gotta' go."

The little boy held out his arms to her and she took him from the horse. Buford resumed grooming the stallion and she turned on her heel and left.

Buford watched her out of the corner of his eye as she departed, carrying Tom over her shoulder. Tom smiled at him and waved. It was then that recognition hit Buford like a thunderbolt.

He finally knew who fathered Tom and it made his knees feel weak. He held on to the horse for support. "Well, I'll be!" he thought. "Tom's that boy's Daddy!" Pieces of the puzzle started to come together.

Emma claimed he was her only customer, but he'd never been sure. He hadn't asked for her fidelity and didn't expect it. It was possible, even probable that she'd lain with his late brother.

He always thought she'd conceived her baby while he was in Ellsworth, but Tom had been with him. Tom must've gotten her pregnant before they left.

It explained why she told Buford the child was his. Tom had been killed and she had nowhere else to turn. He might've been married at the time, but he was alive.

He was relieved that the boy wasn't his but felt a sense of obligation all the same. He wondered what he should do about it. He grew confused and rode into town to see Hi.

He told him of the conclusion he'd come to and Hi laughed.

"He does look a heap like Tom, but he looks like you, too."

"'Course he does. Me and Tom was brothers. Looks more like Tom, though. Hell! She even named the kid after 'im! The whole thing makes sense."

"You still won't admit he's yours, will you?" Hi's blue eyes blazed with anger.

"Don't want to talk 'bout this here no more. Why you so sure he ain't Tom's? Do you know for a fact the boy ain't his?"

"Can't say that I do."

"Well then. That's what I been tryin' to tell y'all. There's only one person who'd know for sure and he ain't with us no more."

"You're forgettin' 'bout Emma. She knows and she says he's yours."

"Fuck what Emma says. That kid looks like Tom. Now that I know he's kin, I'm prepared to help Emma care for 'im."

Hi sighed, "How?"

"I don't rightly know. Gonna' have to think on it. Came as a surprise, I tell you that."

Hi shook his head. He thought it best to let Buford think little Tom was his brother's, if it helped Emma.

Buford did think about it but came to no satisfactory conclusion. After Mabel he couldn't open his heart again, even for his brother's son.

They'd be starting roundup in a few days and he had enough on his mind. In his usual manner both little Tom and Emma were forgotten for the moment. He'd deal with it later.

• • •

One morning Clyde came riding in hard and fast.

"Colonel. The Marshall wants you to come to town right away! We got Injun' trouble. Says for you come quick and bring some of your boys."

"What kinda' trouble?"

"He didn't say."

"Jesus Christ!" Buford swore. "All right. Gimme' a minute." Buford got his gear and some of his crew.

When they reached the jailhouse, Buford was surprised by the number of men that waited outside. All were heavily armed and ready to ride. It put him in a worse temper. He wasn't in the mood for Hi's histrionics. He strode into the jailhouse and Hi noticed his fierce look.

Charlie, Zeb, Junior and two other men were inside.

"I gotta' talk to the Colonel in private," Hi said. "Y'all mind steppin' outside?"

When the door closed behind them, Buford hissed, "What the fuck's wrong with you. Why you botherin' me when you got all these men?"

Hi was in no mood himself and glared at his friend. "James Boutwell and his family was found kilt' in their beds this mornin'. His men, too. All his livestock's gone. One of his hands was at the Longhorn all night and come back this mornin' and found 'em." He suddenly had Buford's attention.

"Apache?" Buford asked.

"Lord, you're quick!" Hi said sarcastically. "Need you to come and help me track 'em."

Buford shook his head in disbelief. "Track 'em? Shit, Hi, ain't gonna' be hard. James had over a thousand head! Don't tell me you can't follow that?"

"All right," Hi sighed. "Truth is you're still the best fuckin' fighter in these parts. You're a good leader, too. I need you if'n I'm gonna' get them red skinned varmints!"

Apaches were bad business and Buford sighed, "Let's go."

They rode towards the Boutwell ranch. When they were a mile away Buford said, "Let me go in first and have a good look. Havin' all these men stompin' 'round is only gonna confuse things."

Hi and the others waited while Buford went to the ranch alone. After a time, he came back and Hi rode out to meet him.

"Apache all right. 'Bout forty of 'em."

"That many?" Hi asked, surprised. He shook his head sadly, "We got twenty-eight men, includin' you and me. Reckon we got enough."

"Against Apache?" Buford laughed coldly. "Need twice as many as we got. In that whole group there ain't more than a handful of fightin' men. The only ones worth a shit are the ones who fought in the war."

"Ya think we should send someone to fetch more?" asked Hi.

"There ain't no time. The Apache left a clear trail. Gettin' cold, though. Figure its 'bout twelve hours old."

They rode up to the waiting men. "The Colonel got a clear trail. Figures there's 'bout twenty of 'em." Hi lied. He didn't want to scare them.

"Gonna' have to ride like hell," Buford mumbled.

Hi continued. "Gonna' have to ride hard. We'll catch up to 'em, though. Them beeves they stole is gonna' slow 'em down."

Buford could see the battle lust in Hi's eyes and wondered if his looked the same.

They followed the trail well into the night. They were getting close when Hi said, "We gotta stop Buford, I can't press these men no more. They's real tired."

"Bunch of ole' ladies," Buford said, his adrenaline racing. "The Apaches ain't that far off. Tracks is fresh. Now's the time to take 'em. You know they don't like to fight at night."

"I know that, but these men need some rest. They ain't gonna' be worth shit if'n they don't get some. Our odds are pretty fuckin' bad as it is."

Buford remained quiet, deep in thought. Finally, he spoke. "All right, Hi. I got a plan. Let the men stop but don't make camp. If'n memory serves me well, there's a spot up yonder that we might be able to use. If'n it's there, the men can rest."

"Well go on and find it then. Don't take too long."

Buford rode on ahead. He returned a short time later and said, "Found it. It's an ole' river bed. There's high ground on either side. We'll set up two groups, you take one side with half the men and I'll take the other. I'll go flush them Injuns out and lead 'em right through the bed. After I come through start shootin'. We'll catch 'em in a crossfire. Figure it's the only way we're gonna' be able to take 'em."

"In the mornin'?"

"Hell no, tonight."

Hi was about to protest but Buford cut him off.

"I know the boys need rest. We'll wait a coupla' hours then I'll go after 'em."

"Reckon, that'll have to do. These men ain't as tough as we are!" Hi smiled.

"Hope you're feelin' tough, Hi. This here fight's gonna' be a mean one."

Hi gathered up the weary men and they followed Buford to the river bed.

"O.K. men," Buford said when they reached their destination. "Y'all can make camp but don't light no fires. When you're settled, I'll tell y'all what we're gonna do."

"This here's my idea," he said when they were gathered around. He explained it to them and drew diagrams in the dirt. "I'll be the first one in so don't none of you girls shoot me!"

The men huddled around the camp speaking low. Without any fires it was dark, adding to their fear. Every heart beat fast. The Apaches were the most frightening of the tribes. Some knew they wouldn't get much sleep imagining what might lay ahead of them.

A few hours later Buford decided to put his plan in effect. "I'm gonna' go find 'em," he told Hi. "Get the men ready."

"You goin' after 'em alone?" Zeb asked incredulously.

"Better that way. Just want y'all to be ready."

Buford got on his horse and the spirited animal reared. He sat large and menacing on the huge horse. The light of the moon illuminated him and his hair flashed silver. To the men assembled he looked like some ancient God of war and the sight of him filled them with awe. His appearance bolstered the courage of more than one man there.

"See you girls soon," he said and rode off into the darkness.

He came across the cattle first. "Whoo cow!" he hollered firing off his gun. He started a stampede and herded them in the direction of Wilder Creek.

The commotion startled the sleeping Indians and they jumped up in surprise. The few on watch were already on horseback and in pursuit of the cows. They were the first to see him.

Buford acted as if he were drunk. He needed to give his noisy behavior some credence, or the Apache would know he was leading them into a trap.

"Eeeeh haaah!" he called out reeling in his saddle and firing his gun again. He led the Indians away from the cattle and straight for where Hi and the men waited.

Although he'd done his best to divert the animals from the camp a few stray steers thundered down the river bed, upsetting everything and scattering horses.

"Buford, you fuckin' moron," Hi swore to himself. Out loud he called, "Reckon, the Colonel ain't far behind them cows. Let's get ready!"

They had been in position only a short time when Buford came flying through the gully, firing his gun and yelling. When he got past the waiting men, he jumped from his horse and ran to join them.

"Steady boys," he said, "here they come!" As the Indians came down the narrow bed, shots rang out. Buford's plan was working beautifully. Caught in a crossfire, most of the Indians were killed instantly. A few jumped from their horses and scrambled up the banks to pursue their attackers.

It was difficult for the men to distinguish friend from foe in the pitch darkness. Buford's eyes and hearing had grown keen during his Ranger years and he had no trouble. Two men rolled on the ground nearby and Buford crept up and quietly stabbed the Indian in the back.

"Much obliged," Charlie panted, his eyes large with fear.

Buford heard a stealthy tread behind him and whirled in time to meet his opponent face to face. Buford grabbed the man and the knife the Indian held swished down and sunk into his massive fore arm. He didn't release his grip and threw the Indian back. When the Apache hit the dirt, Buford jumped on top of him and cut his throat quickly and noiselessly. The battle went on. Hi and Buford were expert marksmen and their shots rang true.

The few Indians who survived fled into the night. When Buford was satisfied that they were either dead or gone, he gathered his men and had them lay quiet. After a while he could hear no sound from the opposite bank and whistled to Hi in Comanche fashion.

On the other side, Hi returned the call.

"All right," Buford said to the men, "fall out."

Slowly the men climbed down the banks and gathered in the middle of the dry bed. Hi lit a lantern and held it up. "Let's count our losses." In the end it was discovered that five men were missing, two from Buford's group and three from Hi's.

The men lit more lanterns and went in search of their comrades. They found two dead and three seriously injured. One of the injured was Junior Converse.

Buford instinctively began to bark out orders and soon the camp was full of activity. Men were busy building fires and helping those less seriously wounded.

Hi and Buford worked side by side, tending the wounded men. It would take all their battlefield skill to help them.

In his weariness it took Hi awhile to notice that the sleeve of Buford's jacket was soaked with blood.

"Buford, you hurt?" he asked.

"What?"

"Your arm."

"Oh, yea. Just a scratch," he said, distracted. He was busy trying to save Junior Converse. He leaned back on his haunches and looked up at Zeb. The older man's face was etched with worry.

As much as Buford disliked Junior, he was fond of Zeb. "Don't worry. Your boy's gonna' be just fine," he said with a reassurance he didn't feel for in truth, Junior's wounds were severe. He left Zeb with his son and walked over to other men who needed attention.

"Take care of that arm," Hi called out after him.

Soon everyone had been tended to and they lay wearily around the blazing campfires.

"Reckon, you don't plan on movin' tonight," Buford said to Hi.

"Fuck, no. These men done rode all day and fought all night. They need rest and I do, too. You're the only one still prancin' 'round like a danged fool. Don't you ever get tired?"

"This here ain't no time for me to set on my ass. We got three men who need to get back to town. They can't wait 'til mornin'."

"Well, they's gonna have to. The men can't go no more."

Buford looked around. "Zeb, are you too tired to head back to Wilder Creek with your boy?"

"Of course not."

"Good. I need one more man. Any volunteers?"

"I'll go," said Charlie.

After the fight, Buford had asked some of the men to make three travoises to transport the seriously wounded. Now he tied one each behind their horses and the three men set off. They made it back to town by late afternoon.

All of them were dirty and bloody and they attracted a large crowd as they made their way towards Doc's.

"You get them fuckers, Colonel?" asked one onlooker. The townsfolk were still stunned by the deaths of the Boutwell family.

"Most of 'em," he answered.

After placing their charges with Doc, Buford suggested they go to the Long Horn for a drink.

"I'll stay with Junior," Zeb said.

The poor man was distraught, and Buford spoke to him gently. "A drink would do you good, Zeb. Besides, I think Doc could tend to 'im better if'n you wasn't hangin' 'round. You can come back in a little while."

"All right," Zeb sighed.

They were too tired to be concerned about their disheveled appearance and it created a stir in the Longhorn just as it had on the street.

Several people rushed over to them asking news of

loved ones. Other's wanted to know about the fight.

Buford answered wearily. "Zeb's boy, Wyn Hudson and Harry Ellis is at Doc's. Y'all have to wait 'til the Marshall gets back for any more news." He'd let Hi talk to the families of the two men who'd been killed.

Dusk was just falling when the rest of the posse straggled into town. Some of the townspeople saw the forlorn group and the two dead men. As news of their arrival travelled, other people came racing out to the street.

A while later, Hi came into the Long Horn with the other men. Buford was the only one of the first group left. Zeb was at Doc's and Charlie had gone home.

"What the hell took you so long?" he teased. "Reckon you'd have three more dead if'n I'd waited for you girls!"

His coolness and nonchalant manner encouraged the tired men and after a few drinks they were full of bravado and strutted around, patting each other on the back. They sported their wounds proudly. To the townspeople they were heroes.

"By Jesus," said one, "we sure showed them fuckin' Indians. I reckon it'll be awhile 'fore they come back here!"

"How's the arm?" Hi asked Buford.

"A little stiff but reckon it'll be all right."

"Did you have Doc look at it?"

"Nah. I already bandaged it up. He got better things to do. Tend to it when I get home, just was waitin' for you."

"Much obliged Buford, coulda' never done this without you. Woulda' been a slaughter."

"We was lucky to have good ground to fight 'em on. Most of those ranchers couldn't hit the side of a fuckin' barn. Havin' all them Apache in a narrow place, meant the men couldn't miss. Now if'n you'll excuse me, I gotta get back to the ranch. I still got roundup. Reckon you can do without me for a while?"

"Reckon, so," Hi smiled. "By the way. You see any of James cows when you come in?"

"No, they probably gone back to 'is ranch. What're you gonna' do with 'em?" Buford asked.

"Don't rightly know. There ain't no Boutwell's left to give 'em to. Reckon the only fair thing to do would be to divide 'em up between you and the other ranchers that come with us."

"Whatever. I'll have some of my men take care of it."

The men who'd ridden out told the townspeople about Buford's strategy in fighting overwhelming odds. They'd been proud to have Buford living in their midst but after that day his reputation grew tenfold.

Some of the men told of Buford sitting tall and thundering in the saddle, his horse rearing like a mad thing. Tales of him charging the Apache alone grew with each telling until the people of Wilder Creek thought him the biggest hero in the territory.

Buford, busy with roundup, didn't go to town, nor to the funeral of the Boutwell family. He meant no disrespect but preferred to stay on the ranch. He wasn't aware that the story of their fight with the Apache grew with each telling.

He went to town to get supplies and was surprised at the reaction his presence caused. People greeted him more congenially than usual and many young ladies blushed and curtsied at his approach.

He stopped by the jailhouse to see Hi.

"What the hell's ailin' everyone in town? They's all lookin' and actin' kinda' strange."

"When word got 'round 'bout our fight with the Apache you become Wilder Creek's most outstandin' citizen!"

Buford laughed coldly. "I ain't no hero, just good with a gun."

"I know that but these folks is impressionable. In fact, all the gals is houndin' Lydia 'bout you. If'n you're ever of a mind to marry again you could have your pick."

Buford snorted. "Ain't got no use for women. They're all a pain in the ass, even Mabel, and I loved her more than life."

"Speakin' of Mabel, you goin' to Dodge this year?"

"Yea, now that the railroad's finished. Me and Victor's meetin' up there."

"I hear it's one hellacious town."

"Can't be worse than Abilene."

"Mebbe' so. Don't mean to pester you but you decided anythin' yet?"

Buford knew what he referred to and his temper flared.

"No, so stop askin'. When I do, you'll be the first to know."

When Buford left the jailhouse, he went to see Emma.

Emma couldn't stay mad at him for long so she beamed when he came in. "Why Colonel, what brings you here?"

"Come to tell you that me and my men is movin' out in two days. I'll let you know when we come back."

"Good enough," she said.

Tom came bounding from the back of the store and ran over to Buford. "Howdy!" he beamed.

"Howdy," Buford smiled back.

"Where's the hoss?" he asked.

"Outside."

"I wanna' see 'im."

"Lord, Tom. You can see all the horses you want, you ain't got no call to bother the Colonel."

Now that Buford knew the boy to be Tom's he was indulgent.   "No bother. I'll bring 'im out."

Emma stood dumbfounded as the two went outside.

"Ain't this peculiar!" she thought to herself. They came in a short time later and Tom's face was flush with excitement. "The boy's almost old enough to learn to ride," Buford said.

"Reckon so, but I ain't got no time and no pony."

If she were the type to complain she would have told him how difficult it was to raise a boy without a man around or anyone else for that matter. She'd been forced to turn her back on Jamie and she had no friends. She and Tom led a lonely existence.

"When I come back I'll see to it. I can bring you one of my ponies and have one of my men teach 'im."

"That's right kind of you."

"I don't wanna' get you riled, Emma, but I want you to take some money. If'n I made you feel beholdin' to me in the past I'm sorry for it. Wasn't my intention. With all the outfits gone it's gonna' be hard for you. Don't wanna' come back and find you half dead with hunger like last year."

"It's all right Colonel. I'll get by. Saved half the money I made washin'. Enough I figure to carry me through 'til they get back."

His face grew hard and his eyes flashed. Emma instantly

regretted her words. Hadn't he told her once that it was her refusal of help that made him angry? She made amends quickly.

"But I'll take it all the same, just in case. If'n I don't use it, I'll give it back to you when you come in."

He still looked fierce. "By Christ if'n you don't use this money to take proper care of you and the boy, I'm gonna shoot you when I get back."

Emma smiled and breathed a sigh of relief. The Colonel was back to normal.

"See you when I get back," he said to her, then looking down at Tom, "You take good care of your Momma, while I'm gone."

• • •

Buford met Victor in Dodge City. The town had been founded four years ago and was a favorite hangout for buffalo hunters, drifters, gamblers and desperados. Last fall they'd run the rail road through and now it was a bustling cattle town as well.

It was twice as big and noisy as Abilene and Buford warned his men to be on their guard.

The law in Dodge that spring was a tall, charismatic man named Wyatt Earp. He'd been a lawman in Wichita and was making a name for himself.

Wyatt had befriended his predecessor, Bat Masterson who'd recently come back to town. It was said Bat had to flee Texas after killing a man and a dancehall girl.

One day as Buford stood outside the hotel talking to some ranchers, the two men came up to him.

"Colonel McLeod?" Wyatt enquired.

"Yea."

Wyatt extended his hand. "I'm Earp, Wyatt Earp. This here's Bat Masterson. We heard 'bout you and wanted to meet you."

Buford shook their hands. "I ain't gonna' cause no trouble," he said solemnly.

Both men laughed, and Wyatt said, "We didn't think you would. I don't think there's anyone in the west who hasn't heard about you when you were with the Rangers."

Buford smiled uncomfortably.

"We'd be obliged if you'd join us for a drink," Bat said.

"Sounds good." Buford excused himself from the group and he and the two men made their way down the boardwalk.

"I've heard that you are one of the best Indian fighters the Rangers ever had," said Wyatt.

"You know how people talk," Buford said modestly, "They tend to exaggerate. I met Wild Bill when he was Marshal of Abilene. He made quite an impression on me. He has a reputation and is a fine lookin' man to boot. Tole' me hisself that he ain't kilt' half the men they give 'im credit for."

"Probably true. His law days are over." said Bat, "They say he got himself married and is in the Dakota territory mining for gold."

"Well I hope he prospers. I thought he was a nice feller."

• • •

Buford decided that he didn't like Dodge City much, nor did he envy Wyatt his job. Although most cow towns were wild and noisy, Dodge was especially so. Most nights the sound of gunfire and brawling kept Buford awake. He was glad when it was time to leave.

On the way back to Wilder Creek he thought of little Tom. He wasn't sure the boy was his brother's child and decided to spend more time with him to make certain.

After he was back a few days he went to town to see Emma.

"Here's that money you loaned me," she said, pushing a handful of bills across the counter. "Didn't need it after all. You ain't gonna' shoot me, are you?", she said with a smile.

He studied her and decided she looked healthy enough. He supposed she hadn't lied about having some money saved.

"Well keep it anyways. Lord knows my ranch is thrivin' and I got plenty to spare."

"Wish I was that lucky", she blurted. She didn't want his pity.

"Well, you know what I think of that. Wilder Creek ain't no place for you. Folks ain't never gonna' give you a break, seems to me. Still don't know why you're so danged stubborn."

"I don't know why either," she said with a sigh. Inwardly

she yearned to tell him that she loved him.

They both remained silent lost in their own thoughts.

"I come to place my order," Buford said after a while. "When you bring it to the ranch, leave the boy with Juan. I tole' you before I left for Dodge that we'd teach 'im how to ride."

"All right," Emma said trying to conceal her surprise. She hadn't expected him to keep his word. Then she remembered how he'd been before he left for Dodge. He had seemed, well, almost human! "I'll be there in the mornin'."

After Buford left the bakery he went to see Hi.

"How was Dodge?" he asked.

"A fuckin' nightmare. Don't know how decent folks can live there. Ain't never seen such carryin' on."

"Bet you're glad to be back."

"That's the truth. Thought I'd come in and tell you what I decided to do 'bout Emma's boy."

"It's 'bout fuckin' time." Hi was clearly irritated with his friend.

"Pretty certain he's Tom's but I plan on spendin' time with 'im to make sure."

Hi tried to hide his growing frustration. "Then what?"

"Still don't know. Figure it'll come to me."

Hi had enough and lost his temper. "Lord, Jesus! You are somethin'! What's your fuckin' hurry? Why don't y'all wait 'til he's full growed. Mebbe' by then you'll decide what to do!"

Buford looked at Hi with a cold stare. It was a look Hi knew well. A look that registered no emotion. Through gritted teeth, Buford said, "I ain't doin' nothin' 'til I know for sure."

Hi shook his head. His anger turned to sadness. When he looked at Buford he had tears in his eyes. "Y'know what? I always knew you had a hard heart, but I never had no idea how bad you was. Even when we was kids you was never one to show your feelins'. I know the war changed you some, changed me too. Joinin' up with the Rangers when we got out didn't help none either. But Lord! I been through the same as you and I ain't the cold-blooded son of a bitch you are. You ain't right. I think sometimes you ain't got no heart a'tall."

"You're right when you say I'm cold blooded. Mebbe' I was born that way. I had no trouble killin' in the war. I was a soldier and it was my job. Because I was a cold-blooded killer they moved me all the way up to the rank of Colonel. I was just a fuckin' kid and they gave me the rank of Colonel!" Buford said, his eyes glassy as marbles. "I had obligations you didn't. I didn't want the goddamn job. When I made the wrong decision, I saw men get slaughtered 'cause of it. Even when we was Rangers they put me in charge, didn't they? You was good at killin' too. Why didn't they put you in charge?"

Hi laughed despite himself. "Ya' know why. I was a fuck up. I liked whores, whiskey and cards too much. You were different. You're always fuckin' serious and don't like no fun."

"I was a fuck up too. I made decisions that got men and some innocent people kilt'. I know it made me hard! I learned a long time ago not to let my feelins' get in the way." He didn't want to tell Hi that he saw their faces in his dreams.

"Mebbe' so, but you ain't in the army or a lawman no more! You ain't in charge of nobody or anything 'ceptin your own self. Ya' gotta' mend your ways, like I did."

"Well, maybe you could. When I left the Rangers I hoped to be like you. Tried to get some feelins' back and Tom was kilt. Tried again with Mabel and you saw what happened with that. Lost 'er and my baby boy." Suddenly the fight went out of them both.

Hi put his hand on Buford's arm and said softly, "It's a shame 'bout them but that was the Lord's will. It's time to be a human being again. Come back to the livin'."

"Tried it and it didn't work out."

Hi sighed heavily. "I know you're a good man. That's why I can't figure you denyin' Emma's boy. I know you're too much of a jack ass to see he's yours but that ain't the point. You think he's Tom's and you still ain't doin' nothin' 'bout it."

"Ain't you heard what I said? I'm gonna spend more time with 'im. Thought it would make you happy."

"You claimin' that chile, one way or the other would

make me happy!"

Don't know why we talk 'bout this here, Hi. Always makes us quarrel."

"It does," Hi sighed, "Just wish you'd do the right thing."

"Well the right thing for you ain't necessarily the right thing for me."

• • •

Emma came to the ranch the next day with the outfit's bakery order and was surprised to see Buford. He was always out with the herd. He walked over to her, with what she thought might be a smile.

"How'd you like to ride the pony today?" he asked Tom.

"Yes!", the small boy beamed.

"Well reckon we should get goin' then." He took Tom's hand in his and started to walk towards the barn. Without looking at Emma he said. "I'll bring 'im back later."

It was a good thing Buford hadn't looked back. Seeing him take Tom's little hand in his big capable one, brought on torrents of tears. She was confused by Buford's sudden interest in Tom. Tom was no longer a baby and easier to care for, but it just didn't seem right. As she wiped at her tears, she told herself not to make too much of it. She didn't want to set herself up for disappointment.

Buford brought Tom in the barn and saddled up one of his ponies. He was a beautiful Welsh Cobb and a gentle creature. The gelding was pure black, with a white diamond shaped mark on his forehead. Juan had named him Diamond because of it.

Buford put Tom on the horse and led him to the corral.

They walked around for hours, Buford showing Tom how to put pressure on the reins to make the pony go where he wished it to.

Buford had built up a lucrative horse business while married to Mabel. After she died, he'd lost interest and although business declined it hadn't vanished. He still had enough to require a few hands to work at the barn all day. They smiled to see him patiently bringing the boy around the corral again and again.

Buford watched the child closely as the day went by. By evening Buford knew for a certainty that the child was

Tom's. Even at the boy's tender age, Buford could see man-
nerisms and expressions that were the same as his brother's.

That night when he brought him back to town he
declined Emma's invitation to come inside.

"Ain't got time to set. I got work to do. Spent all day
with the boy. Next time you come to the ranch, reckon I'd
like to hang on to 'im for a while. He likes the horses," he
said lamely.

Emma didn't know what was going on, but as long as
Buford spent time with her son, she was happy. The only
thing that gave her pause was that he'd grow tired of Tom
and break his heart.

Soon a pattern developed. Every time Emma went to the
ranch with a bakery order, she left Tom. Most times Buford
brought him back but often it was Josh or Juan.

Emma chided herself for over thinking the implications
of what was happening. It was all too strange for her to
comprehend. Although the Colonel was spending time with
Tom, he spent none with her. In the past he'd stop to visit
with her. Now when she asked him to come in for a cup of
coffee or just to sit before the ride home, he always declined.
She thought if she didn't know what he was up to soon, she
might go insane.

One day when Hi came to the bakery she voiced her
concerns to him.

"Y'all know what the Colonel's up to?" she asked him.

"What do you mean?"

"He's been takin' Tom regular and it's got me worried."

"Why's that? I think it's good he's spendin' time with
the boy. After all Emma, you and me both know he's Tom's
Pa."

"Yea, that's what worries me. Tom's growin' fond of
'im and what's gonna' happen? The Colonel ain't claimed
'im and ain't bothered with me a'tall. Brings 'im home and
leaves quick as you please, like I'm gonna' bite 'im or somethin'. Don't know what notions he has. I just don't want my
boy's feelins' to get hurt."

Hi sighed. "I'll tell you what's goin' on Emma. Buford
thinks Tom was the boy's father."

Emma's eyes grew round in surprise. "Tom!" she

exclaimed.

"Now, I know it's foolish but I always done tole' you that the Colonel is a jack ass. Finally admitted to me 'fore he went off to Dodge that he saw some family resemblance in your son. But in his own jack ass kinda' way he thinks it's Tom's kid, not his."

"Well, I'll be. Puts my mind to rest some, even though he's wrong." She had to chuckle in spite of herself. "He thinks Tom's his nephew!"

"Buford sure is somethin', ain't he?" Hi smiled. "Reckon, it don't matter none as long as he thinks Tom's kin."

"Reckon so. At least I know that he ain't gonna' hurt my boy. Buford don't seem the type to turn his back on family."

"What about you?" Hi asked.

"What about me?"

"Now you know why he's been good to Tom. Why do you think he don't wanna' come and set with you no more?"

"I don't know. That man sure does puzzle me. I've known 'im a long time and I still don't know 'im. Does that make sense?"

Hi laughed. "Nothin' makes sense when it comes to Buford. An idea just come to me. Buford's always wanted you to leave town. Hell, most times when he came to see you he was tryin' to get you to leave. Tell me if'n I'm wrong."

"No. You're right." She smiled, "Come to think of it, we had more fights than social visits."

"That's what I thought. Now that he thinks Tom's his nephew, he don't want you to leave no more. To Buford, there ain't nothin' more to talk 'bout."

Emma suddenly looked deflated. "That doesn't say much for me does it. What a fool I've been!" she wailed and crumpled in tears.

Hi put his arms around her and let her cry. "Buford's just a jack ass."

She left his embrace. I'm a bigger jack ass than he is and you know it. He ain't never led me on."

"I know and he ain't never goin' to."

Her face fell with the truth of this and he tried to make amends.

"It ain't your fault Emma. It's him. You're a fine woman

and you been on the straight and narrow for a long time. Kept hopin' that he'd see Tom was his and do right by you. Guess he ain't never gonna come 'round"

"It ain't only him. Nobody comes 'round. I'm so lonely! The only friends I have are waddies and cowpunchers. I been decent a long time and it ain't mattered none. The ole' hens hate me all the same. Half their men folk won't acknowledge me on the street 'cause they's afraid of their women."

She saw the wounded look that came over his face and felt bad for her tactless words. "Don't mean no offence against your wife," she added.

"No offence taken," he said.

That evening when Hi got home he glared at Lydia.

"What's troublin' you?" she asked.

"Stopped by to see Emma," he said.

"What else is new? It's scandalous the way you men is always goin' in and outa' there. Especially you."

He raised his voice to her, something he seldom did. "Scandalous? What's she gotta' do to earn your respect? She ain't been on the line for a few years now. She works hard and takes good care of 'er boy. She don't act unseemly so why do y'all treat 'er poorly? I'm ashamed of you, Lydia, I really am."

Lydia knew Hi was angry, but she spoke her mind all the same.

"How dare you talk to me like that, Hi Johnson! Ain't I the one who helped 'er when she first opened 'er shop? Didn't I get other women to go in?"

"Yea, you did, 'til she got hurt. When she needed y'all the most. Instead you turned your back on 'er and all the others did too. The women here look up to you. When you done business with Emma they did, too. Now you ain't, so they ain't. If'n Emma's in a bad way it's all your fault!"

Lydia's face grew red and she spluttered. "It ain't my fault. Me and you had words over this a long time ago. Why you bringin' it up again?"

"'Cause it galls me! Always did! Stopped arguin' with you 'bout it 'cause it did no good."

"If'n we're gonna' blame anyone, how 'bout the Colonel? He's your friend and a fine man. It ain't like me to question 'im but everyone knows he's the boy's Pa. He's the one who should be takin' responsibility for 'im and that woman, too. Don't blame me!"

"Well, I am. Every Sunday when we's at church I feel like pukin'. It turns my stomach to see all you women singin' hymns to the Lord. Y'all so goddamn pious! Well there ain't an ounce of Christian charity in any of y'all!"

His tone was more than Lydia could bear and she fled in tears. Hi fumed and stomped around the house. He hated to talk to her that way but she had it coming. He couldn't understand her obstinate dislike for Emma.

• • •

Although Buford felt an obligation to little Tom he had no intention of opening his heart to him. Outside of Mabel, it had always been easy for him to shut people out. He'd been doing it for so long, it was something he didn't even have to think about. But as time went by, much to his dismay, Tom wormed his way into his heart. The boy was McLeod through and through and brought back happy memories of his brother.

Buford knew Emma was confused by his new-found attraction to the toddler, but he found it hard to tell her. He was ready to accept the boy as kin, but she wasn't a part of it. He had no wish to encourage her.

One day when she dropped Tom off, Buford noticed that he had a split lip and a black eye.

"What the hell happened here?" he asked Emma gruffly.

"I fighted," Tom answered before she could reply.

"Hush now!" Emma scolded.

"No, I wanna' hear this!" Buford said.

Emma sighed. "I was over to the store the other day and some boys give 'im a hard time. Ain't nothin'."

"Wassa' whore, Colonel?"

Emma's face flushed a deep crimson and tears sprang to her eyes. She looked away so neither Tom nor Buford could see.

Perhaps Tom didn't notice them, but Buford did, and he felt a suffocating rage. He knew he had to decide about Tom's future and it had to be soon.

CHAPTER ELEVEN

Buford began to seriously consider what to do about the situation. He finally decided and went to see Hi.

"Come in to tell you that I'm gonna' claim Tom's boy."

"Well, I'll be damned. You got a heart after all."

"Gonna' ask Emma to let me have 'im."

"What are you loco? She ain't gonna' give 'im up!" "Think she might. I'm gonna give 'im the ranch when he's old enough. Lord knows I ain't never gonna' have no younguns' of my own. Only makes sense he comes and stays with me."

Hi sputtered. "Of all the danged fool ideas! Ain't no way Emma's gonna' let you have 'im. Besides you don't know shit 'bout raisin' a chile."

"Juan's good with 'im."

"Well, Juan ain't his Momma. You ain't helpin' the boy by takin' 'im away from his Ma! You ain't even givin' 'im a Pa! Just a jack ass uncle."

"Yea but I'd be givin' 'im some respectability. The boy's gettin' bothered 'cause of Emma."

"Well that can't be helped. You can't take 'im away from his Ma, it wouldn't be right. You might as well cut that poor woman's heart out."

Buford thought of what Hi said and sighed, "I suppose you're right. Don't know what else I can do."

"You can tell 'er that you think he's Tom's and that's why you been takin' 'im." He didn't tell Buford she already knew. Let Buford tell her his jack ass theory. "Give 'er money for his care. Keep doin' what you're doin'. Spend time with 'im and bring 'im back to 'er. Just the fact that you claim 'im as kin is somethin'." When Buford got to the bakery, he found Emma in the backyard washing laundry for the Converse outfit. Tom ran to greet him.

Emma straightened and rubbed her back. "Howdy," she said cheerfully, wiping her hands on her apron. Buford noticed they were red and chapped.

"I come to talk to you 'bout somethin' important," he said, nervously twisting his hat in his hands.

"C'mon in and set," she said warily. She didn't know what to expect and her pulse raced. "Y'all stay outside for a minute," she said to Tom.

When they were seated Buford began. "I been takin' Tom all this time 'cause I think he's my brother's boy."

Would he get mad if she told him again that Tom was his? She decided not to and looked down at her hands.

"Seein' as he is, I'm gonna' give you money to take care of 'im. Also want 'im to spend more time at the ranch if'n it's all right with you. It's gonna' be his someday."

She looked up in surprise.

"Tom was my partner. It's only right his son should get his half. For now, let me get you and the boy a decent place to live. I'll give you money, so you don't have to work so hard."

"Would be fine but I couldn't let you."

"Why the hell not?" he asked peeved.

Her face turned red and she stammered. "People... people might think you're keepin' me! But I'll take any money you care to give me for 'im. He's growin' like a weed and it's hard to feed and clothe 'im, even with two jobs. I reckon it'll be all right if'n he stayed at the ranch sometime."

"Don't want you workin' so much. I think you should spend more time with little Tom. I'll make sure you got enough money."

"I don't know what to say," she said.

He held up a hand, "Don't say nothin'. Now that I know who his father is, I'm happy to help 'im."

"You don't know who the father is," she said softly.

"Come again, Emma? Didn't hear you."

"Nothin'," she sighed.

Buford continued to take Tom every chance he could. He wouldn't admit it to Hi but he did see a lot of himself in the boy, although he resembled his late brother as well.

One day when Buford was in town he saw Tom outside the general store. He looked longingly at a group of children who played in the street. Buford went over to him.

"How come you ain't playin' with the other boys?" he asked.

"They can't. Their Mommas say no."

"They's just bein' foolish. Y'all go on over there and join 'em."

"Can't."

Buford sighed and shook his head. The child was too young to know the truth but old enough to be hurt.

"Then you just wait for your Ma and don't let them younguns trouble you."

"I won't," Tom said morosely.

• • •

The following Sunday Buford went to Charlie's for Hattie's wedding.

It had taken the distraught girl a long time to get over Tom. Even then, none of the local men appealed to her. It was a cowpuncher that Zeb Converse hired that helped Hattie find love again.

Buford didn't attend many social functions. Now as he mingled through the crowd, he felt the eyes of several single women upon him and it made him uncomfortable. He was the tallest man there and easy to find. A few of the braver belles approached him and flirted with him shamelessly until he had to excuse himself and walk away.

He marched over to Hi, his face red with embarrassment.

"I swear," he said to his friend. "Gal's these days is gettin' bolder."

"When are you gonna' pick one of 'em for the next Mrs. McLeod?"

"Why the fuck do you like rilin' me so much? You know the answer to that as well as I do. Besides, I got Tom now. Don't need no one else."

"Man needs a woman, too."

"I don't."

"Reckon not. When was the last time you had one?"

Buford had to think back. The last woman had been

Emma, the night of Charlie's shindig and that was a long time ago.

"If'n you have to think that long, I know the answer."

"Through with women, even whores."

"I don't know, Buford," Hi's eyes twinkled. "Think you oughta' take one of these fine phillies. They sure is givin' you the eye."

"Ain't gonna' do 'em no good," Buford said grumpily.

The long afternoon was torturous, and he dismissed himself the first chance he could.

He rode home with a feeling of relief. It felt good to be away from the crowd. The sleepy little town was quiet. "Reckon everyone in town's there," he thought to himself, "Except for the whores. And Emma," he added as an after-thought.

A vision of little Tom standing pathetically in front of the store entered his mind. He was an outcast like his mother and didn't understand why. Buford sighed. He wondered if he'd been wrong to listen to Hi. Maybe he should still speak to Emma about bringing the boy to live with him.

He decided to go and speak to her now.

Emma looked out her window at the sound of an approaching horse. Buford came into view and her heart skipped a beat. He looked handsome in his black broad cloth suit.

"Howdy," he said as he entered the bakery.

"Howdy. You're sure all duded up. How was the wed-ding?"

"Same as usual. Can't abide 'em myself."

Emma laughed. "You ain't never been one to socialize."

"Can't see no point in it."

"It's for folks to get together and have fun!" she said. "Though can't say for sure. I ain't had much experience with decent folks."

"That's what I come to talk to you 'bout. Kinda' irks me how the other boys give Tom a hard time."

Emma's face fell. "I know, and it breaks my heart," she sighed. "Beginnin' to think you were right. Now that he's gettin' older I should move and make a fresh start."

Buford grew alarmed. Now that he realized the boy was

his brother's he didn't want them to leave. "I had another idea," he said. "Don't wanna' get you riled. Talked this over with Hi and he said you ain't gonna' like it none, but here it is. Let me have Tom."

"What?" she cried in shock.

"Let the boy come live with me."

"I couldn't!"

"Why not?"

"He's my life! I'd miss him too much."

"You could see 'im any time you want. You gotta' think what's best for Tom. He'd be on a ranch with people, animals and open space. Ain't right for 'im to be holed up in the back of a bakery."

Her face turned pale and she sank into a chair. "I don't know," she said. "I have to think about it." Tears streamed down her cheeks.

"Aw hell, Emma. Didn't wanna' make you cry. This here just make's sense. Stop that snivelin'!"

"I can't. You're askin' me to give up my son! The only person in this world who loves me."

"Don't say that. It'll be the best thing for 'im. You can visit with 'im as much as you want. I give you my word."

Tom came running in from outside and Emma quickly wiped her eyes.

"Colonel!" cried the delighted child. "We go see hosses now?" he asked hopefully.

"Not today. Just come by to talk to your Ma."

Tom's face fell but he held back his tears. "I like the ranch. Nice hosses."

Buford shot Emma a piercing glance. She pulled herself together and forced a cheerful voice, "Would you like to stay with the Colonel?" she asked.

"With the hosses and Juan?"

"Yea. The Colonel wants you to go live with 'im. But only if'n you want to. I'd come and see you every chance I got."

"Can I sleep in the bunk house?" he asked Buford.

"Sure."

Tom's face lit up. "Yes! Let's go!" he said excitedly and grabbed Buford's hand.

After they left, she broke down and wept as if her heart would break. She'd never felt so miserable. Her past was full of hardship and misfortune but giving up Tom was more than she could bear. She would never have done it, but she knew the Colonel was right. Tom was much better off with him. Besides, whether he accepted the fact or not, he was the boy's father.

When Hi learned of the arrangement he came to the bakery.

"Heard Buford took your boy. Is it true?"

"Yea," she sighed heavily. "He come and got 'im yesterday."

"I'm surprised you let 'im take 'im."

"The Colonel convinced me it's for the best. This here's no life for Tom. We was lonely company for each other. At the ranch he'll be 'round folks. Maybe if'n he lives with the Colonel, people might treat 'im decent."

"Emma, you can still take Tom and go."

Emma sighed. "Marshall, bad news travels far. I'd probably have the same problem sooner or later. Besides, he's with his Pa."

The next day she went to the ranch. She found Tom happily feeding the chickens and pigs. He was delighted to see her and ran to her open arms.

Emma embraced him and closed her eyes tight to stop the tears that spilled down her cheeks. She didn't realize that she was being observed by Buford as he stood in the door of the barn.

He felt a twinge of pity for her but knew this was the best arrangement for his nephew.

Tom breathlessly told her of all that transpired since he'd come to the ranch.

Buford gave them time alone then went out to greet her.

"Hear you're takin' good care of my boy, Colonel," she forced a cheery smile.

"That we are. He's a fine boy, Emma. You done good with 'im."

"Ain't been easy but expect no one knows that better than you." He changed the subject. "You bring our order?"

"Yea, Juan's seein' to it now. Brought some donuts for

you Tom."

"The sugar ones?"

"A whole passle of 'em!" she laughed.

"I feed the chicks first," he said and ran back to his chores.

"I can see you're teachin' 'im duty first," Emma tried to smile.

"Reckon."

After that exchange an uncomfortable silence lay between them.

Finally she said, "I best be gettin' on. Little Tom don't seem to need me none." She hugged Tom and left.

The arrangement worked out well for the first few weeks. Emma came to the ranch often and Tom seemed healthy and happy. However, after a while, the novelty wore off and he grew increasingly homesick and lonely for his mother.

One day Juan went to Buford. "Colonel. I'm worried about Tom. He cries all night."

"I know," snapped Buford, "I hear 'im."

"He misses Emma."

"He'll get used to it."

Much to Buford's disappointment, he didn't. Although Tom acted cheerful in front of her, he'd dissolve in tears after she left.

Buford couldn't tolerate it any longer and spoke to the child about it. "You miss your Ma pretty bad, don't you?"

"Yes."

"I like havin' you live here but you ain't got to. You can go back with 'er any time."

"I wanna stay with you, but I want Ma, too."

"You're too young to understand. It wouldn't be proper."

"I want you. I want Ma!"

Buford remained silent and the little boy continued to sob. Buford didn't know what to say or do. The answer came to him a few moments later when Juan entered the bunkhouse.

"Colonel, Miss Smith is outside, says she needs to speak with you."

"What the hell does she want now?" he growled.

"I don't know," Juan shrugged.

Since Hattie's marriage, her sister Maryanne began a campaign to win Buford's heart. The Smith and McLeod ranches bordered one another, and she found several excuses to come by. It was an unbearable nuisance and if not for the high regard Buford had for Charlie, he would've given her a piece of his mind.

He went out and greeted her. "What can I do for you today?" he asked trying not to let his annoyance show.

"Seems like we lost our dog. You ain't seen 'im have you?"

"No, I ain't. If'n I do, I'll bring 'im home."

She was dressed in her Sunday best and batted her eyes at him coyly. "Would be much obliged," she said. He remained silent and she continued, "It's a lovely day, isn't it?"

"Reckon it is. I got work to do."

She wasn't put off by his gruff behavior. She thought she could tame him like Mabel did. "Well, I best be gettin' home."

She peeked out at him from her parasol and left in a flutter of lace and ruffles.

Buford saddled up his horse and rode to town. He went straight to the bakery.

"Is everything all right?" Emma asked alarmed.

"Yea. No. Truth is, Tom's missin' you real bad."

"Really? He don't act it."

"He don't cry when you're 'round but he cries when you leave."

"Oh!" she said dismayed. "You plan on bringin' 'im back?"

"He don't wanna' come back."

"I ain't sure I'm followin' you."

"That's 'cause I ain't sure where this trail's leadin' myself. He don't wanna' come back here. He wants you to live at the ranch with us."

"You know that wouldn't be fittin'. If'n I come stay with you, there'll be a worse scandal over my boy's head."

"Not if'n we was married."

Her eyes grew round and her heart beat fast in her chest. She was too stunned to answer.

"Don't know if'n this is right. I want Tom and he wants you. Figure maybe me and you could get hitched."

He went on nervously. "I ain't in love with you Emma but reckon you know it. Ain't gonna' be much of a marriage. Just doin' it for the boy. What do you think?"

She drew in a deep breath. "I don't know. This is all happenin' so fast."

"For you and me both. Soon as I got the idea I come over here before I lost my nerve. Still don't know if'n it's right or not. Ain't one for bein' impulsive."

Emma remained quiet, her mind in turmoil. She'd loved this man for many years but had given up notions of marriage long ago.

"Do you wanna' marry me?" she asked.

"Can't say that I do. Just seems to be the best thing for Tom. What 'bout you? Do you wanna' marry me? I ain't offerin' you much."

"Yes, you are. I wanna' be with my boy. Bein' with you ain't the worst thing I can think of. It's been real lonely here."

"I guess it's settled then," he said.

"Not exactly," she said nervously. "I'm gonna' tell you this once more and I ain't never gonna' bring it up again. Tom is your boy, not your brother's. I ain't never lied to you 'bout that."

Buford sighed "Reckon, it don't matter much now."

She could tell he wasn't convinced. "When you wanna' do this?", she asked.

"The sooner, the better. Won't have no fancy party or nothin'. Just me, you and the Parson. How 'bout this Sunday?"

"Sounds fine."

When Buford got back to the ranch he told Tom. "Well little buckaroo, your Ma is comin' to stay with us."

Tom's face glowed and he hugged Buford for the first time. Buford was uneasy and didn't respond to the small child who clung to his legs. Finally, he picked the boy up and hugged him close. "All right," said Buford after a moment, untangling himself. "Juan's got vittles ready. We best go get some 'fore them hogs eat it all."

Buford told the men of his plans during supper. The

news came as a surprise to them, and they fell quiet. Josh's face turned pale and he thought he'd be sick. He had ceased wooing Emma some time ago, but he loved her still.

Buford looked at them sternly. "Emma's been out of business for a spell but I know most of you been with 'er. I ain't gonna' tolerate no funny business. Any man here who troubles 'er is gonna' have to reckon with me."

None of the men answered but studied the beans in their plates instead.

Ezra broke the silence. "Congratulations, Colonel. Emma's a fine gal. I'm sure you'll both be happy."

The other men agreed and went over to shake his hand and thump him on the back. Buford for his part, took their congratulations with a grimace.

• • •

He had a lot to do. He had to open the house and get it serviceable again. There was no way Emma could stay in the bunkhouse.

He entered the silent house for the first time since Mabel died. The furniture was covered with a thick layer of dust. He stood trance like, while memories of his beloved wife flooded over him. It was only when he felt his cheeks and beard wet with tears that he realized he was crying.

He dried his face and straightened his back. It would take all his strength, but he would push the memories away and concentrate on the work at hand.

That night the nightmares came in full force. Mabel wailed and called to him and he woke covered in perspiration. He considered not marrying Emma but the sight of little Tom peacefully asleep on the bunk next to him made him keep his resolve.

That Sunday, Buford went to get Emma. Two of his men rode beside the wagon. They'd act as witnesses.

Emma looked radiant. Although she knew Buford's motives for marrying her, she didn't care. She would be reunited with her son and free of her lonely prison at last. She had her meager possessions packed in one trunk and an out of business sign on the bakery door. She looked behind her at the place where she'd spent so many tormented hours. "I ain't gonna' miss that place a'tall'," she said.

The Parson was startled to see Buford's wagon pull into the yard. "The Colonel's here," he called out to Alvirah. "Looks as if he has a few of his men with 'em and that gal, Emma."

"Well go on out there and see what they want," she snapped. "Don't want that woman in my house!"

Alvirah peered out the window full of curiosity. She couldn't figure out what the Colonel was up to.

She watched as Buford helped Emma from the wagon. When the group reached the front door, she scurried into her bedroom. She didn't know what was going on but whatever it was, she wouldn't be part of it.

She sat and waited for what seemed an eternity but in fact was but a few minutes. She finally heard them leave and flew from the room.

"What did they want?" she asked.

"They wanted to get hitched!" her husband smiled.

"No!" she said shocked.

"Yep, they did. Ain't it wonderful?"

"How can you say that! I ain't never seen eye to eye with the Colonel, but I got respect for 'im all the same, but that woman! How could he marry 'er! Especially after Mabel. She was a lady. Now he's marryin' a whore when there's decent gals that'll have 'im."

"Stop it Alvirah. Ya' know what they've been sayin' in town. The Colonel thinks little Tom is his brother's child. Guess he decided to wed the mother." He was speaking to thin air for Alvirah had gone for her cloak.

"Where you goin'?" he asked, as she pulled on her riding gloves.

"I'm goin' to the Smith ranch to see Joanne."

"Alvirah, I forbid it! The Lord don't take kindly to gossip!"

"It ain't gossip," she said, as she brushed by him. "It's news." She was gone so quickly, the Parson could only stare after her in surprise.

She breathlessly told Joanne what transpired, and her friend's consternation was as great as her own.

"That baggage!" Joanne spat. "I can't believe it. If he needed a mother for that boy he coulda' had my Maryanne, a good Christian girl!"

Between Alvirah and Joanne the whole town knew of the wedding before twenty-four hours had passed.

Buford had planned nothing special. To him it was just another Sunday. He didn't feel married and he didn't want to.

He'd warned Emma that this wouldn't be a real marriage. At night he planned to take a husband's privilege, but it would mean nothing. He'd paid her for the same service in the past.

Emma felt nervous and frightened as she walked around the large house. She'd never met Mabel, but the furniture and adornments gave her a hint of the woman who'd lived here before.

"Make yourself at home. I got things to do 'round here", said Buford.

She got Tom settled in his new room and then went to unpack her trunk. When time went by and Buford didn't return, she made herself busy. Jaun's sister Rosa had cleaned the house so there wasn't much to do. She explored the well-stocked kitchen and began to prepare supper. She and Tom ate the meal alone. She waited up for Buford, but he never came back.

The next morning Hi came to the ranch. He was both pleased and angry and he chastised Buford.

"Why you ole' son of a bitch! Why didn't you tell me you was gettin' hitched! Didn't even invite me to the weddin'. My feelins' is hurt."

"Came on all of a sudden. Proposed to 'er on Thursday and got married yesterday."

"Sure is a shock. You was always rantin' and ravin' how you'd never get married again!"

"Well this here ain't what it seems. Done it 'cause of the boy."

"Well, whatever the reason, I think it's fine. 'Bout time, too." Hi laughed, "Lord! You sure got the women folk riled. They're upset you married a soiled dove, meanin' no disrespect to Emma. You left a string of broken hearts behind you."

"They'll get over it. Women always want what they can't

have. Think that was my appeal."

Hi sneered good naturedly, "Lord, Buford. You ain't got no fuckin' appeal that I can see."

"Ain't that the truth! All I know is I ain't encouraged them gals and they was still houndin' me. This here will put a stop to that."

"So that's how you figured it. You get hitched to keep Tom and get rid of pesky women."

"Exactly."

"What 'bout Emma?"

"What 'bout 'er?"

"You got any feelin's for 'er?"

"Nothin' special. I tole' 'er that before we got hitched."
"Ain't you a stupid son of a bitch!"

"You're rilin' me, Hi, like you always do. What the fuck do you want from me? Take in the boy you said. Treat Emma better. Ain't I done that? Why are you still givin' me shit?"

"'Cause her happiness don't mean a damn to you."

Buford sighed. "She's with 'er boy, has a nice house, and don't have to work no more. Sorry I'm mistreatin' 'er," he said with sarcasm.

"Well I am sorry!", Hi said in anger. "She don't mean no more to you than that mule over there."

"I've had enough. We're done here," Buford said. He turned his back on his friend and began to walk away.

Hi sighed. "This here ain't gonna' work. Ya' know why? Cause you ain't nothin' but a cold-blooded son of a bitch." Buford paid him no mind and went in the barn.

• • •

Living with a woman again wasn't the difficult adjustment Buford thought it would be. He had to admit that Emma was easier to live with than Mabel.

Emma was a hard worker and kept the big house spotless. She enjoyed cooking and prepared tasty meals. She continued to bake for the outfit and the kitchen was always fragrant with delicious aromas.

He came and went as he pleased. He didn't coddle her and more often went about his business as if she wasn't there.

Emma was easy to control as well. He hadn't been able

to intimidate Mabel, but he could frighten Emma with a glance.

She slaved over dinners that he often missed and cleaned furniture and floors only to have him soil them five minutes later. The docile Emma didn't complain.

Many nights he slept at the bunkhouse or out on the range. Only when he slept at the house, did he pay attention to her and she accepted it willingly.

This arrangement didn't bother her at all. She had a home and a family to care for. It seemed like a dream come true despite Buford's indifference.

• • •

In the beginning, living in the house brought on a rush of memories for Buford. He'd wake up many nights calling Mabel's name. Emma was hurt but kept quiet. She suspected that being surrounded by Mabel's things was disturbing him.

One day she said, "Colonel, this place is pretty and all, but I was wonderin' if'n we could get some different furniture. What we got is too good for cow punchers and children. I'm afraid Tom's gonna' break somethin'."

"Sounds like a good idea. Truth to tell, I always felt uncomfortable with this fancy furniture. We'll go to town tomorrow."

The next morning Emma grew anxious. She hadn't been in town since their marriage and was uncertain of the reception she'd receive.

As they approached town her heart beat nervously in her chest. She was quieter than usual, but Buford didn't notice.

He also seemed oblivious to the cold stares they received as they made their way down the street. She kept her gaze down and studied the plain gold wedding band on her finger.

When they reached the general store, he helped her from the wagon and was surprised to feel her trembling.

"You ailin'?" he asked.

"No, just a little scared."

"Don't be," he said quietly, and Emma noticed a gleam of determination in his eye.

When they entered the store, the other customers fell silent and turned to stare.

Buford acted as if nothing was amiss. Taking Emma by the arm he made his way to the counter. "Mornin'," he said to the clerk. "Me and the Missus wanna' buy some furniture."

The clerk was nervous in the uncomfortable silence and stuttered, "Over th...th...there," he pointed towards the back of the store.

"Much obliged." He guided Emma in that direction, tipping his hat and greeting people as he went along.

Buford was their hero. They wouldn't dare insult him and greeted him in return.

When Buford went to the clerk to pay for the furniture he said, "Sure is quiet in here, today." He looked around at the dozen or so people in the store. "Somebody die?" he asked.

"N...N...No, Colonel," the clerk stuttered.

"Well since I got everyone's attention, I'd like to introduce y'all to my wife. Sure most of you know who she is."

"The men do," snapped old Penelope Finch.

"True enough, but none of you women do," he said unruffled. "Don't believe you've been introduced."

He took the quaking Emma and brought her around to the ladies, introducing her to each one. They nodded stiffly but remained silent.

"Me and my wife would be much obliged if'n you ladies called on us some time."

"I wouldn't push it, Colonel," said Junior from where he stood in the shadows.

"Just bein' neighborly, Junior."

"Ain't right to ask these decent women to your house."

"Why not? I didn't think my reputation was that bad," he smiled.

"It ain't," said Penelope, emboldened by Junior's outburst. "You got a fine reputation, Colonel. It's the reason folks is shocked. If'n you wanted to marry again, you had plenty of Christian women to choose from."

Buford's patience was at an end. He walked over and towered menacingly over Penelope. His eyes were cold.

He turned to Emma. "Emma, your Ma brung you to church, didn't she?"

Emma, too frightened to speak, nodded in the affirmative.

"You see? I did pick a Christian woman. Now if'n y'all excuse us." He tipped his hat and departed.

"Let's stop and see Hi," he said quietly. "Feel the need to see a friendly face."

Hi noticed Emma's weak smile when they entered the jailhouse. He sensed something was wrong but greeted them cheerfully. "Emma, you look lovelier than ever. Seems that livin' with this varmint ain't hurt you none."

Buford laughed coldly. "You wouldn't say that if'n you been in the store with us just now."

"What happened?" Hi asked, his blue eyes squinting in anger.

"The ladies didn't take kindly to me," said Emma. "I didn't think they would."

"Got 'em to acknowledge you, though," Buford said testily.

"Forced 'em is more like it," she said.

He shot her a dark look. "Reckon I did, but it don't matter none. I swear, if'n I have to hold a gun to folks to accept you I will."

"That ain't gonna' help," Hi said.

"Me and Emma got hitched so Tom could hold his head up in this piss hole of a town. Looks like that wasn't good enough."

Hi looked at the forlorn Emma and his heart went out to her. "How'd y'all like to come to my house for Sunday dinner?"

Emma glanced up in surprise, "But Lydia..." she began.

Hi interrupted her. "Lydia is gonna' be just fine with this. If'n she ain't, she can be the first one ole' Buford holds his gun to."

"Much obliged, Hi. But this here ain't your problem. Don't wanna' 'cause trouble between you and your woman."

"Shit Buford. You know I cause trouble all on my own. I wanna' see y'all at my place this Sunday, hear?"

"Worth a try," said Buford.

On the way back to the ranch, Emma said, "Our bein' married ain't gonna' make no difference."

"'Course it will!" he snapped. "Just gonna' take some time. It ain't easy for good women to accept a whore."

Emma had already endured enough, and that comment cut her to the quick. She turned her back so he couldn't see her silent tears. Buford realized he'd been tactless. "Didn't mean it the way it sounded."

"No, it's true. To folks 'round here, I'm still a whore. They ain't never gonna' change their minds. But I thought after all this time I changed yours."

● ● ●

Hi had his own battle on his hands. Lydia ranted and raved about his dinner invitation and he was furious with her. "I ain't been able to understand what you got against Emma. You was 'er first decent friend. You jealous of 'er?"

"Jealous?" Lydia's eyes flashed. "Why would I be jealous?"

"C'mon' Lydia! You know damn well I poked 'er when she was at the Longhorn! Can't imagine any other reason you're so stubborn 'bout this."

"All right! You wanna' know why? Ever since she opened 'er bakery you've been in and out of there for the whole town to see! She mighta' stopped whorin' but not for you!"

"Lydia, that ain't true," Hi said.

"I don't believe you! I wasn't 'bout to do business with a woman who was pokin' my husband!"

Hi looked at her in disbelief. "You don't trust me!"

"Why should I. When I met you, you had a reputation for two things. Fightin' and fornicatin'."

"I tole' you a hundred times I was helpin' 'er out. No one else would! Why didn't you tell me this before?"

"I was afraid you'd leave me for her if'n I said anythin'."

Lydia appeared to be close to tears and Hi softened. "Lord Jesus, Lydia. You should know that I don't need Emma or any other woman when I got you," he said tenderly.

Now that things were settled between Hi and Lydia, Sunday dinner turned out to be a pleasant event.

Emma had hardly slept the night before in fear of what the outspoken Lydia would say. Much to her surprise, Lydia greeted her cordially.

Little Tom and J.B. got along splendidly, and their happy squeals could be heard from the back yard.

When it got close to dinner time, the women retired to the kitchen, laughing and chatting. Buford and Hi sat out on the front porch.

"What come over Lydia?" Buford asked. "She's bein' nice to Emma. Did us gettin' hitched have anythin' to do with it?"

"No, nothin' a'tall. When I tell you, you ain't gonna' believe it. All this time she thought I was pokin' Emma!"

"Didn't I tell you she'd get mad if'n you kept goin' in the bakery?"

"Yep, and for once you was right."

"So, she's been hard on Emma 'cause you're a jack ass." Buford shook his head and sighed. "I'll never understand goddamn women!"

"For once, I agree with you. I thought I knew Lydia better than that."

"You're slippin', Hi," Buford joked. "You're always tellin' me I don't know shit 'bout women and you're just as bad!"

• • •

A few days later, Josh came to the house to see Buford.

"I'm leavin' town," he said.

"What?" Buford asked, surprised.

"Think it's time I moved on. Been here too long. Might even go home."

"Lord, Josh. Hate to hear this. You been with me from the beginning. You're my best goddamn hand! If'n it's more money you want, I'll be happy to give it to you."

"Ain't that," Josh said looking down at his feet.

"This ain't 'cause of Emma, is it?" Buford asked.

"Reckon, it is. There never was anythin' between us, but can't help the way I feel. I still love 'er."

"You ain't gotta' leave town. Charlie, Zeb or any of the others 'round here would take you in."

"No, I gotta' move on."

Emotion lay thick between them. He and Josh had weathered many a storm together. He cleared his throat and said, "Sure wish you'd reconsider."

"I already have. I can't stay," Josh said morosely.

"When you headin' out?"

"In a day or two."

"I can't change your mind, can I?"

"No, Colonel."

"Well if'n you're gonna' go, I guess you've got to. Take what you need from the store house and any horse you want. If'n you ever wanna' come back you got a place here, don't never forget that."

"I won't."

Josh's leaving put Buford in a foul mood and by the end of the day, the hands stayed clear of him.

"Lord, Josh," said Jimmy Kelly. "What you gotta' go and quit the outfit for? The Colonel's been bitin' everybody's head off all fuckin' day."

"He'll get over it," Josh said, "He always does."

That night at supper Buford told Emma of Josh's plans. "He'll be leavin' in a few days, thought you and Juan could plan some sort of shindig for 'im. Nothin' big, just the men."

Emma was surprised, "I thought he was happy here."

"Just wants to hit the trail I reckon. Been here a long time, guess he's gettin' itchy feet." He thought it best not to tell her the reason Josh was leaving.

"I'll talk to Juan in the mornin'. We'll throw a fine party for 'im," she said.

"Knew you could handle it. I'm turnin' in now. You comin' to bed?"

"In a while. Got more mendin' to do."

"Don't take too long."

His implication was clear, and she put her sewing away and followed him.

• • •

They had a small barbecue for Josh the night before he left. Juan and Emma had out done themselves and the cook house table was laden with all kinds of food and cakes.

Buford provided several bottles of good whiskey. "Drink your fill boys," he said, "Just remember there's work in the mornin'."

The men ate, drank and laughed. Nights off were few and far between and they enjoyed the unexpected treat.

They caroused until midnight and it was a bleary-eyed group who assembled the next morning to bid Josh good bye.

• • •

If Gideon Jones had nothing else, he had good timing. He'd drifted from place to place never reaching California to mine gold as he'd intended.

The son of a Vermont dairy farmer, he learned quickly that there was a huge difference between a dairy cow and a Longhorn steer.

After a few futile years of trying to earn a living on the range he found himself near Wilder Creek. He ended up at Charlie Smith's ranch looking for work. Charlie didn't need him but knew Josh had left Buford's spread.

It was the middle of the day when Buford saw two riders approaching. As they drew closer he could make out Charlie and another man.

Buford greeted them as they reined in.

"This here's Gideon Jones, Colonel. Now that Josh is gone, I thought you might want 'im."

Gideon extended his hand. "I remember you Colonel, you saved my life."

It took Buford a moment to recall the incident, but it came to him.

"You're the feller the Comanche scalped. You was cut up pretty bad. I didn't think you was gonna' make it."

"Thanks to you, I did."

Embarrassed by Gideon's gratitude, he changed the subject. "Let's go on over to the house," he invited.

"Ain't seen you since you got hitched," Charlie said, "Must feel good to have a woman 'round again."

Buford laughed. "Charlie, if'n there's anyone who knows how I feel 'bout women, it's you. All I can say is Emma makes it tolerable. She knows I'm a jack ass and accepts it."

When they reached the house, Charlie greeted Emma warmly. "There's the ole' married lady now," he said, leaning down and giving her an affectionate peck on the cheek. "This here's Gideon Jones."

"Good to meet you," she said.

Gideon was taken back by her blonde beauty. "My pleasure, Ma'am." He didn't tip his hat, knowing the sight of his mutilated scalp wasn't pleasant.

"You men set and I'll fetch you some refreshment," she said.

They sat and talked while Emma went in and out quietly, bearing coffee, whiskey and pie.

She moved around them gracefully and Gideon tried not to stare. When she got close, he noticed the faint trace of scars on her face, but he thought they did nothing to mar her looks.

He filled Buford in on his travels and had the men laughing with some of his experiences.

"So, you're lookin' for work?" Buford asked.

"Yea," Gideon replied. "Though there ain't much I can do 'round here. I have no experience with cattle and I've disappointed more than a few ranchers. I'm better with milk cows than Longhorns."

"Anybody teach you anythin' 'bout 'em?"

"No sir. Never lasted that long. Guess I was useless."

"Well, you're in luck. I got milkin' cows and if'n you're willin' to learn, I ain't got a problem teachin' you how to handle steer. I need another hand. Gotta' warn you though, it ain't gonna' be easy. Learnin' cow's hard work and the men is gonna' pick on a tender foot like you."

Gideon's face beamed. "I'd be thankful for the chance. You've saved my life again, Colonel! I'll learn quick and work hard."

"I hope so. I'm one tough son of a bitch to work for. I ain't no nurse maid and I don't coddle my men. I expect an honest day's work and good behavior. I won't tolerate nothin' less."

Charlie looked at Gideon. "One thing I've got to say. Don't fuck with the Colonel."

CHAPTER TWELVE

Emma wanted to return Lydia's hospitality and approached Buford. "I'd like to have the Marshall and his family over for dinner some time."

Buford looked up from the ledgers he was working on, "Sounds good. Like to invite the Smiths too."

"Do we have to? Charlie's women don't like me none. Can't forget how they treated me at his shindig."

"That was different. You're gonna' be 'round a spell and me and Charlie's good friends. Gonna' have to get y'all together sooner or later. We'll invite 'em. If'n they don't wanna' come, that's their business."

The following Sunday, Emma glanced around the house nervously. Her guests would be arriving soon, and she wanted everything to be perfect. She needn't have worried. The house was so clean it gleamed and wonderful aromas wafted from the kitchen.

Lydia and Hi were the first to arrive and Lydia could sense Emma's anxiety immediately.

"What ails you, Emma? Look like you're goin' to your death."

Emma smiled. "Reckon, I feel that way. Ain't no secret that the Smith gals don't like me."

"Don't worry. Joanne's got a good heart in 'er."

"You coulda' fooled me. She and 'er girls have been hard on me."

A short time later Charlie's wagon could be seen on the horizon. Besides he and Joanne, they could make out Mary-anne and his youngest daughter Nancy.

Emma greeted them all graciously though the women were aloof.

Buford and Emma led them to the comfortable rockers

that lined the front porch.

After exchanging small talk for a while, Buford said, "Charlie, want you to see my new colt. He come into this world just the other day and he's a beauty." The men went to the barn and the women were left in uncomfortable silence.

Lydia did her best to fill it, but it was clear that Joanne and her daughters weren't going to participate.

"Why don't we go into the parlor, where we can be more comfortable," suggested Emma.

"House looks fine, don't it?" Lydia asked the women. "I like these curtains you hung," she said to Emma.

"You changed it 'round some," said Joanne.

"Yea, I did."

"I liked the way Mabel had it fixed better," she said coldly.

"Maybe you do but the Colonel didn't," said Lydia. "It was way too fancy for 'im."

"You ever meet Mabel?" asked Maryanne.

"'Course she didn't," snapped Lydia before Emma could answer.

"She was a fine woman. Beautiful and smart, too. A real lady," Maryanne sneered.

Emma's face colored. "I heard she was," she said softly. "Heard she was all you said and more."

The men came in and joined them and the conversation shifted. If they noticed any tension amongst the women, they didn't let on.

A short time later, Emma excused herself and went to the kitchen to check on dinner. Buford followed her in.

"What the hell's wrong with you?" he asked. "You're skittish as a cat."

"Charlie's gals got me scairt' to death. They done nothin' but insult me since they came."

"Tole' you not to worry 'bout 'em," he snapped. He left the kitchen and she knew he was annoyed with her.

When they were all seated around the large dining room table, Lydia complimented Emma's dinner several times. Joanne and her daughters were doing all they could to make her uncomfortable with plenty of comments of their own.

"Didn't see you in church this mornin', Colonel," said

Joanne.

"Ain't nothin' new. I'm a God fearin' man but not one for sermons."

"You used to go when you was married to Mabel," she said smugly.

"Mabel's gone," said Hi, realizing what they were up to.

"Saw one of your friends in town yesterday, Emma," said Maryanne.

Emma, pleased at being included in the conversation said, "Who?"

"That red headed whore. What's 'er name? The one who wears all that face paint? Oh yea! Jamie."

Emma's face went from beet red to pale white.

"That's enough," said Buford, coldly and quietly from his end of the table. Everyone looked at him in surprise.

"Excuse me Charlie for interferin' with your women folk but this here's my house." His eyes flashed, and he glared at Joanne and her daughters. "Thought when you come here you was gonna' behave yourselves. If'n my wife offends you so much, why'd y'all come?"

"We come 'cause we was invited," Joanne said, glaring back. "I didn't know special behavior was expected."

"Don't want nothin' special," said Buford. "Just thought you'd have better manners."

Joanne jumped from her chair and threw down her napkin. "I ain't stayin' to be insulted one minute longer," she said to Charlie. "Take me home."

Charlie looked at Buford then at Joanne. "Sit down," he said firmly.

"What?" she cried. She was used to getting her own way.

"You heard me. Sit down and eat. You ain't the one been insulted. I'm ashamed of y'all. That includes you too, Maryanne."

Before any more could be said, little Tom and J.B. came in from the porch with empty plates. "These vittles are good, Momma. Can we have more?" he asked.

"'Course you can," she said, glad for the diversion.

Charlie, Hi and Lydia did their best to dispel the uncomfortable mood.

When the dismal affair was over, and everyone had

gone, Emma began to clear dishes and cutlery. Try as she might, she couldn't fight back her tears.

"I'm sorry, Colonel," she said in a small voice.

"Yea, me too. Goin' to town for a spell." She heard the door shut behind him.

"Wonder what he's sorry 'bout?" she wondered. "How them women treated me or that he married me?" Her pain and humiliation would've been complete if she knew it was the latter.

By the time Buford reached the Longhorn he was fuming. Jamie approached him to ask about Emma, but he cast her a scathing glance and she hurried away.

After a few drinks he calmed down and went to speak with her. "Was there somethin' you wanted?" he asked.

"Was just gonna' ask you 'bout Tom and Emma."

"They's doin' fine."

"Sure do miss 'em," she said. "Emma's like kin and I ain't seen 'er to talk to in a long time."

"Emma could use a friend."

"Don't I know it!" said Jamie.

"If'n you wanna' visit with 'er it's all right with me." Jamie's eyes grew wide with surprise. "You serious?"

"I am."

"Much obliged but it ain't a good idea. She's a married woman now and it wouldn't be respectable."

"Don't think it'll make any difference," he sighed.

"Folks still givin' 'er a bad time?" she asked.

"Yea."

"Well, much obliged for the invitation. Y'all be seein' me real soon!"

• • •

On the way back to the Smith ranch, Charlie was in one of his rare fits of fury.

"I don't know why you made us go, Pa," wailed Maryanne, "that woman's unbearable."

"You shut your mouth!" he shouted. "I ain't never been so embarrassed in my whole danged life. What the hell's wrong with y'all?" Charlie was seldom angry and the women kept silent.

"I ain't excusin' the girls, Joanne, but you're their Ma.

What kind of example you showin' 'em?

"I don't like eatin' with strumpets and I ain't gonna' pretend to.

"You were rude to the Colonel, and after all he's done for us! He saved my fuckin' life. How could you act that way to his wife?"

"Don't know why he married that woman," Joanne said stubbornly.

• • •

When Buford finally came home it was late. Emma was in bed but not asleep. She needed comfort badly and thought she'd find it in his strong arms. Outside of his few terse words to Joanne, he hadn't offered her any solace.

Much to her dismay, he climbed into bed beside her and fell fast asleep. He was still cranky the next morning and she tried not to annoy him further.

"Wanna' ride out to the herd with me this mornin'?" he asked Tom.

"Yea!" Tom answered happily.

"Well, then let's go."

Emma blanched when she heard this and spoke up. "Colonel, ain't he a little young?"

"No, he ain't," he snapped. "You baby 'im too much."

One evening when Buford came home for supper, he found Rosa in the kitchen.

"What the hell you doin' here?" he growled.

"I heard you got married. I came to work for your new wife. She hired me."

"What the fuck, Rosa. You ain't welcome here. I hired you to take care of Emma when she got beat up and you left 'er. If'n I recall you don't work for whores."

"She's not a whore any more. She's your wife."

"Makes no fuckin' difference to me. You leave in the mornin'."

"Please Colonel! I need the money."

"I don't give a damn! You ain't stayin'."

He stormed around the house and found Emma upstairs cleaning.

He was furious. "What the hell is that woman doin' downstairs?"

"I hired 'er today," she said nervously.

"You hired 'er! Who do you think you are? Don't give yourself airs, Emma, 'cause you ain't got no right. You're Tom's mother and that's the only reason you're here!"

"I felt sorry for 'er."

"Sorry for 'er? Are you addle brained? Ain't she walk out on you when you needed 'er? How can you forget that?"

"I ain't forgotten but she's desperate. Her son-in-law run out on 'er daughter. Now Rosa got twelve grand-babies to feed. Poor thing walked all the way from the Village. Took 'er all night, too. She was near dead when she got here this mornin'."

"I don't give a shit if'n she died on the fuckin' porch. I ain't runnin' no charity here. Can't believe you, Emma. She's the one who started all your troubles. She ran out on you!"

"That was a long time ago."

"You're too soft."

She couldn't hold back her angry tears. "I got a forgivin' heart unlike most folks 'round here."

"Jesus, I hate it when you cry! She's leavin' in the mornin'," he hissed and slammed out of the room.

Emma wiped away her tears. She'd known better than to hire Rosa but had been too tender hearted to send the distraught women away.

Buford was absent at supper and Emma asked Rosa to join her and Tom at the table.

"The Colonel is angry," said Rosa.

"I know," sighed Emma.

"He doesn't forgive me for leaving you."

"He ain't a forgivin' man," Emma said.

"No, he isn't, but you forgave me. You are very kind."

"It was a long time ago, Rosa. Don't matter no more."

Buford didn't come in that night and Emma slept alone. He came in while Rosa sat at the table drinking coffee. Since she was no longer in their employ, Emma insisted that she do no work.

"Colonel," Emma said shyly, "are you gonna' have one of the men take Rosa back to the Village? If'n they're too busy, I'll take 'er."

He ignored her and shouted at Rosa, "What the hell

you settin' on your ass for? If'n you're gonna' be our house-keeper I suggest you finish cookin' breakfast!"

"Si, Colonel!" Rosa beamed.

He scowled at the two women and went to the dining room, Emma close behind.

"She can stay?"

"I don't pay people for doin' nothin'. If'n I tole' 'er to cook, it's pretty fuckin' obvious, ain't it?" he said, in no good temper.

"Oh, thank you!" breathed Emma. She went over and embraced him. He threw her arms off. "Don't crowd me," he snapped.

"Sorry," she said, her face turning red. She didn't let his mood bother her. He was angry about Rosa, but he'd given in. To Emma it was a small victory.

Buford worked with the horses that day and Tom joined him. Rosa could scarcely believe how Buford doted on the little boy.

"The Colonel seems fond of your son."

"Reckon, he is."

"He should be. It's his son, too, though I never thought he'd admit it."

"How do you know Tom's his?" Emma asked surprised.

"How do I know? Look at him! Even at such a young age he looks like the Colonel. They're cut from the same cloth, those two."

"Well the Colonel don't see it. He thinks he belongs to his brother."

"Why'd he marry you then?"

"'Cause he wants to give my boy the ranch. Little Tom wouldn't stay here without me, so we had to get married for appearances sake."

"And you? What was your reason?"

Emma sighed heavily, "I wanted Tom to have a proper home. I thought the Colonel might realize the boy was his. I don't think he ever will."

"Bah! That's because you won't make him. You are nothing like his late wife. She stood up to him. She was not afraid!"

"She was a lot of things I'm not," Emma said sadly.

As time went by, Buford started to notice things about Tom that nagged at his mind. The boy grew to look more like him and less like his brother. He finally realized Tom was his and it filled him with both wonder and dismay. Emma had claimed that from the start. He decided to keep this to himself.

• • •

With Rosa to do many of the chores, and little Tom frequently with Buford, Emma had time to spare. She decided to try her hand at growing flowers and vegetables in the arid soil.

Although Gideon was proving to be a quick learner and a hard worker, there was something about him that Buford didn't like. He didn't know what it was but kept a wary eye on him.

One afternoon as they talked in the corral, Buford noticed Gideon looking towards the house again and again. He turned to see what was drawing his attention and saw Emma hard at work in her garden. Her long blonde hair hung in a braid down her back and the top buttons of her dress were undone, showing the top of her chemise. Her skin glistened with sweat in the afternoon heat.

"You see somethin' over there that interests you?" Buford asked coldly.

"What?"

"You're talkin' to me and lookin' at my wife."

Gideon blushed. "It's her turnin' the soil that got my attention. I had a first-rate garden in Vermont. Seein' your wife called it to mind."

He seemed sincere, but Buford decided to watch him closer than ever.

When they were through with their conversation Buford went to the house. As he passed Emma he snapped, "Button yourself up! You ain't in the Longhorn no more!"

"Didn't mean no harm, Colonel. It's hot and I didn't see no one 'round."

"Well there was. Can't have you temptin' my men."

She buttoned her dress and her face turned crimson. He'd made it sound as if she purposely tried to entice them. She should've lashed out at him for the insult, but remained quiet.

Much to her surprise Jamie came to the ranch one day. Emma stepped outside to greet her.

"Jamie! Lord you're a sight for sore eyes. What y'all doin' here?"

"The Colonel asked me to come."

Emma looked at her in disbelief, "He did? He ain't said nothin' to me 'bout it."

Jamie got down from her horse. "Coupla' weeks ago, he come in the Longhorn. Tole' me I was welcome here, so here I am."

The two women embraced, and Emma led her into the house and a disapproving Rosa.

"Jamie, this here's our hired woman, Rosa."

"Pleased to meet you," Jamie said.

"Hmph!" Rosa said turning on her heel and walking away.

"Well, I'll be." Jamie laughed, "She sure don't approve, does she?"

"I guess not," said Emma, embarrassed, "but don't matter, none. If'n the Colonel says it's all right, it is. Lord Jamie! How long has it been since you and I visited together?"

"Too long!"

The two women spent a pleasant afternoon, drinking tea and talking. Jamie brought her up to date on goings on at the Longhorn.

She had just left when Buford came in. The odor of cheap perfume hung in the air.

"What the hell's that smell?" he asked, wrinkling his nose.

"Jamie come to visit today. It was good of you to invite 'er," Emma beamed.

"Didn't think it would do any harm. Outside of Lydia you ain't got no friends."

Her face fell. "That's the truth. You must be disappointed. You married me for nothin'."

Before he could reply, Rosa poked her head in. "Is that fast woman gone?" she asked.

"Who you callin' a fast woman?" Buford snapped.

"The one with the red hair! Dio! I'm surprised at you

Signora! Why did you let her in?"

"Rosa, I don't recall hirin' you to pass judgement on Emma's friends. Cookin' and cleanin' is your job and if'n you wanna' keep it, you best get about it," he said in a menacing voice. Rosa looked at him defiantly and went to the kitchen.

"Lord that woman riles me. So do you. Why didn't you put 'er in 'er place? She works for you."

"Didn't have a chance to. You spoke up first."

"Never could abide that woman. Even when she worked for Mabel she was nothin' but a pain in the ass. After what you done for 'er she ain't got no call to judge you."

"Reckon, I'm used to it."

"Well, I'm not. I'm beginnin' to see why you ain't never been accepted in this town. You got no gumption, no back bone. When people insult you, you lay down like a whipped dog!"

Emma felt her eyes filling with tears. "Just don't want no trouble is all."

"Look at you cryin' like a baby. Never saw a woman cry as much as you. Thought you had more spirit," he said with disgust.

"I've got enough."

"You ain't got none a'tall'. Maybe if'n you'd speak up instead of actin' like an outlaw, they might respect you. You're too soft."

"You don't understand," she whispered.

"I'm beginnin' to understand plenty. This arrangement ain't never gonna' work as long as you keep actin' the way you do."

She fled from him, the tears thick in her throat. It wasn't in her to speak harshly to anyone, even a hired hand. She thought of the strong-willed Mabel and sank deeper into despair

The next day he said, "Be leavin' for Dodge in a few weeks and you're gonna' have to do chores in town. I'm takin' you and Tom in today."

"All right," she answered timidly.

"Hope you took what I said yesterday to heart."

"I did."

"Didn't mean to hurt your feelin's, Emma, but God Almighty! When we get to town, don't want you hangin' your head. Want you to look folks straight in the eye! Show 'em you ain't afeared of 'em."

When they got to town, she sat up tall, her back stiff with determination. She kept her gaze level and looked straight ahead.   As they went from shop to shop, Emma displayed a confidence she didn't feel. She acknowledged those they passed. Though few greeted her warmly, the women nodded, and men tipped their hats.

Most people decided to acknowledge Emma to keep on good terms with Buford. This went for little Tom as well. Their children finally let him join them.

On their way back to the ranch Buford said. "Things didn't go so bad today."

"No, they didn't. Folks was downright civil to me and Tom."

"That's 'cause you showed 'em that you ain't gonna' take their shit no more."

They stopped by Hi and Lydia's before returning to the ranch.

Lydia was happy to see them. "C'mon' in and set!" she said.

"Don't wanna' put you out. Just stopped by for a minute," said Emma.

"Ain't puttin' me out a'tall."

"Y'all goin' to Clarence Wilson's shindig next Saturday?" Clarence had the ranch next to Charlie. "His boy just come home. Graduated from one of 'em fancy eastern schools, Harvard, I think. He's a lawyer. Gonna' be the first one in Wilder Creek."

"You know I ain't one for parties. Me and Emma will stay home."

Everyone in town knew that Buford wasn't social. They sent he and Emma invitations, certain that he wouldn't attend.

"Well, me and Lydia, is goin'. Ain't we, darlin'? I never miss a party."

"Can't recall that you ever have. Remember that time in 68' when we had them banditos surrounded on the Mexican border?" Buford asked amused.

"You ain't never let me forget it," said Hi.

"What happened?" Lydia asked.

"We was holed up all day waitin' for these Mexican varmints to come out. There's a little cantina off aways, and when it got dark we hear singin' and dancin' comin' from it. The sound of a good time was too much for Hi, so he takes off and heads for it. The other Rangers across the way finally flush the sons of bitches out and they come straight in my direction. There was five of 'em. I kilt' three but one shot me right here," he said pointing to his side. "I'm layin' there bleedin' while Hi's dancin' and drinkin'!"

"You ole' jack ass! I still come out in time to save your life. So you got shot! How many other times you stop a bullet or an arrow? Besides, couldn't help myself. We waited in that stink hole of a town, what, thirteen, fourteen hours? How was I supposed to know that they'd come out soon as I left?"

"You was somethin' in those days," Buford laughed.

"That I was; til I met Lydia and seen the light! Don't stray off the trail, Buford. We was talkin' 'bout Clarence's party. Ain't fair to Emma and the boy for you to stay home all the time. Come with us, we'll go together. Whatta' you think Emma?"

"It's up to the Colonel."

"We ain't goin'."

When Buford and Emma were leaving Hi called out. "Don't forget, be here at noon Saturday."

"Don't pester me, Hi," Buford said with a dark look.

On the way back, Emma asked. "I'm glad you don't wanna' go."

"Why not? We got as much right as anyone."

"I know but I'd feel funny, besides you tole' Hi we wasn't goin'."

"I changed my mind. We're goin' to the goddamn thing and you're gonna' do just like you done today. Show a little gumption. You're my wife and the sooner folks get used to the idea, the better."

As planned, the McLeod's met Hi and Lydia at their house and they set off to the party together. The women and children rode in the wagon, the men rode alongside.

Emma tried to hide the fear she felt. She wished she was any place else but on her way to this party. Joanne and many other of her antagonists would be there.

When they arrived, Emma glided towards their hosts flanked by Buford and Hi. To look at her, no one would know that she was quaking inside.

"Look at 'er," snorted Joanne to Mary Converse. "Walkin' 'round like she was royalty."

"I'd feel like royalty if I were married to the Colonel. He is a dashing man, isn't he?"

"He is, but y'all know he and I ain't on speakin' terms."

"I think you're being foolish. She's been living decent for a long time. I think it's time we forget the past," said Mary in Emma's defense.

"She was a whore. She slept with men for money, probably our men! Lydia Johnson is a fool for takin' her side. Charlie tole' me that the Marshall always did prefer Emma when she was at the saloon."

"Now, Joanne, I think you should watch that sharp tongue of yours," Mary admonished.

"It's true and now her and Lydia is gettin' cozy. It ain't right."

With a huge smile, Lydia made her way towards the two women, Emma in tow. Joanne turned and made a hasty retreat, but Mary stood her ground.

"Good afternoon. You remember Emma, don't you?"

"Of course, I do," Mary said warmly. "How have you been my dear?"

"Fine thank you."

"Where did Joanne rush off to?" Lydia asked with a scowl.

"Lydia, please," said Emma, "let 'er alone. I don't want no trouble."

"She's right, Lydia," Mary agreed. "Let her stew in her own juice. There's plenty of folks here that Emma hasn't met. Why don't you and I take her around?"

Emma couldn't have had a better ally than Clarence's wife, Mary. Both were highly respected. Mary was well educated and genteel, and set the standards for propriety in Wilder Creek. With Lydia on one side and Mary on the other, Emma received a warm reception.

Joanne was a good woman but not one to be slighted. Strong willed and firm in her convictions, she fumed to see the radiant Emma enjoying the company of decent women. She went about the crowd letting everyone know she wasn't pleased by Emma's presence.

Soon the women broke into two camps. There were those who stood behind Emma and those who joined with Joanne.

Emma didn't notice this at first but as the afternoon wore on it became apparent. She held her head high and tried not to let it bother her. Several women sought her attention and soon she felt like part of the group.

Buford had drifted off and Emma went to look for him. It was then that her happy mood deflated. As Emma approached the Wilson's barn, she heard Joanne speaking to another woman inside.

"Gettin' so decent folk can't go nowheres without rubbin' elbows with that whore."

"I don't know. She seems decent enough. Mary and Lydia like 'er. They say Emma's a nice gal."

"Those women are fools. Don't know 'bout you but I can't be friendly with a woman who slept with my husband!"

"Joanne!" the woman said shocked.

"Well, that's the truth of it. She's probably had your man, too!"

"No!"

"Don't be a goose! 'Course she has. Any man with a dollar coulda' had 'er."

"That was a long time ago."

"Don't matter. I bet every time the men look at 'er, they're thinkin' 'bout 'er naked!"

"Joanne!"

"It ain't right for 'er to be here. Anne Wilson nearly went into a swoon when she saw that baggage. Clarence tole' 'er to be polite, but she ain't said two words to 'er since they got here. Anne only invited 'em 'cause she thought they wouldn't come. Everyone knows the Colonel never goes nowhere, so why's he here today?"

"He used to come to parties when he was married to Mabel."

"That was different. She was a lady. He coulda' had my Maryanne or a dozen decent women, don't know why he married that slut!"

"She done had his baby."

"That's what folks say, but maybe not. The Colonel ain't never admitted to it. From what Charlie says, he thinks the boy's his nephew. But who knows. Could be anyone's. Maybe he belongs to your man!"

"I never! Do you think so?"

"You never know with women like that."

"Well, I ain't gonna' speak to 'er, that's for sure! I got a few words for my husband, though!"

Emma turned and fled back to Lydia and Mary, before she could hear any more.

"The bloom's gone outa' your cheeks," Lydia remarked. "You ailin'?"

"No, I'm fine," said Emma with a weak smile.

"Did you find the Colonel?"

"No, but I didn't look very hard. I'm sure he's hidin' out somewhere."

"You sure you're all right?" Lydia asked concerned.

"Yea, right as the mail."

It wasn't until Joanne cast a scathing glance at Emma that Lydia thought she understood. She took Emma aside.

"Joanne been after you tonight?"

"Don't want no trouble, Lydia."

"She has! I can see it in your face. You ain't a very good liar. I'm goin' over there and give 'er a piece of my mind."

"No, please."

"She's been ignorin' me all day 'cause I'm with you. I guess she don't think much of my friendship. Reckon, it's time I go on over and say hello."

"Please!" Emma begged again but to no avail. Lydia swept away and Emma tried to stop her. Mary held out a restraining hand. "Stay here, dear. Lydia knows what she's about."

Lydia went to Joanne and tucked her arm through hers.

"Howdy, Joanne. Fine day, ain't it?" Lydia smiled and dragged Joanne out of the crowd.

"Lydia Johnson, what's gotten into you?"

"What's gotten into you? How come you ain't spoke to me today?"

"I think you know."

"I do," snarled Lydia. "Hear you're creatin' a stir!"

"Ain't doin' no such thing. I got an opinion and I give it."

"Well, ain't no one askin' for it."

"I don't care. Ain't nobody gonna' force me to set with a whore!"

"I used to feel like you Joanne, but it ain't right! Emma's been outta' business for a long time. She's married to the Colonel, for God's sake! That fact alone oughtta' make 'er worthy of some respect."

"Respect!" Joanne spat. "She ain't worthy. He had his pick of some of the best women in town. Can't believe the choice he made."

"Ain't none of our business who he marries. I don't think he'd like to hear 'bout all your trouble makin' today!"

"Are you threatenin' me?" Joanne snarled.

"Reckon I am. If'n you don't shut your mouth, I'm tellin' 'im. He's plenty put out with you now and I ain't gotta' tell you 'bout his temper. I wouldn't put it past 'im to embarrass you in front of all these people."

Joanne knew this to be true. It was possible that he'd make a scene.

She sighed in frustration. "All right, Lydia. Have it your way. I'll keep my thoughts to myself but not 'cause I'm afraid of you or the Colonel! I don't wanna' ruin Clarence and Anne's party. I'm doin' this for them."

"Good!" Lydia went back to where Emma waited, a victorious look on her face.

"Guess I settled that! Gettin' so I can't abide that woman. Always knew she had a stubborn streak in 'er but Lord almighty!"

"Much obliged to you," said Emma. "I feel bad comin' between you two."

"Don't! The Colonel ain't talkin' to 'er and neither am I.

Pretty soon the whole town is gonna' see what she's up to and no one will speak to 'er. The shoe will be on the other foot. She'll be the outcast."

"I wouldn't wish that on any one, even Joanne!" Emma laughed.

Elsewhere Buford was having problems of his own.

He and the other ranchers were in Clarence's study, drinking and talking about the upcoming roundup. Junior was intoxicated and grew increasingly obnoxious.

After a while, Buford rose to leave. "All this talk 'bout roundup reminds me I got work to do. Best be gettin' home."

"Don't blame you for bein' in a hurry," Junior slurred. "I'd be in a hurry too, if'n I had a fine whore like Emma for a wife."

Zeb spoke to him sharply. "Junior. Watch your manners."

Junior didn't heed him. "She still as fine in bed as she used to be?"

"Now, Junior...," Clarence started to admonish but Buford cut him off.

"She is. I'm a lucky man," Buford said with a cold smile. "Now, if'n you'll excuse me. I don't wanna' keep 'er waitin'. Be much obliged if'n you'd walk out with me, Junior."

"What for?" he asked.

"Just wanna' have a word with you."

"Now, Colonel," said Zeb in alarm. "Junior was out of line but..."

"I ain't gonna' hurt 'im," Buford interrupted. "Let's go," he said, taking Junior by the arm and leading him out of the room.

"I ain't goin' nowhere with you," Junior said sulkily trying to pull away. Buford held him in a tight grip.

When they were outside Buford spoke in a low but menacing tone. "I'm only gonna' say this once. If'n you ever say another word 'bout Emma or bother 'er in any way, I'll kill you."

He turned and strode off before Junior could answer. He had to. It was taking every bit of his self-control not to pound Junior to a pulp.

Buford knew that marrying Emma was going to be

trouble, but he had no idea how much. He was weary of sly
looks and nasty comments. Emma had been off the line so
long, he'd hoped that her charms were but a fading memory
to the men she'd been with. Obviously, Junior hadn't forgotten.

He anticipated more trouble as he walked through the
yard crowded with people. Were the women giving Emma
a bad time?

He found Hi talking with a group of men and joined
them. He glanced around for Emma and saw her sitting with
Lydia, Mary and a bunch of other women. She glowed with
happiness and he heaved a sigh of relief.

Hi and Buford gathered up J.B. and Tom and went to
the women.

"Well ladies, reckon we gotta' head back. Ole' Buford
here done have enough excitement for one day."

Buford looked at him in surprise. How did he know?

As they went back to town in the soft evening twilight,
Hi drew Buford aside. "What was you up to?"

"Don't know what you mean."

"I can see the smoke comin' out your ears."

"Junior."

"Lord, what he'd do now?"

"Opened his big mouth like he always does. Said some
bad things 'bout Emma."

"I'm afraid to ask what you done."

"Done nothin'. Brought 'im outside and tole' 'im I'd kill
'im' if'n it happened again. I ain't never had no use for that
boy."

Hi shook his head, "He's a dead man."

When they reached the Johnson's, Buford declined the
invitation to come inside and he and Emma continued to the
ranch.

He didn't tie his horse to the back of the wagon but trotted along beside. Emma would have welcomed his company, but he rode silently, lost in thought. In the growing
darkness she could barely see him.

"Just as well," she thought to herself. "If'n he could see
my face he'd know somethin's wrong."

Try as she might, Emma couldn't get Joanne's words

out of her mind. Joanne was purposely stirring up trouble. Why should Joanne accept her or their marriage? It was empty and meaningless, and Joanne had the sense to see it.

At the party, Emma watched wistfully as husbands and wives held hands and talked softly together. She would never share that kind of affection with the Colonel. Hadn't he told her that he wouldn't be much of a husband? Unless he was making love to her, he never touched her or spoke an endearing word.

Guilt welled up in her and she chastised herself for these thoughts. She should be grateful. Things had never been better. The Colonel had his faults, but he'd given her and Tom a good home and a decent life. Thanks to him people had been kind to her today. She was determined not to let Joanne spoil things.

Emma didn't realize that it was too late. Joanne had already planted a seed of discontent in her mind.

Buford went out on roundup a few days later and Emma saw him only twice. When he came in from the herd it was to see Tom.

"Can I do roundup, too?" the little boy pleaded.

"Maybe in a year or two. Besides, if'n' you come with me, who's gonna' handle things here? You ain't thinkin' of lettin' the womenfolk do it! Ranch needs a man to keep things runnin' smooth."

Tom smiled. "All right. Reckon, I can stay."

After a few days, the novelty of being in charge wore off and he'd mope.

"Better get used to it," Emma told him. "The Colonel's gonna' be goin' up to Dodge soon and we ain't gonna' see 'im a'tall."

Buford would be leaving some men behind when he went to Dodge. He knew that Junior Converse was not making the long drive this year and he instructed them, "If'n that sorry son of a bitch shows up here, I want 'im shot on sight."

His men didn't know what Junior did to warrant such deadly passion from their boss, but there was no doubting the sincerity of his request.

Buford slept at the house the night before he left. It had

been weeks since he'd been with Emma and he made love to her several times. The next morning, this emboldened her to kiss him good bye. He suffered her embrace but didn't respond.

Tom put on a brave smile, but his tears lay close to the surface.

"I'll be back before you know it," Buford said. "I'll bring you somethin' from Dodge. Would you like that?"

The little boy could only nod.

"You take good care of your Momma and the men. I'm leavin' you in charge of this outfit."

That evoked a small smile and Tom threw himself in Buford's arms. Buford hugged him back and it warmed Emma's heart. "Someday, you'll know the truth," she thought to herself.

She would've been surprised to know that he already did and leaving his son was the hardest thing he'd ever done.

She and Tom settled into a routine and the weeks flew by quickly.

Much to Emma's delight, Mary, Lydia and other ladies invited her to their homes. She reciprocated and entertained them at the ranch. As time went by, the pleasant Emma won their affection.

Jamie came to call, and Emma didn't turn her away, even if it meant jeopardizing her new friendships. As much as Emma liked her new friends none were as dear to her as Jamie. To Jamie's credit, she used discretion, and no one learned of her visits.

On a hot, sultry day in July, Buford and his men returned. Tom was beside himself.

"Momma! Momma! The Colonel's back!"

Emma rushed out to the porch and saw a huge dust cloud in the distance.

When the dust settled, Emma saw the men going to the cook house and barn while Buford rode up to the house. His face glowed at the sight of Tom.

"Howdy, Emma," he said casually, making no move towards her.

"Howdy."

Tom stood on the side, dancing with anticipation.

"Little buckaroo!" Buford said warmly. "Looks like you took good care of the place while I was gone."

Tom ran to him, and Buford swept him up in his arms. Emma was pleased with this display of affection. She wished he was happy to see her, too.

"What you bring me, Colonel?" Tom asked.

"Come to the barn and see."

"Come with us, Ma!" Tom invited.

"I don't know..." she trailed off, not knowing if her presence was wanted.

"Want you to see it, too," Buford said.

The three of them set off and when they got to the corral, he told them, "Y'all wait out here."

He disappeared into the barn and came out leading a beautiful Shetland pony.

Tom's eyes grew wide when he saw the magnificent beast.

"This critter's yours. I ain't named 'im yet. That's gonna' be up to you. You like 'im?"

"I love 'im'! Can I ride 'im?"

"The Colonel's tired," said Emma interceding. "Let 'im rest a while."

"I'm all right. C'mon' up boy." He hoisted Tom on to the bare back of the pony.

Tom's face split in a huge grin. "My own hoss, Ma! Ain't he fine?"

"That he is," Emma smiled.

"Think you could rustle me up somethin' to eat?" Buford asked.

"Sure, I'll have it ready in a jiffy," said Emma, knowing she'd been dismissed.

CHAPTER THIRTEEN

Three months after Buford came back, Emma learned she was pregnant. She was afraid to tell him, so kept it to herself.

Gideon Jones had been in Wilder Creek long enough to learn of Emma's past. This pleased him immensely. He'd been attracted to her from the start and now thought he could have his way with her.

One day when Buford went to town, Gideon decided to make his move. He found Emma in the barn grooming her horse.

"Hello, Mrs. McLeod."

"Howdy, Gideon. What you doin' here? Thought all you men was out with the herd."

"I was, but Ezra sent me back for another branding iron. How's that garden of your's comin'?"

Emma laughed. "All right, I reckon. Been a chore, though. Soil ain't fit to grow nothin'."

"Just takes a little work and a little know how."

"I got the work part down, but I ain't got much know how."

"I wouldn't say that. I heard you know a whole lot."

"Whoever tole' you that was fibbin'," Emma said.

"I'd like to find out what you know for myself."

Emma shot him a puzzled look.

"Understand you were one the finest whores in Wilder Creek. They say you really know how to please a man."

Emma felt the hair on the back of her head stand up. "That was a long time ago," she said, trying to remain calm.

"Don't matter to me. I'm sure you haven't forgot. I'll pay you good money."

"Lord, Gideon! Are you loco? I ain't a whore no more,

I'm a married woman! You better leave. If'n the Colonel comes back and finds you here, he's gonna' get mad."

"I don't expect he'll be back soon, do you?" he said walking towards her menacingly.

"Stay away from me!" she hollered picking up a pitch fork and pointing it at him.

"They said you was a wild cat," he said, fire in his eyes. He lunged at her and she jabbed out. He swung around, barely avoiding the long tines that threatened to spear him. He grabbed her arm and wrenched the weapon away.

He held her in a tight grip. "Come on, honey. Don't tease me. I know you want it," he said, his foul breath on her face. "I heard you and the Colonel don't have a real marriage."

"Let me go!" she said trying to release herself from his grip. She couldn't escape and kicked him in the shin.

He cracked her hard across the face. "I'm losin' my patience with you, woman."

He wrestled her to the ground and pinned her down. She struggled to get loose, but the harder she fought the more violent he became. Half-conscious, she lay still. He tore at her petticoats and pantalettes. Just at that moment a gunshot rang out and the top of Gideon's head blew off. Blood and tissue spattered her face and he collapsed on top of her.

Mad with fear, she shoved him off and sat up. She saw Buford with a smoking gun in his hand, then everything went black.

When she came to, she found Rosa hovering by her bed-side.

"Oh Lord!" she said, "My innards are burnin'."

"You lost your baby when that man attacked you," Rosa said.

"Oh, God!" she moaned, "I never tole' the Colonel I was expectin'.

"That explains it. After the Doctor told him about the baby, he went loco."

It was true. Buford had lost his senses, but it wasn't Emma he was thinking about. It was Mabel and the baby she lost. He wasn't aware of going to the barn and emptying his gun into Gideon. After, he jumped on his horse and rode off, not knowing what he'd do or where he'd go.

The demons who occupied his sleeping hours assaulted him. He was back in the war and heard the crack of guns and the cries of the wounded, he smelled the stench of gunpowder and burning flesh. Then he saw the outlaws and Indians he killed when he was a Texas Ranger. They were writhing in agony. Over all this chaos he saw Mabel. She cried pitifully. "Why me? Why me?" she asked him mournfully.

He rode across the plains, trying to ignore these gruesome images. After a few hours, his mind cleared but more guilt assailed him. He knew he should be with Emma. He rode slowly back to the ranch

When the men came back for supper, they found Gideon's body and the sight filled them with dread. The bloodspattered barn was a grisly sight. Ezra went to the house and Rosa told him all that transpired.

"Reckon, we oughta' get rid of the body and clean the barn before the Colonel gets back. More than likely, sight of that son of a bitch will set 'im off again." The men went about it and soon there was no trace of the carnage.

It was well after dark when he returned. Although he was emotionally exhausted, he went to see Emma. She lay on the pillows, her face bruised and swollen.

"How you doin'?" he asked softly.

"I lost your baby, Colonel," she moaned, tears streaming down her face.

"Don't cry. I didn't know you was expectin'."

"I didn't know how to tell you, but it don't matter."

"No, it don't. We got Tom. Truth to tell, I don't want any more younguns. You know how to prevent that sort of thing, don't you?"

Emma was mortified. "I didn't know you felt that way."

"Well, I do. Hope you can prevent it in the future."

"I'll do my best. She sighed. "I bet you blame me for what happened."

"'Course not! What gives you that notion?"

Emma laughed bitterly. "Ain't you accused me of temptin' your men? If'n Gideon didn't know I was a whore he wouldn't of tried what he did."

"Reckon, that ain't your fault. Always knew Gideon was

a bad apple, just didn't know how bad. I shoulda' never took 'im into the outfit.   "What did Doc say? You gonna' be all right? You ain't got no permanent damage, do you?"

"No. He said all I needed was a few days bed rest."

"Reckon, I oughta' leave you to it. You look a might peaked. I'll see you in the mornin'."

"Ain't you gonna' sleep here?"

"No. Don't wanna' keep you up with my snorin'and thrashin'." Emma had trouble sleeping. Buford's indifference ate at her. She knew he didn't love her, but it seemed to matter little to him whether she lived or died.

When Buford came in the next morning, he was taken back by her appearance.

"Lord Emma, you ain't lookin' good."

"Don't concern yourself," she said.

Her tone startled him. Had there been sarcasm in it? He ignored it.

"You gotta' rest like Doc said. I'll take Tom out with me today."

When they were outside, Tom asked, "What if'n Ma died?"

"She didn't."

"I'd be alone. I ain't got no Pa."

"You got me. You can call me Pa if'n you want to."

Tom's face lit up. "Yes, Pa."

It was after supper when the two of them got home. They went to see Emma.

"Howdy, Ma! How you feelin'?"

"Just fine now that you're here."

"You look a heap better," Buford said.

She'd slept most of the day and felt better physically but not mentally.

Rosa knocked on the bedroom door and entered. "You and the child come eat. I'll bring Emma a tray."

"The boy worked hard today," Buford told Emma. "He's probably hungry."

"I am Pa, but I wanna' come back to see Ma."

"We will."

"What in tarnation is that all about?" Emma thought. "Pa?"

When they came back, Tom chatted non-stop. He told her of the calf he'd seen born and his face glowed with excitement.

After he went to bed Emma and Buford were alone. An uncomfortable silence filled the room.

Emma finally spoke. "Why you havin' Tom call you Pa?"

Buford got up and began to pace. "Reckon' 'cause I think I am." he said softly.

"'Bout fuckin' time."

Buford had never heard her cuss and it startled him. "Well, couldn't be sure."

"I tole' you he was yours. I had no reason to lie," she said sullenly.

Her tone annoyed him. "Well, don't matter none. It ain't gonna' change nothin' between us," he growled.

"Don't expect it will."

"What's wrong with you? Why you actin' nasty all of a sudden. I've given you a good life. Is it 'cause I don't want no kids?"

"No." She gave a harsh laugh. "It's 'cause you think I'm dirt. You don't care if'n I live or die. I'm only here for Tom."

"I never tole' you different. I had no choice. I wanted Tom and he wanted you."

"Ya' know what Buford?"

"No, what?"

"You can go fuck yourself." She rolled over and put the blankets over her head.

Buford was stunned by her words and was in a foul mood when he entered the bunkhouse. It didn't help that the men looked at him strangely and shied away from him.

"Y'all got a problem?" he snarled.

"No," they mumbled.

Buford went back outside for some air and encountered Ezra.

"You all right, Colonel?" he asked, noticing Buford's scowl.

"Yea."

"Reckon you had a rough day yesterday. You and Emma can have more youngens."

Buford laughed harshly. "That ain't what's botherin' me. It's the men. They ain't actin' natural."

"To speak plain, Colonel. Seein' Gideon kinda' give 'em a fright."

• • •

A week later, Emma was up and around. She mourned the loss of her baby in silence.

Rosa was deeply shocked by what passed as a marriage in this house. Emma's eyes were empty and sad. The Colonel barely acknowledged her. Rosa recalled the gentleness and love he showered on Mabel and her heart went out to Emma. She'd grown to love her and wanted to help.

One afternoon when Emma came in from her garden, Rosa cried, "Dio! You are a sight. Quick! Go make yourself presentable before the Colonel comes in for supper."

"He probably won't eat with us and if'n he does, he ain't gonna' give me a glance."

"Miss Mabel, now there was a woman who knew how to get a man's attention. Dio, how she dressed! Always, perfect. Perhaps, the Colonel would look at you if you dressed up pretty for him."

Emma smiled. "Much obliged for the advice. I don't think it'll change anything but reckon it wouldn't hurt."

Buford and Tom were already seated at the table, when Emma appeared. She wore one of her best dresses and her hair was piled high, held by a silver and turquoise comb.

"You look pretty, Ma," Tom glowed.

"Why, thank you, honey."

"What are you all dressed up for?" Buford scowled. "We got company callin'?"

"No. Just felt like dressin' for dinner."

"Hope you don't expect me to."

"'Course not. Don't mean nothin'. I was workin' in the garden and had to change, so I gussied up a little is all."

"After what happened with Gideon, you oughta' have more sense. You're only askin' for trouble prancin' 'round in your finery."

"I didn't think of that. I won't do it again," she said close to tears.

Buford didn't reply and ate in silence. Emma put her

face down to hide how she felt.

"You gonna' cry, Ma?" Tom asked with concern. "You look like you're gonna' cry."

"I ain't. Be quiet and eat your supper."

Buford looked up from his plate and studied her. His face grew dark. "Jesus Christ!" he swore, and picking up his dish, he left the room.

Word spread quickly about Emma's mishap with Gideon. A smug Joanne told a group of women at the general store, "Didn't I tell y'all? The woman ain't no good. Gettin' the Colonel's men all worked up. Was only a matter of time before someone took liberties with 'er."

During the following weeks Emma tried not to give in to the depression that threatened to overwhelm her. Every day she counted her blessings and put on a cheerful smile, but her unhappiness lay just under the surface.

Jamie came to call one day, and Emma poured her heart out to her. She cried against Jamie's shoulder and for the first time, grieved out loud for her unborn child.

Jamie held her tight and let her cry. When Emma regained control, Jamie said. "I know this ain't gonna' be no comfort to you but I always tole' you the Colonel was a hard man. The Marshall tole' you, too."

"He's not I tell you. He loved Mabel and loves little Tom. The Colonel's got love in 'im, but not for me."

"He ain't never cared for you and tole' you plain a hundred times, so why you carryin' on? What did you expect?"

"I don't know. I never thought he'd love me, but he could treat me better."

"Well, darlin'. Y'all gotta' live with it or move on. He ain't never gonna' change."

"Move on," Emma said glumly. "I can't leave Tom and he won't leave the Colonel."

"Can't see no other way," Jamie sighed. "Thinkin' of clearin' outta' town myself. Gettin' too old for whorin'. Thought I might move some place and open a saloon. Why don't you come with me?"

"I can't, though it sounds temptin'. It wouldn't be fair to Tom."

"Well, think on it."

• • •

Now that she was healed Buford slept with her again. Her sleep was disturbed by the frequent nightmares he had.

He'd shout orders to his men or yell for them to take cover. In his sleep he mourned the dead he buried, and it broke her heart. He dreamed of Mabel and called for her pitifully.

After one such night Emma could bear no more, and her feelings were apparent.

"Christ Emma, you ain't been right since that day with Gideon. I know losin' the baby was hard on you, but you gotta' get on with your life."

"It ain't that."

"Then what? You're always bitchin' 'bout somethin'."

"It don't matter."

"For Christ's sake, don't gimme' that bull shit. I've knowed you a long time and there's somethin' wrong."

"What if there is? Ain't nothin' for you to worry 'bout." He sighed in exasperation. "Someone botherin' you?"

"No."

"Then tell me what it is. Wanna' get to the bottom of this. You walk 'round like a ghost."

"How the hell would you know?" she cried out vehemently. "You don't pay me no mind!"

"Is that what's botherin' you? I already tole' you..."

"That you weren't gonna' be no real husband. You ain't gotta' say it again! Strange how you don't mind bein' my husband at night."

His brows furrowed in anger, "That's business just like it always was! Payin' you for it just like before. Maybe not in cash money but I put a roof over your head and take care of you and the boy. You live pretty good here, you're obliged to gimme' somethin'."

Emma's eyes opened wide "Obliged! How dare you! I ain't a whore no more! When you gonna' realize that?" She burst into tears. "Sometimes I just wanna' die how you treat me!"

"Lord, Emma, I ain't gonna' stay here and listen to another word!"

She ran to block his path.

"You ain't leavin' 'til I say my piece! Everyone always tole' me you had no feelins', but I seen some good in you. I lost your baby and you don't care!"

"No, I don't! We didn't need another chile'. We got one already. I tole' you that Tom belongs to me. What more do you want?"

"All I want is for you to stop treatin' me like a whore! It troubles me how little you think of me."

"Goddamn it, Emma! I done a lot for you! Didn't I make an honest woman out of you?"

"An honest woman out of me?" she snorted. "You can barely look at me. You think I'm no account. God help me, I love you still."

"What did you say?"

"I said I love you! I love you, you son of a bitch!" she screamed at him.

"Well, don't," he hissed. He pushed her out of his way and left.

Buford didn't come to the house all that day and at night he slept in the bunkhouse.

Emma went to bed early but couldn't sleep. After tossing and turning for hours, she got up and dressed. She had to leave the ranch, or she'd go insane. She saddled up her horse and rode off in the darkness. She needed time to think. Before she knew it, she was in town. She thought she'd ride up towards Hi's, circle around and head home.

She passed the Long Horn on her way and didn't see the shadowy figure of Jamie on the balcony.

Jamie heard the slow tread of a horse make its way up the street and hid in the darkness. As the rider got closer, Jamie could see it was Emma. She let out a sigh of relief.

"Emma?" she called softly.

Emma looked up at the silent, dark building.

"Oh, Jamie. Thank God! Can I come up?"

"'Course you can. Tie your horse 'round back. I'll be right down." Jamie ran downstairs on stealthy feet and unlocked the saloon door for her friend.

Emma's face was streaked with tears and she'd thrown her dress on hastily. Her hair tumbled to her waist.

"Lord, Emma. You is a sight! What's wrong?"

"The Colonel and I argued. I couldn't sleep and went out ridin'. I ended up here."

"Well, come up to my room 'fore we wake the place. Does the Colonel know you're gone?"

"No, but I'm sure it wouldn't matter to 'im. I tole' 'im how I feel and all hell broke loose." She recounted their argument.

In the bunkhouse Buford also found sleep illusive. His feelings swung back and forth between rage and confusion. It troubled him that she was in love with him. Hi had told him that but he hadn't believed it. This was going to ruin everything.

When Buford came in the next morning, Emma was nowhere to be found.

Tom was in the kitchen eating breakfast.

"Where's your Ma?"

"She ain't here."

He spoke to Rosa. "You seen Emma this mornin'?"

"No."

"Goddamn it!" he swore. He went out to the barn and saw that her horse was gone. "Where the hell did she go off to?" he asked himself.

He saddled his horse, his hands shaking with fury. He had no trouble following her tracks and reached town just as the first light of day filled the sky.

The door of the Long Horn was locked, and he banged on it. After a few moments a bleary-eyed Frenchie greeted him.

"Colonel! What can I do for you?"

Buford didn't answer but pushed the little man aside and stormed up the stairs. He knocked loudly on Jamie's door and entered.

Emma sat up on the couch, half asleep. The dark look on his face startled her awake and her insides turned to ice water.

"What the hell's goin' on here?" Jamie asked rising from her bed.

"I've come to fetch Emma," he glared at her.

"Maybe she don't wanna' go."

"Is that so?" he asked, his voice filled with venom. "Can

I have a minute alone with 'er?"

"You want I should leave?" Jamie asked her.

Emma nodded and Jamie left.

He walked to Emma and slapped her soundly across the face. "If'n I ever catch you here again, I'll kill you. Now get the fuck home," he said between clenched teeth. He turned on his heel and bolted from the room. Emma touched her face. Her jaw ached and she could taste blood.

Jamie came running in. "What happened? Lord! Did he hit you?"

"Yea."

"That son of a bitch! You ain't goin' back there!"

"I gotta' go," Emma said, getting up to tend her bleeding mouth.

"Why? He'll hit you again, you mark my words."

"I ain't got no choice, I want what's best for Tom."

Emma slipped out the back door and left town without being seen. Her face throbbed and began to turn a deep shade of purple.

"Dio!" cried Rosa, when she saw her. "What happened?"

"Nothin'. Where's Tom?"

"He's with his father. I must warn you, the Colonel is in a fearful temper. When he sees your face, he's going to go loco. Who hurt you?"

"Don't matter," Emma said softly. "I'm goin' to the barn to do my chores."

Realization of what happened struck Rosa and her face screwed up with indignation.

A few hours later Buford and Tom rode in. They could see Emma in the corral exercising the horses.

"There's Ma!" Tom cried, pointing.

"So it is. Go on up to the house and eat your lunch. Me and your Ma will be up in a minute."

"All right, Pa," Tom said, riding slowly towards the house.

Buford dismounted and led his horse into the barn. As he unsaddled the animal, he wondered what to say.

Emma wished she could climb over the fence and run away. She had no desire to see him. She decided to stay out in the corral until he left.

When Buford showed no sign of leaving, she took the bridle of one of the horses and entered the barn. Buford looked up at her approach and saw the ugly bruise on her face.

"Jesus Christ!" he swore softly to himself. He was filled with shame and couldn't bring himself to speak to her. Silently, she brought in the rest of the animals and left for the house.

Buford followed her a few minutes later. At lunch neither of them could think of anything to say. Tom chatted away filled the silence.

"Ma, what happened?" Tom asked.

"One of the horses," she lied.

"Be careful. Pa, says they're ornery critters!"

Buford's face turned a deep shade of red.

It wasn't until nightfall and Tom had gone to bed that Buford finally spoke to her.

"Come here by the light, Emma," he said softly.

She walked towards him slowly, not knowing what to expect. When she reached him, he tilted her chin up gently. He studied the bruise in the lamp light.

"I'm real sorry 'bout this, Emma. I had no right. Sometimes my goddamn temper gets the best of me, but that ain't no excuse. I ain't never hit a woman in my life."

"Well, I ain't no regular woman. I'm a whore." Before he could protest, she continued, "I'm goin' to bed. Good night."

Shoulders sagging, she retired to the bedroom and shut the door. She was exhausted. She'd slept only a few hours the night before. Soon she sank into the oblivion of sleep.

Buford sat up awhile longer, deep in thought. He felt the need to make amends. When he entered the bedroom, he was disappointed to find her asleep. He quietly slipped into bed with her.

They both awoke at dawn and he gathered her in his arms and kissed her neck. She pushed him away and got out of bed.

"I ain't got time for that," she lied. "I got a heap of washin' to do."

At first, he was stunned by her refusal. His shock soon turned to anger, and he looked at her with flashing eyes.

She turned from him and started to dress hastily. He noticed that her hands trembled.

As the days went by Emma tried to bury her discontent. She wanted what was best for Tom so she'd have to endure.

Buford was puzzled by her behavior. She no longer moped. She seemed cheerful, but had grown indifferent. This detachment carried into the bedroom. In the past she'd given herself to him with abandon, now when they made love she was unresponsive.

He tried not to dwell on it. "Who gives a damn how she feels?" He could push her from his mind easily but for a reason he couldn't fathom, it bothered him tremendously. "My fuckin' prides hurt, that's all," he thought.

He rode out to see Hi one day. When Hi asked after Tom and Emma, Buford answered, "Tom is doin' fine," then blurted, "I'm worried 'bout Emma."

Hi chuckled. "Well, I'll be damned. Is that little gal finally gettin' to you? It ain't like you to worry 'bout no one!"

Buford scowled at him. "No, she ain't gettin' to me, Hi. I'm only worried 'cause I gotta' live with 'er is all. You notice anythin' strange 'bout 'er?"

"No. I can't say I have."

"She ain't been right for months."

"Do tell," Hi said.

"Since that thing with Gideon she's been actin' strange. I figured it was losin' the baby. But it ain't that a'tall. She don't think I treat 'er right. I don't know what the hell she wants from me! I provide for 'er and the boy, don't I?"

"Reckon you do but that ain't what's important to 'er. When you got hitched didn't I tell you this here arrangement wasn't gonna' work? You're treatin' this marriage all wrong, and it ain't fair to 'er."

"That's bull shit," Buford snapped.

"Is it? Then why you here with a long face? You don't care 'bout 'er and that's plain."

"She knowed that and married me any way. She even seemed happy for a while."

"Yea, well I reckon she realizes her mistake now."

"You think?"

"Lord, Buford! You're such a jack ass! Sure, I do. She

was never one to complain, but that don't mean she got no feelins'."

Buford sighed. "Well that's the thing. She done tole' me she loved me." Buford put up a hand. "Before you open your fuckin' mouth I know you tole' me that, too. I can't help it, but I don't love 'er."

"That's the sadness of it all, ain't it? You ain't human. Outside of Mabel and Tom you ain't got love for no one. It's a shame. Emma's a good woman and you don't appreciate 'er."

"Didn't say that."

"You don't have to. Why do you think Joanne and some of the others don't take to 'er? You don't take to 'er and they see it."

"That ain't true!"

"Sure, it is!"

"Christ what a mess!" Buford said sadly.

"Yea, it is."

"Don't know what to do."

"Try talkin' to 'er and don't let your temper get in the way."

"Ain't got nothin' to say she'd wanna' hear. Last time I done talk to 'er I ended up hittin' 'er."

Hi looked at him with narrowed eyes. "You what?"

"You heard me."

"Jesus Lord! You ain't never hit no woman that I know of."

"No, never did, but she can rile a man!"

"Don't know what to do with you," Hi said, shaking his head. "Well, if'n you can't talk to 'er, and you can't be good to 'er, reckon the only thing left is to cut 'er and Tom loose."

"Can't do that either."

"Why not?"

Buford lost all sense of pride when he said, "Tom's my son."

Hi laughed coldly, "You really are one sorry son of a bitch ain't you? How long did it take you to figger' it out?"

"Don't get on your fuckin' high horse! I've known for a while. Didn't say nothin' to y'all 'cause I knew you'd give me grief just like you're doin' now."

"Did you tell Emma?"

"'Course I did, but it didn't change nothin'. I still ain't got no feelins' for 'er."

"Well, at least you know she wasn't lyin'.

"It don't matter none."

Hi snorted, "and you wanna' know why she ain't actin' normal! God! Are you really that stupid?"

Buford rose to leave. "Why the fuck did I come here? You ain't understandin' a'tall."

Hi's blue eyes flashed in anger, "No, that ain't true. Reckon I understand too much."

"Well, you ain't helpin' any. Guess, I'll have to figure this out myself."

Buford was almost to the door when Hi called him back. As Buford turned, Hi gave him a punch to the jaw that made Buford stagger. "What the fuck was that for?" He asked rubbing his chin.

"That's for Emma," Hi said rubbing his hand.

When Buford left, he could feel blood in his mouth and running down his chin. "

When he got home, he said, "Emma, I gotta' say a few words."

"'Bout what?" she asked.

"We gotta' settle this. It ain't no good. I ain't never hit no woman before. Ain't never lost my temper on a woman like I did you."

"I been hit before."

"Expect you have but that ain't the point. You seemed happy enough when we got hitched. Don't think you like livin' here no more."

"Truth to tell, I don't."

"Reckon that's my fault. But I can't help it. You want more from me than I can give."

Emma looked down at her hands but didn't reply.

"I don't love you, but I like you. I don't like the way things are between us. Wish they were like before."

Emma tried to remain calm, but fury flamed within her. "What before you talkin' 'bout? Before I married you or after?"

"For Christ's sake, Emma," Buford said sadly.

"Oh, I get it!", she said. "I ain't received you kindly in bed lately and you don't like it none. I guess you feel you ain't gettin' your money's worth. I promise to act like I'm enjoyin' it from now on. I always have," she lied.

He stood up, his face rigid with anger. "You bitch!"

"I guess you didn't know I was puttin' on a good ole' show. Ain't that what a whore's supposed to do?"

Buford clenched his huge fists and paced the room. "Shut up, Emma. Ain't never had a woman rile me like you."

"Don't mean to rile you," Emma said recklessly. She started unbuttoning her dress. "But don't matter none, I guess I ain't keepin' up my part of the bargain. Ain't that right? You wanna' do it here or in the bedroom? Maybe you don't wanna' do me a'tall. Want me to satisfy you?" she said licking her lips lewdly. "Take down your pants, I don't mind."

Her intention was clear, and Buford's eyes nearly bulged from his head. Whore or not he'd never heard any woman talk that way. He stormed from the house.

After he left, Emma's anger faded, and she trembled with embarrassment. She knew she'd acted badly, but she wanted to shock him. The desperation of her situation made the words spill out before she could stop them.

The next morning, neither mentioned the incident but things remained strained. They didn't make love and barely spoke to one another.

Rosa had to shake her head. If they thought they were giving Tom a good home, they were mistaken. Fortunately, he was too young to feel the tension between them.

Buford went on roundup and then to Dodge. Tom pined for him, but Emma was glad to be rid of him.

When Buford returned, he had gifts for everyone but her. He'd even brought Rosa a black and red silk shawl.

"For me?" she asked incredulously.

"You been with me a long time, Rosa. Both wives considered," he smiled.

"Whatta' 'bout Ma?" asked Tom.

Buford didn't know what to say. Emma helped him out of the awkward situation, even though it was with tongue in cheek.

"Why honey, the Colonel ain't gotta' bring me nothin'! Just havin' 'im return to me is present enough!"

That night he apologized to her. "Sorry, I didn't bring you nothin'."

"Don't fret. I learned not to expect nothin' from you."

Buford was tired and out of sorts after the long drive. "I can see you're still in a mood," he growled.

"I ain't in no mood. Just ain't pretendin' no more."

"You are a pain in the ass, you know that? Don't reckon I want to live with you no more."

"Don't think you ever did!" she said to his retreating back.

Buford slept with his men that night and for many nights after that. If they thought anything of it, they kept their thoughts to themselves.

He couldn't bear her coldness any longer and one night he confronted her.

"Emma, it's been a spell since we..."

"Since we what?" she asked watching him squirm.

"You know."

"You can have me any time you want. I'm a whore."

"Goddamn it, Emma! I hate when you talk like this. I'm your husband and I got a right."

"I ain't stoppin' you," she said.

Any passion he might have felt dwindled.

"Never mind. Don't want you no more. Reckon, I'll go see Jamie."

This comment sent Emma into a panic and she called out after him. "Colonel, wait!"

Buford paid her no mind and left the house. He got on his horse and thundered off.

When he reached the Long Horn it was crowded. He searched for Jamie and finally found her.

"How much for a poke?" he asked.

"You ain't got enough money," she said.

"What the hell? Are you in business or ain't you?"

"I am, but not for you. What happened, Emma finally come to 'er senses?"

"You don't like me much, do you?"

"No, I don't. I love Emma and you been 'er down fall.

Her life's been ruined and all 'cause of you."

"Yea, I been real bad to 'er. Give 'er my name and a decent place to live. I even claim 'er boy as my own. Decent women call on 'er. Yea, I've been a real son of a bitch," he said sarcastically.

Jamie looked at him and laughed coldly. "Yea, you been a real fuckin' prince. That's why you're here. Emma won't have you no more. I ain't got time. Mebbe' one of the other girls will oblige you." She got up and left.

Buford felt rage well up in him and left the Long Horn. He rode fast towards home. It was late when he reached the ranch, and everyone was asleep. He burst into the bedroom and Emma sat up with a start.

"Somethin' wrong?" she asked.

He didn't answer but stripped off his clothes and got in bed beside her. He grabbed her forcefully and crushed his lips to hers. She struggled for only a moment and then gave in to him. It had been several months since they'd been together, and she couldn't help herself.

They made love with all the fervor that abstinence brings.

When they were done, he said, "Lord, Emma, you sure feel good. Missed you more than I thought." He took her again and again and they stayed awake until dawn.

He got up to dress and she sighed with contentment. "I lied Colonel, it ain't never been an act with you."

"Glad to hear it. Reckon, you don't owe me no more."

"What?"

"You said last night you owed me. You cleared your debt. You sure are somethin'," he said with a smile.

"Why you..." she said jumping up from bed, unaware of her nakedness. She lunged at him and slapped him hard across the face. "I hate you!" she wailed and burst into tears.

"Aw Christ, Emma. What're you cryin' for? I didn't mean no harm."

"I know. That's what bothers me. I'll get a job. I'll open the goddamn bakery or take in washin' again. I'll anythin' I have to, to pay my way, but I ain't bein' your whore no more!"

"Jesus, Emma! Stop it. What's wrong with you? We was

both smilin' a minute ago."

"Well, I ain't smilin' no more," she said through her tears. "You just don't get it, do you Colonel?"

"No, I don't. Women! I'll never understand y'all!" he said leaving the room.

That night when he came in for supper, Emma was gone.

"Where the hell's Emma?" he snapped at Rosa.

"She's in town. Said something about opening her bakery again."

His face turned to a mask of fury. "Feed Tom and put 'im to bed. I'm gonna' go fetch his Ma."

When he got to the bakery Emma was removing baked goods from the oven. A bottle of whiskey sat by the stove.

"What the hell you doin'?"

"What's it look like?"

"It looks like you're gettin' drunk."

"So, what if I am? What the hell do you care?"

"You're really tryin' my patience. I put up with your moods long enough. You ain't openin' this fuckin' bakery!"

"Gotta' pay you for my keep somehow," she said.

He grabbed her roughly by the shoulders and shoved her into the wall.

"I'm tired of this, Emma. Can't abide no more."

He could be frightening when he was angry. Emma was five feet four and he towered a foot above her. She swallowed her fear and tried not to let his size intimidate her.

"Did you expect the same from Mabel?" she asked. "Did she have to go to bed with you to pay 'er way?"

He let her go and she nearly fell to the ground. "Don't talk 'bout Mabel like that! I swear, Emma, if'n you ever mention 'er again, I'll kill you! Do you hear me?"

His big frame trembled with rage and his eyes burned with a frightening glow. Emma knew she'd gone too far. Her courage faded and she collapsed in a heap of tears. "I ain't a whore no more, I ain't a whore no more," she repeated.

He looked at her where she lay sobbing and his anger turned to impatience.

"All right, Emma, you done made your point. Now get up and let's go home."

CHAPTER FOURTEEN

Emma and Buford rode back from the bakery in silence He finally grasped the situation and chastised himself for being such a fool. "Damn," he thought, "I should know by now to keep my goddamn mouth shut!"

When they got home it was late and everyone was in bed.

Emma went to the bedroom and Buford followed. He began to gather up some of his belongings.

"What are you doin'?" she asked.

"I'm movin' to another room."

"Why?"

"Why?" he repeated, in a cold voice. "Should be pretty goddamn obvious. Lord, you're peculiar! You don't want me to treat you like a whore. Ain't that what you said?"

"That ain't what I meant. You said you got my point."

"I did. If'n my layin' with you makes you feel like a whore, I won't do it no more." He sighed heavily and looked her in the eye. "When we got married, I figured you wouldn't mind satisfyin' my needs. Guess I was wrong."

"Guess you was," she said sadly.

"Don't gimme' those cow eyes. You don't want me pokin' you no more is the way I understand it."

"Ain't that a'tall! It's why you're pokin' me. It makes me feel cheap."

He looked at her with an icy gaze. "Cheap? Lord, I've paid for you more ways than one and believe me you ain't never come cheap."

Emma didn't know what to say and her eyes filled with tears. "Don't start your goddamn cryin'! I ain't never seen a woman cry as much as you!" He picked up his things and strode out of the room.

The next morning, he glared at her across the table as

they ate breakfast. She fidgeted but said, "How do you expect me to pay my keep?"

"Reckon, you do enough work 'round here."

"Sounds fair to me."

"Glad you finally approve of somethin'," he growled.

Buford left the house with his mind in turmoil. He wasn't pleased by this new arrangement at all, but he could see no alternative.

When he'd married Emma, he thought she'd be grateful. She serviced him willingly before she learned he saw it as terms of payment. He wished again that he'd known enough to keep his mouth shut.

Life settled down at the ranch once again. Emma went about her chores cheerfully. She tried to hide the empty void inside her and this time was successful.

Buford paid little attention to her as he'd always done. He became resigned to the situation. "There's plenty of whores if'n I need a poke," he thought to himself.

At social functions and to their friends they kept up appearances. No one knew they were estranged, not even Hi.

"Settle that problem with Emma?" he asked Buford one day.

"Yea. Things is fine."

"Thought so. Emma seems happy enough."

The only two who knew were Rosa and Juan.

"Dio!" said Rosa to her brother one day. "This is the worst marriage I've ever seen."

"Si, I agree with you, but you know the Colonel."

"I do, and he is a fool. He doesn't treat Emma anything like he did Mabel."

"He loved Mabel. He has no love for Emma."

"You don't have to tell me. Never does he show her any tenderness! Mabel, may she rest in peace, was a good woman, but Emma, Dio! She is ten times the woman."

"I thought you didn't like whores?" Juan asked bemused.

"Whores, no, but Emma is no longer a whore. Why do you think she is having all this trouble with the Colonel? I hear them when they argue. He still thinks of her that way."

"Ah!" Juan said, "Perhaps that is why he has been in

such a mood. He hollers at everyone. Nothing pleases him!"

There were many nights when Buford went to town and didn't come back until late. Emma wondered if he was seeing the whores at the Long Horn and asked Jamie about it when she came to visit.

"No, he ain't been to the Long Horn. If'n he's pokin' anyone, it's at the Bell Star 'cause none of us gals is gonna' service 'im."

"I heard of that place. I hear they got some real pretty gals there," Emma said in dismay.

Jamie scowled. "Nah! A bunch of amateurs. The men-folk still prefer us. That place ain't hurt our business none."

"Well, reckon he's goin' somewhere," sighed Emma. "Ain't gettin' nothin' from me. Probably got a gal at the Bell Star."

Her speculation was accurate. Buford had been going there frequently to visit a pretty Mexican named Angelina. After a while she became clingy and greeted him with more urgency than he cared for. He thought it best to stay away from her and his visits ceased.

• • •

When Buford and the men left for Kansas, Emma relaxed. She no longer had to live by his rules.

Buford came back a few months later. It was near dark when he came in but there was no mistaking the man who rode beside him.

Buford had found Josh in Kansas. Josh had been dissat-isfied
with his new employer, and eagerly accepted Buford's offer to return to the McLeod outfit.

When they reined in, Tom ran and jumped in Buford's arms.

"Howdy, Tom, Emma. Look who I found!" he said joy-fully.

"Howdy, Emma," Josh said, "Sure been a long time."

"Good to see you again, Josh," Emma beamed.

"Good to be back," he said.

"Found this ornery critter in Dodge," Buford said. "Talked 'im into comin' back."

Tom let go of Buford and ran to hug Josh. "We sure did

miss you!" he said.

Josh laughed. "Not as much as I missed y'all. Lord! Look at you, Tom. You growed a piece since I been gone."

"I'm big for my age," he said, looking down at his shoes, his face growing red.

"Reckon, you are. But ain't nothin' to be sorry 'bout! You're gonna' be a big man like your Pa. No one is gonna' fool with you!"

"I call the Colonel, Pa, but don't know who my real Pa is."

Josh and Emma both looked askance at Buford.

"Come see what I got for you," Buford said, changing the subject.

Buford brought gifts for everyone including Emma. He handed her a velvet box. Inside was a gold locket in the shape of a heart.

"It's the most beautiful thing, I ever seen," she said, her eyes all aglow.

After giving her the gift, Buford paid little attention to her. He, Tom and Josh went into the house leaving her behind. It didn't bother her as she'd come to expect it. "I'm finally learnin' my lesson," she thought. It was Tom's comment that troubled her mind.

That evening she mustered the courage to talk to Buford.

"Got somethin' on your mind?" he asked.

She held the locket he gave her clutched in her hand but didn't comment on it.

"Yea. Tom said somethin' today that struck me strange."

"What's that?"

"Said he didn't know who his Pa was. I thought you tole' 'im you was his Pa."

"Not exactly. Tole' 'im to call me Pa is all. Thought that was enough."

"Well it ain't. You heard 'im today. He wants to know!"

Buford sighed. "Thought he woulda' figured it out. Reckon, he didn't. I'll tell 'im."

"Be much obliged," she answered. Buford turned back to his ledgers.

"Reckon, that's all I have to say," she said turning to leave. She remembered the locket pressed in her hand.

"One more thing. Was nice of you to buy me this here gift. It's beautiful," she said holding it out.

"How come you ain't wearin' it?"

"Can't seem to manage the clasp. I'll get Rosa to help me."

"C'mon' over here. I'll help you. Wanna' see what it looks like on."

She went over to him and lifted her hair. He put it around her neck and glanced down. Her slender white throat and heaving bosom below made him light headed. He felt the first stirrings of passion and had a hard time controlling himself.

He fastened the clasp and she turned around to face him.

"How's it look?" she asked.

"Looks right pretty. It's real gold. Glad you like it."

"I love it," she said, standing close.

She smelled of flowers and he felt light headed again. Before he knew what he was about, he reached for her and held her tight.

She made no move to free herself and he bent forward and kissed her tenderly on the lips.

She threw her arms around him and time seemed to melt away.

When Emma awoke, she was disoriented. It took her a few seconds to realize Buford was in her bed.

She thought of the night before and shuddered with pleasure. In all their years of lovemaking, never had she known such a night. Her feelings of wellbeing crumbled when he awoke.

"I'm real sorry, Emma. Hope you didn't take last night the wrong way. Ain't 'cause of the locket or nothin'."

"Huh?"

"I don't want you to get the wrong idea 'bout last night. It won't happen again. Don't want you to feel beholdin'."

"I don't."

"Good," he said, not meeting her gaze.

After that night, Buford didn't cross the line again. They kept to their separate lives.

Buford found himself thinking of Emma from time to time

and scolded himself. "What the hell?" he thought to himself. "I'm wastin' time thinkin' of things that ain't important."

One thing he did think important was straightening things out with Tom.

When an opportune time presented itself, Buford spoke to him. "Tom, why'd you tell Josh you don't know who your Pa is?" he asked him.

"'Cause I don't."

"Sure you do. I'm your Pa. Kinda' figured you knew that."

"You are?" Tom asked breathlessly.

"Wouldn't of tole' you to call me that if'n' it was otherwise. One thing you gotta' learn son, a man don't mince words."

"What's mince, Pa? Like what Ma puts in a pie?"

Buford laughed and ruffled Tom's hair. "Means, a man don't say more than he has to."

"Oh, well if'n you's my real Pa, how come you and Ma didn't live together before?"

"Well, that's a long story, one that I'll tell you some other time. But we're all together now. That's what's important."

Later that night, Tom told Emma, "Pa, tole' me I was his son."

"Yea."

"Was he my Pa when we lived at the bakery?"

"Yea, he was."

"Well, reckon it don't matter none. We're all together now. That's what Pa says."

Emma's eyes filled with tears and she turned her head so Tom wouldn't see. How she wished it was true.

It was late when Buford came in and he was surprised to see her still awake.

"It's late. What are you doin' up?"

"I had to talk to you."

"Can't it wait 'til mornin'?" he said impatiently. "I'm tuckered out, been sittin' up all night nursin' a sick calf."

"It's 'bout Tom."

"I tole' 'im I'm his Pa. Ain't that what you wanted? Now if'n you don't mind, I'm goin' to bed," he said turning his back on her and walking away.

"He's askin' questions," she said dryly, stopping him in mid step.

"Yea, I know. I tole 'im I'd explain another time. Seemed to satisfy 'im."

"Maybe we should share a bedroom again."

Buford laughed coldly. "What the hell for?"

"Just think it would look more normal to Tom."

"He's too young to know 'bout such a thing. You got anythin' else you wanna' talk 'bout?"

"No, sorry I troubled you," she said quietly.

He entered his room and shut the door. Buford lay in bed a long time unable to sleep. He should've accepted her invitation to move back in their room.

The next morning, he approached her. "Emma, what do you want?"

She spun around, startled by the sound of his voice.

"Don't know what you mean."

"I'm gettin' confused, can't quite follow your tracks. Do you wanna' be together again or not?"

She still looked puzzled and he tried to explain. What you said last night 'bout sharin' a room. Was you serious?"

"Well…"

He interceded before she could gather her thoughts. "Just answer my question. You wanna' share a room again, or not? If'n we do, things are gonna' be like they was before and I ain't gonna' have you runnin' off every time I touch you."

Emma sighed and leaned against the door. "I don't wanna' argue with you, Colonel, but don't think I could go back to the way things was. I don't like feelin' obliged."

"Well, you are Emma."

She opened her mouth to speak but he held up a hand to silence her. "Not in the way you're thinkin'. But you are my wife and a man has a right to his woman when he wants 'er."

"His woman!" she thought happily, "He called me 'his woman'. Is he startin' to care for me?"

"I suppose you're right," she said calmly, though her heart beat hard in her chest.

"'Course I am. So what's your answer? I ain't got all

goddamn day."

"Yea, Colonel. I'd like it if you shared a bed with me again."

"It's settled then. Glad you come to your senses."

Emma was happier than she'd been in a long time. He said he had a right to sleep with her, not because she owed him anything, but because she was "his woman", two of the sweetest words she'd ever heard.

To Buford it was immaterial why she relented, so long as she did. He had needs and he thought it unseemly for a married man to have to resort to whores to satisfy them.

Any hopes Emma had that things would be different were dashed in a few day's time.

Buford did move back in and took her night after night. However, during the day, he went about his business like he'd always done, speaking to her only when necessary and ignoring her the rest of the time.

Emma realized with dismay that once again, the only tenderness he showed her was behind closed doors. She knew it wouldn't do to make a fuss and kept silent. They'd been married almost three years and standing up to him had accomplished nothing. If anything, it made things worse.

Emma often went to do errands in town. Now that she was accepted, Buford had no qualms about it.

One day as she rode over the plains, she saw a woman off in the distance. The woman staggered as if drunk. Emma whipped the horses and quickly brought the wagon to her side.

She was stunned to see Joanne Smith, stumbling about beaten and half naked. Joanne didn't seem to be aware of Emma's presence.

"Joanne!" Emma called out in shock, but Joanne made no response. Jumping from the wagon, Emma went to her and shook her hard.

"Joanne!" she cried again. Joanne's glazed eyes finally focused on her, but she remained silent.

Emma had enough experience to know what happened. "Who did this to you?" she asked.

"Indians," Joanne whispered.

"Lord, Joanne," Emma said softly. She examined her

quickly. "Don't look like you're hurt except for...c'mon', I'm takin' you home."

Emma helped Joanne into the wagon and covered her nakedness with her shawl. "What happened?"

"I was out ridin' at the edge of our land." Joanne paused unable to speak.

"Then what happened?"

Joanne took a deep breath and continued. "Three Indians come out of nowhere. They...they...they forced me to... then stole my horse." She burst into tears.

Emma placed a comforting arm around her. "Cry, Joanne, it'll do you good. It don't do to keep it in."

She continued to comfort Joanne on the way back to the Smith ranch when she saw a sight that turned her blood cold. The three Apache, with Joanne's horse in tow, made their way towards them.

"Lord, here they come again. Take this," she handed Joanne a colt revolver. Picking up another gun, Emma took careful aim and squeezed off a shot. Far from adept, she was lucky and one of the Apache fell from his horse. The other two came on, whooping and yelling and soon reached the wagon before Emma had a chance to fire again.

The two men circled the wagon. Emma stood up and flailed at them with her whip. One of them grabbed her arm and she fell out of the wagon with a thud. He jumped from his horse and threw himself on top of her while the other wrestled with Joanne.

As Emma struggled in the dust, she heard a gunshot. Joanne had killed her attacker. She managed to knee her opponent in the groin and jumped up. She had killed another of their attackers. Emma's foe got up. He was furious and unsheathed his knife. Emma screamed and tried to climb back in the wagon, to no avail. The Indian slashed her back and she fell to the ground. Another shot rang out and he fell dead.

"You sure is a good shot," was all Emma could say. She leaned heavily against the wagon, blood and sweat streaming down her face.

Joanne remained silent. After Emma caught her breathe, she climbed back in the wagon and rode to Charlie's as fast as her team would go.

"Much obliged to you" Emma said. "Where'd you learn to shoot like that?"

Joanne didn't respond at first but then answered. "Been shootin' since I was a girl."

Emma had suffered a nasty gash on her head when she fell from the wagon and she had to keep wiping the blood from her eyes so she could see. She was unaware of the knife cut to her back.

The arrival of the disheveled women caused a panic at the Smith ranch. A panicked Maryanne went to find Charlie and in a short time he came running.

"What in tarnation happened here?" he said. Joanne just stared at him.

"Apache," Emma said, starting to feel dizzy. "I was on my way to town when I found 'er. They'd already been at 'er. Was bringin' 'er back here when they come for us again. We kilt' 'em. Your woman's fine with a gun, Charlie." That was the last thing she said before she passed out.

"Go fetch the Colonel," Charlie shouted to one of his men.

When Buford arrived, Charlie led him to the room where Emma lay. She had come to and Maryanne was trying to tend to her. Maryanne's hands were shaking, and she was ineffective.

"I'll take care of 'er, Maryanne."

He didn't speak to Emma, but gently and carefully cleaned and bandaged her wounds.

"Feel strong enough to go home?" he asked when he was done.

"Yea. But wanna' talk to Charlie first."

"It'll have to wait, he's with Joanne and nearly out of his mind over this."

"That's what I gotta' talk to 'im 'bout. Please, Colonel!" she said, panic in her voice.

"All right," he sighed. He led her to the bedroom door and knocked softly.

"Charlie, it's the Colonel. Emma wants to talk to you. Can you come to the door? Don't wanna' disturb Joanne."

When Charlie opened the door he said, "Thank God,

they didn't get you, too," he said, his voice shaking with fury.

"That's what I wanna' talk to you 'bout. Ain't none of my business, but ain't no one gotta' know 'bout this, do they? Wouldn't benefit Joanne, none. If'n they gotta' know anythin' we say we was attacked and kilt' 'em. What else they done, ain't nobody's business."

Joanne, who lay silent all this time, spoke. "Emma?"

"Yea, Joanne, I'm here," she said going to her bedside.

Joanne grabbed her hand. "I'm sorry, Emma. I'm sorry for all the harm I done you."

"You ain't got nothin' to be sorry 'bout. You saved my life! That red skinned varmint woulda' kilt me sure if'n not for you."

Joanne put Emma's hand to her cheek and held it there. "I was wrong 'bout you."

Emma didn't speak, too touched by the display of affection. It was Buford who broke the silence. "Emma's got a point, Charlie. Ain't nobody gotta' know."

"Yea. No one has to know and they won't, but I know, goddamn it. I know!" he shouted rising from Joanne's bedside, his face red with rage.

Emma let go of Joanne's hand and grabbed Charlie's arm. "C'mon' outside with me a minute," she said, leading him out of the room. She closed the door so Joanne couldn't hear.

"What the hell's wrong with you, Charlie Smith? You ain't helpin' Joanne actin' like this! I know what you're thinkin'. You don't want 'er no more 'cause of what happened."

"Damn right. She's spoilt' goods now. Them fuckin' Indians done ruined 'er."

"Lord, Charlie," Emma said furiously. "You think she wanted this to happen? You was one of the few people in town who was decent to me when I give up whorin'. What I done in the past didn't bother you none, and I had a choice. Your woman didn't have no choice. It's a miracle they didn't kill 'er. She's been through bad enough without you actin' like a fool. You gotta' treat 'er like you always done, even better! You ain't got no idea what she's goin' through."

"You got no idea what I'm goin' through. I can't help thinkin' 'bout them with their filthy hands on 'er."

"You can't punish 'er for what happened! You got more heart than that, Charlie."

Buford opened the door and said to Charlie. "Joanne's callin' for you."

Charlie looked at Emma and was about to speak but changed his mind. He went in the bedroom and shut the door.

"I'm ready to go home." Emma said weakly. The last of her strength was spent and she sagged against the wall.

Buford picked her up and carried her down the stairs. He gingerly put her in the wagon, and they were on their way.

Neither of them spoke. When the house came into view, Buford said, "Why the hell did you go back to the ranch, Emma? Joanne tole' you them Indians was there. You shoulda' gone in to town."

"I wasn't thinkin' straight. Besides, if'n I went to town, everyone woulda' knowed what happened to 'er. Folks would treat 'er different. Ruin her reputation."

"Why you worried 'bout that? She ain't had a good word for you in years. You're too fuckin' soft."

Emma thought of all she'd just been through. "Soft!" she thought. She and Joanne had fended off a serious attack and killed three Apache warriors.

"I'm always a disappointment to you, ain't I?" she said sadly.

"You just ain't got no sense, is all."

Emma sighed. She could do nothing right as far as he was concerned. She'd nearly been killed, and he offered her no comfort, but criticized her instead. She changed the subject.

"I think you oughta' talk to Charlie."

"'Bout what?"

"Joanne. He don't feel the same 'bout 'er 'cause of what them Indians done. He don't wanna' poke 'er no more. Says she's spoilt goods. You know 'bout that."

"It ain't the same."

"No, it ain't. I tole 'im she had no choice. But he don't

seem to care."

"Joanne's a good woman. Never had any other man 'cept Charlie. 'Course he's feelin' bad 'bout it. It's natural."

"Yea, I guess it shoulda' been me they done," she said in a trembling voice.

"Lord, Jesus, Emma! Don't turn this here around. Ain't sayin' that. Just sayin' you was spoiled when I got you. You'd been with everyone in town and I knew it. It's different for Charlie. Joanne was pure when he got 'er."

She wished she had the strength to speak up to him. She knew better than to expect any sympathy, but as usual he added insult to injury. Her feelings hurt more than her body, but she kept silent.

When they reached the house, Rosa fussed over her and put her to bed. She fell asleep immediately. When she awoke it was dark and she was alone. She ached all over but got out of bed. She wanted to look in on Tom.

As she slipped on her robe, Buford entered the room.

"Where you goin'?"

"Was gonna' look in on Tom. Does he know 'bout today?"

"Knows you was hurt. Tole' 'im you fell outta' the wagon. He come in and seen for himself that you was all right. He's sleepin', peaceful. Just come from his room."

"Oh," she said softly. She sat on the bed and winced.

"Come in to check on you. Since you're awake let me look at you. You sure got banged up some."

"You ain't tellin' me nothin' I don't already know. Feel like I been in a buffalo stampede."

He redressed her head wound and said, "Take off them night clothes."

"Not tonight. I'm feelin' poorly."

"Jesus! Not for that. Gotta' check your back. Ain't too deep but still needs tendin'."

"Lord, gonna' have as many scars as you pretty soon," she said.

When he was done, she put her night gown back on and got out of bed.

"Now, where you goin'?" he asked.

"To the kitchen. I'm hungry. Rosa got any vittles left over?"

"Yea. I won't be here when you get back. Plan on bunkin' in my old room 'til you're feelin' better."

"Good night, then," she said. As she made her way to the kitchen, she fought back her tears. Once again, she'd been through a terrifying experience and he could care less. She took a deep breath and successfully choked them back. It wouldn't do to cry. This was the way it was and always would be. She couldn't spend the rest of her life feeling miserable.

A week after the incident Emma went to see Joanne.

Joanne's wounds were more emotional than physical, and Emma found her cleaning the parlor.

"Hope you don't mind me callin' like this," said a timid Emma.

"Lord, no. Was gonna' come see you but didn't know if'n you'd receive me. Charlie said I apologized to you but don't recall it."

"You did, but you got nothin' to feel sorry 'bout. I come here to thank you for savin' my life."

"Don't recall doin' that neither."

"Can we speak plain, Joanne?"

"Guess so."

"How much do you remember?"

"Remember seein' them Indians and then don't remember nothin' 'cept comin' to in bed."

"Did Charlie tell you what happened?"

"Yea, he did. Woulda' guessed the worse part of it anyhow," she said with a crimson face. "I'm sore as hell. He tole' me you found me and everythin' else that happened after that."

"Well, it's a blessin' you don't remember, Joanne, it really is. I ain't felt right since Gideon tried to do me. Even a gal like me don't like to be forced."

Joanne cleared her throat, "Don't remember nothin', that's why I wanted to come to you. I'm real sorry for what I said and done to you. Surprised you didn't leave me there to die."

"Lord, no, Joanne! Woulda' never done nothin' like that. I'm sorry I brought you back to the ranch. Nearly got us both kilt' and the Colonel was put out with me for it."

"Why did you come back here instead of goin' to town? It was closer."

"Truth to tell I wasn't thinkin'. I thought them red skins was gone."

"You was worried 'bout what folks would think."

"No, really, just thought it best to take you home. Guess I was wrong."

"You're a poor liar, Emma. I'm glad you didn't go to town. I'd rather been kilt' by them Indians then lettin' folks see me like that. I'm ashamed of myself," she said, tears welling in her eyes. "You tried to protect my reputation when all I done was try to ruin yours."

"Don't think like that, Joanne. You done what you thought was right."

"God forgive me," Joanne wailed.

"If'n I do, surely He must," she said.

"'Course still ain't on speakin' terms with the Colonel," Joanne said through her tears.

Emma laughed, "Neither am I half the time. You don't remember but he sat and held your hand while' I was talkin' to Charlie. He was a might put out with them Indians. Good thing we kilt' 'em. Hate to think what woulda' happened if'n Charlie and the Colonel got to 'em first."

"I know what you mean," Joanne said wiping her tears.

After that Emma and Joanne became close friends. Although, Joanne never did remember that awful day, she felt a bond with Emma.

They learned they hadn't been the only ones to see Apache so close to town. Several people reported seeing them and panic spread through Wilder Creek.

Buford went to Hi one day. "What's this I hear 'bout there bein' Indians 'round."

"Ain't nothin'. Me and my men go out every time someone sees one but we ain't found nothin' yet. Think every one's lettin' their imaginations run away with 'em. Ain't seen any and don't know of anyone who's been bothered by 'em."

"Shoulda' tole' you this before but those fuckers are out there. Joanne and Emma was attacked by Apache 'bout two weeks ago."

"Jesus Christ, Buford!" Hi said, jumping from his chair. "Why the hell didn't you tell me this earlier?"

Buford gave him the details.

"Don't make no never mind, you coulda' tole' me. Jesus! Don't you trust me no more?" Hi said, clearly furious.

"'Course I do. Thought they was just a few warriors lost on Charlies land. Outside of what happened at the Boutwell ranch, ain't never had no trouble with Indians here."

Hi sat deep in thought. When he spoke again, he was no longer angry. "You think we got a situation, here?"

"The folks who seen these Apache, are they reliable?"

"Some of 'em."

"Where they seein' 'em?"

"All over the fuckin' place! And when we get there, we don't find shit. That's why I thought we had nothin' to worry 'bout."

"Seems to me like they're watchin' us but they ain't gettin' too close."

"This ain't good."

"No, it ain't. Goddamn army's got 'em riled up, again. Already figured it was gonna' be hell gettin' through the Nations this year. Seems like we got trouble now and at our own front door to boot."

"Well, Colonel, what do you suggest we do?" Hi said the word "colonel" with sarcasm.

"Organize patrols. Put men out on our borders 'round the clock. Should be enough men in this piss hole of a town for that."

"I'd be much obliged if'n you'd help me with this here. I know you ain't no law man, but no one knows Indians as good as you 'ceptin mebbe' me and I can't do it alone."

Buford sighed. "Reckon, so. I got a bad feelin' 'bout this."

"I'll call a meetin' for tomorrow night. I'll let you do the talkin'. Hell, I'll just put you in charge."

"How'd I go from helpin' to bein' in charge?" Buford snapped.

"I got responsibilities here, too! Can't be everywhere at once."

"Yea, responsibilities! Settin' at the Long Horn with

whores all day and goin' to the Village to scare drunken Mexicans."

"This is serious, Buford! If'n you come to me in the beginnin' mebbe' wouldn't have this trouble now," said Hi, his eyes flashing in anger.

"All right, Hi. Seems we got a situation here."

Emma was mortified when Buford told her about the meeting. "You're gonna' have to tell 'em 'bout me and Joanne, ain't you."

"Can't be helped. Don't have to tell 'em everythin'."

The next evening the men gathered together. Buford questioned those who'd seen the Indians. He told them about Emma and Joanne's encounter.

"How come you and Charlie didn't speak up sooner?" a man in the crowd asked.

Buford thought quickly. "Didn't want to start a panic. There was only three of 'em and they was more interested in stealin' horses than killin'. Besides Joanne and Emma done kilt' 'em," he said proudly. "When I tole Hi 'bout this he said y'all been seein' them close to town, so now we're takin' this serious."

He continued, "Me and the Marshall decided it was time to take some action. We think the best thing for now would be patrols."

Buford had a map of Wilder Creek and outlined the areas to be watched. He assigned two men to ride together and had enough pairs to provide adequate protection. He told them what he expected of them. "Don't want no dead heroes," he concluded. "Y'all see any of 'em varmints you come ridin' in fast."

• • •

One morning, Buford came in and found Emma fastening her bonnet. "Where you think you're goin'?"

"Got chores in town."

"Lord, Emma. You can't go alone."

"Don't want to but got no choice. We got nothin' in the pantry. I ain't got no sugar, no salt, no flour...nothin'. Ain't lookin' forward to it, but I gotta' go."

"I'll get Josh to go with you."

"Be much obliged."

So it was that she and Josh went off to town together, heavily armed. As they rode along Josh wished things had turned out differently between them. During the years he'd been in love with her he'd become expert in knowing her every mood. She acted light hearted enough but he could tell she wasn't happy.

"Ain't seen you to talk to since I come back. How you been?" he asked.

"Been fine."

"Colonel, treatin' you all right?"

"Yea, got no complaints, why?"

"You ain't got no more sparkle in your eyes."

Emma laughed but it sounded force. "Sparkle? Never knew I had any!"

"You did, Emma. Always had a twinkle in your eye. No more. Shouldn't say this but I don't think you're happy."

"I am."

"Then how come you don't look it?"

"Stop it, Josh! Don't wanna' talk 'bout this."

"Do you good. Me and the other men ain't blind. We know what's goin' on."

"Don't know what you mean."

"Don't lie to me, I knowed you too long. If'n it wasn't for Tom he wouldn't bother with you a'tall."

"Ain't no one's business but my own."

"Run away with me, Emma," he said in a strained voice.

"What?" she asked in shock.

"Let's me and you high tail it outta' here."

"I couldn't leave Tom."

"I know. We'll take 'im with us. We'll go to Mexico. No one would have to know we wasn't man and wife."

"Josh, please stop," she cried. "I don't wanna' hear no more. Think I'd rather face the Apaches alone than listen to any more of this kind of talk."

Her distress moved him, and his face grew red with embarrassment. "Sorry, Emma. I don't know what come over me. I'm ashamed of myself for even thinkin' it."

"It's all right, Josh. Can we still be friends, or would it be hard for you?"

"No. I'd like to be friends."

"You ever hear of Gideon Jones?" she asked.

"Yea, the men tole' me what happened. Glad I wasn't here at the time. After the Colonel kilt' 'im, I woulda' butchered 'im."

"I know you never woulda' done to me like he did. Even if'n the Colonel don't love me, he don't take kindly for anyone on the ranch lookin' at me."

Josh knew she was right and kept his feelings to himself.

When they returned later that afternoon, Buford was in the house. He could hear Emma laughing at something Josh said.

He peered out the window and noticed a glow about her. Did Josh's hand linger a little too long on her waist when he helped her from the carriage?

He was aware of how Josh felt about Emma but was certain he'd never take liberties. Josh and Emma had known each other a long time and enjoyed each other's company. He knew he was being foolish but for some reason their easy banter bothered him.

He came out to help Josh with the supplies.

"Well, glad to see y'all back safe and sound. Coulda' been dangerous out there all alone." He emphasized the last two words and shot Josh a withering glance that turned the younger man cold.

"She was safe with me, Colonel. Wouldn't let nothin' happen to 'er," he said, trying to hide the guilt he felt.

"Didn't think you would," Buford said knowingly.

Emma noticed the glances they exchanged and realized their words had double meaning. She wasn't aware that although Buford knew nothing about women, he knew a lot about men.

CHAPTER FIFTEEN

One night, Buford was woken by someone hammering on the front door. He found Zeb and Junior on the porch in a state of agitation. They had been on patrol.

"We come across somethin' not far from here," Zeb said when they were inside.

"Indians?"

"I think so."

"How many?"

"It's too dark to see. By the sound, I'd say not too many. Coulda' swore I heard one of 'em speaking Spanish," Zeb said puzzled.

"We waited 'til they rode off before comin' here," Junior said.

"Think you can show me where they was?"

"Reckon, so," said Junior.

"Let me get my gear," Buford said.

He finished dressing in a second and went out to the bunkhouse to wake Ezra.

"We got trespassers. Get everybody up to watch the herd and have a few men stay at the house with Tom and Emma. I'll be back soon as I can." He quickly saddled a horse and the three men rode off into the night.

Zeb and Junior brought him back to where they'd heard the horsemen.

"Sounded like they headed off that way," Junior pointed.

Buford dismounted and lit a lantern. He kept the flame low and hunching down, looked around the area. After a while he came across their tracks. "Jesus, Joseph and Mary," he swore to himself.

Out loud he said, "Phineas and Charlie is up yonder. Hope they don't run into no trouble."

"You gonna' be able to track 'em?" Junior asked.

"Wish I could," he answered. "It's too fuckin' dark. Ain't no moon a'tall. Should be daylight soon. Reckon I'm just gonna' have to wait. Why don't y'all finish your shift and warn the other men when you go in."

"You're not thinking of going after them alone?" Zeb asked.

"Ain't goin' after 'em. Just gonna' do a little scoutin', is all. You go on." The two men rode off and Buford looked back down at the ground. What he saw filled him with dread.

When the first faint light of dawn reached the sky, he set off.

Emma didn't think anything amiss when she woke and found Buford gone. It wasn't until she entered the kitchen and found two of his men sitting at the table that she knew something was wrong.

"Don't fret, Mrs. McLeod," said Bill Harper. "Ain't sure what's happenin' but don't seem to be no cause for alarm. The Converse boys done seen or heard somethin' last night and the Colonel went to investigate."

"Apache?"

"Reckon."

• • •

It was late afternoon when Buford went to the jailhouse.

Hi rose when he entered. "'Bout time you got back. Been waitin' on you, since Zeb and Junior come in. What you find out there?"

"Somethin' you ain't gonna' like. We got ourselves a real renegade bunch."

"'Course I knew they was renegade! Peaceful Indians ain't gonna' be creepin' 'round town."

"Worse than you think. We got a mixed group. The Apache are ridin' with outlaws, some of 'em is Mexican. You're gonna' have to wire the army. We ain't no match for this here."

Hi's face turned white and he sat down heavily. He'd been a Ranger long enough to realize the trouble they were in.

"What do you think they're up to?" he asked.

"Ain't rightly sure, but I plan on findin' out."

"Whatever it is, it ain't good. You don't find that kind of outfit ridin' together unless they're up to somethin'," said Hi, "but do you think we need the army? We must have close to eighty fightin' men. How many you figure there is?"

"I ain't sure. They're ridin' in small bands. Found different sets of tracks all 'round town, but they's all headin' north. Thought I'd come in and see you 'fore I go back out. I wanna' see what we're up against. Looks like you're gonna' have to put Marshallin' aside for a while and start Rangerin' again."

Hi scowled. "I'll tell the army to come right quick. Put this in their hands. Want me to send word to Emma?"

"Would be obliged, might be out a few days."

"Want me to go out with you?" asked Hi.

"I think it'll be better if'n I go alone."

"Watch yourself," Hi said with concern when Buford got up to leave.

"Don't I always?" he asked with a smile.

Buford followed the tracks until it grew too dark to see. He paused to sleep for a while but was up at first light and on the trail again.

He had an uncanny ability for stealth and he and his horse blended into their surroundings. It was near dusk when he finally found what he was looking for.

He looked down from a ledge onto an Apache camp below. From what he could see there were close to sixty warriors and near that number of outlaws.

He climbed down from his perch and crept as close to the camp as he dared. The sound of the camp bounced off the canyon walls and he was fortunate to find a place to hide where he could over hear conversation. He settled in for a long wait.

He lay there many hours before he heard two outlaws talking. They were the only members of the camp still awake and sat in front of a fire, passing a bottle of whiskey between them. Buford had no trouble hearing them in the silence of the sleeping camp.

"Donny, how many beeves you figure we're gonna' get?" asked the first man.

"Don't know for sure but probably a whole passal. Great Moon says his people don't want none of 'em. All they want is their land back," Donny replied.

"What you gonna' do with your cows?"

"Probably sell 'em when we get to Mexico," said Donny.

"Not me," said the first man. "Gonna' ranch mine."

"Reckon, it don't matter," Donny sighed. "Gotta' get 'em first. Ain't gonna' be easy."

"You're loco. Gonna' be like takin' candy from a baby."

Donny shook his head, "Don't know 'bout that. Hear tell they got some mean law men down there."

"Y'all worry too much. Law men, my ass. They got two ole' retired Rangers. One of 'em's Marshall and he got two deputies. That's all there is. Rest of 'em is all ranchers. Besides we're gonna' surprise 'em."

"I don't know," said Donny. "Them Rangers figured out somethin' was up. You saw the patrols yourself."

"Yea, but they don't know what and they don't know when."

"True, enough," Donny laughed. "They's all gonna' be in church singin' hymns. We're gonna' be takin' their town right from beneath their prayer books."

Buford couldn't believe his good fortune. These men had given him every detail. He left his hiding place and made his way to his horse without a sound.

As he rode, he thought of Great Moon. Years ago, he'd pursued the warrior and renegade all over Texas, but Great Moon alluded him. It had been a test of skill and cunning between the two men. Buford had been frustrated by the illusive Apache but as time went by with no word of him, Buford thought he might've driven him out of Texas after all.

Buford didn't stop to sleep but rode through the night. He made it back to town by mid-day. Hi let out a sigh of relief when Buford, haggard and dusty, entered the jail house. "Good to see you back."

"Good to be back. Get a message to the army?"

"Yep. Now just gotta' wait."

"We got 'til Sunday," Buford replied and told him what he heard.

"Lord! Don't make sense. Why do you think them Indians want Wilder Creek? Army would just come and take it away from 'em. Don't seem like Great Moon's style a'tall."

"Couldn't agree with you more. Got a feelin' there's someone else behind this. The Apache made a deal with them outlaws. But figure someone else made a deal with the Apache. Just wish I knew who. Whoever it is wants Wilder Creek."

"Just hope the army's here by Sunday."

"You and me both. We're gonna' have to work with 'em, though. Gonna' need every able-bodied man in this here town.

• • •

Tom, burst into the kitchen, "Ma! Ma!"

"Goodness," Emma scolded, coming from the pantry. "What's all the ruckus 'bout?"

"Pa's comin'!"

Emma ran out to the porch and she and Tom watched Buford approach.

When he dismounted, Tom ran to him and hugged him around the waist. "Thought the Indians got you," he cried.

Buford hugged him back. "Well, as you can see, I'm fit as a fiddle! Just a might weary. Now c'mon. I wanna' wash up and get some grub. What's been happenin' in this outfit since I been gone?"

Tom chattered away and followed Buford to the pumphouse. "Get some food on the table, Emma. I'm hungry as a horse," he called as they walked by.

Emma went to the kitchen and said to Rosa. "You heard the man. Let's get 'im some food."

"Seems the banditos would've done you a favor if he did not return."

"Rosa!" Emma scolded. "That ain't nice!"

"I know, but he makes me loco, that one! When I think how he treated Mabel and how he treats you..."

"Enough, Rosa. I won't have no more of that kind of talk. It don't help any. Now go and fetch me an apple pie from the pantry."

Rosa went off muttering a steady stream of Spanish.

Buford came in the house with nothing but a towel

wrapped around his middle. She couldn't help the flutter in her stomach at the sight of his hard, muscular body.

"Ain't you a scandal!" she laughed. "Put some clothes on and I'll have your vittles on the table by the time you're ready."

• • •

As Hi and Buford suspected, there was someone else behind the planned attack of Wilder Creek. He was Lord Lawrence Evans Barr of England.

A wealthy man, he'd left his native country to traverse the great American continent. Like many Englishmen he was enamored of the great expanse of land in the west. He'd come to the New Mexico Territory with hopes of raising sheep.

He settled in the north east corner of the territory, north of Ute Creek and close to the Nations. Much to Lord Lawrence's amazement he learned that local ranchers loathed sheep herders.

They claimed the sheep ate the grass down to the roots, then cut the roots with their hooves. Sheep secrete a sticky substance from their hooves which did further damage to the grass. Ranchers also believed cattle were repelled by the smell. Wars between sheep herders and ranchers were common place in the territory.

Lord Lawrence met with resistance at every turn and decided he must find a different place for his operation.

He didn't want to raise cattle which he knew nothing about. His father and grandfather had raised sheep back in England and that's what he had his heart set on. He traveled the territory and could find nothing that suited his needs.

It was during this time he made the acquaintance of Great Moon, an Apache scout and no friend to the white man. Great Moon would've taken his life, but Lord Lawrence made a bargain with him. If the Apache could find a suitable location for his ranch, he would give Great Moon his original holdings which were vast. The Apache warrior was glad to take on the task.

Great Moon travelled far and wide and thought Wilder Creek a perfect spot. It had plenty of water and grazing land and was far from any other town. The only obstacle was the people who inhabited it. Small and isolated, Wilder Creek was vulnerable to attack. Great Moon thought with enough men, he could take it easily.

He didn't have enough warriors, but a plan began to form in his mind. Once Wilder Creek was taken, there'd be thousands of steers that neither Great Moon nor Lord Lawrence wanted. With stolen cattle as a reward, he had no trouble procuring outlaws to help him. He outlined his plan to Lord Lawrence who gave him full control of the operation. Everyone would benefit. The Apache would get his land, the outlaws would get the cattle and he would get Wilder Creek.

Great Moon and his men made scouting expeditions to the area. Some of his men went into town posing as legitimate cow punchers. They confirmed Great Moon's suspicions. The hundred or so people in town posed no problem to them.

Lord Lawrence had no qualms about wiping out a small town. A cold and calculating man, he had a singular purpose in mind and would let nothing deter him from it.

• • •

After a good's night sleep Buford returned to the jailhouse. "We're gonna have to hold a meetin' and tell the men what's goin' on."

"Already done it. Yea, while you was eatin' and sleepin' like a hog, I sent word out to meet tonight."

Buford looked discouraged. "We're gonna' have to come up with a plan. It's fuckin' Wednesday. We got four days to get ready for them sons of bitches."

"You're forgettin' the army."

"I ain't forgettin' 'em. Doubt they'll get here in time. We gotta' make other plans in case."

Hi sighed, "All right. This is gonna' be a fuckin' bitch."

At the meeting Buford took the floor. He told them what he found. "It ain't just Indians we gotta' fight. They hooked up with some mighty bad white men. We're lookin' at 'bout a hundred twenty of 'em. Maybe more. We're all gonna' have to fight, even if'n the Army gets here in time. This band are a bunch of professional killers."

"What 'bout our cows and our women folk?" Charlie asked.

"Got some ideas but if'n the army shows up it'll be their call. For now, think y'all better bring your herds in, keep 'em close and your women folk closer. Keep everyone and everything on your ranch. Arm your men and keep a rider ready to go. If'n there's any trouble have 'im come to town."

"Try not to panic your women folk but let 'em know what we're up against. If'n any are good with a gun, give 'em one."

• • •

When the army arrived on Friday, Buford and Hi were in the jailhouse making plans. Captain Jackson came in and introduced himself.

After introductions were made, he said, "Well, what do we got here, gentlemen?" Buford told him about the planned attack.

"Looks, like we got here just in time," said the Captain. "although, I've only got thirty men."

"You got 'bout another eighty here," said Buford.

"That'll have to do. I'm hopin' y'all will help me with the plan of attack. There's no finer Indian fighters in the west," said Captain Jackson with respect.

The Captain chose the hotel as headquarters and the three men began to plan their course of action.

They knew no one on the outskirts would be safe and wanted everyone in town by Sunday morning. The Captain also wanted to bring the cattle in.

"I agree we have to bring folks in, but not the cattle. If'n we do, they'll know we're waitin' for 'em. Didn't think there was no harm havin' the beeves on the ranch. Roundups startin'."

Buford wanted to ambush them while the Captain wanted to fight them outside of town.

"Can't do that," scowled Buford, "It would be a slaughter. Ain't got enough men to fight them varmints and guard the women, too. Besides, we got some veterans but most of 'em are ranchers not fightin' men."

"What do you think we should do?" Captain Jackson asked.

"I think we gotta' hide the women, children and those who can't fight in these here buildins'," he pointed out the window to the structures that lined the main street. "Then we'll set up the men this way," he indicated various locations. "The rest of us go to church and observe the Lord's day. We want 'em to come into town just like they planned."

Some women, like Joanne, wanted to be involved. They could shoot as well as any man, and better than some. Buford reluctantly agreed. They needed all the firepower they could get. Emma and a few other women volunteered to stay at the church to nurse the wounded.

By Sunday morning everything was in place. The women and children huddled in back rooms and dirt cellars all up and down the street. The men were strategically placed in every door, window and roof of these same buildings. The rest would be at the church.

January Watson, a spinster who played the organ, volunteered to stay so things would appear normal. Buford was grateful to the feisty old lady. At 8:00, he instructed her to play and the group in the church began to sing the first hymn.

Josh got an eerie feeling as he looked around the church. The men waited at the windows, singing to the Lord while they loaded their weapons and checked their gear.

Great Moon and his men circled the town. Some of his men thought it strange that there wasn't a soul around. The ranches and houses were empty.

"Ain't strange a'tall," said one. "They's all in church. These are God fearin' folks."

"Well, they're gonna' be meetin' their maker soon enough," said another.

"Here they come," said Charlie. Everyone kept singing.

When Great Moon and his men came within range, the men commenced firing.

What followed was a hellacious battle. The men loaded and fired until they're hands were raw and burned. Joanne was shooting from the bell tower and Lydia loaded her guns. Great Moon's men still came on.

A bullet thudded into the sill two inches from where Buford stood, and splinters of wood flew in his face. "Son of a bitch, that was close," he swore silently as he took aim and fired.

Bullets thudded all around them in the church, many of them finding their mark. The wounded were brought to the pews and tended to by the women.

Soon the gun fire at one end of the street stopped. It grew more sporadic at the other end.

"Wish I knew what the Captain and Hi was up to," Buford thought. The three men had split up. The Captain and Hi at either end of the street and Buford in the middle at the church.

He peered out a window and had his answer. Great Moon had gathered his forces and surrounded the church. Soon Buford observed men stealthily moving up from each end of the street. They had left the safety of their hiding spots to fight outside the besieged building.

The battle raged on. Caught between the army and townsfolk, it was late afternoon when Great Moon rode off with less than a dozen survivors.

The men gave a cheer. It was cut short by the smell of smoke and the first flicker of fire reaching the sky.

Great Moon didn't leave in total defeat. He set fire to everything he passed on his way out of town, though Captain Jackson and his men were in close pursuit.

Many of the buildings that were ablaze had women and children in them, and pandemonium reined. Buford rode up and down the street calling out orders and soon some semblance of order was maintained.

The street was full of activity as men and women ran here and there forming fire brigades and helping the wounded.

Everyonr had been able to flee the burning buildings except one unfortunate group hidden in the blacksmith shop.

Josh rode down to him, "Colonel, come quick. We got folks trapped."

When he got there he instructed the men to throw buckets of water on the back wall where the agitated blacksmith told him the women and children were hidden. Buford charged in through smoke and flames.

His eyes teared from the heavy smoke, nearly blinding him. He picked up a sledge hammer and made his way to the back where he could hear the terrified cries of the occupants.

Picking his way gingerly through the flames he finally reached them and led them to the area the men doused with water.

With one mighty blow he banged a whole in the wall. Two more blows made it large enough for the women and children to pass through. He'd just gotten the last person out and was gulping fresh air into his burning lungs, when Emma ran to him.

"Colonel! Come quick. It's the Marshall. They just brung 'im in and he's hurt real bad."

Buford jumped back on his horse and reached out to her. She clambered on behind. "Where's Tom?" he asked in a voice made hoarse by smoke and exertion.

"He's safe, brought 'im and J.B. to the Long Horn, Jamie's keepin' an eye on 'em."

"The Long Horn?" he scowled.

"Yea. Rosa's helpin' with the wounded, everyone's busy, didn't know what else to do with 'em."

The hotel had previously been chosen for a makeshift hospital and equipped with medical supplies. Now people went in and out, bringing in the wounded and carrying out the dead.

To Emma, it seemed like the end of the world. Flames lit up the sky lending an eerie glow to the dead men and horses that littered the ground. Frenzied people dashed here and there, going from one emergency to another. The scene was one of panic and confusion.

When they reached the hotel, Buford jumped from his horse and ran into the building unmindful of Emma, who followed behind.

He found Hi on the dining room floor with a distraught Lydia beside him. His face was covered with sweat and blood.

"Buford, you ole' son of a bitch. What the hell happened to you? You's as black as a darkie."

"Fightin' fire when Emma fetched me."

"Well, glad you come 'fore I died."

"You ain't gonna' die. You're too fuckin' ornery."

"Sure I am. I'm gut shot. Doc says there's nothin' he can

do."

"Ain't gonna' let you die that easy, Hi. If'n Doc says he can't do nothin' I might as well give it a try."

"I ain't gonna' die by your hand, Buford."

Hi said this to thin air as Buford had already gone in search of the things he'd need. He came back a moment later.

"If'n you gals got no stomach for this, y'all better leave. Ain't gonna' be pleasant but could use your help."

"I'll stay," said Lydia, through her tears.

"Me, too," said Emma.

"Get the hell away from me, Buford. I know what you're about."

"Gonna' knock you out, Hi. You ain't gonna' feel a thing."

"As I recall, you done this to Stuart Reed." To the women, Hi explained, "Reed was in the Rangers with us. Got 'imself gut shot and ole' Buford here tended to 'im."

"Well, he lived, didn't he?" Buford snapped.

"Yea, but claimed he never shit right again."

Buford ignored him and placed a rag soaked with chloroform over his face.

Emma almost retched as Buford cut into Hi's stomach. He worked steadily and silently, speaking only when he needed something.

Finally, he produced the bullet. Buford staunched the flow of blood and investigated the wound. He cleaned it out and asked for the needle and heavy black thread Emma had by her side. She handed it to him, and he began to sew.

When he was done, he leaned back and wiped his brow. "Well, Lydia, I done what I could."

"Reckon, Doc couldn't have done no better," she said.

"That ain't true. If'n Hi pulls through, he might never be right again. Doc mighta' been doin' 'im a favor, leavin' 'im be."

"To die?" Lydia asked in a trembling voice.

"Sounds hard, I know," said Buford quietly. "But he wouldn't suffer."

He remained quiet, choked with emotion. He cleared his throat and said, "Get some of my men and take 'im home."

He went out and found the situation in utter chaos. He

wearily climbed on his horse and fired three shots into the air. He frightened some who thought the outlaws came back, but he got everyone's attention. He organized work details and attended to hundreds of other things. No one resented him taking charge, if anything they were relieved. Calm and collected, he had an authority that made people obey him without question.

When Captain Jackson and his men rode back to town the next day, they were amazed at how orderly things were.

Men were ripping down the charred ruins of the buildings while others dragged horse carcasses to be buried in a pit outside of town.

Women were busy cleaning broken glass and other debris from the board walk and street, while children went about doing errands and helping where they could. A burial detail was at work, digging graves in the hard earth.

Captain Jackson found Buford at the hotel, where he was tending the wounded.

"Can I have a word, Colonel?" he asked.

"Sure," said Buford. "Kinda' hectic here, how 'bout we go to the saloon."

When they got to the Long Horn the Captain told Buford of his progress. "We followed them sons of bitches as far as we could but lost 'em in the hills. We got three more but not before they killed five of my men. What were your losses?"

"Fourteen dead, twenty-three wounded," said Buford, "some of 'em women and children. I wanna' know who's behind this," he said angrily. "I know someone put Great Moon up to it."

"I don't know as you'll ever find out. I don't reckon you'll have trouble with Great Moon again. He didn't have many men left."

"Don't mean a goddamn thing," Buford growled. "He can always round up plenty more if'n he's got a mind. Shoulda' gone after 'em with y'all. I gotta' find out."

"I wished I'd a' done that for you, but I couldn't. I had wounded men and orders to move out as soon as this business was over."

"I ain't blamin' you," said Buford. "Know you can't follow 'im all over the danged country."

"Why are you so certain this wasn't his idea?"

"Just know is all. Wilder Creek is perfect ranch country. The Apache ain't ranchers. Someone else wanted this town."

"Reckon you're right. If it's any comfort, we followed them a far piece and they didn't have a single cow."

"Sent out hands from each outfit to check on their beeves. They all come back and reported no livestock missin'. Didn't think they'd stop with y'all on their tail. Without you and your men, I believe it woulda' been a slaughter. We're much obliged."

Captain Jackson looked embarrassed by Buford's heart-felt thanks. This man was a legend and the Captain was in awe of his fighting skills. He also had never seen anyone take charge as effortlessly as Buford had. This made it unnecessary for him to stay and restore order. The Comanche were stirred up and he was needed elsewhere.

"Well, looks like my work here is done. I'm leavin' the town in good hands. Ever think of goin' back into service? The army could use a man like you."

Buford gave him a weary smile. "My soldierin' days is over. I like bein' a rancher. I don't have to look over my shoulder all the fuckin' time."

• • •

Great Moon was angry. His plan had failed, and he'd lost many warriors. He suspected that Buford was responsible for the ambush and he vowed to get revenge.

The next few days were busy ones for the people of Wilder Creek. Buford wished he could leave but he was needed here. He and Emma were staying at Lydia's helping her with Hi who clung to life by a slender thread.

The Parson performed a service for the fourteen souls who'd lost their lives. Almost every outfit had lost men, including Buford. Reuben Buzzell had been killed and Bill Harper lay seriously wounded.

The warriors and bandits were buried unceremoniously in a mass grave. Some of the women argued that the white men deserved better, but Buford held firm.

"They was outlaws and is goin' straight to hell. Don't see no need to put everyone out on their behalf. Y'all got better things to do."

"That's not the point, Colonel," said one of the women with disapproval. "It ain't Christian not to bury the white men proper."

"Christian?" Buford echoed, with a harsh laugh. "Well, if'n you got a mind to dig their graves, go right ahead. I ain't wastin' the man power."

Joanne Smith entered the hotel while this conversation was taking place. "Elizabeth Raymond, what you doin' botherin' the Colonel?" she snapped. She glared at the other women. "Ain't there enough to do without worryin' 'bout some riff raff that tried to kill us? Now skedaddle, I got important business with 'im."

They cleared out in a huff and Buford heaved a sigh of relief. "Much obliged, Joanne. What was it you wanted to see me 'bout?"

"Nothin'," she smiled. "Just didn't want them hens givin' you trouble is all."

"You're a pistol, Joanne," he laughed. "I guess this means you ain't mad at me no more."

Joanne blushed. "I've been a jack ass. It was none of my business who you married, but I was a might disappointed in you. Me and you had words over it. I found out when Emma saved my life what a good woman she is."

"Well it took you long enough," he said with mock anger. After she left, he drank a generous glass of whisky and went to see Hi.

When he entered the bedroom, Emma looked up. Buford noticed how tired she looked.

"Why don't you get some sleep, he said.

"Reckon, I will. I tole' Lydia I'd wake 'er up soon any way. When she gets here, want you to get some sleep yourself. You look plum tuckered out."

"I'll sleep when I got a mind to," he said. "Let Joanne be."

Hi drifted in and out of consciousness and Doc kept him heavily sedated. After a few more days with no change, Buford and Emma decided to go back to the ranch.

The gentle swaying of the wagon put little Tom fast asleep and Buford saw an opportunity to speak his mind.

"Wasn't good that you brought Tom to the Long Horn,"

he said.

Emma had forgotten about it.

"Didn't know what else to do. All hell had broke loose. Buildin's in flames, people runnin' 'round like chickens with their heads cut off. Figured he'd be safe there with Jamie. He's knowed 'er his whole life."

"He ever ask you 'bout 'er?"

"No?"

"He never asked you why she wears all that paint and fancy clothes? Or why she lives on top of the saloon?"

"No."

"Well, he asked me."

"He never been curious 'bout it before," Emma replied.

"He's gettin' older."

"What you tell 'im?"

"Tole' 'im she was a singer there. You better start usin' your head, Emma. Good thing the other gals wasn't there. They was all out helpin'."

Emma's already taught nerves snapped. She kept her voice low but her anger was apparent.

"Goddamn it to hell. I can't never do nothin' to please you. Every fuckin' thing I do is wrong. Why don't you just shoot me and be done with it. Put us both out of our misery."

"Watch your mouth," he hissed, angry at her show of temper. "Ain't that a'tall. You just ain't got no sense, never did neither as far as I can tell."

"Ain't that the truth. If'n I did, woulda' never joined up with the likes of you. Findin' fault with everythin' I do. I ain't perfect like Mabel!"

"Tole' you not to talk 'bout 'er, didn't I?" he growled.

"Yea, you did, but can't help it. Rosa's always tellin' me how you was with 'er. I know you don't love me none but Lord! I get raped, lose a chile', get attacked by savages and you don't bat an eye."

"That ain't true. I cared. Just kept it to myself, is all. I didn't wanna' encourage you any. You've known how I feel 'bout you from the beginning so don't act all hurt and pathetic like. I ain't never lied to you."

What he said was true and she remained silent. Besides, she didn't have the energy to argue any more. She sighed heavily. "You're right, Colonel. Sorry for what I said. Guess I'm wore out and ain't thinkin' too clear."

"Reckon, you are."

Even though it was early afternoon when they reached the ranch, the three of them went to bed. When Emma woke it was morning and Buford was gone."

"Where's my menfolk?" she asked Rosa.

"Out working with the herd."

"Did Tom sleep straight through?"

"Tom!" Rosa laughed. "Not that one. He woke up in time for supper. I let him eat then put him back to bed."

"The Colonel?"

"I don't know. He didn't eat with us last night and he was gone this morning when I woke up. He came to get your boy about an hour ago. Would you like me to fix you breakfast?"

"I'm not hungry. Been feelin' kinda' queasy, lately."

"Oh?" said Rosa with a twinkle in her eye. "For how long?"

"Coupla' weeks now."

"Are you expecting?"

"Lord, no! The Colonel would tan my hide if'n I got myself in a family way. It started the day me and Joanne were set upon by those red skins. Reckon, it's just nerves."

Buford and Tom returned home at supper time.

"You feelin' poorly?" Buford asked Emma. "You look a might peaked."

"That's what Rosa said. Just tired is all."

"We've all been through a lot."

"Yea, we have."

"Gonna' go in town and see Hi," he said.

"Can I come, Pa?"

"No, Tom. Reckon you and your Ma should stay home. It's a long ride and it'll be late when I get back. Thought you'd have your fill of town by now."

When Buford reached Hi's, Lydia met him outside, tears in her eyes. "Was just comin' to fetch you," she said. "Hi ain't doin' too good. Doc's in with 'im now." Buford squeezed her arm reassuringly and led her back into the house.

Doc was changing the dressing when Buford entered

the bedroom.

"Ever think of becoming a doctor, Colonel?" Doc asked without looking up.

"No can't say that I have."

"You did a fine job on the Marshall, here, although I don't think he's going to make it. I've done what I can, now it's up to God," he said, closing his bag and rising to leave.

Buford looked down at Hi, his heart nearly bursting in agony. He couldn't imagine what it would be like without his lifelong friend.

Lydia looked at him mournfully. "My man's gonna' die," she said in a trembling voice. Buford held out his arms to her. She rushed to him and sobbed against his chest. "What am I gonna' do if'n I lose my man?" she wailed.

"You ain't lost 'im yet. He's a tough ole' bird. He'll pull through," Buford said with a confidence he didn't feel. "I'd like to bunk with y'all if'n you ain't got no objection."

"Much obliged, Colonel, but can't let you do that. You gotta' get your herd ready and Emma might get worried."

"My men can take care of things and Emma won't fret. I don't keep regular hours, she ain't gonna' think nothin' of it."

Lydia looked at him. "If'n you think it'll be all right, I'd like you to stay."

Curiosity about Emma and Buford penetrated her grief. She wondered if they were happy. She'd always thought Emma would confide in her if she had a need to. It wasn't that she saw anything wrong between them but neither did she see any affection.

Her musing was broken by Buford's voice.

"Lydia?" he said for the third time.

"Sorry, Colonel. Reckon, my mind was elsewhere."

"You're tired. Y'all go on to bed, I'll sit up with Hi. If'n there's any change a'tall. I'll wake you."

"Be much obliged, been sittin' by his side since yesterday."

"You got any whiskey?"

Lydia smiled despite herself. "'Course I do. You know Hi," she said and then burst into tears again.

"Lydia..." Buford started to say.

"No, it's all right, Colonel. I'll fetch it." She brought him the whiskey and a glass.

"Now go get some sleep," said Buford gently. "A few hours shut eye's gonna' make you feel a heap better."

Lydia looked at him. "Don't know what I'd do without you. You done saved my man so many times. Even if'n he... you done everythin' you could."

"Go to bed," he said pouring himself a glass of whiskey. The chair was too small for his large frame and fidgeted trying to get comfortable.

It was some hours later that Hi spoke. "Lydia?" he called out in a hoarse whisper.

Buford was by his side in a second. "She's sleepin'. I'm here."

"Jesus, Lord!" Hi laughed weakly. "Bad enough I'm dyin' but Lydia leaves me with a jack ass."

"You're the jack ass, if'n you think I'm gonna' let you die," Buford said, his eyes full of tears.

"You son of a bitch," said Hi, "my guts is burnin' and it's all your fault."

"Reckon, it is. Here drink this," said Buford administering a hefty dose of laudanum. Hi drank it and fell back to sleep before Buford could get Lydia.

She came in hours later. "How's he doin'?"

Buford smiled. "Good. He come to for a minute last night and cussed me out. Reckon, that means he's gonna' be all right. He passed out again before I could fetch you."

"I knew he'd wake up when I wasn't with 'im! I set there for two whole days." She started to cry.

The reticent Buford took her in his arms.

"Don't fret, Joanne. He'll wake up again. Don't matter whose here long as he gets better. If'n you don't mind I'd like to bunk out with you awhile."

"That would be fine, if'n you could. You seem to have away of rousing him."

Buford laughed. "That's 'cause I piss 'im off. I'll go fetch some things and come back."

A bleary-eyed Emma greeted him when he returned.

"Colonel, you had me scared to death," she said. "I thought you mighta' got bushwhacked by one of them varmints."

"I don't think they'll come back for a spell. I spent the night at Hi's. He ain't doin' well and Lydia was plum tuckered out. I stayed to give 'er a hand. Just come for some clothes. I'm goin' back."

"You want that I should go? she asked.

"No. It ain't necessary. I wanna' be there with 'im in case....," he got choked up and couldn't go on.

CHAPTER SIXTEEN

Buford stayed on at the Johnsons. Hi never spoke again except to ask for laudanum. After, he'd go into a drug induced sleep.

A week passed when he awoke. He struggled to sit up and Buford helped him.

Hi looked at his friend. "Am I in hell? How come every time I open my eyes, you're here?" He winced, "Lord, I hurt."

"No, you ain't in hell. The first words you've spoken and you fuckin' complain," Buford scowled. "I'll get you some laudanum."

"I don't want it," said Hi.

"Don't want none of your bullshit," said Buford, going to his bedside with a draught.

"No, I mean it. Makes me addle brained. I wanna' stay awake for Christ's sake. Wanna' see Lydia and J.B."

Buford found them in the backyard. He cracked a huge smile. "I got good news. Hi's awake and wants to see y'all. But I gotta' warn you he's in a foul mood. I can tell you he ain't got no love for me right now," he laughed.

When they entered the room, Hi said with mock anger. "Lydia, what you doin' leavin' me with this jack ass?"

"Hi, darlin'," said Lydia dissolving into tears.

J.B. planted a kiss on his father's head. "Pa. I thought you was gonna' die."

"I woulda' but ole' Buford here won't let me." His tone softened and he put an arm around his wife and son. "Sure is good to see y'all. I thought I never would again." His eyes filled with tears, but he recovered quickly. To change the mood he said cheerfully, "I'm hungry as a hog. You got any vittles?"

"Sure, I do. I'll fix you a steak."

"That would be fine."

"Would be," said Buford, "but reckon you ain't havin' any. Get 'im some soup."

"Soup? I'm hungry! I want me some food."

"Can't have it, yet. You heard what I said Lydia, get 'im soup."

"God damn it, Buford! This is my house and if'n I want..."

"Lydia, the soup!" Buford snapped. She scurried to the kitchen.

"You can't eat no solid food yet. It'll tear you up."

"All your fault, too. As I recall you was the one pokin' in my innards."

"Yea. You don't wanna' be like Reed, do you? Thought you'd wanna' shit proper."

Hi laughed and then winced. "Lord, I feel bad. Feel weak as a kitten and hurt like hell."

"Gonna' take a while to get your strength back. Don't rightly know if'n the pain'll leave you."

"Why ain't I surprised. Knew I was in for trouble when I saw that knife in your hand."

"No need to thank me for savin' your fuckin' life," Buford said.

"Sure, would like to get outta' this bed."

"Let's go," said Buford, ripping the blankets off. He scooped Hi up in his arms.

"Lord, Buford. I ain't no woman! Reckon I can walk by myself."

"Not today."

He sat Hi in a chair.

"There," Buford said. "Now you're ready to eat."

"Eat, nothin'," Hi groused. "Fuckin' soup."

"Coupla' days, Hi. Have some patience."

"It's roundup time, ain't it?"

"Yea."

"Then go back to your goddamn ranch. As you can see, I'm gonna' be all right."

Buford laughed. "Yea, and you'd be eatin' ham and eggs, soon as my back is turned."

"So, what if I do?"

Buford dropped his joking banter. "Goddamn it, Hi. You don't know what your woman and son been through. Almost lost you, two, three times. You're gonna' do as I say."

"That bad?" Hi asked.

"Worse."

"All right, Buford. Don't wanna' worry Lydia and J.B. I promise to behave."

"You ain't gotta' promise nothin'. I ain't leavin' you. Gonna' stay and make sure you behave."

After a few more days, Hi was sore but much better.

"Hate to say it Buford, but you done a good job. Hurtin' plenty but I can eat all right. Shit right, too," he smiled.

"You was shot higher up than Reed."

"Much obliged to you. Remember that Doc give up on me. You saved my life again."

"Didn't mean to," Buford joked. "Thought I'd kilt' you for sure."

Satisfied that Hi would recover, Buford went back to the ranch.

"Pa, Pa!" Tom cried running to him. He jumped into Buford's arms almost knocking him over.

"Whoa, there boy. You're gettin' too big for this here."

"You been at the Marshall's all this time?"

"Yea."

Emma came out to the porch, looking wan.

"Howdy, Emma."

"How's the Marshall?" she asked.

"He's gonna' be just fine."

"Thank God," she said sagging against the rail.

"What's ailin' you Emma?"

"Nothin'."

"She's been sick," Tom said knowingly. "She throws up a lot."

"That right, Emma?" he asked.

"Nerves," she said.

"What do you got to be nervous 'bout?"

"Been sick since me and Joanne was attacked by them Indians."

"That was a month ago."

"I know."

"Shouldn't still be sick over it."

"I'm a nervous Nellie. First it's the Indians, then Great Moon. Reckon I got a reason to be a nervous."

At dinner he looked over at Emma. He couldn't remember the last time he'd made love to her and they slept little that night.

"Lord! I missed you," she sighed.

"Reckon, I missed you, too," he said.

"Really?"

"Don't make more out of it than it is. Ain't seen you in a spell, is all."

● ● ●

Even hard work couldn't free Buford from his thoughts. He wished he had the time to find out who put Great Moon up to the attack and he wouldn't rest easy until he found out. When he did there would be hell to pay. He needn't have worried for Great Moon had already done it for him.

Lord Lawrence made a serious mistake by under estimating Great Moon. When the Apache met with him and told him what happened he grew furious.

"You didn't take the town?"

"No. They knew we were coming."

"How?"

"They have a Ranger, a great white warrior. He knew and he and his men were ready for us. They called in the army."

"That's impossible! He couldn't have known. Do you think one of your men told him?"

"I don't think so."

"Damn! Well, I suppose you'll have to find another place."

"I am done with you. I've lost many warriors. I want your land as promised."

"Don't be absurd. You didn't fulfill your part of the bargain," said Lord Lawrence with scorn. "I've been in this God forsaken place for ten months and I still don't have a suitable site. Bloody cattle ranchers! The deal we made is you'd get the land when you found me a place to ranch. You didn't. I fear our relationship is over," said Lord Lawrence with an air of dismissal.

Great Moon said nothing. Instead, he grabbed him and stabbed him through the heart.

The Englishman's eyes grew wide with surprise as he grasped the knife buried in his chest, then he fell dead.

Great Moon looked down at the body with satisfaction. He would take what the white man promised him and lead his people there, but he had one more score to settle first.

Great Moon couldn't stop thinking of Buford. He and the Ranger had matched wits in the past and Great Moon wanted this to end.

• • •

A calf had gone astray and Buford he was teaching Tom how to cut sign and find the errant animal.

They found it and were returning to the herd, when a shot rang out and Tom fell from his pony.

Buford jumped from his horse and ran to him. "Lord!" he moaned, his mind reeling. He put his fingers on the gaping hole in Tom's neck. Blood spurted all over his face and chest. Quickly he tore off his bandana and tried to fill the hole, but it was no use. Tom was dead. "Lord!" Buford said again.

Another shot fired and Buford fell over. He scrambled up with a wild look in his eye and got on his horse. The shots had come from a large out crop of rocks.

"What the hell was that?" Josh asked Ezra.

"Sounded like gun fire."

"I don't know. Mebbe'," Josh said with uncertainty.

"There's another one!" said Ezra.

"Heard that one clear enough," Josh replied. "The Colonel might be in trouble."

Josh and Ezra rode off as fast as they could.

As they approached, they saw an Apache warrior riding away, Buford close on his heels.

They saw the small figure of Tom lying on the ground and Ezra rode over and swung from his horse.

"Lord, have mercy!" he cried.

Josh was beside him in a second. "Shit," was all he could utter.

Buford was stunned when he saw Great Moon charge

from behind the rocks. He squeezed off a quick shot and missed. It was all the opportunity Great Moon needed. He had a good horse and he thundered off.

Buford doubted he'd be able to catch him on his cow pony, but he'd kill the beast trying.

The distance between them lengthened and Buford was mad with rage. The cow pony could not keep up and Great Moon was out of firing range.

Suddenly, Buford saw Great Moon's horse go down and the Apache landed in the dirt. He spurred his horse and soon reached the Apache. He leaped from the galloping animal and landed on top of him.

They scuffled in the dirt but Great Moon, renowned warrior that he was, was no match for the enraged Buford. He drew his knife, but Buford took it away from him. He threw the dagger out of the Apache's reach.

In his fury, Buford had the strength of ten men. He placed his huge hands around Great Moons neck and slowly squeezed. The Indian fought for his life, punching, kicking and thrashing, but Buford was oblivious. He enjoyed watching the life ebbing from his foe. He could've done it quickly, but he wanted to make sure Great Moon suffered. When he was close to death Buford released his grasp and stood up over him.

Great Moon began taking hard, gasping breaths. His eyes fluttered open and then grew wide with terror. Unsheathing his own knife, Buford reached down and with a Kiowa war yell, scalped the Apache, then cut his throat.

Buford caught his breath and then mutilated the corpse in Indian fashion. He wanted to give Great Moon a dose of bad medicine. A superstitious people, they believed a soul from a mutilated body would never rest in peace.

When he got back to where Tom's body had been, there was nothing but a puddle of blood. He saw Josh and Ezra's familiar tracks and rode back to the herd.

He found most of the outfit standing around the body of his son and saw that they had cleaned him as best they could.

They looked at him with tear filled eyes but spoke not a word.

He dropped down beside Tom and did something his men had only seen once before; he wept.

It was as he knelt crying that Josh noticed something, "Lord, Colonel. You been shot!"

Buford made no response.

"Where?" Ezra asked.

"Right there in the shoulder."

"He's right," Ezra said peering close, "You got a hole clear through you. Better let me tend to it. You're bleedin' some."

Buford shrugged out of his grasp.

"Ain't got time for that now," he said, wiping away his tears. "Reckon, I better bring Tom home to his Ma." He cradled Tom gently in his arms as he made his way back to the ranch.   Some of his men followed, staying a good distance behind to give him privacy. Josh could hear Buford weeping, heart wrenching sobs that shook the big man's body.

Emma heard horses in front of the house and ran to the window.   She saw the small body covered with blood and her heart dropped. She wanted to run outside but her legs turned to jelly, and she couldn't move. "Oh God," she wailed, "please don't let this be bad."

"What is wrong?" asked Rosa rushing from the parlor to stand beside her mistress.

Buford entered the house with the lifeless body and walked by them as if they weren't there. Emma crumpled to the floor in a heap of tears. It was Josh who picked her up and led her to where Buford lay their son.

Buford looked at her with tortured eyes, "I'm sorry, Emma," he said in a husky voice.

Emma threw herself on Tom's body and sobbed. Rosa, with tears streaming down her cheeks, placed a comforting hand on her.

When Emma looked up again, Buford was gone. Josh had managed to get him to tend to his own wound.

"Emma, let me take the boy and clean him," said Rosa.

"Don't touch 'im!" Emma screamed, her eyes wide with grief and shock. "Ain't nobody gonna' touch my baby!"

Buford, buttoning his shirt, dashed back to the parlor at the sound of her shrill voice.

Emma looked at him and stood up on shaking legs. She went to him and wrapped her arms around him. He did not return her embrace but stood woodenly, staring over her head at Tom. He pushed her aside gently and walked to the small body.

Emma's sorrow was complete, even now, he offered no comfort. She stood looking down at the floor, tears pouring down her cheeks and her body trembling.

Josh nudged Buford and gestured towards her, but Buford ignored him. The room was silent, their sobs the only sound. After a while Buford cleared his throat and spoke. "We should get 'im ready for burial."

Emma ran to Tom's body and took him in her arms. "I'll kill you if'n you touch 'im!" she screamed. "You ain't takin' my baby away from me!"

Buford sighed and led Josh out to the front porch where Ezra and some of the others waited. Buford wiped his eyes and pulled himself together. Even in his grief he had do what was necessary. He sent men to town on various errands. To some of the others he said. "I need a grave dug next to Mabel." Looking at some of the others he said, "Plan on buryin' Tom later today, bring the men in before sundown. Reckon, that's all," he said wearily.

Buford walked back in the house. Emma still clung to Tom's body, rocking him in her arms as she wept. She sang snatches of lullabies through her tears and seemed mad with sorrow.

The sight was too much for him and he left the house. He saddled up a horse and rode off.

He wandered the plains, thinking and crying. He found some comfort in the thought that Tom was now in heaven with Mabel and his baby boy. He said a silent prayer and asked her to watch over him.

He'd been on the edge for years and finally cracked. His nightmares came to haunt him in broad daylight.

He thought of the attack on Wilder Creek and the death and destruction of the small town. He saw his son falling from his pony, dead before he hit the ground. One awful thought led to another. He thought of his brother and Mabel and his still born son.

He was unaware that he had fallen from his horse and was laying in the dust. He saw soldiers in grey and blue and heard the sound of battle. The screams of the wounded deafened him. Next, visions of those he killed as a Ranger came. He had killed to protect Texas from those who sought to destroy the peace. Killing had been part of his life for too long, and his past deeds came back for revenge. He had lost all those he loved. When he came to, he had no idea how long he'd been lying there.

He returned to the ranch and Hi came out to greet him, holding his stomach and weeping for Buford's loss. He was better but not fully recovered. He made the painful journey to be with his friend.

"This is a bad day," he said, "bad as any I ever fuckin' seen."

"How's Emma?" Buford asked.

"Drunk. I had to give 'er spirits to calm 'er down. Reckon, I give 'er a little too much, but she'll be O.K."

"The undertaker. Did she let 'im..."

"Yea. It took some doin' though. She fought us like a wild cat."

Buford nodded glumly. He knew he should go in and comfort his wife, but something held him back. He walked by the bedroom where Joanne and Lydia had taken her. He headed for the parlor and a bottle of whiskey.

The Parson and undertaker were involved in quiet conversation. Buford, Hi, Josh and Charlie sat in silence. There was not a dry eye in the room.

A short while later Ezra entered. "All the men's in, Colonel," he said.

"Let's get this over with," Buford said. "Ain't doin' Emma no good to wait."

A quiet sermon was held over Tom's grave. Emma, too drunk and bereaved to stand on her own was supported between Joanne and Lydia. Buford stood dry eyed, still as stone.

After the ceremony, Joanne put Emma to bed.

"You want we should spend the night?" Lydia asked Buford.

He shook his head. The misery etched on his face tore

at her heart.

"Ain't no call to. Ole' Hi over there looks plum tuckered out, probably shouldn't be outta' bed."

When everyone was gone he looked in on Emma. The women had continued to give her whiskey and now she was asleep.

Buford took his bed roll and went to sleep beside Tom's grave.

He lay down and threw an arm over the small heap of freshly dug earth. He gazed up at the star filled sky, his heart and mind numb with grief.

In the morning he found Emma still fast asleep and went out to join his men. If he didn't keep busy, he would go out of his mind. He would come back and see her later.

After a few hours he couldn't put off facing her any longer. As he made his way back to the house, he wondered what he'd say.

When he reached home, Rosa greeted him with tears in her eyes.

"Emma. She is gone!"

"Gone? Gone where?"

"I don't know. She was loco. She had a suitcase. Said now that little Tom is dead, you don't need her anymore."

"Goddamn it!" Buford scowled.

He went to the barn to see which horse she'd taken and went in pursuit. Her tracks led him straight towards town.

"Wouldn't be surprised if'n she's back at the Long Horn," he grumbled.

When he drew close to town, he noticed her trail veered off. He decided to go to the Long Horn. Jamie might know where she went.

When he entered the saloon, it fell quiet. "We're sorry to hear 'bout your boy," one of the men said.

"Where's Jamie," Buford asked, ignoring the man's comment.

"Upstairs," said Frenchie, surprised at the Colonel's unexpected visit and afraid of the dark look on his face.

He took the stairs two at a time and knocked on Jamie's door.

"I'm busy," Jamie shouted.

"It's Colonel McLeod," he said.

"Be right there," she said in a gentler tone.

A moment later, a disheveled cowboy, carrying his boots and hat came out and squeezed by Buford's large frame.

Jamie appeared next, dressed in a satin robe.

"Sorry to hear 'bout Tom," she said, tears in her eyes. "How's Emma doin'?"

"Reckon, you know better than me. Where is she?" he asked impatiently.

"How the hell should I know?" she said.

"She didn't come here?"

"I'd tell you if'n she had," Jamie snapped.

"Shit!" he swore. "If'n she shows up, keep 'er here."

"Colonel! Wait!" Jamie called but he was down the stairs in a flash.

"Where the hell could she be goin'?" he wondered as he rode back to pick up her trail.

Emma had been going back to the Long Horn. She planned on taking up Jamie's offer to open a saloon together. Now they could flee and start new lives.

She was almost there when she changed her mind. She was through with that kind of life and wanted something better.

Out of her mind with sorrow, she thought little of her safety and headed west.

Buford followed her trail until it was too dark to see. She was hours ahead of him.

"Goddamn women!" he thought to himself. "What is she up to? Should just say the hell with it and let 'er go. Ain't got the time to be travellin' the country lookin' for 'er. Besides, just gonna' send 'er away again."

He felt like turning around but knew he wouldn't. He couldn't leave her out there alone and vulnerable. "Emma, I'm gonna' tan your hide for this," he thought. After a few hours' sleep he was on her trail again.

As he rode, he thought of Tom and couldn't control the steady stream of tears that poured down his face. He was fighting hard to keep himself focused. He found another set of tracks heading in the same direction as Emma. In awhile he saw two horses tied to a tree. The scrub brush nearby began to rustle. Buford got off his horse and stealthily went to investigate.

He saw two boys resting in the shade. One looked to be about eight. The other was a teenager. The teen looked up sharply as if he'd heard something. Buford almost laughed out loud. "Yea, that's right son, you heard somthin'. What you heard was the wrath of God," he thought coldly. He cocked the trigger and was about to shoot the older brave when his hand faltered.

Instead he decided to question them. "C'mon' out with your hands up," he said in a thundering voice. The braves came out slowly with their hands in the air. The older brave, White Bird, looked at him with defiance.

"You know who I am?" he asked.

"A pale face, like any other," spat White Bird.

"I'm Colonel Buford McLeod, Texas Ranger, ever hear of me?"

"I've heard of you. They say you are the devil," the young man said coldly.

"What they say is true. Now I'm gonna' ask you some questions and I want some answers. If'n you don't give 'em to me, I'm gonna' use some Indian tricks I learned from y'all 'til you tell me what I wanna' know." He glared menacingly at them.

"Go ahead white man. Ask your questions."

"Do you know Great Moon?"

"He is a fierce warrior and my father's brother. He has sworn to protect us. He will come after you!"

Buford laughed coldly. "I don't think so. Great Moon is dead."

"You lie, Ranger!" White Bird said angrily.

"It's the truth. I kilt' 'im myself."

"No wonder they say you are the devil!" The young man said. "He walks with the ancestors now. They will honor such a great warrior."

"Don't think so. Took his scalp and cut 'im up some."

The little brave who had remained silent cringed and looked at him with renewed horror.

"You have much hatred for my people," White Bird said.

"I done battle with 'em in the past but that was my job.

This here's different. It's personal."

"What did he do?"

"He burnt down my town. He kilt' my friends, then kilt' my son. The only person I love. I chopped 'im up good. Hope that fucker went straight to hell." Buford said in fury. He calmed some. "Did you ever hear of Wilder Creek?"

White Bird remained silent and Buford pointed the gun at the younger boy. "Don't push me!" he growled. "Wouldn't trouble me none to kill y'all."

"Yes, I've heard of it," White Bird answered sulkily.

"Who sent Great Moon and his men there?"

"Another white man."

"Who?"

"An Englishman. A great warrior in his country."

"For what purpose?"

"He wanted the land to raise sheep. He offered Great Moon much land if he could get it for him."

"What do you know 'bout the outlaws that was with 'em."

"They were extra fighting men, nothing more."

"What was they gonna' get outta' this?"

"Cattle."

"Where's this Englishman now?"

"Dead," said White Bird. "My uncle killed him. Like all white men, he made a promise and didn't keep it."

"What are you doin' here. This ain't Indian territory." White Bird didn't answer. Buford swung out with one huge hand and cracked him hard in the face.

"Just as I thought, you was up to no good." With one swift motion he reached out and grabbed the younger brave and pointed the gun to his head.

"Gimme' all your weapons," he said to White Bird.

The brave moved to the horses and did as Buford asked.

"Go slow and easy," he instructed him. "You ain't no match for me. If'n you try anythin' funny, I'm gonna' blow this boy's head clean off."

"Do as he says," said the other boy in Apache, his voice trembling.

"You heard you 'em. Do what I say."

White Bird looked at him with surprise. "You know our

language?"

"The devil knows everythin'," he said.

When he was satisfied that the brave had no weapons, he said, "I got a message for your people. Tell 'em to leave us alone or by God I'll kill everyone of 'em. Now untie your horses and bring 'em over here."

White Bird hesitated sensing a trap.

"Guess you don't care 'bout your partner here." He put the gun on the boy's temple. "If'n you don't get the fuck over here with them horses, he's a goner."

When White Bird came over with the horses, Buford gave a low whistle. In a while his horse came out of the shrubbery and trotted over to him. He clambered on with the small brave, his eyes never leaving White Bird. The frightened boy didn't weep but Buford could feel his body trembling.

He rode over to White Bird and gently handed him the young brave. "Now get on your horses and go back to your people, tell 'em what I said."

White Bird was surprised that Buford was letting them go. "You grow soft, Ranger!" he said.

"Don't count on it. Now skeedaddle!" he replied.

Knowing who hired Great Moon didn't seem to matter with everything else that happened. He continued to follow Emma's trail.

A short while later a nasty storm came up. Black clouds rolled and boiled above the plains, sending down a torrential rain. "Christ!" Buford swore, his mood growing worse every minute.

An expert tracker, he had no trouble following her faint trail. It was close to dusk when he found her horse next to a rocky overhang. He peeked inside and found her with a blanket over her head to keep out the rain.

"Jesus Christ, Emma. Was thinkin' I was never gonna' find you."

"Go away," she said. "You don't need me no more."

"Maybe so, but this ain't no way for you to leave. Come home with me."

"What for?" she asked peering at him through wet blonde tresses.

"Because I said so!" he snapped.

"I ain't goin' nowhere with you."

"Lord, Emma, I ain't got the fuckin' patience for this."

"I didn't ask you to come lookin' for me."

"I know that! I ain't gonna' stop you from leavin', just want you to do it proper. I'll give you a ticket to anywhere you wanna' go. Give you money, too. You can't be travelin' out here alone with nothin'."

"What do you care?" she said. "Tom's dead!" she wailed, "you ain't gotta' bother with me no more."

"For Christ's sakes, let's go," he said gently trying to dislodge her from the narrow space.

"Stay away from me," she shrieked.

He could see that she was becoming hysterical and his tone softened.

"C'mon, Emma," he said.

"Let go of me!" she hollered fighting to get out of his grasp.

"Hate to do this," he said and hit her on the head. She sagged and he pulled her from the crevice.

He stripped off his coat and wrapped it around her. After gathering her meager gear, he set off with her propped up in front of him. Her horse was tied behind.

She came to a moment later. "I'm cold," she said with chattering teeth.

"Ain't surprised, you're wet through."

She noticed the blood stain on the shoulder of his shirt.

"Colonel, you're bleedin'."

"Ain't nothin'."

"There's a lotta' blood."

"The rain makes it look worse than it is," he said.

A vision of him walking in the house covered in blood penetrated her foggy mind.

"Was you hurt, too?" she asked.

"Yea, bullet went clean through. Nothin' serious."

She didn't respond but slumped against him. He could feel her shivering.

Emma either slept or fainted, Buford wasn't sure which. He knew he had to get her home as soon as possible and rode through the night.

When they reached the ranch, he carried her into their room and set her down on the bed.

"Rosa, take care of 'er," he said.

"Si, Colonel," Rosa said full of concern.

Buford rubbed his aching shoulder and went in search for a bottle of whiskey.

Rosa came out of the bedroom to speak to him. "She has a fever, Colonel."

He went in the bedroom and put his hand on Emma's forehead. It was burning hot, although her teeth still chattered.

"Reckon, I should fetch Doc," he said.

"You are nearly dead yourself," Rosa snapped. "Send one of your men."

"Can't spare 'em."

"Stubborn like a burro, you are!" Rosa exclaimed and then muttered something in Spanish.

"English! Goddamn it!" he growled.

As he rode into town, he thought of how quickly his life had been turned upside down. Tom was dead and Emma lay sick.

He and Doc returned at nightfall. The lamps were turned up inside and the house looked welcoming. Cold, tired and hungry, Buford was glad to be home.

It was the first time he ever thought of the ornate house as home. As much as he loved Mabel, he'd found the house hard to live in. He disliked the fancy knick knacks and delicate furniture. Emma had replaced it with things more comfortable.

He tried to imagine how it would be once she left. He'd close the house. He couldn't bare the memories of Mabel and Tom it would evoke.

He thought he'd be glad to see her go, but instead felt an overwhelming sense of loss. "What the hell?" he wondered. He didn't have time to dwell on it.

As they entered the house, Doc said, "You better go on and take care of yourself, Colonel. You look like shit. Get some dry clothes on and drink something hot. You're ready to fall over."

Buford did as Doc suggested. After changing his clothes,

he poured a generous slug of whiskey into the steaming cup Rosa handed him. He sipped at it gratefully.

Although Buford angered Rosa constantly, she felt sorry for him. He sat slumped in the kitchen chair, gaunt and disheveled.

"Let me get you something to eat," she said.

He was too weary to speak but nodded. In a moment she set a steaming plate of food in front of him. He was hungry but could only pick at it.

Doc came in and sat down at the table.

"How is she?" Buford asked.

"Not too good, I'm afraid. The strain of the past few days weakened her. She was foolish to take off like that in her condition."

"What condition is that?"

"The baby of course."

"Of course," Buford repeated, his heart thudding in his chest.

"I've given her somethin' to bring the fever down. We'll have to wait and see."

Doc noticed Buford's chalky pallor. "You've had a rough time and could use a little doctorin' yourself. Let me look at that shoulder." Buford took off his shirt like a man in a trance and let Doc clean and redress his wound.

"Baby!" Buford thought, stunned by the news.

When Doc was through, he said. "I suggest you get some shuteye. When was the last time you slept in a proper bed?"

"I can't rightly remember."

"You see? Get to bed! Have Rosa give Emma a dose of medicine every six hours."

After Doc left Buford went to see Emma. He sat in a chair by her side and fell asleep instantly. He slept soundly and didn't hear Rosa as she came in and out to tend Emma.

Rosa wondered if she should wake him. His big frame sprawled from the chair and he looked uncomfortable.

"He sleeps like a baby all the same," she thought and left him where he was.

He awoke near dawn to the sound of Emma's voice. She still burned with fever and called for her son in her delirium. The sound of her pitiful wailing nearly broke his heart and his own grief engulfed him.

He got up and went to her. Taking her hand, he knelt on the floor by her side. He could no longer control his emotions. Resting his head on the bed, he cried great sobbing tears.

After a while he got up and dried his eyes. Every muscle in his body screamed out in agony. He knew he should go to bed. It seemed like eons since he'd had a decent night's sleep.

"One more night ain't gonna' kill me," he thought.

He went to the kitchen and made a pot of coffee. He brought it back to the room along with a bottle of whiskey.

He studied Emma. Her silky blonde hair lay spread on the pillows and her face was composed.

"Damn, she sure is pretty, scars and all. Been a long time since I noticed."

He felt a flood of tenderness for her that startled him. He thought of what the brave said. Maybe he was growing soft.

He sighed. He had a lot to think about, although he doubted he could do so clearly. He was nearing the end of his physical strength. His musing was broken by Rosa.

"Dio!" she said peering in the door, "Are you still here? Go to bed."

"Gotta' stay with Emma," he said.

"Why? She's been ill many times and you didn't stay. Go to bed. I'll sit with her."

Rosa was right. Why did he suddenly feel protective of her? Was it because of the baby?

"Reckon, you're right. I'm goin' to the bunkhouse if'n you need me."

Buford stumbled to the bunkhouse and fell heavily onto a bunk. He was asleep before his head hit the pillow. That evening when his men came in, they looked at him with pity.

"Poor son of a bitch." Ezra said.

"He's been through hell, that's for sure," said Josh.

"Wonder why Emma run off like that?" asked one of the hands.

"Who knows. She ain't in 'er right mind. She never had nothin' but that boy," replied Ezra.

"Well, she's back now," Josh said.

"Sick as hell, though," Ezra added.

"Colonel, ain't lookin' too good hisself'," said Phil, another ranch hand.

"I've known the Colonel most of my life," said Ezra, "and I'm worried 'bout 'im. I know he's havin' a hard time but he's had 'em before. He never lost his courage, but now….."

"We's all worried 'bout 'im," said Phil, "that's why you boys gotta' keep workin' hard. We gotta' get this here herd ready. Should be leavin' for Kansas soon, though don't know if'n the Colonel's up to it."

The men's talking woke Buford up. He smelled a wonderful aroma wafting from the cook house and his stomach growled. He didn't know what time it was or what meal was being served but he planned to get up and find out.

His men stopped talking and accompanied him to the cook house.

"Good to see you rested and hungry, Colonel." Ezra said.   "Ain't certain I'm awake, yet. What time is it and what're you eatin?"

"It's seven o'clock and this here slop's supposed to be supper," Josh smiled.

"Slop or not, them vittles smell fine, Juan."

Juan jumped up for a plate. "Sit, Colonel. I will serve you."

"How's Emma?" asked Ezra.

"She was no better last time I seen 'er. Goin' over there after I eat."

"If'n there's anything we can do," said Josh.

"You boys done enough already. I ain't been worth a damn to this outfit for a long time. If'n it wasn't for y'all this here spread woulda' gone straight to hell. I appreciate all you done for me."

"It's the least we can do," Josh said. "Hell, you saved the whole dang town."

"Ain't saved nothin'. Plenty of people got kilt'," he said sadly.

"Woulda' been lots worse if'n not for you," Jimmy replied.

"My boy's gone. Protected a fuckin' town but couldn't

save my own son."

A sad silence filled the room. The men were saddened by the loss of Reuben and Bill, two of their crew. Bill had died in the battle against Blue Moon and Reuben succumbed to his wounds and died a few weeks later. They were especially devastated at the loss of little Tom. He'd been a good boy and all the men doted on him.

It was Ezra who spoke first. "Me and the boys wanna' know if'n you'll be goin' to Kansas with us."

"Reckon so."

"You feelin' up to it?" Josh asked.

"I'm right as the mail," Buford lied, for in truth he felt old and tired. Tom's death had sapped the strength out of him. He didn't know how he managed to put one foot in front of the other. He decided he was running on instinct.

When he got to the house, he found Rosa in the bedroom with Emma.

"How's she doin?"

"Her fever broke late this afternoon, but she is weak and full of sorrow. She just fell asleep a little while ago."

"Why didn't you fetch me when she come to?" he snapped.

She glared back at him, "Dio! You needed to sleep! Besides, why would I! You never troubled with her before."

"Ain't none of your business whether I trouble with 'er or not."

"Dio!" Rosa said again. "Let me get you something to eat."

"Ate grub with the boys. Now you skeedaddle. I'll set with 'er awhile."

Rosa came back a short time later.

"You still look bad yourself. Go back to the bunkhouse and sleep."

"I had enough sleep. You been settin' with 'er all day. Reckon I'll set with 'er now."

Rosa beamed, "You are starting to worry about her, just like you worried about Mabel. No?"

"No! Emma's had a rough time of it, is all," he scowled.

"Stubborn as a burro, you are."

"I tole' you to git!"

"All right, but you must change that bandage. The Doctor himself told me."

"I'll do it later."

"No! I will help you now, you can't manage alone."

"Jesus, Rosa! I always said you was a pain in my ass."

"Don't call His name. He doesn't listen to a man like you. Now let me help you!"

"All right," he growled taking off his shirt. "Don't know why I keep you on."

After she left, Buford took off the rest of his clothes and slipped into bed beside Emma. He couldn't believe how good his own bed felt to his weary bones. He fell asleep but awoke when he heard Emma crying. He lay there in the dark and tried to get back to sleep but couldn't ignore her muffled sobs.

With a sigh he reached over and scooped her in his arms. She laid her head on his chest and sobbed until the front of his night shirt was drenched. He felt his own eyes filling and let the tears flow.

CHAPTER SEVENTEEN

Buford joined his men that morning for work. It helped him think. Now that he knew Emma was pregnant, he didn't know what to do. His plan had been to send her away.

He was furious with her for getting pregnant. He'd made it clear that he didn't want any more children. He pondered the situation and came to one conclusion. He was certain he never wanted to love again, especially a child. Every time he opened his heart it had been broken.

He decided to stick with his original plan. Pregnant or not, he'd send Emma away to any place of her choice. He had enough money to provide her and the baby with a good life. He didn't have to live with them.

With his mind made up he rode back to the house to see her.

She was sitting up in bed, picking at her breakfast. Her face was pale and her hands trembled.

She put her fork down when he entered the room.

"How you feelin' Emma?" he said.

"Poorly," she sighed.

"Why the hell did you run away?"

"Tom's dead. Figured you wouldn't want me 'round no more."

"Wouldn't be because of the baby, would it? Tole' you plain I didn't want no more."

She laughed weakly. "I didn't know 'bout the baby myself 'til Rosa tole' me."

"Don't gimme' that bullshit! A woman knows these things."

"Not always," she snapped. "I ain't that far gone. Sometimes it takes a while to know. Besides, I took steps to prevent it. I guess it didn't work. Just like it didn't when I got in the family way with Tom." Her eyes filled with tears at the memory. "Besides, you ain't got nothin' to worry 'bout. I now you don't want it."

"That's what I come to talk to you 'bout. I know you don't wanna' stay here. Truth to tell, don't want you here. When you get better, I'll send you anywhere you wanna' go and support you and the baby."

"There ain't gonna' be no baby. There's a gal at the Long Horn who knows 'bout such things. Then I'll make my own way. Ain't gonna' be obliged to you no more."

"You ain't sayin' what I think you are?" he asked, his eyes wide with shock.

"Yea, I am," she sighed. "I don't want this chile' any more than you."

"It ain't right, Emma!"

She glared at him and her blue eyes turned cold. "You son of a bitch! You ain't got nothin' to say 'bout it. It's my body that carries this chile'. I been pregnant twice and don't wanna' go through it again." Since Buford was going to send her away, she'd rather abort the baby than raise it alone.

"You're talkin' foolish! You ain't gotta' get rid of it. Settle down somewhere and I'll send you money regular. Take care of you and the chile' for the rest of your lives."

"No. I ain't forgettin' all them lonely days and nights me and Tom had. It's hard raisin' a chile' alone. Ain't good for the chile' neither. Poor Tom. He didn't have a decent life 'til you took 'im in. His happiness didn't last long." She burst into tears.

"This is gonna' be different, won't be like last time. I'll buy you a nice house. You won't have to work or worry 'bout nothin'. The good Lord took Tom but he give you another one."

"Maybe so, but it ain't no good. We both don't want this baby. I never forgot the day Gideon hurt me and I lost the baby. You was glad!"

A pang of guilt pierced him, and he grew furious. "God-damn it! Don't start with me."

She looked at him mournfully. "I can't raise another chile' on my own."

"Can't see where you got any choice. Ain't gonna' let

you do nothin' foolish."

"How you gonna' stop me?"

He jumped from his chair, his huge hands curled into fists. "Don't push me, woman! I lost my son, too."

Her sadness turned to anger. "Don't think it pains you any, neither!" she said maliciously, trying to hurt him. "You didn't want 'im in the beginning and you don't want this one. I ain't havin' this baby. Git outta' here. I'm tired and I wanna' be alone."

"I'll leave, but you ain't," he said between clenched teeth. "Gonna' keep a man watchin' you night and day, you hear? Don't try runnin' off again."

"Get out!" she shrieked, close to hysteria.

Buford was at his wit's end. "How can she say I didn't care 'bout Tom? How can she say that?" he thought angrily. He was stunned that she wanted to end her pregnancy. "What kinda' woman would do a terrible thing like that?" he wondered. He decided it was the shock of losing Tom.

When he joined his men, they could see he was in a bad mood.

"Jimmy and Phil, want you to go back to the house and keep an eye on Emma. Don't want 'er runnin' off. Since Tom..." he paused too choked up to go on. His voice grew husky, "She ain't right. She ain't to leave the house."

He didn't have to worry. Emma didn't try to leave again. She was too tired and heartsick. Besides, she was sick most of the time. She hadn't been like this with her other pregnancies.

She had never known such misery. Her son was dead, and the Colonel wanted to be rid of her. Bitter reality settled in and she knew he never would care for her. She had to get away. If she was going to end this pregnancy, it would have to be soon. She'd do it when he went to Kansas.

She didn't know he wasn't going. She was amazed to find him in bed on the morning he was to leave. As she lay there, she noticed how quiet it was. The ranch had been teaming with men and cattle and now the eerie silence filled her with anxiety. "They left without 'im," she thought and jumped out of bed.

Her sudden movement woke Buford and he sat up with

a start. "What the hell, Emma?"

She gazed out the window to the empty scene below. "They're gone," she said softly.

"They left at first light. What's it to you?"

Her face fell. "Nothin'. Thought you was goin' with 'em."

"Couldn't go. Knew you'd run off soon as I did. You look a might disappointed. That's what you was plannin', wasn't it?"

She looked at him sadly but didn't answer.

"Goddamn it!" he growled, getting out of bed and beginning to dress.

"Let me go, Colonel," she said in a tremulous voice.

"Was gonna' but now I can't. Got no one to blame but yourself. You ain't right in the head, Emma. You ain't been since Tom died."

"I don't wanna' argue with you..." she began when her stomach heaved. She ran for the pot under the bed and vomited.

Her face was chalky white and beaded with sweat. She looked at him with pleading in her eyes, "Please don't make me go through this."

"Must be somethin' wrong. I'm goin'for Doc."

He instructed Rosa, "Don't you dare let 'er leave. You understand?"

"If she wants to go, I will not stop her!" Rosa said, her face lifted in defiance.

He was ready to yell at her but thought better of it. "You don't like me much, do you?" he asked.

"No."

"Did it ever occur to you that I ain't always wrong?"

"No."

He sighed, "You can't let Emma leave. She wants to get rid of the baby."

"Dio!" Rosa cried, crossing herself. "I can't believe it. Emma loves children, she wouldn't do such a thing."

"She ain't thinkin' straight, that's why we gotta' take care of 'er."

"I won't let her go."

Buford stopped at Doc's and sent him to the ranch. "I'll

meet you there later," he told him. "I got business with the Marshall."

Hi was sitting on his front porch when Buford rode up.

"What the hell you doin' here?" Hi asked. "Thought you left for Kansas."

"Didn't go."

"Obviously."

"How you feelin'?"

"Good. Real good. Wish Doc would let me go back to work but says it's too soon. Hate doin' nothin' but sit on this fuckin' porch all day long."

Buford pulled up a rocker next to his friend.

"Got a problem," Buford said sadly. "It's Emma."

"Lord Buford, when you gonna' tell me somethin' I don't already know?" Hi scowled in exasperation.

"She's havin' a baby."

Hi's face registered surprise and his eyes glowed with happiness. "Well that's fine! Best thing for you and Emma. What's the problem?"

"I don't want another youngun'."

"You can't be serious. After all, with Tom gone..."

"That's the point," Buford interrupted. "Can't go through that again. Figure I'd send 'er away. Buy 'er a nice house or whatever she wants, support 'er and the chile'."

"You cold blooded varmint," Hi snarled. "I can't believe you! You'd send that gal off in a family way?"

"Yea, reckon I would."

"Is she gonna' go?"

"She wants to get rid of it."

"What?"

"Says there's a gal at the Long Horn who could do it for 'er.

She says she can't bring it up alone."

"And why should she? You are somethin', you really are. Can't believe you'd send your wife and chile' away."

"She ain't really my wife."

Hi looked at him in amazement. "Is it me, or do you get more fuckin' stupid every day? What the hell do you mean she ain't really your wife? Y'all been hitched for a long time. She's havin' your baby!"

"I mean I married 'er for Tom. He's gone now. I don't need 'er no more."

Hi was furious. "If'n I was feelin' myself, I'd get up and tan your hide. Lord Jesus, you rile me! You don't need 'er no more. You talk 'bout 'er like she was somethin' you was gonna' throw away. Besides, what 'bout the baby? You know this one's yours."

"Listen to me, Hi," Buford said in a cold, quiet voice. "When I left the Rangers, I was gonna' live alone and work my spread. Then Mabel come along. She was the best thing that ever happened to me. When she was with chile' I didn't know a man could feel so good. When her and the baby died, I thought I would, too. I took in little Tom and he made me happy again. I was so fuckin' proud of that little feller. Look where it got me. All love ever give me was heartache. I don't want Emma to do anythin' foolish, but I can't get attached no more. I'm sendin' 'er away and ain't nothin' gonna' change my mind."

Hi's mouth snapped shut. He noticed the smoldering look in Buford's eyes. It was one he'd seen many times before and knew this was no time to anger him.

Buford continued. "You ain't got no idea what it's like to have your woman die birthin' your chile'. Sometimes I swear I can still hear 'er screamin'. I see my baby boy, too. Dead 'fore he had a chance to live. Then watchin' little Tom bleed to death...," he burst into tears. "I need to be alone. I need some peace. Ain't had any in I don't know how long." Tears continued to run down his cheeks.

Hi's heart ached for him. He reached out and patted Buford's arm reassuringly.

I don't agree with what you're doin' but guess I understand why. What are you gonna' do? Soon as you set 'er loose, she's gonna' get rid of it."

"Thought of that. Reckon she's just gonna' have to stay with me 'til the baby's born."

When he got back to the ranch, Doc was waiting for him.

"There's nothing to worry 'bout," he said briskly. "Emma's healthy enough. Just a touch of morning sickness. I want her to stay in bed a few more days, though. She's as weak as a kitten. Now let me look at that hole in your shoulder."

When Doc left Buford went to see her.

"Emma, I want you to stay 'til the chile's born."

She heaved a sigh of relief. She didn't know what had come over her when she said she didn't want the baby. The Colonel was right, she wasn't right in the head. Grief and despair enveloped her like a tomb.

"Sorry for what I said before," she apologized softly. "I ain't gonna' do nothin' foolish. But I'd be much obliged if'n you'd let me stay. Don't wanna' be in a strange place when my time comes."

"Now you're usin' your head. When it's born, I'll take y'all to some place decent and set you up fine."

"Guess I ain't got no choice," Emma said glumly.

Buford could see the agony on her face and grew uncomfortable. He got up to leave, "Got chores to do," he said gruffly.

He couldn't find any solace in work that day and the torment in Emma's eyes came back to haunt him.

A few days later, Emma got out of bed and tried to resume the routine that had been so brutally shattered by Tom's death.

She mourned her son silently and let no one see her tears. She knew Buford grieved, but like her, he did it in private.

One morning, Rosa told her she had to leave for a few days. She received word that her daughter was ill.

That night after supper Emma began to clear the table.

"Let Rosa do that, that's what I'm payin' 'er for. Want you to take it easy."

"She ain't here," she said.

"Ain't here? Why the hell not?" he growled. "A woman in your condition needs help."

"Am I hearin' things?" she thought. "It almost sounds like he cares." Out loud she said. "Her daughter's feelin' poorly. She went to stay with 'er for a spell."

Buford realized that this was the first time they'd been completely alone in the years they were married.

He studied her as she bent to clean the table and noticed how her swelling breasts strained against the thin fabric of her dress.

He reached for her and pulled her to him gently. He sat

her on his lap and began to kiss and caress her.

Emma responded with all the passion of her tortured soul. She needed his physical comfort badly. She vaguely remembered when he held her one night while she cried but it seemed like a long time ago.

It wasn't until he began to unbutton her dress that she came to her senses. "I can't," she said jumping from his lap.

"What?" he said breathing hard with his urgency.

"I can't. This ain't right. I don't even know what I'm supposed to be. Am I your wife or just a boarder?"

His face grew red with rage and frustration. "Lord, Emma! Reckon you're a little bit of both. What the hell difference does it make?"

"Makes a whole lot," she pouted.

It made her look more desirable and his anger faded.

"You're my wife," he said softly, trying to placate her.

She didn't respond but stared down at the floor. He got up with a sigh and went to her. Lifting her chin, he leaned down to kiss her. She offered no resistance and he led her to the bedroom.

The weather grew extremely hot and Emma's nausea grew worse. She was sick every morning and many an afternoon. Buford stopped in in to see Doc. Once again, Doc assured him it wouldn't last.

For a reason he couldn't fathom, Buford found her presence comforting. He decided it was because they both lost Tom and shared that sorrow. Once again, he tried to think what it would be like when she left.

• • •

By the time the men came back from Kansas, Emma was feeling better. The color came back to her cheeks and she began to gain weight. She no longer looked gaunt and haggard.

One day she was out in the barn when Josh came in.

"Howdy, Emma! You're sure lookin' pert today."

"That's right kind of you, Josh. At least I ain't green no more."

"Uhhh...Emma," Josh stammered. "Know this ain't none of my business but they say the Colonel's gonna' send you away after the baby's born. That true?"

"Yea, it is," she said sadly, her color fading. "He wants to settle me in someplace else. Says he'll support me and the youngun' for the rest of our days."

"Is he divorcin' you?"

She looked at him startled. "I never asked 'im that."

"You should. Mebbe' you might want to marry again."

"I don't think so."

"You might. I tole' you once before I wouldn't trouble you none, but..." he paused, looking awkward and embarrassed. "Well, I just thought since the Colonel don't want you no more mebbe' you wouldn't mind throwin' your lot in with me. I wanna' marry you."

"Oh, Josh," she said wearily. "I don't know. I'll think on it. I'm much obliged for the offer, though."

That night she broached the subject nervously, "Colonel, are you gonna' divorce me?"

"Never thought of it."

"Wish you would. Think we should end it clean. After all, I might wanna' marry again."

He tried to mask his surprise. He hadn't thought beyond sending her away. That she might want another man never occurred to him. He felt a jealous pang and scolded himself for it.

"We'll worry 'bout that when the time comes," he said and went back to his newspaper.

The next day, Josh took him aside. Buford could see he was nervous.

Josh licked his lips and began. "Colonel, when it's done with you and Emma, I'd like to court 'er."

Buford glared at him. "Are you the one she wants to marry?" he said in a cold voice.

"No!" Josh faltered under the frigid stare.

"What's goin' on between you two?"

"Nothin'. You know how I feel 'bout 'er but I ain't never done nothin' dishonorable! I asked 'er to marry me but she said she don't know yet. I know she don't love me but I wanna' take care of 'er and the baby. You won't have to worry 'bout nothin."

"She's still my wife, Josh. I'll let you know when I'm done with 'er."

"Yes, sir. Was just askin'. Didn't mean no disrespect," Josh said red in the face.

Emma noticed Buford's bad temper that night at supper. She found his presence intimidating and tried to keep her distance from him.

He noticed how she scurried out of any room he entered, and it made him angrier. "Why are you avoidin' me?" he asked with a dark look.

"Looks like you got somethin' on your mind. I thought you might wanna' be alone."

"I got somethin' on my mind," he snarled. "Talked with Josh today. Says he wants to marry you."

"He tole' you that?"

"Said it, didn't I? You gonna' marry 'im? Is that why you want a divorce?"

Her face grew pale. "I don't know yet, but even if'n I don't marry 'im, I might wanna' marry someone else someday."

"Well, let me know when you decide. Warnin' you, though, long as you're livin' under my roof, you're my woman. If'n I hear anythin' 'bout you two, I'll kill you both."

He turned on his heel and stormed out of the house. He was full of fury and didn't know why. He'd known for years how Josh felt. It made sense that he would want to marry Emma if she were free.

The next few months flew by. Emma was big with child and had the glow common to pregnant women. Buford he thought she'd never looked more beautiful.

"What the hell's wrong with me?" he thought. "Can't get 'er off my mind." He would be glad when she was gone.

As she neared the end of her term, she grew melancholy.

"What's eatin' at you?"

"Still ain't decided what I'm gonna' do or where I'm gonna' go."

"Well, you're close to your time. Reckon y'all better give it some thought."

She didn't want her pregnancy to end. The Colonel had never been as kind to her and she wondered about the subtle change. He had never cared what she did before but now it was different.

One day he scolded her, "Lord, Emma! Put that fire wood down! Ain't I payin' enough people on this fuckin' place that you ain't gotta' work? Go sit and put your feet up. Look like you're gonna' pop!"

From that time on, he wouldn't let her do anything. She spent her days knitting and sewing clothes for the baby and trying to decide her future.

Often Emma would look up and find him staring at her. He always averted his gaze, but she thought she'd seen a flicker of something in them, but what was it?

On a cold November day, Emma gave birth to a beautiful baby girl. "Lord, she sure is tiny," Buford said in wonder.

"'Course she is. I have no doubt she'll grow to be tall like 'er Daddy."

This comment sobered him, and he got away from the cradle. It would do no good since he was sending her away. He was glad it wasn't a boy. It would be harder to let him go.

Emma didn't know what to name her. "You have any ideas?" she asked Buford.

"Not really. What's your Ma's name?"

"I don't wanna' name this chile' for 'er. What's your Ma's name.

"Katherine," he replied.

"That's a right pretty name. We'll name 'er Katherine and call 'er Kate."

"Reckon that's as good a name as any. You'll be leavin' here soon. Have you decided what you're gonna' do?

"I have," she sighed. "I'll marry Josh if'n you'll gimme' a divorce."

He felt like someone had knocked the wind out of him. "You sure, Emma?"

"I'm sure. I don't wanna' raise Kate alone. I can't go through that again. Josh is a good man. He knows I was a whore, but don't hold it against me."

Buford was quiet. After a while he said, "Well, since your minds made up, reckon I should have a talk with 'im. I'll support you and the baby just the same, after all, she's mine. I'll go see the lawyer tomorrow 'bout the divorce. He can draw up the papers."

He turned to leave, and she called out to him, "Colonel!"

"Yea?"

She wanted to tell him how much she loved him and beg him not to send her away, but she lost her nerve.

"Nothin'," she said glumly.

"You sure you want to marry Josh?" he asked again.

"The only thing I'm sure of is that I ain't raisin' this chile' alone. Tell you plain, you're the only man I ever loved, so it don't matter who I marry. Josh loves me and will treat me good."

Buford cleared his throat. "Reckon you're right. Know he will."

"Ask 'im to come to the house. I might as well tell 'im."

Buford found Josh on the line. "Emma wants to see you and I wanna' talk to you to. You go on to the house and I'll be there shortly."

Josh went not knowing what to expect. When Emma told him she'd marry him, he gave a whoop that woke the baby. Emma laughed in spite of herself. "Guess you're gonna' have to learn to be quiet."

When Buford came in he said to Josh, "I expect she'll be ready to leave in a few weeks. Want you to take the wagon, extra horses and anythin' you need. Have any idea where you're headed?"

"I've been savin' my wages. Reckon, I'll buy me a little place here in the territory somewhere."

"Good," Buford said softly.

Josh was ecstatic. "There ain't no hard feelins' is there?"

"No, there ain't. Glad she's joinin' up with you. At least I know she's got somebody decent."

While Emma healed, Buford ignored her and the baby. He was anxious for them to be gone.

The day they were to leave was a sad one for Emma. She wept as she hugged Rosa and bid the men goodbye. Josh flashed her a reassuring smile and she dried her eyes.

Buford stood by stoically, no emotion on his face. This no longer surprised his men. They, like everyone else in town were shocked that he could send his wife and baby away. "Just like I always said," Alvirah told anyone who would listen, "the man ain't got no heart."

Once she was in the wagon he said, "Let me know when

you're settled, and I'll send them divorce papers to you."

Emma tried to hold back her tears. "I will," she said in a strangled voice.

The men went back to work but Buford stood and watched until the wagon was out of sight.

He went back to work, but the next few hours were excruciating. He couldn't stop thinking of Emma and the baby. "They'll be fine with Josh," he tried to convince himself.

"Colonel?" Ezra asked, interrupting Buford's thoughts. "What?"

"You want me to bring them beeves down to the creek?" he asked.

"Yea."

"You all right?" he asked. It was obvious that Buford was preoccupied.

"Yea, why wouldn't I be?" he snarled.

Ezra didn't reply but rode off to move the herd.

"Damn it all to hell," Buford swore to himself. He rode over to Juan. "I got some business to tend to." Much to Buford's dismay he felt he had to go after Emma.

• • •

Emma couldn't stop crying as she and Josh traveled. "Are you havin' second thoughts 'bout marryin' me? he asked.

"No. I'm gonna' miss Wilder Creek and my friends. I already miss the Colonel," she wailed.

"You ain't never gonna' love me, are you?"

"Lord help me, no. I'll never stop lovin' 'im."

Josh stopped the wagon and turned to her. "This ain't no good. I can't marry you no more." That made Emma cry all the harder.

"I don't mean it the way it sounds, but maybe we shouldn't marry up. I don't wanna' force you. I'll still take care of you and the chile'." His gallantry moved her.

She dried her tears. "What a mess. You love me but I don't love you. I love the Colonel and he don't love no one. You're better'n I deserve. I'd still like to be your wife."

Josh didn't respond. He was lost in thought.

They were travelling with a wagon full of goods and

their progress was slow. Buford caught up with them easily.

They heard a horse galloping behind but gave it no thought. It was a well-travelled road. When the rider approached both were surprised to see him.

"Colonel!" Josh exclaimed. "What're you doin' here?"

"I ain't sure myself. Can I talk to you for a spell?" "Sure, Colonel," Josh said getting down from the wagon.

Buford didn't acknowledge Emma's presence even as he led Josh away.

Buford began, "When y'all left I realized I wanted my wife and baby back. If'n you both wanna' go on, I'll leave."

Josh sighed. "Emma's been cryin' since we left the ranch. She wants you but will settle for me. Reckon she'd never be happy with me."

"If'n she comes back with me, what 'bout you?"

"I don't rightly know."

"This is just a thought. When I met you, you'd put a little gal in the family way and her Pa run you outta' town. You was a boy then, but now you're a man. Did you ever think of goin' back?"

"That was a long time ago. She probably married, but it wouldn't hurt to see my chile', even if it's from afar."

Buford looked at him. "Take all the supplies and a couple of horses. Whatever you want."

Emma had no idea why Buford was there or what he and Josh had discussed. When they came back, she expected the worst. Josh spoke first.

"Emma, the Colonel convinced me to go home and face what's comin' to me. It's time I went back to see the gal I left and my chile."

"Oh," said Emma with a sigh.

"If'n you gotta' mind to, I wanna' bring you and Kate home."

Emma began to cry. "No. I can't live with you like before."

Josh walked away to give them privacy. He started packing for his journey.

"It ain't gonna' be like before. Found out somethin' today. Reckon it was somethin' I knew all along but was too much of a jack ass to admit."

"What's that?" she asked.

"I love you and I reckon I have for a long time. When you and Josh left I knew I had to come fetch you. I can't live without you or the baby."

"I wish I could believe that. You've only loved one woman and I can't compare to 'er."

"Yea, I loved 'er, but I love you, too. It's 'cause I was comparin' you to 'er that I couldn't see what a fine woman you are."

Emma looked away and remained silent.

"Shit Emma. I love you, I want you, and I want our baby. Why are you makin' this so fuckin' hard?"

Emma grew angry. Nothing had changed. He had a funny way of showing his love. She turned to look at him. He had one of his rare smiles on his face and love and tenderness in his eyes. She softened. "Why ain't I surprised at how you put things?"

"Because I'm a jack ass, now let's go home."